BRIDE
by coronation

THE
Underworld

MAGGIE COLE

PULSE PRESS INC

To all my romance addicts who've met a broken stranger, obsessed over him until it hurt, and couldn't understand why your family & friends didn't see his magnificence... Dive back into that place because this love story needs a permanent spot on your bookshelf...next to all the love letters he may have sent!

xoxo-

Maggie

Mafia Wars universe

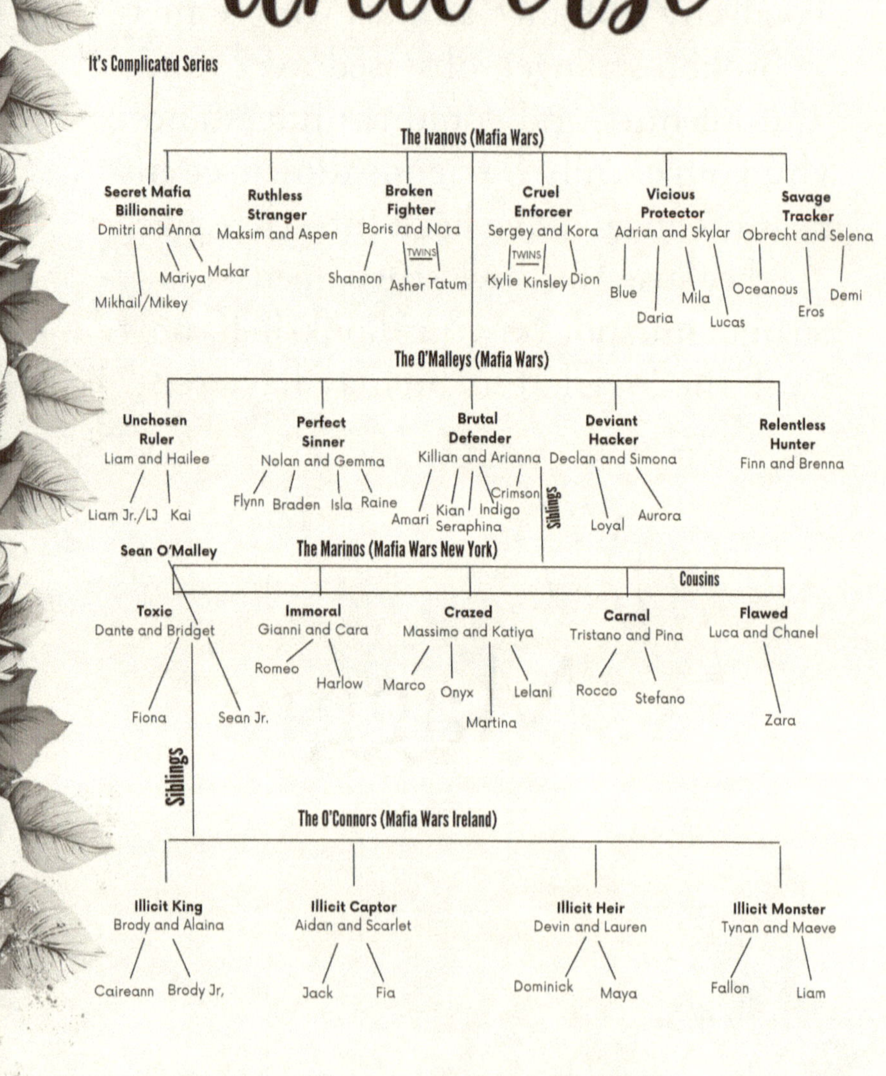

THE
Underworld

Fiona
O'Malley

Prologue

Memories of my father keep fading. Sometimes, I have to look at photos to remember his smile. There are only a few videos of birthday parties where I can hear his voice. And the more years that have gone by, the more confusion evolves regarding who he was and what he was involved in that led to his murder.

As much as I want to know, I don't think anyone will ever be honest with me. Everyone wants to protect me and keep me isolated. So I stay inside my world full of people who are beautiful on the outside but lack the one thing I never forget my father taught me: True beauty is a scarred masterpiece. It runs deeper than we initially see, digging into the core of who a person is and blooming into a blinding light. It's so magnificent that only those who take the time to closely examine it can appreciate its uniqueness and recognize its rarity. Even fewer people exist who can see it immediately, becoming blinded by the brightness of another upon the first gaze.

Everyone wants me to find my guy and settle down, but there's a problem with every man I date.

No one is really beautiful. They lack the glow of imperfect blemishes the world sees as ugly. But as my father taught me, the world is wrong. The imperfections the world doesn't appreciate are exquisitely beautiful and rare, and that's the type of man I ache to know...to hold close...to ultimately love for eternity.

Fiona

Chapter ONE

Bitter cold slams into me the moment I step outside the Pilates studio. The wind whistles louder, and a blanket of thick, wet snow covers buildings, streets, and cars. Oversized flakes fall, making it nearly impossible to see what's ahead of me.

I reach my bare hand into my pocket, feel my credit card sleeve, and nothing else.

Great. I forgot my phone.

"Idiot," I mutter, shivering and digging my hands into my pockets deeper, cursing myself for not anticipating the weather. My alarm didn't ring, and I ran out of my apartment in my sneakers, leggings, and a thinner winter jacket just in time to catch the last advanced class of the day.

The moment I stepped outside, I knew I needed more clothes. But it wasn't snowing then, so I ran the entire eight blocks, happy to burn off the wine I drank at the dinner party I went to last night.

Now I'm regretting putting my workout over my attire. My hot cheeks and sweaty skin only accelerate the chill creeping into my bones. I push myself against the harsh gusts, trying to walk faster, but every step is a fight. And the rising sun only serves to mock me, adding no warmth anywhere.

It takes me three times as long as it normally does to travel a few blocks. Nostalgia fills me from when I was a little girl and taxi cabs lined the streets. These days, you only get a ride if you order one, and since I don't have my phone, I'm out of luck.

Michigan Avenue appears, and I almost cross it, but I turn at the last second. My brother, Sean, and his wife, Zara, who's also my best friend, live on the next corner. So I decide I'll visit them and my new twin niece and nephew. I'll call my driver when I'm ready to go home.

Four doors and I'm there, I tell myself, picking up the pace, then the strongest blast of wind so far barrels into me. I duck slightly, but it knocks me back two feet.

"Forget this," I mutter, yanking open the coffee shop door. I lunge inside, relieved to escape the torturous wind, and take a spot at the back of the line.

The rich, warm aroma of roasted coffee, nuts, caramel, and pastries fills the air. Hints of chocolate, cinnamon, and vanilla dance around it, comforting me. Indie music, grinding, hissing, whistling espresso machines, and whirring blenders fight for attention.

I study the menu, decide what I want, and step forward when the line moves, staring at the back of a well-built, broad-shouldered, tall man wearing a black wool peacoat and matching cashmere scarf. His dark, thick, wavy hair is four, maybe six inches long in some parts. It's clean and styled but reeks of messy, and it's the opposite of the country club men I usually date.

Wonder if he likes women tugging on it?

The bell over the door rings, and a violent burst of cold air hits my back. I lose my balance and step forward, knocking into the man.

"Crap! I'm so sor—" My mouth turns dry and air catches in my lungs. I gape at him, unable to believe it, feeling the same ache I haven't been able to escape whenever I allow myself to think about the stranger.

Surprise fills his sharp features, and a large dimple pops out under his scar. It's a quarter-inch faded white line with just a hint of pink. It starts at his right temple, moves diagonally over his eyelid, through his nose and cheek, and down to the left side of his jaw. His short-trimmed beard fits his face perfectly, except for the area around the scar that doesn't grow.

I wonder how long he's had the scar. I assume he's in his mid-forties, between ten to fifteen years older than me. The mark looks aged. In the last year, I've devised a dozen scenarios about how he got it.

Butterflies take flight inside me, and the cold chill gets beaten back by the heat flooding my veins. I've only seen this stranger once. I ran into him at a club when I was out with Zara. He sent a bottle of the most expensive champagne to my table, then disappeared.

His lips twitch. His Caribbean blue eyes light up, and his deep Russian accent hums in my ears when he says, "I think you have an obsession with barreling into me."

I beam at him. "Or maybe you have an obsession with being in my way, so I'm forced to bang you?"

He arches his eyebrows in amusement.

My cheeks heat. "I mean, bang into you," I quickly amend.

"Next," a whiny barista calls out.

He turns, steps in front of the counter but off to the side, then pins his heated stare on me. "What do you want, Fiona?"

"You know my name?" I blurt out, my pulse skyrocketing so fast I get dizzy.

He opens his mouth, then shuts it.

I bite on my lip.

"Can I help you?" the barista interjects in an annoyed tone.

The man claims, "Your friend said your name outside the bathroom."

"Oh, I forgot," I admit, recalling Zara interrupting my hot moment with Mr. Bad Boy.

"Sorry, but there's a line forming," the barista snaps.

The man narrows his gaze, scolding, "You're being rude."

The probably high-school-aged boy, wearing a name tag that says Theo, shrinks and cringes. In a nicer manner, he offers, "Sorry. How can I assist you?"

"Fiona?" the man asks, motioning for me to step next to him.

I obey and give my order. "Long macchiato, one pump caramel, one pump mocha, add whip." I turn to the man. "What's your name?"

Amusement flares in his eyes. He states, "Kirill."

"And what would you like, sir?" Theo pushes.

Kirill doesn't take his stare off me. He answers, "Large coffee. Fiona, have you tried the oatmeal raisin cookies here?"

I shake my head. "No."

He turns toward Theo. "Add on two cookies."

"Name?"

"Bob."

I stifle a laugh. "Bob?"

"No one can spell or pronounce my name."

I add, "You definitely don't look like a Bob."

"That'll be eighteen forty-five," Theo announces.

Kirill taps his card, displaying a tattoo of a hand necklace. Tiny pink hearts on top of crossed bones hang off a black chain. It runs over the sides of his thumb and pointer finger.

My knees weaken, and I grab the counter to steady myself. I had a guy hold my neck once and apply a tiny bit of pressure, but that relationship didn't last long because other than that, he bored me to death. I've craved for another guy to hold me like that, but I haven't had much luck. Everyone I date seems to be duller in bed than the previous one. So I blurt out, "You have a hand necklace?"

He freezes, then studies me, and the ache in my core turns into an inferno.

"Sorry. I'll agree your tattoo is rather fascinating, and I don't mean to be rude, but would you please step down to the end so other customers can order?" Theo interrupts.

Kirill shoots him more lethal daggers with his glare, then steps back. He motions toward the pick-up counter, his hand necklace on full display. "After you."

With wobbly legs, a racing heart, and zings flying through me, I force myself to move to the end of the counter.

A young girl with bright-green hair, four nose rings, and three eyebrow hoops slaps two cookies, wrapped in paper sleeves, on the quartz. "Your drinks will be up in a moment."

"Thank you," I reply.

Kirill steps closer to me and unbuttons his peacoat, and the same delicious scent he wore the night we met in the club slinks around us.

I hold in my groan. The number of times I tried to find that smell at cologne counters is uncountable. I inhale deeply, basking in the leather, rosewater, saffron, jasmine, and other notes I can't identify.

"You aren't dressed very appropriately," Kirill states in disapproval, his gaze drifting over my body.

I squeeze my thighs together, babbling, "I was late for Pilates. When I got outside, it wasn't snowing, so I ran, thinking I'd sweat last night's wine out of me. I was at a dinner party. I didn't get drunk or anything. I just had a few more glasses than normal. Anyway, when I left class, the weather had turned, and I forgot my phone." I stare at him, my heart thudding so hard that I'm sure he can hear it.

Tiny wrinkles crinkle around his blues. He teases, "It's a good thing you didn't turn into an icicle. I'd have to defrost you in front of everyone."

My breath catches in my lungs. The throbbing in my core accelerates. I add, "I detoured to my brother and sister-in-law's place since the snow was beating me up too badly."

Something passes in Kirill's expression, but I don't understand what it means.

"Bob," the girl calls out.

I bite on my smile.

Kirill winks, picks up our drinks, and holds mine out to me.

I reach for it and freeze, gaping as goose bumps cover my skin.

What is he doing with that on his hand?

Kirill has the same skull adorned with roses that my deceased father designed and then branded on his hand. It's in the same spot, near his thumb and index finger. It's also the same mark my brother branded on his hand and Zara got on the back of her neck. The only difference is theirs have soft pink accents while his has gold.

I've asked Sean and Zara to explain what it means, but they only say they did it when they married as a tribute to my father. I don't buy it, nor does my mother or stepfather, Dante.

Kirill puts my drink in his other hand, then picks up his.

My voice shakes when I ask, "Why do you have my father's mark on you?"

Guilt flickers over his face, then turns to a hardened expression. "It's nothing."

"Like hell it is!" I object.

"Take your drink, Fiona," he orders in a low tone.

I grab it, my hand trembling.

He snatches the bags of cookies and then slides his arm around me so I'm forced to walk with him.

After several steps, I push away. "Tell me how you got my father's mark!"

"It's just a design I found. I don't know how it could be your father's," he claims.

I seethe, "Liar! My brother and sister-in-law have one too!"

His eyes turn darker. He clenches his jaw, then sets his drink and the cookies on the table. He pulls out a chair. "Sit down."

"Tell me. Now," I insist through gritted teeth.

He steps closer, slides his arm around my waist, and tugs me into him.

A surge of electricity races through every one of my cells. I gasp, my body molding against his looming frame.

His lips graze my lobe as he murmurs in my ear, "I said sit, Fiona."

I glance at his darkening features, illuminated by the faded scar, unsure what to do.

"Sit," he quietly repeats.

I cave, sitting and holding the macchiato too tightly.

The lid pops off, and my hot drink spills over my hands.

"Ouch," I cry out.

"Shit!" Kirill sits, grabs napkins off the table, and secures my hands in his. He dabs the liquid until it disappears onto the paper, and assesses my hand. With relief in his voice, he states, "I don't think you're going to blister or scar."

"How'd you get your scar?" I blurt out, then my chest tightens.

His head jerks backward, and pain crosses his expression. It's a small move but enough to notice. He recovers, putting on a poker face, but grinds his molars.

I almost apologize, but I don't. He's wearing my father's skull design. I want answers, and he hasn't given them to me yet. So it's time he starts talking.

He picks up his coffee, takes a large mouthful, then sets it down, refocusing on me.

I fight the ache in my core with the fear over who he is and what he might be involved in. Since he doesn't answer me, I question, "Did you know my father?"

He maintains his silence and takes another sip of coffee, studying me.

Tension builds between us, creating an intense anger inside me, pushing me to the point I might explode.

I'm tired of asking for the truth about my father and getting nowhere. No one lets me in on anything. Not my mother, Dante, Sean, or even Zara. It's not even her father, and she has more information about my dad than I do.

I fume, "I want answers."

"It's not the right time," he declares.

Shock fills me. "Not the right time? You have my father's mark on you, and you have the audacity to tell me it's not the right time?!"

"Keep your voice down," he reprimands.

"No. Don't you dare tell me what to do!" I cry out.

Disapproval appears in his gaze, and he pins it on me, breathing through his nose.

"Tell me," I demand.

He doesn't move for a moment, then unwinds his scarf from his neck. He leans forward, loops it behind my neck, and secures the soft cashmere around me. He grabs the material in his hand and tugs me closer.

The ache resurfaces, numbing out the anger.

Kirill's hot breath teases my lips. He warns, "When I say it's not the right time, I mean it. It was nice having you run into me again. Don't forget to try the cookie. Have a good day, Fiona." He releases me and rises.

I stare at him.

He picks up a cookie, slides it in my jacket pocket, then shoves the other in his coat. He turns and walks away, exiting the building.

I jump up, race toward the door, and face the bitter cold head-on. The outline of his body is hard to see through the snow, but I jog as best as I can on the slippery pavement and catch up to him. I grab his arm, screaming, "You don't get to do that!"

He spins, wraps his arm around me, and moves me around the corner. He pins me against the wall, caging his body around mine. His fingers close around my throat, and he uses his wrist to lift my head.

Millions of sensations flame to life inside me, singeing me so I can't even feel the cold air.

"Listen to me closely, little bird. It's not the time," he warns.

I take bated breaths, staring at his lips, craving for him to kiss me and squeeze tighter while anger and frustration swirl among my needs.

Surprise fills his expression. His erection pushes into my stomach. Seduction replaces the rage in his leer. He mutters, "Ah. I was wrong about you." His fingers tighten, loosen, then tighten again as he watches me.

My knees buckle, and I whimper, not flinching.

He presses closer, mesmerized by my reaction, and then his face hardens. He releases me.

I take deep, shallow breaths, keeping my glare pinned on him.

"A queen obeys her king. Don't forget it, Fiona," he asserts.

I furrow my brows at his words.

He steps back, ordering, "Make sure you dress appropriately from now on. I wouldn't want you to get frostbite and ruin your beautiful skin."

I gape at him.

"Until next time," he adds, then backs away, disappearing within seconds in the snow.

It takes several moments for me to recover. I don't understand how he could be so seductive when I want answers he won't give me.

I finally push off the wall, hurry past the coffee shop, and step into Sean and Zara's building. I nod at security and get into the elevator. I punch in my code and quickly rise to the penthouse.

The doors open, displaying the magnificent cherry blossom tree in their foyer. I brush past it and open the door, stepping directly into the living area. The stunning view of Lake Michigan is barely visible, with ice frosting the penthouse windows in every direction you look. Flames flicker in the oversized fireplace, creating a soft glow. Slow music plays on the surround sound system.

Zara and Sean are on the floor with River and Willow. One of the babies giggles from Sean's tickles.

"Don't worry! Daddy's coming for you next!" Zara coos.

"Sean, I just ran into a man with Dad's skull on his hand in the same spot you put yours!" I announce.

They turn their heads toward me. Zara's eyes widen. Alarm fills my brother's face. He demands, "Who?"

I rush over to them, sit on the couch, and cross my arms. I'd normally pick up a baby, but I'm too upset. "Tell me what the skull's about, and don't give me your usual song and dance."

"Fiona, who did you run into?" Sean demands, picking up Willow and holding her close.

Zara rises, leans down, grabs River, and states, "Nap time. Give Daddy a kiss." She holds the baby in front of my brother.

Sean kisses him, then Willow, and hands her to Zara.

Zara shoots me an apologetic look.

I fume, "You're not innocent in this conversation either!"

She takes a deep breath, then replies, "I'll be back after I get the babies down." She exits the room.

Sean gets off the floor and sits next to me. "I need to know who you talked to and what they said."

I grab his hand with our father's mark. "A man who had this. He told me he couldn't tell me what it's about because it 'wasn't the time,'" I spout, making quotation marks with my fingers.

Sean's jaw twitches. "Who was it?"

"A man," I repeat.

His greens glow hotter. "Who, Fiona? Stop playing games and tell me who."

"Don't you dare accuse me of playing games! You and Zara need to stop hiding and spill whatever you know about Dad's mark," I insist.

Sean scrubs his hands over his face, then releases a stressful breath. "What did he look like?"

"Why? Are you going to tell me who he is if I tell you?" I ask.

He opens his mouth and then shuts it. He taps his fingers on his thigh, staring out the windows.

"Seriously?" I scoff.

Zara steps back into the room. "Sean," she interjects.

They lock eyes.

"Stop hiding the truth from me!" I cry out.

"Keep your voice down. The babies need to take their nap," my brother reprimands.

"Then you better start talking because—" My pulse pounds between my ears.

"What is it?" Zara asks.

I point at her. "You knew who he was, didn't you?"

"Who?" She pins her eyebrows together.

"The man in the club with the scar," I reveal.

The color in her face drains, and she turns a fearful gaze to Sean.

Shocked, my brother asks, "You met Kirill?"

"Yes. Who is he, and why does he have Dad's skull?" I push.

Sean stares at the ceiling momentarily, grinding his molars, then answers, "I know you don't want to hear this, but he's right. This isn't the time, and any further information will only harm you."

"Meaning what?" I ask.

"You have to trust me," Sean insists.

I rise. "I'm supposed to trust you?"

He nods. "Yes."

I turn toward Zara. "I need to know."

She winces. "I'm sorry. Sean's right. We need to keep you safe."

"Keep me safe?"

"Yes," they say in unison.

Full of frustration and rage, I shake my head at them and spit out, "Thanks for nothing." I move toward the door.

"Fiona!" Zara calls, grabbing my arm.

"Don't!" I warn, shaking out of her grasp.

Guilt floods her expression. She holds her hands in the air. "Okay. But we love you. Please trust us."

I scoff. "You two deserve each other." I step into the foyer, slam the door, and vow that whatever they're hiding from me, I'll stop at nothing to find out, even if it's dangerous.

Kirill Petrov

Several Hours Later

Chapter
TWO

"Come on," I mutter, pushing the elevator button for the third time and shaking my head at Jasper, the daytime security guard.

"It's getting fixed today, Mr. Petrov," he reassures.

"About time. This is ridiculous," I grumble, just as the number one lights up and the steel doors open.

The redhead, who lives on the floor below me, tries to hide her disgust. Like always, she can't. She takes one look at my scar, cringes, and plasters a tight smile on her face.

My chest tightens. "After you," I offer, motioning for her to get off the elevator so I can get in and forget this little encounter.

She squeaks out, "I forgot my gloves. I have to go back upstairs."

Awesome. A ride with Ms. Uppity.

I step inside, press my palm against the screen, then hit eleven for her floor.

The doors shut, and there's no movement.

I press my hand against the screen again.

The redhead offers, "It's just taking a while."

"Totally absurd," I bark, a little louder than I should.

She jumps, then steps closer to the back corner, as far away from me as possible. The back of her black boot heel hits the wall.

I sigh. "Sorry. Didn't mean to scare you."

The thin line on her mouth forms again. She refocuses on the doors and tightens her black wool coat around her scrawny body. Her cheeks flush a shade of maroon, darkening her freckles.

The elevator creaks and slowly begins to lift.

I lean against the wall, cross my arms, and try to ignore the clawing in my gut.

She doesn't speak, but I can feel her sneaking glances at my face from the corner of her judgy eyes. She does it whenever I see her, so today is no different.

I shove my hands in my coat pockets and squeeze my fists tightly, cursing myself for letting her judgment affect me.

She's a bitch.

No different from every other woman.

Fiona didn't give me that look.

Don't fool yourself. She only hides it better, I scold myself. But I can't escape what's been flaring in my mind since I left her in the snow.

I misinterpreted it.

I didn't.

I did.

Fiona's greens, dancing with a challenging excitement while I squeezed her throat, won't leave my mind. They mix with the recollection of her thumping pulse pushing against my hand.

The small box continues to move at a snail's pace. The next number lights up, but it's blurry.

Fiona's parted lips and hot, shallow breath torment me further. It's so real, it's like she's in front of me.

The metal doors part in a loud screech, tearing me out of my thoughts.

The redhead shoots out of the elevator and into the hallway. Her frizzy hair bounces out of sight.

I press my palm on the screen and hit the close button, but it's another painstakingly long process before I get to the penthouse. The elevator finally stops, and I step out into my foyer, remove my jacket, and put it on the coatrack.

The elevator doors shut. I reach for the front door and enter the main area. The bell rings.

The hairs on my arms rise.

I don't get visitors. Not unless it's someone in The Underworld, and almost always one of my fellow Omni. Lately, those visits only turn into arguments.

It's my fault. I brought it on myself when I stepped in and interfered during Sean and Zara's final test to earn their seats at the table. I offered my only token. For it to be accepted, and for Sean and Zara not to die, we had to agree we'd owe the Omni.

Little did I know they already knew what they wanted from me. They set me up so I'd have to do the one thing I've worked hard to avoid—get married. Now, no matter how hard I try, there doesn't seem to be any way to escape it.

I may be king of the Omni, but right now, I'm powerless. And I should have prepared myself better. I've gotten away without a wife at my side longer than I theoretically should have. The rules are clear, and I'm to rule with a queen by my side.

Ironically enough, the Omni has chosen the one woman I've been unable to stop thinking about since our first random encounter. And when they ordered me to marry Fiona O'Malley, it only strengthened my obsession with her, no matter how much I've fought to make them change their minds.

Today's innocent reappearance of the sexy blonde who doesn't grimace or seem afraid of me isn't helping the ache digging deeper in my core. Her initial flirting, which I have to be wrong about, fucks with my head the same way it did the night I first met her. And every ounce of anger, frustration, and determination to learn the truth about her father's mark and why I branded it on my hand creates a guilt I'm not used to feeling.

The bell rings again.

I slam my hand against the button, demanding, "What is it?"

"A Sean O'Malley is here to see you," Carmen from the front desk states.

"Of course," I mutter, then instruct, "Send him up."

"Yes, sir."

I open the front door, then walk to the window, staring at the iced-over water. The flakes are as big as they were earlier.

What was she thinking, not dressing appropriately? I wonder, wishing she hadn't seen the skull and we could have had a more pleasant conversation.

What's the point?

I have to marry her.

I'm not doing it.

There's no getting out of it.

When she learns the truth, she's going to hate me.

Maybe she won't.

Stop kidding yourself.

She might as well hate me from the start.

By the time Sean arrives, my head is spinning with all the self-loathing and sins of the past I try to keep buried but fight every time I think of what's to come. It slaps me so hard that a cold shiver runs through my bones.

"Kirill," he booms.

I spin away from the white blanket, blinking a few times until he comes into view.

"Why did you corner my sister?" he accuses.

"I didn't."

"Bullshit."

"Watch your mouth," I warn.

"Or what?" he challenges, stepping closer and intensifying his scowl.

I remind him, "You may have earned your seat at the table, but I'm the king. Don't push me. Not today."

"A king who takes unnecessary risks with my sister?" he spouts.

Fiona's beautiful face, full of warmth and excitement when she first saw me, bursts into my mind.

She'll never look at me like that again.

Why did she to begin with?

"Why would you do that? You could have put her in danger," he points out.

My pulse increases. He's right. And the last thing I want is to hurt her. So I back down and sigh, admitting, "I was in the coffee shop. I didn't know she was coming to your place and would come inside, or I wouldn't have been there."

He studies me.

"Believe what you want, but that's the truth."

"She isn't marrying you," he declares, then grinds his molars.

My chest tightens. There are plenty of reasons Sean wouldn't want me marrying his sister, and the scar across my face is only one of them. What's worse is if he knew the secrets I live with, he'd try to kill me.

He leers harder at me.

I cross my arms, stating, "I don't want to marry your sister. But why don't you tell me how we're getting out of this, because the last time I checked, you were in this as deeply as I am."

Guilt floods his features. His breath quickens, but he stays quiet.

"That's what I thought. You're up against the wall as much as I am. And you're welcome again for saving your ass," I hurl, pissed that we're in this situation and both powerless to change it.

He clenches his jaw.

I walk to the fridge, open the door, and pull out two beer bottles. I snap the cap off one, take a long drink, then open the second one. I hold it out to him. "Here."

He stays frozen.

"Fine. Suit yourself," I say, putting it on the counter and downing half of mine.

He finally moves, grabs the bottle off the island, and takes a large swig.

"I wouldn't intentionally put Fiona in danger," I insist.

He pulls a barstool out and sits. He puts his forearms on the counter, stating, "We have to find a way to change the Omni's minds."

I grunt. "Good luck."

"I'm serious."

"You don't think that's what I've been working on?"

He sits back and crosses his arms, glaring daggers at me.

I scoff. "You're something else."

He snarls, "What's wrong with my sister? Most guys would drool at the prospect of marrying her. You think you're better than her?"

Just the opposite, I think, but keep it to myself.

"My family isn't going to allow her to marry a Petrov," Sean adds with more disdain.

I curl my fists at my sides, threatening, "You seem to not understand how The Underworld works. For someone who has a seat at the table, I suggest you study the rulebook your father put together."

His face hardens before he turns and stares out the window.

I continue, "The point is to work together, not continue the families' wars."

"Yeah, I know," he claims, pinning his greens on me again.

I finish my beer, then grab another out of the fridge, cracking the cap off.

Sean asks, "Why did you do it?"

"Do what?"

"Save Zara and me."

My heart races faster.

Tense silence fills the air.

"Well?"

I put the beer down, then admit, "I promised your father."

The blood drains from Sean's face. He holds his breath, studying me, then questions, "What are you talking about?"

My gut clenches, but I push the emotions down. "Your father helped me once when no one else would. I wanted to pay him back. He made me promise that when the day came, and you and Fiona needed help, it would come from me," I confess.

Sean gapes at me.

I step back and lean against the counter, squeezing my fingers against the quartz, taking deep breaths, and remembering the day I wish I could erase from my memory.

But I can't.

It'll never disappear, nor will the dominoes that fell after it.

"Don't fuck with me, Kirill," Sean warns.

"I'm not. Trust me, if I could erase that day, I would," I snarl, grab my beer, and return to the window. The blanket of cold snow I previously wanted to escape, I now wish I could disappear into forever.

Sean seethes, "I doubt my father would approve of you marrying Fiona."

I snort. "Nope. I'm sure he wouldn't. But part of that isn't my fault, now is it?" I spin and lean against the cold glass, barely feeling it.

Fresh guilt pops up on Sean's face. He lowers his angry voice, stating, "I couldn't let them do that to Zara."

My chest tightens. I nod, but he's not getting off that easily. "The moment I accepted the position of king, my fate was sealed. But Fiona's only on the table for one reason. It has nothing to do with your final test, and that's on your conscience, not mine."

His eyes turn to slits. "What the fuck does that mean?"

I swallow a large mouthful of beer, waiting until the bubbles hit my stomach. Then I answer, "You disrupted what was to be on the night of your initiation. You did that, not me."

"What are you talking about?"

"There was a plan, and you decided to go rogue. You were warned there would be consequences," I point out.

Sean opens his mouth, but nothing comes out. Understanding fills his expression, and he looks away.

"Ah, that's right. You didn't just change Zara's and your fate. You changed your sister's and mine. So, you can sit there and accuse me until you're blue in the face, but this is on you," I assert.

He pales further.

I let it sink in a moment, then add, "I respected your father. I would never do something that would upset him, but unless you can change the Omni's minds, we're going to have to figure out how to deal with the situation. The only other option gets everyone killed. And I don't think you want your twins to be orphans."

He jumps up. "Don't you dare—"

"It's reality, and you know it!"

He takes large breaths, his face red with anger and fear.

I soften my tone. "I'm not here to hurt you, your sister, or anyone in your family. When I say I respected your father, I mean it. But this conversation is pointless unless you can come to me with a viable solution."

He slowly meets my gaze and states, "I want to know what went on between you and Fiona today."

I shrug. "Nothing."

"It wasn't nothing!" he barks.

I step closer. "She saw the skull. That's it."

Sean studies me closer and then asks, "What else happened?"

"That's it."

"But she's seen you before?"

My pulse skyrockets. I nod. "Yes. Your wife was there. I thought you knew about it."

Anger flickers across his features. He spews, "Are you following Fiona?"

"Don't ask stupid questions."

"Are you?" he roars.

"Of course not. I wouldn't put her in that position. We both know what happens if we attempt to bypass whatever the Omni wants for her initiation," I state.

His jaw twitches.

More tension erupts between us.

He warns, "My sister can't go through what Zara did for initiation. You can't let that happen."

"I don't get to choose, Sean. Just like you didn't, I don't either," I claim.

"You're the fucking king!" he booms.

Disappointment fills me. I hate having no control over this situation. But it is what it is, so I reply, "Nothing regarding Fiona's initiation is up to me. We gave up our tokens. We traded in our choices on this matter. Now, I don't like it any more than you do, but the sooner you accept it, the easier it will be for you."

He scrubs his face and shakes his head. "There has to be another way. My sister isn't going to agree to marry you. And I'm not forcing her."

My heart races. I hide the sting of his words, even though I already know Fiona will never want me. She's eleven years younger than me and beyond gorgeous. Her thriving career in the fashion world means she understands and values beauty. The men she dates are country-club perfect and belong on the covers of magazines. Plus, she's already proven she's not scared of me and isn't afraid to fight for what she wants.

And that's what worries me the most. I'll be a man and deal with my fate, but I'm fearful that same spirit might be the cause of Fiona ending up dead on initiation night. So I can blame Sean all I want, but that's on me if that happens.

If she does go through with it, she'll end up dead anyway.

No way will she survive being married to me.

She'll hate herself for allowing me to ever touch her.

Her embarrassment that I'm her husband will show every time we walk into a room together.

"Find another way, Kirill. If you really did respect my father, then you'll figure this out."

Beyond frustrated, I roar, "You're not listening!"

He jabs me in the chest. "No, you're not. Find another way. Fiona is off-limits!" He spins and stomps out of the room.

I follow him. "Sean, I'm not the enemy. I know you think I am, but I'm not. Trust me, I don't want this any more than you do."

He smacks the button a few times until it lights up, then demands, "Go marry someone else. That'll solve this issue."

I scoff. "You know they'll kill me if I do that."

"So? My sister would be safe."

I grab his coat and yank him toward me, pointing my finger in his face and snapping, "Stop saying irrational things. If I do anything of the sort, we all die. Is that what you want? Zara, your sister, and you lying in a pool of blood next to me?"

He pushes me away, snarling, "Don't ever touch me again unless you want to be laid out on the floor."

"The threats aren't going to make this go away, and neither is blaming me, so I'll tell you what your dad would tell you right now. Grow the fuck up."

New hatred fills his expression. He fumes, "Don't ever talk to me like you know what my father would say."

I stay silent, realizing I'm fighting a losing battle.

The elevator opens, and Sean leaps into it. He hits the button, but the doors stay open.

I add, "We have to find a way to work together. There are Omni who have seats, and they're working against us. The sooner we make peace, the better off everyone will be."

"Get us out of this nonsense with my sister, and I'll happily work with you," he declares.

I groan. "You're not listening to a damn word I've said!"

He glares at me, warning, "Fiona will never agree to marry you. Don't put her in a position where her life's on the line."

"Do you honestly believe that's what I want?"

"You're the king. Figure out a way," he orders.

"I'm trying," I insist.

"Try harder, because you're not marrying my sister," he snarls as the doors shut.

The hum of the lift belt fills the air, and I close my eyes, wishing the solution would present itself.

Nothing comes. All I see is Fiona and everything she represents.

The longer I try to make her image disappear, the worse the dread in my stomach grows. And I can't escape it. There are a few things I'm sure of regarding Fiona becoming my queen: She could never want me, accept me, or be happy calling herself my wife.

Fiona

A Week Later

Chapter
THREE

"What do you think about this?" Blue asks, holding up a hot-pink miniskirt.

I shake my head. "That'll be a negative."

Her face falls. "Really? I think it matches perfectly. And I love this material."

"We had a similar skirt two years ago. Last year, Condora opened their show with a nearly identical one."

Blue wrinkles her nose. "Of course they did. They're always copying my mom's line."

"Yep. Welcome to the fashion world," I chirp.

"It's so unfair!" Blue complains.

"What's unfair?" Skylar questions, stepping into the wardrobe room.

"Condora copying our pink skirt from two years ago," I explain.

Skylar glances at the material in Blue's hand and smiles. "They say it's better to be copied than to be the copier."

Blue whines, "It's cheating. And now I can't do anything with this design I created."

Skylar reaches for it and stretches the waist, studying it. "I don't know about that."

"It looks like the Vixen we launched," I remind her.

"Right. Which is why you need to do your homework and study our releases from the last ten years," Skylar reprimands Blue.

Her face falls. "Sorry. I just had this in my head."

Skylar assesses the material for another moment and then hands it back to Blue. "If it's in your head, then finish it."

"It is finished," she protests.

"Not if you want it in the line this spring," Skylar challenges.

Blue grabs the skirts. "Fine. I'll see what I can do."

"That's my girl," Adrian booms in his Russian accent as he enters the room.

Skylar's face lights up. "What are you doing here?"

He tugs her into him, kisses her, then announces, "Hoping to take my wife to a long lunch." He wiggles his eyebrows.

Blue wrinkles her nose. "Ew. Get a room, you two."

I laugh.

Adrian surprises Skylar almost weekly, sometimes more than once, to take her to a "long lunch." I'm sure it's code for sex. Sometimes, Skylar doesn't even return to the office.

Skylar frets, "I can't. I have to meet with Ramone over at the Skyline."

"Can't Fiona do it?" Adrian asks.

Skylar pins a hopeful gaze on me. "What's your schedule like for the rest of the afternoon? You know how he likes to gossip for an hour before getting down to business."

I glance at my schedule on my phone, then relay, "Nothing I can't do tomorrow."

"I could do it," Blue offers.

Skylar's face turns stern. "Sorry, but you don't have the experience yet. And don't you have work to do on your skirt? We only have a month before we solidify the spring line."

Blue's expression falls. "Ugh. Fiona always gets to have all the fun."

"Fiona put in the time. You haven't, and you sound like a brat," Adrian scolds.

Skylar adds, "Plus, Ramone has a relationship with Fiona and not with you. It's another thing you haven't developed. This business won't accept you just because you're my daughter."

Blue sighs, then glances at me, offering, "Sorry. Didn't mean it to sound so bad."

"It's okay," I assure her, then point to where we keep pieces of metal in different sizes, shapes, and colors. "That skirt might look great if you mix gold or other metals into the design. No one has done anything with that color pink and metals in over ten years, and I think it would be super fashionable right now."

Her eyes light up. "Okay. I'll see what I can do."

"Great idea," Skylar praises.

"No problem. Where's the book for my meeting with Ramone?" I question.

"In my desk," Skylar answers and then exits the wardrobe room.

I follow her down the hall and into her office.

She pulls a six-inch binder out of her drawer and holds it out to me, declaring, "He's not seen any of these. It'll probably take your entire afternoon. Are you sure you're good to go in my place?"

"Absolutely," I insist, taking the book, happy to have Skylar's trust for such an important meeting.

Ramone owns some of Chicago's and New York's top boutiques. He places millions of dollars of business a year with us. It took years for Skylar to feel confident in my ability to meet with him alone, and I don't take the responsibility lightly.

"Thanks again. And I appreciate you taking Blue under your wing. I know she can get a little ahead of herself sometimes," Skylar says.

I smile. "All good. She reminds me of me when I started working with you."

"You didn't have the entitlement she does," she asserts.

I scoff. "Sure I did. You just thought it was cute because I'm not your daughter."

"Which is why she needs to prove herself more than anyone," Skylar adds.

"She will. Plus, she's way more talented than I was right out of fashion school," I insist.

Amusement fills Skylar's expression. She shakes her head. "I don't know. I think younger Fiona and Blue would give each other a run for their money."

I beam. "Maybe."

"Ready?" Adrian asks, poking his head past the door.

"I'll see you later," I say, brushing past him to head to my office. I put on my coat and the scarf Kirill gave me.

Leather, rosewater, saffron, jasmine, and the other notes I still can't identify waft around me.

Why am I still wearing this?

It's cold.

So? I have hundreds of scarves.

I inhale deeper, wrap the soft cashmere around my neck, and text my driver. Then, I slide the binder into a huge briefcase. I leave the building, and a gust of wind hits my face.

Cillian waits next to the SUV. He questions, "Where to?" and opens the back door.

"Skyline," I state, sliding across the leather.

"Yes, ma'am," he replies, then closes the door and goes to the driver's side. He gets in and veers into traffic.

I sit back, staring at the buildings and the pedestrians on the sidewalk, inhaling Kirill's scent.

What is wrong with me? I need to stop wearing this.

Why does he have my dad's skull on him?

Like every time I've asked that question this past week, I have no answers. It nags at me until Cillian pulls up to the restaurant.

He gets out and opens my door.

Another harsh burst of wind slams against me as soon as I step outside. I push the scarf over my nose, rush into the building, then take the elevator to the top floor where Skyline is.

"Fiona!" Ramone sings, jumping off the bench as soon as I exit the elevator.

"Hi!" I reply, embracing him and kissing him on the cheek as he gives me one.

"Is Skylar not coming?" he questions, glancing behind me, the crinkles around his eyes popping out.

"She wasn't feeling well. I hope it's okay I came in her place?" I ask.

"Sure, sure, darling," he says, removing his top hat, and moves me toward the hostess stand. He lowers his voice, leans into my ear, and adds, "You can fill me in on what Skylar's been up to. You know, everything she won't tell me about herself." He winks.

I laugh, knowing full well I won't be disclosing any of Skylar's private affairs.

He opens the door, and the sound of guests chatting and moody music floods the atmosphere.

"Ramone! It's great to see you. Your table is ready," the hostess gushes.

"Great." He runs his hand through his dark hair, then slides his arm around my waist. He ushers me through the dimly lit restaurant. There are gold and black booths against the wall and tables with chairs next to the window. We get to our table. It's against the glass and showcases downtown Chicago with the lake behind it. Ramone circles his finger in the air.

I spin.

He helps me out of my coat, then pulls out my chair and motions with a "Sit, darling."

I obey.

He sits across from me and states, "Thanks, Fawn."

"Sure," the hostess says and then disappears.

"Good afternoon. I'm Kyle. I'll be serving you today," a twenty-something guy announces.

"Great. A bottle of Cristal, a dozen Oyster Rockefellers, and the caviar trio, please," Ramone orders.

"Yes, sir," Kyle replies, then disappears.

Ramone's eyes light up, and he leans forward, reaching for my scarf. "You look fabulous, darling. And where did you get this scarf? Such a bold statement to make, but, girl, the masculinity is working for you."

I softly laugh, not realizing I forgot to take the scarf off.

He points at me. "And your dress! It's from the line three years ago, right? What did you call it? The...the Mankiller!" He snaps his fingers.

I laugh harder, asserting, "You have a great memory."

"That little black dress sold out in minutes!" he gushes.

"I remember."

"Well, it still looks amazing on you! But that scarf with it...wow! Just wow!" he praises.

I don't have the heart to tell him I only had it on with my coat. But I also don't want to think about Kirill, so I change the subject. "And what have you been up to lately? Seeing anyone new?" I bat my eyelashes, grinning.

He smirks. "You know me well, dear."

"So, who is he?" I question.

"Well..." Ramone glances behind us and then leans closer. He murmurs, "He's a little younger than what I typically go for."

"Really?" I ask, biting my smile. Ramone's in his fifties and always dates guys in their late twenties to mid-thirties.

"Darling, he's barely legal to drink," Ramone states.

"Cristal," Kyle interjects, and a loud pop fills the air. He pours the bubbly liquid into a flute, hands me one, then fills a glass for Ramone.

"Thank you," I offer.

"You're welcome. I'll be back soon with your caviar trio," he relays.

Ramone holds his champagne in the air. "To our fabulous selves."

I clink his glass. "Salute."

"Salute," he echoes.

I take a sip, and the refreshing bubbles slide down my throat. "So what's the name of your new boo?"

A blush crawls over his cheeks. He answers, "Lazarus."

"Lazarus?"

"Yes." Ramone's eyes light up.

"That's a unique name."

"It is. And he's a unique man," Ramone adds, then takes a large mouthful of Cristal.

"Where did you meet?" I inquire, knowing the trick with Ramone is to keep him talking about himself so he doesn't push for private info on me or Skylar.

His eyes darken. "If I tell you, it has to stay between us."

I pretend to zip my lips and throw away the key.

He glances behind him again, then whispers, "He's a dancer at the Cat's Meow."

I catch myself from gaping and nod, offering, "Guess he's got a killer body if he's dancing there."

"Oh my God, he does!" he raves.

"So, how long have you been seeing each other?"

Nerves fill his expression. He admits, "About six months."

Surprise fills me. Ramone never keeps anyone around longer than a month, so I ask, "Is this serious?"

He stares at me a moment, then nods. "I asked him to move in with me."

"Aw. That's awesome. I'm happy for you," I declare and mean it. Ramone has always been so sweet to me. Over the years, I've heard one horror story after another about why he's ended things with others, so if he's happy, so am I.

"Thanks. Enough about me, though. What about you? Are you seeing anyone?" he inquires.

I shake my head. "No. Not right now."

He scrunches his forehead. "What happened to the last one? What was his name?"

"No one memorable," I state.

Kyle appears with a tray. He sets down a trio of different caviars. Then he puts a platter full of crackers, thin breads, unsalted pitas, and sliced gouda and cheddar cheese. He picks up the bottle of Cristal and tops off our flutes.

"Looks divine," Ramone gushes.

"Agreed," I affirm.

Before excusing himself, Kyle adds, "The Oyster Rockefellers will be out shortly."

Ramone puts caviar on a buttery cracker and hands it to me.

I pop it in my mouth. "Mmm," I moan as it melts against my tongue.

Ramone eats one and nods. "Never a disappointment." He washes it down with champagne and then continues, "So, no one has caught your interest lately?"

Kirill's face appears, but I push it away. "No," I lie.

Ramone studies me.

I nervously ask, "What?"

"Fiona O'Malley, did you just fib to me?"

I put caviar on a piece of gouda and push it past my lips, shaking my head.

"Are you sure?"

I nod, chewing my food.

"Well, I don't understand how a woman like you is so fabulous and single," he states.

I laugh. "Thanks for the compliment."

Relief fills me when he asks, "So, how's the new line coming along?"

"You're going to love it! We're still working on a few pieces. And Blue might get her first design in the show, but let me show you what we have so far," I declare, pulling the binder out of the briefcase.

Excitement flares on his expression. He opens the book and points at the back of the restaurant.

I refrain from rolling my eyes.

Ramone is the only buyer we trust to look at our line before it's live. With everyone else, we guard our book with our life. However, he was one of Skylar's first major buyers and has an eccentric way of assessing a line. We excuse ourselves to the bathroom, where he studies our book, and then we return and discuss.

I rise, put my napkin on my seat, and say, "If you'll excuse me, I need to use the ladies' room."

"Sure, darling. Take all the time you need," he replies, as if he thinks I need to use it, and it's not his rules I'm abiding by.

I pat him on the shoulder and brush past him, strolling toward the back of the restaurant. I'm almost to the bathroom when I glance at a couple in a booth, and freeze. My heart pounds so hard that I get dizzy, so I grab the back of the booth to steady myself.

What's he doing here?

Who is she?

She's beautiful.

His hand is over hers.

I'm going to kill him.

What am I saying? He's not mine.

Who is she to him?

Kirill sits beside a woman with long, curled dark hair and gorgeous hazel eyes. She has flawless skin, and I'd bet all my money she's Italian. Her lips are the perfect shade of red. She looks powerful but distraught. From what I can tell, she's taller than me based on her long torso and crossed legs, complete with killer stiletto knee-high boots.

Who is she?

Kirill has a compassionate expression on his face and squeezes her hand. He declares, "It'll be soon. You have to remain patient."

She says something I can't understand, but I pick out the phrase, "It's already been years," and know enough from living with my stepdad Dante to realize it's Italian. Her eyes well with tears and she blinks hard.

Kirill frowns. He softens his tone further, insisting, "Valentina, you're so close."

My insides quiver harder.

Is she with him?

My lips tremble, and my knees wobble.

Valentina opens her mouth and then slowly pins her gaze on mine. Her eyes widen. "Oh *merda.*"

Why is she saying oh shit?

Kirill follows her stare, freezing momentarily when he catches sight of me, his glassy blue gaze burning through me until I'm trembling. When he recovers, he says, "Fiona. What are you doing here?"

I open my mouth, but nothing comes out. I grip the back of the booth tighter until my knuckles hurt.

His scar twitches over his jaw. "Fiona?"

I glance at Valentina. "Sorry." I rush past them, willing my legs not to fail me, and find the bathroom door. I jiggle the knob, finally open it, and step inside.

My pulse pounds between my ears, drowning out other sounds. I press my hands on the counter, staring at my reflection, trying to catch my breath.

Who is he?

Why did he buy me coffee if he's with someone?

Why am I putting any stock in whatever I thought was happening before I found out about the skull design?

I turn, lean against the counter, and put my hand on my gut, feeling sick.

The door flies open, and Kirill steps inside.

I leap off the counter. My voice cracks when I scold, "This is the women's room."

His lips twitch. He reaches for the lock and turns it, stating, "Sue me." He stares at me, and I must be losing it. It appears heated, but I have to be wrong.

I point at the door and blurt out, "Your girlfriend is right outside this door!"

Surprise fills his expression, but he doesn't move.

"You're going to have a lot of explaining to do to her when you leave this bathroom after intruding like this!"

His mouth curves, and he teases, "What should I tell her about what happened between us here?"

My core catches fire, and I hate myself for it.

I don't engage in cheating.

I don't engage in cheating.

I don't engage in cheating.

He lunges closer, puts his hands on both sides of my hips, and cages me between his body and the counter.

I inhale sharply, staring at the skin on his chest peeking out of his dress shirt. His scent flares around me, stronger than what's left on the cashmere scarf.

He tilts my chin up, pinning his gaze on me, asserting, "She's not my girlfriend."

My voice shakes as hard as my insides when I say, "Sorry. Your wife." It stings my heart as it comes out.

He slowly shakes his head. "Not that either."

"Mistress?" I offer, still unable to take a lungful of air.

He chuckles. "Nope. None of the above. And I don't pay for sex either, so don't ask if she's a prostitute."

I bite on my smile, trying to stop it from exploding into existence.

"Why are you here?" he asks.

"Why are *you* here?" I retort.

His eyes light hotter. "I asked first."

"I asked second," I push back.

"Ah, you've already forgotten it, Fiona," he murmurs.

I squeeze my legs together, wishing my body didn't throb every time he said my name, and wonder how he could have this effect on me. I barely get out, "What's that?"

His expression turns serious. "A queen obeys her king. You don't seem to be very good at following orders."

My heart races faster, and butterflies attack my stomach with full force. I grip the counter, taking shallow breaths.

He slides his thumb over my jaw, then slips his hand under the scarf, stroking my neck over my pulse.

Tingles race down my back. I shiver and gasp, closing my eyes, drowning in his ability to overload my senses. It's to the point I'm burning with something I've never felt before.

He moves his mouth to my ear. His hot breath creates more chaos within me, and he warns, "You're going to have to learn how to obey your king, little bird."

I swallow, not understanding what this king and queen talk is all about, and stop myself from turning my head to touch my lips to his.

He circles his fingers around my throat, barely applying pressure, and a whimper flies out of me. He groans, then holds my head so I can't avoid his gaze.

The world stops moving. Time freezes, as do I, unable to tear my stare away from his.

In a firm tone, he claims, "I'm having lunch with a friend. And you?"

"Work lunch," I mutter.

His gaze drifts to my lips, then back to my eyes. He adds, "It was nice seeing you, Fiona. Have a good lunch." He studies me another moment, then releases me and steps back.

I gape as I watch him disappear through the door. When I exit the bathroom, neither he nor Valentina are anywhere to be seen.

Kirill

Chapter FOUR

"What was she doing here?" Valentina frets once we get into my car.

"Work lunch," I state.

Worry floods her expression. "If the Omni finds out I've spoken to her without permission, I'll never get a bid for a seat at the table!"

I sigh. "That's not happening."

"I've worked for years!" she cries out.

I turn and put my hands on her shoulders. "Valentina, listen to me closely. Nothing is happening. You'll eventually get a bid."

"You know the rules! If they find out—"

"You did nothing wrong. I will take full responsibility for this occurrence should there be any consequences. You have my word as king," I assure her.

She lowers her voice. "Kirill, I have to get a seat."

"You will. Now, don't think twice about this," I order, then sit back against the leather seat, staring out the window, trying to cool the hot blood flowing through my veins.

What is it about her?

Why doesn't she seem scared of me?

She didn't cringe when she saw me.

Valentina tears me out of my thoughts, asking, "She knows nothing, right?"

"No," I answer, continuing to look out the window.

"So how does she know you? She knew your name," Valentina points out.

"I randomly met her at a club when she was out with Zara. She ran into me," I admit, fighting a smile as I remember the night she literally ran into me.

"When?"

"Over a year ago. Then, a week ago, we bumped into each other at the coffee shop near Sean and Zara's place," I confess.

"Randomly?"

"Yeah," I affirm, wishing I could get Fiona's face out of my mind so my erection would completely disappear.

We drive several blocks, and Valentina softly claims, "You like her."

My chest tightens and my jaw locks.

Valentina adds, "You do. Don't you?"

I turn my head and open my mouth to deny it, but nothing comes out.

Valentina's lips twitch. She arches her eyebrows. "Well, I'll be. The impossible has happened."

An uncomfortable tightness forms in my chest. "The impossible?"

She nods. "Yeah. You. A woman. Feelings."

"Stop talking nonsense," I order.

Excitement grows on Valentina's expression. She shifts in her seat, turning more toward me. "You do. And from what I saw, she's into you too."

More unfamiliar sensations plague me. "Why would you say such a silly thing?"

She softly laughs. "She's a gorgeous woman. You're a super-fit, sexy man. What's so silly about it?"

"Stop talking nonsense," I snap.

Her face falls, and her voice turns stern. "Your scar doesn't eliminate you from the relationship-worthy pool. I've told you before. You're a good catch."

I grunt and turn toward the window again. Valentina's the only person on Earth I'd call a friend. It took years of working with her before our friendship grew and she got to the point she no longer cringed when she saw me. Now, I fully trust and respect her. And unfortunately, there's no one else I'd put in the friendship category since Sean and Fiona's dad was murdered.

The guilt I feel whenever I think of Sean Sr. mixes with my self-loathing.

Fiona will always hate me.

She can't find out.

It'll be impossible to hide it forever.

She'll want out of the marriage before it even starts, so I shouldn't worry about this.

"You should get over yourself. Fiona's into you."

"She's not, and your radar is off. Once she's forced to marry me, you'll see the disgust come out," I insist.

She scoffs. "She will have her choice to marry you or not, just like everyone else. It's an arranged marriage, not forced."

"Are you going to claim that when the Omni determines who you'll marry? Because we all know what happens if you don't do what they want."

Valentina takes a deep breath and swallows hard. Silence builds between us.

The driver veers to the right and parks in front of her building.

I get out, reach in to help her out, and she takes my hand. She exits the SUV, and I walk her into her building. When the elevator opens, I put my hand against the door and reiterate, "Don't worry about anything. You have my word your bid is coming soon. But I need you to be patient."

She casts another worried glance at me.

"I promise. You'll get your seat. Soon," I vow.

She sighs and nods. "Okay."

"Have a good rest of your day," I state.

She steps into the elevator and presses the button. She smiles and replies, "You too. Thanks."

"Anytime," I add, and the doors shut. I return to the SUV. My driver accelerates several blocks.

My phone rings. I glance at the screen, and my gut drops. It rings again, and I answer, "Ulrich."

"Meet me for a drink," he says in his German accent.

I glance out the window, replying, "I've got a busy day."

"It's not a suggestion," he states and then hangs up.

I close my eyes, squeezing my fists. For the first time in years, I'm not fully in charge. The Omni revoked my power regarding anything having to do with marrying Fiona. They voted to give Ulrich Koch the powers taken away from me during this time period. So, any decisions based on my nuptials are out of my control. If he's demanding I meet him, he no doubt wants to discuss my upcoming marriage.

I stare at my reflection in the divider glass, cursing the scar running across my face.

I have to get out of it for Fiona's sake. It's not fair to her.

I roll down the divider window and direct my driver, "Ivan, take me to Nostrovia."

"Yes, sir," he replies, and makes a U-turn.

I put the divider up, lean my head back, and close my eyes. All the arguments I've had with Ulrich and other Omni regarding this arrangement roll through my mind. I think about all the rules of The Underworld I know inside and out, trying to find a loophole, but it's pointless. There isn't one. Sean O'Malley Sr. didn't make loopholes. He created the rules for everyone to obey, and the king has to abide by them too.

Nostrovia isn't far, and the drive seems faster than normal. When Ivan stops outside the bar, I wait a moment, making one last-ditch effort to find something that will stop my pending marriage.

Ivan opens my door before I'm ready, but it's not his fault. I'm never going to be ready to ruin Fiona's life, but unless we want to both end up dead, there's no way to avoid it.

I slide out of the SUV, nod to the bouncer, Victor, and step inside. It's midafternoon, before happy hour, but the worn-down neighborhood bar is busy. I shove through the crowd of regulars and slip into the kitchen. I nod to the line cooks and step inside the walk-in fridge.

My breath comes out in a fog from the chilled air. I continue to the back, reach for the pull handle, and the frosted metal sends a jolt of cold through me. I open it and enter the private, dimly lit space.

Underworld men from all walks of life play poker at several round tables. A scantily-dressed bleached blonde struts around distributing drinks, mostly vodka. Alexsi, a balding, overweight bookie, records bets coming in from his cell.

Ulrich sits in his usual spot, alone in the corner, not participating in the fun. He hates being in Nostrovia, preferring to be in the German Underworld bar based on his heritage. Yet he doesn't have a choice. I'm still the king. This Underworld secret spot is the one I'm most comfortable with, so he has no choice if he wants to meet with me.

He takes a puff of his cigar, then lifts his drink toward me as I grab the chair across from him and pull it out. He nods. "Kirill."

Natalka, another scantily-dressed young woman, brings over a crystal tumbler. She picks up the fifth of vodka and pours. "Can I get you anything else tonight?" She bats her long, fake lashes at me, but her face hardens in a way it doesn't for the others. Her gaze darts to my eye that has the scar cutting through the lid before she quickly tries to refocus.

"No," I say, which is the same response as always. The other men here don't think twice about buying her sexual services, but I wasn't lying to Fiona. I don't entertain prostitutes.

"We're good," Ulrich states.

She pats him on the shoulder and then leaves, swaying her hips.

I take a large mouthful of vodka, relishing the burn as it travels to my stomach.

"The time is near. The moon will soon be in position," Ulrich announces.

My gut curls. I know all about the moon's positions and phases, and the different rituals surrounding them. Yet I protest, "You've not given her time to decide if she wants to be part of The Underworld. She knows nothing about it."

Ulrich's eyes turn to slits. "You shouldn't be seeing her."

My chest tightens. Another thing I've lost due to this debacle is my privacy. The Omni are watching me like they did before I earned my seat at the table. My privileges as king no longer exist. They'll only be restored when I've got a wedding ring on my finger.

Ulrich chuckles. "Ah, you forgot we see everything."

"Then you know it was pure coincidence we ran into each other. And Valentina had nothing to do with it either," I insist.

Ulrich takes a drink, then studies me.

Panic hits me. "Valentina isn't to blame. She had no knowledge Fiona would be there, just like I didn't."

He taps his fingers on his crystal glass. "For every action, there is a consequence. When things occur that shouldn't, the course changes."

My heart races faster. In an assertive tone, I reiterate, "Valentina had nothing to do with Fiona and I running into each other. And don't forget, Ulrich, when this is over, I'll be in charge again."

"That a threat?"

"No. It's a promise," I warn.

He purses his lips.

I lean closer, insisting, "Valentina is not to be punished."

"She will take one step backward," he states.

I clench my fists tight, arguing, "She is innocent."

He repeats, "For every action, there is a consequence. The course must change."

I grind my molars, pissed he's holding this against Valentina. She's worked hard to earn a bid. She deserves to have a seat at the table. It's not right she has to take a step backward.

He adds, "Her consequence will be—"

"She'll convince Fiona to go through with initiation," I interject, knowing it's the easiest consequence Valentina can be assigned.

Ulrich studies me.

"I'm still king. That is what will happen. Move Sylvia off the project," I order.

"Sylvia was chosen for Zara and Fiona," Ulrich points out.

"Like you said, the course must change," I declare.

Tension builds, thickening between us. Ulrich keeps his leer pinned on me, and I don't flinch.

I break the silence first, adding, "There's no reason you can't grandfather me as king without a queen."

"That was reserved for Sean Sr. only. You know this," Ulrich asserts.

My gut drops. I push, "He made the law for us to use. I don't need a queen to rule. I've done fine without anyone by my side."

Arrogance fills Ulrich's expression. He finishes his brandy, and asks, "What do you hate the most? The thought of having sex without your mask on or fucking Sean's daughter?"

Anger rushes through me, flooding every cell I have. I scowl, staying quiet, afraid of what I might say or how it'll sound. Both options scare the hell out of me.

Ulrich's lips curve. He continues to assess me and finally says, "You can't hide behind a mask forever. All snakes eventually shed their skin. The time has come for everyone in The Underworld to understand who their king really is without the mask."

I stare at my drink, clenching my jaw, gripping the glass so tight I'm surprised it doesn't break. My stomach quivers, and the thought of what's to come makes me ill.

Before I was scarred, I didn't have a problem with sex. After my disfigurement, I couldn't look at the disgust on a woman's face and stay hard. My skull mask gives me freedom. It allows me to participate in rituals without seeing the repugnance that's pinned on me on a daily basis whenever a woman glances at my face.

"My mask stays on," I insist.

Ulrich shakes his head. "No. Your mask will not be on when you marry your queen. It will not be on during any part of your ceremony. The time has come for you to stop hiding."

"I don't hide," I claim. But it's a lie.

Ulrich sits back and crosses his arms. "There's no point fighting about this. It has been decided."

My hand shakes under the table, and I grip my thigh. The thought of Fiona staring at me with abhorrence makes me ill.

Then another thought hits me. I blurt out, "What ceremony are you giving me?"

Evil crosses Ulrich's expression. He answers, "Unveiling of the Bride."

"No. I won't have it," I protest.

"All the members of The Underworld should be allowed to witness the nuptials. It is a great day of celebration," Ulrich claims.

My stomach twists. I mentally scan the list of rituals and then demand, "I want Knights of the Round Table."

"But that's more private," Ulrich points out.

"I'm king. I have a right to Knights of the Round Table. It's in the laws," I insist.

He takes another mouthful of brandy, then caves. "You're right. I can't stop you."

A bit of relief fills me, but I repeat, "There's no reason I can't be grandfathered in with no queen."

Ulrich opens his mouth, then shuts it.

I lean closer. "Say whatever it is you were about to say."

"I'm thinking."

I stay quiet initially, but then push, "Grandfather me in."

He motions for another brandy.

The server brings him one and he takes a large mouthful. Then he sets down his glass and stares at me.

"Grandfather me in," I beg.

His lips twist and he replies, "I'll make a deal with you."

"Go on."

"What's the only other way to avoid having a queen at your side?" he questions.

I take a minute, wondering what I've missed, then a cold chill flares down my spine. I gape at him in horror.

Excitement expands in his expression and voice. "During the Knights of the Round Table, she can tap out and stay your queen. Or she can choose not to tap out and...well..." His grin grows and he finishes with, "You can rule alone for the rest of your life."

The air in my lungs turns stale.

"What's wrong, Kirill? Isn't that what you want? To rule alone?" he asks.

"I'd have to kill her," I blurt out.

He shrugs. "It would be her choice. If she can't tap out, then that's on her, not you."

My mouth turns dry.

He leans closer and murmurs, "She'll never have to look at you again. All the fears you have of her giving you that look? Well, you'll only have to see it on your wedding night. After that, that expression will be eliminated. At least on her."

The air stifles my lungs. I hate how he knows my fears and how much enjoyment he's getting out of my discomfort.

He rises. "Get Valentina to start the process. And remember, the choice is yours."

I stare at him.

He continues, "Everything in The Underworld comes with choices. Just don't make the wrong one." He winks, pats me on the shoulder, and disappears through the door.

I don't move for a long time, unable to get the different scenarios out of my mind.

I can't kill her.

It'll save her from a lifetime of disgust and hurt.

Why am I even contemplating this?

She'll never get over fucking me without my mask on.

I'm not killing her.

It'd be a blessing in the end for her.

I go over and over scenarios, cringing at every one, hating myself for each option I'm presented with and how I don't eliminate it right away.

This entire situation is wrong. Every ending only brings misery.

"Can I get you anything else?" Natalka offers, giving me the same grimace as before, then quickly covering it up.

I don't answer her. I rise, down the rest of the vodka, and hurry out of Nostrovia. Instead of getting in my car, I walk the city streets for hours, numb to the cold and unable to escape the nightmare of choices in front of me.

Fiona

The Next Day

Chapter
FIVE

*E*verything feels off since my encounter with Kirill yesterday. I made it through the rest of my lunch meeting with Ramone. There was plenty of time to return to the office and get in a few more hours of work, but I couldn't do it. I went home, replaying Kirill's and my exchange in the bathroom.

To make matters worse, Valentina haunts me. She's beautiful, and their lunch seemed intimate. Surely, she's more than just a friend to him?

It doesn't matter, I tell myself for the millionth time.

The alarm blares into the silence. I groan and hit the button on my phone, exhausted from no sleep and partially relieved it's time to get up.

I have to stop thinking about him, I scold myself.

It doesn't work. I can't escape Kirill's face, intoxicating scent, and strong fingers around my throat. I jump in the shower, and all I hear is my name rolling off his tongue or his Russian accent, declaring, *"A queen obeys her king."*

Why does he keep saying that?

Suds run down my body, and Kirill's hand over Valentina's sends a wave of nausea through my gut.

Friends, my ass.

Maybe he's telling the truth.

No way.

They looked super close.

Another flare of jealousy hits me until I see green.

"Ugh! Stop these stupid thoughts. It doesn't matter," I reprimand myself as I turn off the water. I grab a towel and add, "Awesome, now I'm talking to myself."

I dry off, grab my robe off the hook, and secure it around me. I continue to go through the motions of getting ready. Once dressed, I enter the kitchen, turn the coffeepot on, and remove the creamer from the fridge.

"Can I have one too?" I hear a woman with a somewhat-familiar Italian accent ask.

The hairs on my arms rise. I spin and freeze in place, my mouth going dry.

Valentina smiles but doesn't say anything more. She's wearing a red designer minidress, and she looks as amazing as yesterday.

I grab a knife and snarl, "What are you doing in my house?"

She holds her hands up. "Easy there. I'm not here to hurt you."

"You have two seconds to answer my question," I warn, stepping closer and pointing the knife at her.

Amusement fills her expression. "You're holding that wrong if you're going to stab me."

I glance at the weapon.

She adds, "You have to hold it up in the air like this." She demonstrates how to hold it, as if she has a knife in her hand, and continues, "The force coming down will dig the blade deeper into me."

I gape at her, unsure what to do.

"Fiona, put the knife down. And please, give me a cup of coffee. It's early," she orders, pulling out a barstool and sitting at the island.

I don't move, repeating, "What are you doing in my house?"

She points at the coffeepot. "Caffeine first. We both need to function, and from what I can tell, you didn't sleep too well last night."

My insides quiver. I open my mouth, but nothing comes out.

How does she know that?

I glance behind me.

"No one is here but you and me. Why don't you sit? I'll get the coffee." She gets up, takes two mugs out of my cabinet, as if she already knows where everything is, and pours a cup. She sets it on the counter and places the cream and sugar next to it. Then she opens a drawer, pulls out a spoon, and sets it down.

"How did you get in here?" I ask, knowing my stepfather Dante has decked out my building with the highest level of security.

"I'll explain everything, I promise. And you want to learn about your father's mark, right?" She arches her eyebrows.

My pulse skyrockets. "What do you know about my father?"

She points to the seat. "Sit." Then, she pours a mug for herself. She adds a spoonful of sugar and then leans against my back counter. "Sit so we can talk, Fiona."

Not knowing what else to do, I keep the knife by my side and take a seat.

"Fix your coffee and then we'll talk," she commands.

I obey and take a sip.

"There. Better?" she asks with amusement.

"Start talking," I demand.

Her amusement intensifies. "You're a lot like your brother."

"You know Sean?"

"Of course." She takes another sip, keeping her gaze on me.

I grip both hands around the hot mug and demand, "Spit out whatever it is you're here to say."

She lowers her gaze. "You don't like me, do you?"

"Am I supposed to? You did break into my house," I point out.

She studies me for a moment, and a knowing expression appears on her face. She states, "That's not why you don't like me. Is it?"

My heart races faster. "That's not a good enough reason?"

Her lips purse, and she studies me closer.

I want to smack her arrogance off her. Instead, I grip the hot mug tighter.

She blurts out, "You don't like me because of him."

"Him?" I ask, but my chest tightens. I already know who she's referring to.

She answers, "Kirill."

My cheeks heat. "I don't know what you're talking about," I lie.

"I can assure you that we're only friends."

"Sure you are," I mutter, then curse myself.

"You should also know I'm his only friend."

"That's an arrogant statement to make," I accuse.

"It's true. You'll see one day."

More confusion fills me, but I'm not buying that a man like Kirill isn't surrounded by a ton of friends.

Are they all women?

I don't care.

Ugh. They probably are all women, flocking around him to get an ounce of attention.

"It's only me. He's a very private person," she adds.

The air turns thick. I hold my breath, wrapping my mind around her statement.

So she's privy to his private life?

"You don't have to worry about me," she adds.

"Why would I worry about you?" I snap.

She takes another sip of coffee and smiles. In a cheerful voice, she chirps, "Glad we got that out of the way. So, time is running out. The moon will soon be ripe, and you'll have to make the biggest decision of your life."

"Still not following."

She sets her coffee down, reaches up, and twists her hair into a knot. She turns so her back is to me, revealing the same brand Sean, Zara, and Kirill have, except her skull has red coloring.

Goose bumps pop out on my skin, and my breath catches. "Why do you have my father's mark on your neck?"

She releases her long, dark hair and turns back to face me. She questions, "Since we're low on time, I assume you want the quick answer?"

I still don't know what she means about the moon or this timeframe, but I affirm, "Yes."

"Great. I hate sugar-coating stuff." She drinks more coffee.

I wait for her to speak.

She steps closer to the island and puts her mug down, saying, "The skull is the mark of The Underworld. Your father created a secret world so all crime families could coexist harmoniously. Inside The Underworld, it doesn't matter what family's blood runs through your veins. Everyone respects each other. We aren't enemies."

I scoff. "Right. And Santa is real, sliding down millions of chimneys one night a year."

"It's true," she insists.

"Did you know the tooth fairy exists, too?" I sarcastically add.

Her voice turns stern. "I understand this is a lot to take in, but The Underworld is real. Your father created it so you and your brother wouldn't have to deal with the wars and bloodshed of his time."

"Bullshit."

Her eyes turn to slits.

I don't flinch, lifting my chin and matching her glare.

She points at me, warning, "The appropriate phase of the moon is almost upon us. We don't have time to waste."

I roll my eyes. "Not following your moon talk. Next, you'll tell me that my father was a hippie."

Anger lights her eyes. She reaches down, pulls a phone out of her boot, and swipes the screen. She sets the phone down in front of me.

I glance at the screen and see a contact entry with my brother's name and photo.

I shift in my seat.

Two rings fill the air, then he answers, "Valentina. What can I do for you?"

"I'm at your sister's. Can you confirm your father created The Underworld, and that its purpose is for crime families to live harmoniously?"

Silence fills the line.

"Sean?" Valentia questions.

He clears his throat. "Fiona? You're there?"

I swallow the lump in my throat. "Yes."

"At your place?"

"Yes."

"I'm not far. I'll be right over."

My gut spins. "Sean, is she telling the truth?"

There's another beat of silence before he confirms, "Yes. It's true. I'll be there shortly." The line goes dead.

I gape at the phone, attempting to decipher what all this means.

Valentina softly says, "I know this is a lot for you to take in, but we don't have much time. It's imperative we fast-track you for your coronation."

I jerk my head upward. "Coronation?"

She nods, and her expression is stern. "Yes."

"Sorry, I'm lost again," I admit.

She grabs the coffeepot, refills our cups, and places it back on the burner. Then, she strolls over to the couch and picks up an oversized bag. She opens it and pulls out a huge black binder.

I question, "What is that?"

She sets it before me, announcing, "The Royal Doctrine. It's the rule-book for the monarchy."

"The monarchy?" I ask, running my fingers over the raised gold skull of my father's design and then the two crowns. They're slanted against one another, as if holding each other up.

Valentina takes the seat next to me. "Yes. You and your brother were always meant to have a seat at the table. Since he changed the course of how things were to go, your role is now bigger."

I lock eyes with her. "My role?"

She nods. "Yes. Everyone strives to become an Omni. No one dares to dream of wearing the crown. But you? Well, you're meant to wear it."

Speechless, I study her and realize she believes this talk about monarchies and crowns. Suddenly, this all seems funny to me. Maybe it's my lack of sleep, but an uncontrollable laugh erupts from me. I can't stop it, and tears roll down my cheeks.

Valentina stares at me like I'm crazy.

Her expression only makes me laugh harder.

"What's so funny?" she asks.

I can't answer her. I look at the cover of the binder and think about her crazy talk, and it finally hits me.

My brother and Zara set me up. They're playing a sick joke on me and have been telling the truth all along.

My father's skull design is just a mark, nothing more.

"Did I miss something?" Sean's voice booms across the room.

I wipe my face, glance at him, and try to pull it together.

"I think she's in shock," Valentina offers.

Sean pulls out the barstool next to me and sits. He asks Valentina, "What have you told her?"

"Not much. I'm trying to explain her role."

I stop laughing and blurt out, "Nice one, Sean. I'm going to get you and Zara back for this."

His face remains stern. "Back for what?"

"Stop playing dumb," I order.

"This isn't a game, Fiona. It's the furthest possible thing from a game," he declares.

I start to laugh again. "Nice try."

He slams his hand on the counter, barking, "This isn't a joke!"

I jump. "Jesus—"

"The Underworld is real, Fiona. Dad created it. He died because of it. And you have to decide whether to take your place in it or not. But if you don't, Zara and I are dead," he announces.

Shock fills me. I gawk at him.

He closes his eyes for a minute and shakes his head. He mumbles, "We didn't know you would be pulled into this. I swear neither of us knew."

Fear ignites within me, rushing through me like water from a damn that's broken. My voice is shaky when I whisper, "Sean, what did you get me involved in?"

He pins his greens on me, full of sympathy and something I never see on my brother. I realize it's trepidation.

Valentina interjects, "Both of you were meant to have a seat at the table. The course just got slightly changed."

"Slightly?" Sean seethes.

She accuses, "Byrne and Sylvia prepared you and Zara. The decision to go against his instructions was yours and Zara's. That changed your course."

"Everyone died. It should have no bearing," Sean argues.

"Who died?" I ask.

They exchange a heated look, and Valentina answers, "No one you ever met. And you don't have the clearance level to know anything about it until you've gone through your coronation."

I turn toward my brother. "What is she talking about?"

He glances at Valentina and then his anxious expression meets mine. "The Omni have decided you will be queen."

Unlike before, nothing seems funny, just even more confusing. I inquire, "What is the Omni?"

"*Who* is a better question," Valentina states.

Exasperated by this entire situation, and still not trusting her, I shrug. "Okay, who?"

She looks at Sean.

He divulges, "The Omnipotence, or Omni, are the rulers of The Underworld. The seat at the table refers to the Omni. I gave up my token, and now you're to become queen."

I scoff. "Token? Like from an arcade?"

"This is serious, Fiona!" he reprimands.

"You know you both sound crazy, right?"

"Yeah, but it's all real. I lost my token, and now your seat at the table is the throne!"

"This is a joke," I state, but the pit of my stomach tells me differently.

Sean lowers his voice. It's full of dread and remorse. He offers, "I didn't know what would happen. I didn't know they would make me..." He swallows hard and looks away.

"Make you do what?"

He takes several breaths, then pins the guiltiest look I've ever seen on him, announcing, "Give you to the king."

My breath catches in my lungs. I stare at him in disbelief.

Valentina interjects, "It's an arranged marriage. No one is forcing you to marry him. It's your choice to take your rightful place as queen or not enter The Underworld. But your father wanted you to be a part of it."

"I'm not marrying some stranger! I don't care what my dad wanted!"

"It's not that easy, Fiona," Sean asserts.

I spin on him. "Why is that? Seems pretty simple to me. Forget I know anything about whatever this is." I tap the binder and continue, "Or me marrying a stranger. I'm out."

Sean cries out, "They'll kill Zara and me! The twins will be orphans!"

Horror fills me. The thought of River and Willow growing up without parents pains me. I lost my father at an early age, and that sucked. Thankfully, I had my mom. I can't imagine what life would have been like with both my parents dead.

Sean's desperate tone fills the air. "I know it's a bad situation. And I've gone round and round with the Omni, but they won't change their mind."

"A bad situation? That's what you call making me marry a stranger so my niece and nephew don't end up parentless?"

He sighs. "Fiona, I know this isn't ideal—"

"Ideal?" I shriek. "You're putting me in a horrible position. I swear to God, Sean, this better be a sick joke!"

The color drains from his face, and he slowly shakes his head.

My gut dives and then spins into chaos. I put my hand over it, swallowing down bile.

He puts his palm on my thigh. "I'm so sorry. Honestly. I would never have intentionally put you in this position."

I remove his hand, snarling, "Don't touch me, Sean."

Shame fills his expression.

Valentina offers, "If it makes it any easier, your seat is more powerful than your brother's."

I snap my head toward her, seething, "Get out."

She shakes her head. "I can't. We aren't done yet."

"I said to get out," I repeat sternly, pointing at the door.

"She's right. She can't go," Sean says.

I rise, pick up my mug, and slam it into the sink. It's harder than I wanted, and several pieces chip off the ceramic. I roar, "Dammit!"

"We need to go through the book," Valentina urges.

"I need to get to work," I declare.

"You're not going today. I already told Skylar you came down with the flu," Sean discloses.

Rage fills me. I explode, "You have no right to mess with my job!"

"The Underworld doesn't work on your timeline, Fiona. We work on theirs," he explains.

"I don't care about this Underworld!"

Valentina asks, "Then you're okay with Sean and Zara dying?"

I take deep breaths, my glare drifting between the two of them. I finally point at Sean. "How could you let something like this happen?"

A lifetime of regret crawls deep into his expression until my strong brother looks like a weak and helpless man. It's something I've never seen on him.

"Well? Answer me," I push, angrier than I ever remember being.

He closes his eyes and laments, "I didn't know. I'm so sorry to put you in this position."

My lungs tighten, only allowing shallow breaths of oxygen. I glare at Sean, and the more I study him, the more this situation sinks in until my bones turn cold.

Valentina picks up the binder and opens it. She taps her finger on the page. "Time is running out. You have to not only understand the Royal Doctrine but memorize it."

I gape at her. The binder is at least four inches thick. I glance at my brother again, then ask, "Who do I have to marry?"

Disgust fills his expression and he grinds his molars.

My insides quiver harder. "Who, Sean?"

"I'm sorry, but I'm not allowed to tell you."

"Are you serious right now?"

He nods. "I'm sorry. If I could, I would."

I glare more daggers his way, then finally order, "Get out of my house, Sean."

"Fiona—"

"No! Leave! Now!" I demand, stalking to the door and opening it.

He slowly gets up and stops in front of me. "I'm sorry. If I had known—"

"Get out," I seethe.

He hesitates but finally leaves. As I watch him disappear down the hall, my anger only grows.

My brother and I have had our differences in the past. We've had times where we needed some space from the other. Right now, I'm unsure if I can ever look at him again.

Kirill

The Next Day

Chapter
SIX

"How did she take it?" I ask the minute I open the door.

"Well, hello and good morning to you too," Valentina chirps, brushing past me. She shrugs out of her long coat and drapes it over the black leather sofa.

My irritation level is at a high. I bark, "I don't have time, Valentina. How did Fiona react?"

Valentina's face turns stern. She points at me. "No need to get snippy."

"Talk," I order.

She puts her hand on her hip and discloses, "She's pissed off, hates Sean, doesn't want her niece and nephew to grow up as orphans, and is smarter than I credited her as being."

My chest squeezes tight. "Why is that?"

Valentina goes to the kitchen, opens the fridge, and grabs a bottle of water. She pops off the cap, takes a long sip, then reveals, "She already has the Royal Doctrine memorized."

Pride sweeps through me, along with surprise. It took me over a week to remember every tedious law. I cautiously probe, "She understood the intricacies?"

"Yes. Much faster than I expected."

That's my little bird.

She adds, "She's a pistol. Don't piss her off, or you're going to pay for a long time."

"Why do you say that?"

Valentina scoffs, "She thinks I'm the devil. I'm pretty sure it has more to do with her belief we're fucking than me being the messenger."

Panic hits me. "That's impossible. I told her we were friends."

Valentina nods. "Yep. I reiterated that, but little Miss Sunshine didn't want to accept it."

An uncomfortable tugging sensation in my chest erupts. I can't help myself and ask, "What did she say?"

"Nothing much. But I'm a woman. I can tell these things," she insists.

The hope fizzles. As I expected, Valentina is making something out of nothing.

Stop acting like Fiona will be any different than any other woman, I scold myself, then reprimand Valentina. "Let's stick to the tasks at hand, please."

Valentina rolls her eyes. "Fine. Have it your way."

I'm hit with a wave of relief. The last thing I want to do is wallow in my misery all day. I prod, "So she's going through with it?"

"Of course. She loves her niece and nephew too much. I suppose for Sean and Zara, too, although I'm pretty sure they're on her shit list for life."

My gut dives, and guilt assails me. The last thing I want is for Fiona to hate her family members. And she and Zara are more than sisters-in-law. They're best friends.

Valentina points out, "There's only a week until the ceremony. Have you done everything on your end?"

I arch my eyebrows.

Valentina shakes her head in disappointment. "Really, Kirill?"

"What?"

She huffs. "This isn't a normal initiation. It's a coronation, and you're the king."

"So I've been told," I sneer.

"Snap out of it, Kirill!"

"I don't know—" I shut my mouth, another jolt of panic striking me.

"Ah, reality is hitting you," she coos.

My heart thumps hard against my chest cavity. "There's only a week left."

"Right. Do you want me to help you pick things out?" she offers.

I shake my head. "No."

"Are you sure? I can offer a female perspective."

I hesitate but then sternly reply, "No. I'll do it on my own."

Valentina shrugs. "Okay. Suit yourself." She finishes her bottle of water, tosses it in the trash, and puts her coat on. "If you change your mind, let me know."

"I won't," I insist.

She gives me an I-don't-believe-you look, then steps out my front door.

I pace my house for an hour, making a mental list of everything I'm required to do. Then I text my driver and flight crew. I exit the building and get into the SUV.

Traffic is heavy, and the drive to Chicago Executive takes longer than normal. It only serves to make me antsier. By the time I get on my plane, my palms are sweating.

My flight attendant, Arina, greets me with a curtsy. "Your Majesty. Nice to see you. Can I get you a drink?"

"Vodka," I state, then take a seat.

She brings me a crystal tumbler with three fingers of liquor and asks, "Would you like something to eat?"

I grumble, "No. Please tell the pilot to get off the ground as soon as possible."

"Yes, sir," she replies, then disappears. She returns a moment later, stating, "He said three minutes."

"Great. Thank you," I respond, then stare out the window, my heart racing faster.

What if I pick the wrong one?

I should have brought Valentina.

No. This is my responsibility.

The flight to Monaco takes almost eleven hours. I normally sleep on flights, but I can't today. When I arrive, the hours of self-loathing and remorse over ruining Fiona's life hit a high.

The plane door opens, and I walk through the hallway, lit only by the flickering flames from the candles inside the sconces. There are several turns before I get to the first door. I put my hand on the knob and pause.

What am I doing?

There's no way out of this.

Man up.

I open the door and enter a room with a table, a locked wooden box, and two oversized chairs. It's in the back of a jewelry store, which happens to be the most exclusive and expensive supplier of wedding rings in the world. I sit and wait.

A few minutes pass until Ahmed, an old Moroccan with wrinkled skin and who is The Underworld's only jeweler, appears. He bows reverently. "Your Majesty."

I rise and hold out my hand. "Ahmed. Good to see you."

He shakes my hand and smiles, replying, "And it is always a pleasure to see you, sir."

I motion to the chair. "Please. Sit."

He obeys.

I follow suit and wait.

His brown eyes gleam. He unlocks the box and removes the lid, claiming, "These are the best in the world, reserved for your queen."

Diamonds glitter with brilliance, making the situation I'm in more real. My pulse skyrockets as I pick up each one, assessing them.

"Perfect clarity, color, and cuts," Ahmed assures with pride in his tone.

"Yes, I can see that."

"Did you have a specific cut in mind?" he probes.

The hairs on my neck rise in apprehension.

She has to love it.

The air turns thick, and my palms sweat again.

Ahmed picks up a ring and holds it out, suggesting, "What about a princess cut?"

"She's not a princess. She's a queen," I remind him.

"Ah. Forgive me," he says and sets it down.

I study the rows of diamonds again, trying to breathe through my panic.

"I'm so sorry. I didn't mean to be rude. Can I get you a drink?" Ahmed questions.

"Maybe a water," I respond.

"One moment." He rises, disappears through the door, then returns with a glass of water and a smaller, gold metal box.

I down half the water and point at the box. "What's in there?"

His expression turns serious. He states, "There's one last diamond. Since you're marrying his daughter, I believe you should reconsider your declaration to keep it as a relic."

My stomach flips. I lock eyes with Ahmed, asking, "You mean Sean's ring?"

He nods. "Yes. The one reserved for Bridget for when she joined The Underworld."

I hold my breath, staring at the box.

Ahmed unlocks it, removes the gold lid, and scoots the box across the table.

I pick up the seven-carat, marquise-cut diamond attached to a gold band, mumbling, "I forgot about this ring."

Ahmed admires it, stating, "I miss the era where marquise cuts were the big rage. Bridget really loved them. Silver was making a big state-ment, but she preferred gold. And the inscription was classic Sean." He hands me a magnifying glass.

I spin the ring and look through the glass, reading, *Mine for eternity.* My skin erupts with goose bumps. I stare for several minutes at the exquisite piece, imagining it on Fiona's finger.

It's perfect.

Ahmed informs, "A lot of women don't like marquise. Do you know if Fiona does?"

I shake my head. "No. But if she doesn't like it, I'll get her a different one."

"Do you want to pick a second choice just to be safe? These other ones are more popular right now," he asks, pointing at the big box.

"No. I'm taking this one. Is it the correct size, or do you need to make adjustments?" I prod.

He smiles. "She is the same size as her mother. It'll fit her perfectly."

"Then it's meant to be," I state, feeling a swell of relief.

He puts it in the box, replaces the lid, and locks it. He hands me the key, declaring, "If you lose this, I have another."

"I won't," I insist, putting the box in the inside pocket of my sports coat.

"Good. And congratulations," he offers.

A strange feeling hits me. I nod. "Thank you." I rise, shake his hand, and exit through the door I entered. Then I walk down a different hallway and open another door, stepping into an empty room with one chair.

That anxious feeling reappears. I pace the small space, then sit and tap my fingers on my thighs.

The door finally opens. Colette, a petite woman with a tight bun, glasses hanging around her neck, and just as many wrinkles as

Ahmed, beams at me. She curtsies and chirps in a French accent, "Your Majesty. What an honor to see you again."

I lean in and kiss her on the cheek. "Colette. How have you been?"

"Very good, sir."

"And your family?"

"Just as well," she informs.

"Glad to hear it."

She motions to the chair. "Please sit. Can I get you anything to drink or eat?"

"No, thank you."

"Alright. One moment." She opens the door and belts out orders in French.

Two younger women appear in the doorway. They curtsy, then wheel three racks of dresses inside the tiny space.

Colette motions toward the door. "Thank you." She says something in French, and they disappear. She turns toward me with a huge smile. "What an exciting decision you get to make!"

My stomach clenches. I never understood why Sean Sr. created a rule that the king picks the queen's wedding gown. It seems like it takes away the excitement from the bride.

Fiona's far from excited, I remind myself.

Maybe this is better for her if I do it.

Who am I kidding? I know nothing about wedding dresses.

"Sir, may I show you my top picks?" Colette asks.

"Please," I beg, not wanting to screw this up but feeling like I'm going to.

Colette pulls a dress off the rack and hangs it on the wall hook. She selects two more and points to the first. It has a super-puffy skirt and reminds me of a princess.

"Not that one," I say.

"No?"

"No. She's a queen, not a princess," I state.

What aren't these people understanding about this?

Colette nods. "Understood, sir." She moves to the next dress. It's form-fitting and all satin.

"Too plain," I say.

She moves to the third dress. "This one has more beading. Is it more your taste?"

I stare at the pearls and lace, then give Colette a frantic look. I admit, "I don't know how to do this."

She softly laughs. "It's okay. We'll find your queen the perfect dress. Don't worry."

I rise and move toward the racks. "Do you mind?"

"Not at all," she says.

I sift through the heavy dresses, bypassing most of them, pausing on a few, then get to the last rack.

"Saved the best for last," Colette states.

"I hope so," I mutter, my palms wet again. I wipe them on my pants and carefully touch only the hangers. I slide four dresses across the rack, then freeze.

The dress is a golden cream color with an intricate geometric design and just the right number of crystals and pearls. And it has a dove on the chest.

My little bird.

Colette claps her hands, practically singing, "It's such an exquisite couture piece! The entire dress is hand-embroidered with sequin crystal beading and elegant pearls. The bird holds the corset together, and did you know that doves represent love?"

Love.

Not in the cards for me.

"Feel the luxurious lace! It's so soft," she continues.

I trail my fingers down the skirt, unable to refute her claim. I confess, "I thought lace was itchy."

She smiles. "Not the most elegant kind!" She steps next to me and pulls it off the rack, then takes it to the wall and hangs it on the hook. "Can you see Fiona in it?"

I study the dress, unable to imagine anyone but her in it.

Colette gushes, "Ah! You can imagine it! I see it dancing in your eyes!"

My cheeks heat, and I shift on my feet. "Sorry?"

She points at me. "That look! Right there! This is the dress, isn't it?"

I study the wedding gown, trying to imagine Fiona in anything else, but it's useless. I ask Colette, "What if she doesn't love it?"

She shrugs. "Pick two backups. I'll send you with all three."

I think about it for a moment, then declare, "I'd appreciate it if you pick the others."

She nods. "No problem, Your Majesty."

"Thank you."

She quickly selects two very different gowns, hangs them on the wall, and inquires, "Are these good?"

"Sure."

"Great." She enters the hall, says something in French, and the young women return. They curtsy again.

"No need to curtsy anymore today."

"Sir?" a dark-haired girl asks.

"It's okay. I'd prefer you don't," I tell her.

"If the king says no, just obey," Colette reprimands.

The girl's cheeks heat. "Yes. Sorry, sir."

"No problem."

Colette speaks in French again, and they wheel out the dresses. She turns toward me with a new gleam in her eyes. "Are you ready for the fun part?"

I arch my eyebrows.

Colette questions, "I was told you'll have a Knights of the Round Table ceremony?"

My chest tightens. I had forgotten about my upcoming moment of horror, not just for myself but for Fiona.

"Just one moment," she says, and peeks out the door again, rattling off a string of French.

Another rack, this one full of lingerie, is wheeled inside, and the girls disappear.

Colette asks, "Is there a specific body part you'd like to focus on?"

Jesus.

"No. Whatever you think she'll like is fine," I answer as I take a seat. I put my ankle on my knee, trying to look casual and not appear embarrassed.

Colette holds up two barely-there white pieces of fabric. "Are you thinking separates or one piece?"

The image of what I think Fiona will look like pops into my mind. My mouth waters and my dick hardens.

I'm the fucking king. Stop acting like a child.

"I'm not picky," I admit, trying to sound normal, but it comes out strangely.

Colette wrinkles her forehead, turns to the rack, shifts through several pieces, then pulls out a creamy white one-piece with tiny hints of gold and blue. She boasts, "Fiona will look great in this!"

Hot blood shoots through my veins. The space in my pants reduces further.

She adds, "It'll solve the blue requirement too."

"What's that?" I question, tearing my eyes off the lingerie.

She beams. "You know. Something old. Something new. Something borrowed. Something blue."

"Oh. That's an American tradition, right?"

"It was from the Victorian era in the U.K. America ran with it," Colette states.

Old. New. Borrowed. Blue.

Stress begins to stir within me.

Colette shakes the delicate piece and asks, "Is this the winner? Can you see her in it?"

I rise, grumbling, "I'll take it. Can you package everything and have it taken to the plane?"

"Of course."

I move toward the door and then freeze. "Shit!"

"What's wrong, sir?" Colette frets.

"How do I know it'll fit her?" I question.

She smiles. "You must have pre-wedding jitters. You know all the dresses and undergarments are already sized to those about to be initiated."

"Oh. Right. Sorry, I have a lot on my mind," I fumble, then nod. "Thank you for your help."

"Anytime, Your Majesty," Colette says with a curtsy.

I exit the way I came in, and when I reach the plane, I brush past Arina.

Old. Borrowed. Blue.

"Drink?" Arina offers, holding out a tumbler of vodka.

I grab it with a nod and tap the crystal, looking out the window. Every second that goes by stresses me more.

Arina stops in the aisle next to my seat. "Sir, the packages have arrived. I stored them up front. Is there anything else you need before we leave?"

"No."

"Okay, I'll let the pilot know," she says.

Within minutes, we're in the air.

I reach for the gold box and unlock it, staring at the ring.

Something old.

A splinter of relief lodges itself in my chest. "Old, new, and blue is taken care of, but what about borrowed?" I mutter, taking a sip of liquor and grimacing as it burns my throat.

The eleven-hour flight doesn't go any faster than the first time. I pace the majority of it, wondering what Fiona could borrow.

The pilot announces, "We're about to land. Please take your seat and secure your seat belt."

I obey, leaning my head back against the seat and closing my eyes.

Think!

We land, and I'm no closer to an answer. My SUV waits on the runway, and I don't waste time getting into it. The dresses and lingerie are loaded into the trunk, and within twenty minutes, my driver pulls up to the curb in front of my building.

I go inside, wait for the elevator that still hasn't been fixed, and worry about what Fiona can borrow.

"What a stupid tradition," I mumble, stepping into the penthouse. I pace the family room until the packages arrive.

Once I'm alone again, I take the dress with the dove, the lingerie, and the ring out. I put them on my oversized bed and stare at them.

I need to know if she likes any of this.

Worried I made the wrong choice, I glance at the items and then go over to my desk. I open the drawer, tear off the top of my letterhead so I don't break any rules, and remove the cap from my fountain pen.

A thousand things race through my head, and I take a few moments to sort through them, then begin writing.

My dearest Fiona...

Fiona

The Next Day

Chapter
SEVEN

My doorbell rings, and I groan. It's been a long few days. I've barely slept, and avoided countless calls and texts from Zara and Sean. I even kicked them out of my house when they came over last night unannounced.

The one saving grace came from my work. As usual, it's been hectic. Between mentoring Blue and moving forward on the upcoming spring line, it was the only time my mind wasn't thinking about what's ahead of me.

Am I really going to marry a stranger?

I can't.

I have to. My niece and nephew will be orphans if I don't.

The few moments I spent holding them last night before I insisted Sean and Zara leave didn't help me find a way to let them sink into the consequences of whatever they got themselves into.

How could my father create something so insane?

The rulebook Valentina insisted I memorize made me realize I didn't know my father. He seemed obsessed with the numbers 7, 13, and

666. He created laws so black and white there's no room for gray between them. And the punishment almost always is death.

How could he create peace if death is involved?

My curiosity got the worst of me, and I cornered Sean on my lunch break earlier today. He told me that the wars were so bad when we were kids that Dad created The Underworld to protect us. Yet I can't see how it can.

Sean also insisted our mom knew nothing about the secret society. So I question if she had any idea who the man she married really was, which only serves to break me.

It all hurts my heart. The moments in my life I've grieved for my father, remembering the loving, generous man he was to all of us tear through me. Somehow, this new realization taints my memories. And it seems even more unfair to my mother, who still carries pain over his death.

Did he really love her if he hid something so important to him? He grandfathered himself so he didn't have to have his wife at his side at the table, so it leads me to believe he must not have loved her.

The more I think about everything, the more pain I feel. Right now, I want to crawl into bed and not deal with anyone, especially Sean or Zara, who I'm sure are the ones knocking on my door.

The banging turns louder.

"Go away," I call out.

The doorbell rings several times.

I rush over to the entrance, angrily whip open the door, and scold, "Stop ringing and banging—"

"Good evening, Ms. O'Malley," a bald man offers. He has several large packages next to him.

The hairs on my neck rise. "Who are you? And how did you get past my security?"

He smiles and holds up his fist, showcasing my dad's skull, but there's no color on it. It looks freshly branded and has plastic wrapped around it. He announces, "Don't worry. I'm just a messenger."

I wince, wondering why my father chose such a barbaric thing. It could have been a beautiful tattoo instead of a painful brand.

Why put himself and others through extra pain?

How could he not love my mom?

He did.

He couldn't have, or he would have brought her into what he created, especially since a lot of the laws are around spouses. He had to have valued marriage.

The man declares, "I have a delivery for you from the king. Can I bring everything inside?"

My pulse skyrockets. I blurt out, "What is it?"

He shakes his head. "I am not privy to that, ma'am." He reaches into his coat pocket and pulls out an envelope. "This is for you as well."

Goose bumps pop out on my arms. I stare at the expensive cream envelope with my name written across it.

"Ma'am? Can I bring everything inside? I'm not allowed to leave until I can assure the king the items are safely within your possession," the man frets.

Not seeing any other way around this, and curious about what's in the packages, I open the door wider. I motion past me. "Go ahead, then."

He looks relieved as he nods. "Thank you," he says, and brings inside several garment bags and a white box with a gold bow around it. He carefully places the bags over the back of my sofa and sets the box on the coffee table. Then he turns and studies me.

"Sorry. Let me get my wallet to tip you," I say.

He holds his hands in the air. "No, ma'am. I apologize. I didn't mean to stare. I just wanted to get a glimpse of the future queen. I don't know if I'll ever be this close to you again. Please forgive me for any offense I may have caused."

I gape at him, shocked he knows so much about my situation and his enthusiasm to meet me.

"Please, don't hold this against me. I truly am sorry if I offended you," he begs.

"You're fine and didn't offend me," I assure, then ask, "What's your name?"

Nerves fill his expression.

I softly laugh. "It's okay. I just thought it would be nice to know your name."

"It's Vaughn," he offers.

"That's a great name."

"It is?"

"Absolutely!"

He blushes. "Thank you, ma'am. I look forward to the day I can call you queen."

I arch my eyebrows, stunned by this entire encounter.

He rushes past me and calls out, "Have a great evening." He exits my apartment, closing the door behind himself.

I turn and assess the packages, then realize I'm still holding the envelope. I debate opening it, then set it down, unzip a garment bag, and pull out a long, form-fitting wedding gown.

My stomach flips.

Is this really happening?

"I'm not wearing that," I mutter, holding the bright-white dress with a lacy floral design. I set it down and open the next bag. To my surprise, it's another one, only more wrong for me.

This one has way too much tulle and is also bright white. There's so much I'm sure I'd get lost under it.

"Is this all they can do for a queen?" I sarcastically mumble, then unzip the third bag. I pull out the dress and freeze, unable to take my eyes off it.

I've never seen anything so unique. The intricate placement of crystals and pearls is fabulous, and the lace is soft, which means it's top-of-the-line and hand-sewn. There's a dove on the corset. Best of all, it's a creamy white, hinting toward gold.

For several moments, I run my fingers over the bodice, studying every unique part of the design.

"So couture," I praise, continuing to talk to myself.

I glance at the tag, trying to see who the designer is, but it only reads in a script font, Queen Fiona.

I carefully set it down and then look inside the other dresses. The others have no labels on them.

Queen.

I'm dreaming this entire situation.

No, I'm having a nightmare.

I glance at the dove dress and can't stop my smile.

At least I'll look amazing.

I open another garment bag, and my heart races faster. It's another fabulous piece of fashion, but this time, in the form of lingerie. I slide my fingers over the tiny flecks of gold and blue, admiring the piece.

He thinks he's going to fuck me.

He's not.

"You've got a lot of balls, thinking you're going to touch me," I scold the king, even though he can't hear me.

I'm going to have to change my morals and become a cheater. There's no way I'm not having sex for the rest of my life, and I'm not letting that man touch me. I don't care if he's the king or not.

I put the lingerie next to the dress and then sit down. I pick up the white box, carefully remove the gold bow, and open the lid.

There's a gold key and matching box with my father's skull design on it. My chest tightens.

What is this?

I unlock the box, remove the lid, and my mouth turns dry.

The biggest marquise diamond I've ever seen, with a gold band, is nestled inside.

I pick it up and swallow hard, examining it closer. It's beautiful and unlike rings most women have. The diamond appears flawless. The inside of the band has something engraved on it, but it's too small to see.

I curl my fist around it, taking deep breaths, trying to wrap my head around everything.

I can't. It's all too much.

I haven't read the letter.

I open my fist, put the ring back in the box, and pick up the envelope. I turn it over. There's a seal with a gold skull on it. I carefully pop it off, pull out a matching piece of paper, and unfold it.

What the heck?

Someone ripped the top off. I assume it's the king's letterhead.

This secrecy is ridiculous.

I take a deep breath and read.

MY DEAREST FIONA,

THIS IS THE FIFTH LETTER I'VE WRITTEN TO YOU TODAY, AND I'M GOING TO HAVE TO TRUST WHATEVER I WRITE WILL BE THE CORRECT THING. AS WE BOTH KNOW, TIME IS RUNNING OUT. THE MOON WILL SOON BE RIPE FOR YOUR CORONATION, AND YOU MUST MAKE THE BIGGEST DECISION OF YOUR LIFE.

FOR THAT, I'M SORRY.

YOU DESERVE BETTER. IF I COULD GET YOU OUT OF THIS, I WOULD. PLEASE BELIEVE ME WHEN I TELL YOU I'VE TRIED. YET YOUR FATHER'S WORLD GIVES NO ONE FULL POWER, EVEN THE KING.

HOWEVER, I WILL TAKE FULL RESPONSIBILITY FOR THIS SITUATION. I WAITED TOO LONG TO CHOOSE A QUEEN, NOT WANTING TO SUBJECT ANY WOMAN TO MY FLAWS. WHEN YOU FIND OUT WHO I AM, YOU WILL REALIZE WHAT THIS MEANS, BUT THIS HAS PUT YOU IN A POSITION I DO NOT WISH FOR YOU. AGAIN, I EXTEND MY SINCEREST APOLOGIES.

IN A FEW DAYS, YOU MUST CHOOSE TO TAKE YOUR SEAT OR NOT ENTER THE UNDERWORLD. I WON'T BLAME YOU IF YOU DECIDE NOT TO TAKE YOUR PLACE AT MY SIDE. YES, THERE ARE CONSEQUENCES, BUT YOU HAVE THE RIGHT TO NOT ACCEPT YOUR CROWN.

MY PEERS TELL ME YOU ARE LEANING TOWARD TAKING YOUR RIGHTFUL SEAT. IF THIS IS THE CASE, PLEASE CHOOSE THE DRESS YOU WOULD LIKE TO WEAR. I PICKED ONE, AND THE seamstress chose the other two. If all three are horrible to you, please let me know. I will fly back to Monaco and retrieve more.

I just realized I didn't give you choices on the lingerie. The same applies, and I extend another apology. I know you value beauty and uniqueness and have your pulse on what's fashionable and what's not. I will admit to you I claim to know nothing. If my personal shopper didn't select my outfits, I wouldn't know what to wear. So, full disclosure, if you marry me, you'll be the fashion expert in our relationship.

It was merely a gut feeling that made me choose the dress and lingerie, but I know I might be wrong. I can see you in it, but let me know if you don't like it. You'd look incredible in anything or nothing. Okay, I'll stop this part of the conversation before I have to crumple this up and write a sixth letter.

The ring is also your choice. It is my wish that you love it and are proud to wear it, but if it is not to your taste, I will get you another one to wear in public. Regardless, you should have it. This ring was your father's. He had it made for your mother. It's seven carats. Your father had a thing for numbers, but I'm sure you already know that from memorizing the Royal Doctrine. By the way, I'm super impressed with how quickly you memorized it. It took me a lot longer. Seems like you've got brains and beauty.

Anyway, there's an inscription on the gold band that can only be seen with a magnifying glass. It reads, Mine for eternity.

Your father was going to present it to your mother when he was assured it was safe enough to tell her about The Underworld. It was always his vision that she would sit by his side, but not until it was safe for her. I cannot tell you how sorry I am he was unable to

FULFILL THAT WISH. YOUR FATHER WAS A GREAT MAN. HE
HELPED ME AT A TIME WHEN I WAS AT MY LOWEST. IF IT
WEREN'T FOR HIM, I WOULD NOT BE HERE. IT WAS VERY
PAINFUL FOR ME, AND STILL IS, TO THINK ABOUT HIS DEMISE.
NOW THAT I'VE WRITTEN THIS LONG, DRAWN-OUT LETTER TO
YOU, PLEASE KNOW THAT TOMORROW MORNING, BEFORE
WORK, THE COURIER WILL ARRIVE TO COLLECT THE PACKAGES.
FEEL FREE TO WRITE BACK TO ME REGARDING YOUR WISHES.
SINCERELY,
THE KING

P.S. – IF YOU CHOOSE TO ACCEPT THE ITEMS, I'VE FULFILLED
SOMETHING OLD, NEW, AND BLUE. I'M STILL WORKING ON THE
BORROWED. PLEASE FORGIVE ME. I'M STRUGGLING A TAD WITH
THAT ONE.

A short laugh comes out of me as tears fall down my cheeks. I reread
the letter and then reach for the ring. I slide it on my finger, and it fits
perfectly.

My father did love my mother.

How could I have doubted it?

More tears fall, blurring the diamond. And maybe it's the stress of the
last few days, but my tears turn to an outright sob.

After a few minutes, I pull it together. I keep the ring on my finger,
then read the letter so many times I could recite it from memory.

Something about it rips through my heart while also frightening me.

What flaws are so bad that he doesn't think he deserves a wife?

Is he a horrible man?

I reread the letter again, deciding he can't be. If he were, why would
he keep apologizing? And something about him sending me a letter
seems overly kind. How could any man who took the time to write

five versions of this letter be unworthy of having a woman by his side?

I stare at his handwriting, wondering what he looks like and what his name is. Is he as old as my dad since they knew one another?

I wrinkle my nose. Older is fine, but there's a point I don't want to cross. I'm unsure what it is, but I know anyone my parents' age is too old.

I don't have a choice.

He's funny and complimentary, at least.

I stare at the writing, smiling at different parts, then finally set the letter down. I pick up the lingerie and the dress with the bird. Then I take them into my bedroom.

I take off my clothes, slide into the lingerie, and stand in front of my full-length mirror. Butterflies break out in my belly, and I mutter, "For a guy who claims to have no fashion sense, you have a knack for sexy lingerie."

Because he wants to fuck me.

The butterflies mix with dread. I swallow hard, then carefully undress. I pick up the dress, spend several minutes figuring out how to open it, then step into it. I secure it as best as I can and then return to the mirror.

More conflicting emotions erupt within me. The dress is a stunning piece of artwork. It showcases every curve I have in a tasteful way. The attention to detail is superb, better than most high-end pieces I deal with at work.

My mom would flip over this.

Oh my God! My mom!

A rush of panic and guilt fills me. Sean and Zara almost killed my mom when they got married without her.

I hightail it to the kitchen, grab my phone, and hit the button to call Zara.

It rings once, and she softly chirps, "Hey! I was hoping you'd call."

"My mom needs to be at the wedding," I blurt out.

Silence fills the line.

"Hello?" I fire in an irritated voice.

Zara replies, "Fiona. I'm sorry, but that can't happen."

"I'm not doing to her what you and Sean did!" I spout.

"Trust me. If it were possible, I'd tell you how. But it's not," she claims.

"Then I'm not doing it, so find a way!"

"I'm telling you the truth. No one can be present unless they're part of The Underworld. Your mom knows nothing about it, so they won't let her be there. And if you tell her anything, they'll kill you and her. Loyalty and secrecy are not negotiable," she warns.

"It's unfair for her to endure this again."

Zara lowers her voice. "I know. And I'm sorry. Maybe you can change the rules once you're the queen."

"How's that going to help my mom?"

Tension buzzes between us over the line.

Zara finally offers, "It won't help your mom. But if you become queen and change the rules, it could help other mothers avoid going through what she will."

I snap, "Gee, thanks. That makes me feel better."

"Fiona—"

"Thanks for ruining my life and hurting my mom," I snarl, then hang up.

I toss my phone on the counter, pace the room, then return to the bedroom. It takes a bit to figure out how to get out of the dress, but I finally do. I put my clothes back on. Then, I return to the living room and repackage the garments.

My phone dings. I pick it up and read the message.

> Zara: I hate myself for being the reason you're in this situation.

> Me: Then why don't you tell me what was so bad that my own brother had to promise me to a stranger?

> Zara: I can't until you're the queen. I know you don't want to keep hearing me say that, but if I tell you, I'm dead. So are you.

"Whatever," I mumble and turn off my phone, not wanting to hear any more excuses. I put my cell down and stare at the huge diamond still on my finger.

My mom will go nuts when she sees this.

It should be hers.

I feel guilty. I glance at the gold box but can't seem to take the ring off. Instead, I go to my desk, sit, and open the drawer. I pull out a piece of paper and reach for a pen in the holder.

For several moments, I think about how to start. Then I realize it doesn't matter. I'll make a different version if I'm not happy with it.

Dear Stranger The Underworld Calls King...

Kirill

The Next Morning

Chapter
EIGHT

I tell the front desk, "Send him up," and glance at my watch.

I'm disappointed and anxious with the amount of time it's taking for Vaughn to return.

It's been too long.

Why isn't he back?

I pick up my phone and text him.

Me: Where are you?

Vaughn: Not far. There was an accident. It took me a bit to get past it.

Me: The items are secure?

Vaughn: Yes.

Me: Did she want you to tell me anything?

Jesus, I sound desperate.

Vaughn: No. She's really kind, though. She'll make a good queen.

Me: I agree, but what makes you say that?

Vaughn: I don't know. She has an aura about her.

Is that what you call it?

Me: Come directly to my place.

Vaughn: I am.

Me: Did she send a letter back?

Vaughn: No.

My gut sinks.

How will I know if she likes any of the dresses?

What if she refuses to get initiated into The Underworld?

The Omni will have no choice but to behead me.

The elevator opens, and Brax appears with a bored expression. He leans against the wall with his arms crossed. His knee is bent, a sneaker flat against the metal. He gripes, "When are they fixing this thing?"

Irritation floods me. "Get your shoe off the wall. Show some respect."

He pushes off and steps into my foyer, arguing, "Seriously. You live in one of the most expensive buildings in Chicago. When are they fixing this piece of shit?"

I grunt and move into the living room. The sun's high in the sky on a cloudless day, turning the cold waters of Lake Michigan into a sparkling, breathtaking scene. It's one of the things I appreciate about my penthouse the most.

I should have sent the shorter version of the letter.

Brax inquires, "So what's the big emergency?"

"Who said anything about an emergency?" I retort.

He scowls. "You pulled me out of my workout. I was in the ring with Sean. I had to make excuses to Finn about why I had to leave, and he knows I'm lying. It was written all over his face. He's starting to not trust me."

"Not my problem," I say.

Where is Vaughn?

I shouldn't have given him such an important job.

I need to stop instilling so much faith in these new members.

I glance at my watch again.

Brax warns, "Don't tell me I'm late. I left as soon as you beckoned."

I match his scowl, leering at him.

He scrubs his face. "Come on, Kirill. I have an entire list of things to do today. If I don't get them done, Liam is going to be all over my ass."

"Once again, not my problem," I state, scolding myself another time for not sending the shorter letter.

"Well, well, well! Look who the cat dragged in," Valentina's voice chirps.

I turn as she walks through the door, smirking at Brax.

He whistles. "It's the sexy little minx, gracing us with her presence." His gaze drifts to her cleavage, then the bottom hem of her miniskirt.

She bats her eyes and chirps, "Are you in trouble again? Does the king need to get out his belt and whip you?"

Brax unties his sweatpants and turns his back to her. He drops his pants, displaying his muscular ass, and looks over his shoulder, taunting, "Assume you want to volunteer?"

"Enough!" I bark, then order, "And pull up your goddam pants in my house!"

"Such a barbarian," Valentina adds.

"Enough from you as well," I reprimand.

She widens her eyes. "Someone got up on the wrong side of the bed."

"He's been like this since I arrived," Brax interjects, tying his pants.

"What's wrong?" Valentina questions, pinning her concerned gaze on me.

The sound of the door buzzer shrills through the air.

I rush over to it and push the button. "Yes."

"Vaughn is back," Jasper informs me.

"Send him up," I instruct, my pulse racing.

"Letting our little baby Brax learn something new from Vaughn today?" Valentina asks saucily.

Brax scoffs. "Please. He got initiated two seconds ago."

"And you had your special night over eight months ago. Yet your mark is still colorless. Why is that?" She purses her lips together.

"You can't forget that night, can you? My ceremony haunts your dreams," he jeers.

I roar, "Will you two shut up?"

Valentina's head jerks backward.

Brax clenches his jaw.

My chest tightens. I step out into the foyer, slamming the entry door behind me. Those two never stop. I normally find some humor in it, but not today.

I pace the small area, cursing the building management for not fixing the issue with the elevator. Time drags by until it finally opens.

Vaughn has the garment bags over his arm and the white box in his hand.

My mouth goes dry as a desert. I point at the perfectly tied gold bow, probing, "She didn't open it?"

"She said to tell you to open it," Vaughn answers.

I narrow my eyes. "I asked you if she wanted you to tell me anything and you said no."

He nods. "That's correct."

I step closer, glaring down at him. He shrinks back, and I continue, "You just told me she instructed you to tell me to open this box." I tap it.

He nods. "Yes."

"That's a message!"

"It is?"

I slide my hands under the garments, grab the box, then demand, "Get out of here."

"Sir, I didn't—"

"Go!" I roar.

He pushes the elevator button.

I enter the main area, brush past a heated conversation between Brax and Valentina, and go into my bedroom. I shut the door, put the garment bags on my bed, then sit next to them.

My heart races faster. I take a deep breath and untie the bow, remove the lid, and pick up an everyday white envelope. It says, *Underworld King* on it. I flip it over and freeze, except for the grin exploding across my face.

It's sealed the normal way, but there's an F in red lipstick. There's a small imprint at the bottom of the letter that leads me to assume it's Fiona's fingermark.

She's creative.

I chuckle and slide open the envelope. I pull out a piece of white copy paper.

> *Dear Stranger The Underworld Calls King,*
> *Thank you for sending me the items. Unfortunately, I*
> *cannot return the ring. I have not been able to take it*
> *off, knowing it was my father's and meant for my*
> *mother. I'm sure you understand. And don't worry about*
> *another one. I'd prefer to wear this everywhere.*
> *Although I do feel guilty my mom never got the chance*
> *to wear it.*
> *By the way, how old are you? Since you said you knew*
> *my father, does that mean you're his age? No offense,*
> *I hope you're not. And if you are, don't expect me to*
> *call you Daddy.*

I start laughing so hard, tears well in my eyes. I calm and continue reading.

> *Regarding the dresses...*

The first two are not me. However, the third one I opened I was rather impressed with. You say you have no fashion sense, but my guess is you have more than you give yourself credit for. And yes, it's the one with the dove. Since that one had my name on the tag inside, I assume that was the one you selected? Am I right or wrong?

So you know, the lingerie fits. Can't dock you for fashion points for that one either.

A visual of what I think Fiona looks like in the lingerie explodes in my mind. My cock hardens and the blood in my veins turns to fire. I continue reading.

I would love to say this is the first version I've written, but believe it or not it's the seventh. Do you think I inherited my dad's eccentricity with the number?

That leads me to another point of my confusion. As you pointed out, time is running out. This thing with the moon is another obsession I didn't realize my father had. Maybe I should have since he always took us outside whenever there was a full moon to stare at it. Yet I never knew it had more meaning to him.

I will admit to you, I don't understand any of this Underworld stuff. This king and queen thing is bizarre to me. Do you get used to people referring to you as royalty? I'm not sure if I will.

Well, that's assuming I go through with this. As mad as I am at Sean and Zara, I love them and the twins. However, I also love myself, and want to know what

I'm getting into. This secrecy might be the worst part about this. And it's not fair that you get to know who I am but I don't get to know anything about you. So if you want me to go through with this, or even just feel a bit better should I force myself to do it for the safety of those I love, I would like to know something about you.

You said you had flaws. I don't know what that means. But doesn't everybody?

Or are they so serious I need to be scared?

Like, are you an axe murderer waiting to chop me into a million pieces?

Will you physically, sexually, or emotionally abuse me until I'm broken into pieces?

Or maybe your flaws aren't quite as severe but would still drive me insane until the end of time.

Do you refuse to shower and stink like my brother's room when he was in high school?

Are you a vegetarian? I'll be totally honest with you. That's a deal-breaker. Don't keep my meat from me.

Perhaps you take phone calls in public, speaking so loudly the entire building can hear you?

It would be nice if you would write to me and tell me if I need to worry about any of these flaws.

I chuckle again, but then my face falls.

No, little bird. My flaws are nothing you can imagine.

I stare out the window a moment, then continue reading.

I'll confess I don't understand how I'm in this position because of something my father created. I have a million questions ranging from the reason my brother promised me to you, to why my mom can't come to the wedding.

It's going to break her heart again. If you knew my dad, then don't you think she's had enough heartache? Could you please reconsider?

I sigh, hating how Bridget has to endure more hurt. Fiona is right. She's had a lifetime of pain, and I wish I didn't have to bring her more, but there's no way she can be there. I finish reading the letter.

I guess this is all I wanted to say. Seventh time's a charm for me! Forget that saying about a third! Oh, I did think it was nice of you to write to me.
I wish I could tell you I knew for sure what I'll do, but as of now, I'm still torn.
Sincerely,
Fiona

P.S. I'm curious if you figured out something borrowed yet.

The panic I've been feeling resumes. I still have no idea what to give her as something borrowed. So I rise and pace the room with the letter, rereading it several times.

A knock interrupts me.

"Kirill!" Valentina shouts.

"Yeah?"

She opens the door, glancing at the bed and then the letter. She meets my eyes. "What's that?"

"Nothing. I'll be out in a minute."

She arches her eyebrows. "Are you okay?"

"Yes."

"Okay. I need to go. I've been ordered to check on one of the newbies," she states.

"Lucky you," I offer.

"The little-brained peon is still out there," she adds.

I groan. "You two are impossible. When are you going to get along?"

She scoffs. "When he grows up."

"You're not innocent," I point out.

"I am," she insists.

"No. You're not."

She beams, chirping, "Gotta go! See you later!" She shuts the door.

I sit down at my desk and take out my letterhead. I rip the top off and grab my pen, then study Fiona's letter.

My DEAREST FIONA,

THANK YOU FOR YOUR LETTER.

"Kirill, what did you call me here for?" Brax booms from my bedroom doorway.

"Ever hear of knocking?"

"You've been in here forever. I have a lot to do today. Tell me what my task is so I can go on with my life," he orders.

I point at him. "You better watch your tongue, or I'll cut it out."

He closes his mouth and grinds his molars, shooting me a look of death.

I glance at the letter, then change my plans for him. "I'll tell you what. Go sit on the couch until I'm ready for you. Instead of the six-hour task I had for you, I'll give you a quicker one. But stop your bitching, or I'll make you work all weekend."

"Fine," he grumbles, then shuts the door harder than he should.

Ignore him, I tell myself, refocusing on the letter.

I carefully go through it and address Fiona's concerns. At least the ones I know won't violate any rules. I reread what I wrote, then get to her PS.

I have to figure this out, yet it seems impossible.

What to let a queen borrow.

I pace for several moments, then stop in front of the window.

I mutter, "How stupid could I be?"

I return to the letter and add a PS.

I fold up the note, stick it in the envelope, then add the skull seal. I write *Fiona* on it, then take it out to the main room.

Brax crosses his arms. "Can I please start my task?"

"Your Majesty," I remind him, tired of his disrespect. I don't throw my rank around a lot, but he's getting on my nerves.

He shifts in his seat. "Sorry. Your Majesty."

I point at him. "You need to change your attitude. Understand?"

His face hardens. "Yes, sir."

I study him for a moment, then nod. "Good. Now, I have an extremely urgent matter, and it's important. I need to know I can trust you."

"You can," he claims.

"If you fuck this up, your head's on a platter, understand?" I warn.

His expression turns serious. "What is it?"

I hold out the letter, announcing, "I need you to go to Fiona's work. Give this to her and tell her she needs to read it immediately. Then wait for her to respond."

His eyes widen.

"Too much for you to handle?" I question.

He runs his hand through his thick locks, asserting, "She doesn't know I'm in The Underworld."

"Yeah, well, time she found out," I declare.

"Is that a good idea?"

"Are you the king?"

He shakes his head. "No."

"Good. Then leave the decision-making to me. Now, are you able to complete your task?" I prod.

"Yeah." He reaches for the letter.

I snap it back.

He freezes.

"Tell me your orders."

"Seriously?"

"Yes. Tell me what you understand your orders to be."

He protests, "Contrary to what your little pet Valentina tells you, I'm not an idiot. I do have a brain."

"You do?" I taunt.

He scowls.

"Don't call Valentina my pet. She's my friend. Don't be disrespectful."

He grunts. "But it's okay for her to be?"

I scoff. "Sorry. I thought you were a man."

"I am a man," he claims.

"Then grow the fuck up. Stop being disrespectful to her and you'll see a different side of her. That's what you want anyway, isn't it? To get to know the real her?"

His jaw twitches. "I don't know what you're talking about."

"Sure you don't."

He pins his hardened eyes on me. "Can I go now?"

"Tell me again what your job is," I repeat.

He rolls his eyes. "To get Fiona the letter and wait for her response. Then run back here and tell you."

I pat him on the shoulder. "Good. And remember, she can't know who I am, or you're in violation of the law."

"Got it," he says and snatches the envelope from my hand.

I need to see this through.

I follow him to the elevator, grab the letter from him, and push the button. "On second thought, I'll take you there myself."

He scrunches his forehead. "Why? I can do it."

"I told you this is important." I grab my coat and slide into it.

"And I assured you I can handle the job."

I text my driver, and a miracle happens. The elevator opens. I motion for Brax to get in.

"This is ridiculous," he mumbles under his breath, brushing past me.

"Watch your mouth," I remind him, stepping beside him and hitting the G button for ground level.

The elevator takes forever to move, then stops on the next floor. The doors open and the redhead appears, sees me, and cringes.

"Get in or stay out," I bark, hitting the close button.

She huffs, then steps in on the other side of Brax. She bats her eyes at him. "Hi. Are you new to the building?"

"No. I'm visiting."

She glances at me, wrinkles her nose, then pins another flirty smile on him. "Oh."

I try to ignore her and my growing irritation as the elevator stops at every floor, even when no one is waiting for it. When we finally get outside, my driver is waiting.

I slide into the SUV, direct him to go to Fiona's work, then sit back, wondering what she'll reply.

Fiona

Chapter NINE

"How's the revamp coming?" I ask, handing Blue a latte.

She scrunches her face. "Not good. I can't see anything. It's just my pink skirt as is." She reaches for the cup and takes a sip. "Thanks."

"Sure. So you don't have any ideas?" I ask, not believing that nothing is coming to her. Blue has a lot of her mother in her and is one of the most creative people I know.

She shrugs. "Nothing worthy of the runway."

I sit in the chair across from her. "Want to run your ideas by me? Maybe you're onto something and need to develop it further."

She groans and dramatically puts her arms on the desk and buries her face in them. She whines, "There's nothing worth your time."

"Are you sure about that?" I question.

"Fiona! There you are," Brax booms.

I turn my head in the direction of his voice. "What are you doing here?"

"Is that any way to treat your brother's bestie?" he teases.

Blue sits up and runs her hand through her hair. Her eyes light up, and she breathes, "Hey, Brax."

He nods at her. "Blue. How's it going?"

"Good. Well, not good. I need to figure out my design. But other than that, things are going well. I'm great. And you? Are you doing well? Can I get you a drink? Or a cookie? One of our clients sent us a surprise order of a dozen chocolate chip ones," she babbles.

Oh, Blue. I've told you that you're way too young for Brax.

She's had a crush on him since she was sixteen. It doesn't matter how much I try to get her to set her sights elsewhere. Nor did it help when Adrian saw her flirt with Brax and warned her that he was off-limits.

After that, he threatened Brax not to touch his daughter. Brax said it wasn't a problem because he wasn't interested in little girls. He's always insisted he would never go there, but it doesn't stop Blue from wishing or trying.

Brax gives her barely any attention, saying, "No, thanks. I'm good." Then he focuses on me, adding, "I need to speak to you privately, Fiona."

"What about?" Blue asks.

"None of your business," Brax scolds, then exits the room.

Blue's face falls.

I sigh, lean down, and mutter, "He's way too old for you. There are tons of guys closer to your age who want to date you."

Her face hardens and she looks away.

I pat her shoulder. "I'll be back later, and we can look at your project." I leave and go into my office.

Brax stands near my desk with his arms crossed.

"You didn't have to snap at her," I reprimand.

He grunts. "She's a child. It's never happening between us, and she needs to move on. Besides, I don't need Adrian accusing me of anything."

I glare a few daggers at him.

"Be mad at me all you want," he replies in response to my look.

I put my hand on my hip. "You're as annoying as my brother."

"So you've told me a million times."

"Why are you here?"

He clenches his jaw and holds out an envelope. "I've been ordered to give this to you."

"Ordered?" I glance at his hand, and my breath hitches. I gape as I reach for it.

He yanks his hand back and mutters, "Here we go."

I lock eyes with him. "You're wearing my father's mark."

"Yep."

"You're..." A shiver runs down my spine.

He nods. "Yeah. Let's move on. I've got a lot of shit to do today, and I need to make sure you read this immediately. Then I have to take your response to his Royal Highness," he sarcastically informs.

I stare at him.

He wiggles the envelope in front of me. "Time's ticking, Fiona."

I snatch it from him and pull out my chair. I sit, staring at the skull on the back.

"I need you to open it and read it."

I point to the door. "Get out."

"Did you not hear me? I have to give him your response," Brax asserts.

"So? Take two steps out the door, shut it, and I'll get to you when I'm ready," I order.

He pins a challenging scowl on me.

I toss the envelope on my desk, sit back, then cross my arms. "Fine. I'll read it later."

"Fiona, I have shit to do!"

"Then do what I said," I bite back.

He takes several deep breaths and then caves. "Don't take too long," he grumbles. He stomps out of my office and firmly shuts the door.

I pick up the envelope, read my name on the front, then turn it over. I carefully break the seal, pull out the torn, cream linen letterhead, and unfold it.

MY DEAREST FIONA,

THANK YOU FOR YOUR LETTER.

I'M HAPPY YOU LOVE THE RING. I UNDERSTAND YOUR GUILT,
BUT YOUR MOTHER DOESN'T KNOW ABOUT THE UNDERWORLD.
SHE NEVER CAN. HER TIME TO KNOW WAS WHEN YOUR FATHER
WAS ALIVE. NOW THAT HE'S GONE, HER PLACE AT THE TABLE
HAS EVAPORATED. SO THE RING WOULD HAVE SAT IN THE BOX
FOREVER HAD YOU NOT CHOSEN TO WEAR IT.

I glance at the brilliant diamond gleaming on my finger. The sadness I feel regarding my parents mixes with joy. It's too pretty to stay locked away in a gold box forever.

I continue reading.

UNFORTUNATELY, THOSE SAME REASONS ARE WHY I CANNOT
GRANT YOU THE WISH TO HAVE YOUR MOTHER AT OUR

WEDDING. NO ONE CAN ATTEND ANY UNDERWORLD CEREMONY OR RITUAL EXCEPT MEMBERS OF THE UNDERWORLD. SHE CAN NEVER KNOW OUR WORLD EXISTS. PLEASE TRUST THAT IF I COULD CHANGE THE RULES, I WOULD. I DON'T WANT TO CAUSE HER ANY MORE PAIN, YET THIS DECISION IS NOT MINE TO MAKE. YOUR FATHER CAREFULLY CRAFTED OUR LAWS, WHICH WE MUST ABIDE BY.

The little hope I had fizzles. I shake my head, hating the laws my father created, and still not understanding why he thought they were so necessary.

I return to the letter.

YOU ASKED ABOUT MY AGE. WHILE I CANNOT DISCLOSE IT, I CAN ASSURE YOU THAT I AM YOUNGER THAN WHAT YOUR FATHER WOULD BE, AND WILL NEVER ASK YOU TO CALL ME DADDY.

I bite on my smile.

MY FLAWS ARE NOT ANYTHING YOU LISTED. I WILL NOT ABUSE YOU, OR CHOP YOU UP IN MILLIONS OF PIECES. IN FACT, IF ANYONE TRIES, THEY WILL BE THE ONES SLICED INTO UNRECOG-NIZABLE PIECES.
I LIKE TO ASSUME I DON'T SMELL BAD, BUT I'LL LET YOU TELL ME WHAT YOU THINK WHEN WE'RE FINALLY ALONE. AND, NO, I DON'T DECLARE MY BUSINESS OVER THE PHONE TO THE WORLD. IN ADDITION, I CAN ASSURE YOU THAT MEAT WILL ALWAYS BE ON THE MENU

"Good to know," I mumble, smiling, but then my face falls.

If those aren't his flaws, then what is so bad?

I can't think of anything else that would annoy me for all eternity or hurt me, so I return to the letter.

IT DOESN'T SURPRISE ME THAT YOU HAVE A MILLION QUES-
TIONS. YOU'RE AN INTELLIGENT WOMAN, AND THE SECRECY
DROVE ME NUTS TOO, BEFORE I BECAME KING.
SO, I'LL TELL YOU THE TRUTH. ONCE YOU'RE MY QUEEN, I'LL BE
ABLE TO ANSWER WHATEVER QUESTIONS YOU HAVE. THERE WILL
BE NO MORE HIDDEN AGENDAS OR RESTRICTED SCENARIOS.
YOU WILL HAVE AS MUCH ACCESS AS I DO TO THE UNDER-
WORLD'S PAST, PRESENT, AND FUTURE. AND YOU WILL RULE
WITH ME. IT WAS YOUR FATHER'S VISION FOR HUSBANDS AND
WIVES TO PLAY AN EQUAL ROLE, AND WE WILL ACHIEVE HIS
DREAM TOGETHER.

Together.

A flash of anticipation mixes with the fear of the unknown.

I take a sip of my latte, then continue reading.

IT'S FUNNY THAT SEVEN WAS YOUR NUMBER. YOUR FATHER
DID HAVE AN ECCENTRIC OBSESSION WITH NUMBERS. HOWEVER,
THEY HAVE MEANING, SO IF YOU INHERITED THAT TRAIT, IT'S
SOMETHING TO BE CELEBRATED.
THANK YOU FOR SHARING YOUR MEMORY OF YOUR FATHER
WITH ME. I CAN IMAGINE YOU AS A LITTLE GIRL, SITTING ON
YOUR FATHER'S LAP AND STARING AT THE SKY, LIT BY THE
MOON'S LUMINESCENCE.

I blink hard.

How did he know I sat on my father's lap?

I wait until the nostalgia passes, then read more.

SINCE YOU SHARED YOUR STORY WITH ME, I'LL DISCLOSE ONE
TO YOU. IT MIGHT GIVE SOME INSIGHT INTO WHY YOUR FATHER
LOVED THE MOON SO MUCH.
ONE NIGHT, YOUR FATHER TOOK ME OUTSIDE. HE POINTED TO

THE SKY, AND THE MOON WAS UNLIKE ANYTHING I'D EVER SEEN. HE TOLD ME, "THE MOON'S SURFACE IS COVERED IN CRATERS. TO THE UNEDUCATED, IT WOULD APPEAR DAMAGED. YET THE POWER HELD WITHIN IS GREATER THAN ANYTHING ELSE IN THE UNIVERSE. IT'S SO STRONG, ITS GRAVITATIONAL PULL STABILIZES THE EARTH'S TILT. IT CREATES TIDES, WHICH HUMANS HAVE USED SINCE THE BEGINNING OF TIME FOR GUIDANCE. IT HAS MOONQUAKES AND WATER AND TIDAL LOCKING, SO IT ALWAYS FACES OUR PLANET."

I REMEMBER STARING AT THE RADIANT BALL IN THE SKY, SURPRISED BY ALL YOUR FATHER KNEW ABOUT IT.

THEN HE SAID, "THE CRATERS ONLY TELL A STORY OF ITS HISTORY. BILLIONS OF YEARS AGO IT WAS BOMBARDED WITH A HEAVY COLLISION OF SPACE ROCKS. ASTEROIDS, COMETS, AND METEOROIDS... THEY ALL TRIED TO DESTROY IT, BUT THEY COULDN'T. EVEN TODAY, THERE ARE COLLISIONS. SOME SCIENTISTS THINK IT'S ATTACKED ON A DAILY BASIS. YET THE MOON CONTINUES TO REMAIN POWERFUL, CONTROLLING OUR OCEANS AND GLOWING IN THE DEAD OF NIGHT FOR ALL TO SEE."

HE JABBED HIS FINGER IN MY CHEST AND ADDED, "THAT'S WHAT YOU HAVE TO REMEMBER ABOUT YOURSELF. THE POWER YOU HOLD ISN'T WHAT OTHERS CAN SEE UNLESS THEY CHOOSE TO LOOK AT IT, AND THE ONES WHO CHOOSE TO LOOK AWAY CAN BE DAMNED UPON YOUR CHOOSING. EMBRACE BEING UNDERESTIMATED. YOU CAN ALLOW CRATERS TO DEFEAT YOU OR EMPOWER YOU. SO DIG DEEP TO UNDERSTAND HOW FORMIDABLE YOU ARE, BECAUSE THE ROCKS WILL ALWAYS FLY AT YOU. IF IT WASN'T THIS, IT WOULD HAVE BEEN SOMETHING ELSE. IT'S UP TO YOU HOW YOU PROTECT YOURSELF AND STILL DEVELOP THE POTENTIAL I SEE IN YOU THAT NO ONE ELSE DOES."

"If it wasn't this it would have been something else?" What does that mean?

I reread the section, not coming to any answers, then continue.

SINCE YOU'VE BEEN HONEST WITH ME, I'LL ADMIT THAT YOUR FATHER SAVED MY LIFE THAT NIGHT FOR A SECOND TIME. IT SHAPED WHO I BECAME AND HOW I LEARNED TO DEAL WITH THINGS.

What things?

I reread the entire section then continue on.

ON ANOTHER NOTE, I CAN'T TELL YOU HOW RELIEVED AND PLEASED I AM THAT YOU LOVE THE LINGERIE AND DRESS WITH THE DOVE. YES, IT'S THE ONE I CHOSE FOR YOU. MAYBE I DO HAVE SOME GOOD FASHION SENSE IF YOU SAY I DO. HA. HA.
I HOPE THIS ANSWERS YOUR QUESTIONS.
SINCERELY,
THE KING
P.S. I'M SURE YOU'RE BUSY, BUT CAN YOU TAKE A MOMENT AND WRITE ME A NOTE? I HAVE FIGURED OUT THE BORROWED ITEM. I NEED TO FLY FAR TO RETRIEVE IT, THOUGH. I HAVE A SMALL WINDOW OF TIME TO MAKE THE ROUND TRIP. I DON'T WANT TO GET THIS WRONG, SO PLEASE TELL ME IF YOU PREFER NEWER OR OLDER THINGS. THANK YOU.

Newer or older things? And what is he getting that he has to fly so far?

I sit back in my chair, drink more of my latte, and reread the letter, pondering his question, unsure how to answer.

There's a knock on the door.

I put the envelope and letter on my lap, calling out, "Yes?"

The door opens, and Brax sticks his head inside. "Are you done yet?"

I glare at him.

"Fiona, I'm going to be in some big shit with Liam if I don't get this task completed," he whines.

"Not my problem." I smirk, not happy he's interrupting my thoughts and pressuring me to figure out my answer.

"Jesus. You two are meant to be together," he mumbles.

My heart pounds harder. "What was that?"

"Nothing. Just hurry. Please," he begs.

I wiggle my finger at him.

He groans and disappears, shutting the door.

I stare at the PS again, then grab company letterhead out of my drawer. I stare at it, then pick it up and tear off the top.

Smiling, I click my pen and reply, then fold the paper. I stick it in an envelope and seal it. Then I grab my lipstick from my purse, draw an F, and trace my finger over the letter, pushing down on the bottom to showcase my print. I draw a tissue out of the box and wipe the excess off.

I rise, stick my letter in my purse, and then grab the reply. I open the door.

Brax pushes off the wall. "What do you want me to tell him?"

I narrow my eyes.

He crosses his arms. "I don't have time for games, Fiona. Spit it out."

"Do you really think I'd give you a verbal message to mess up?" I question.

Brax's face turns red. He fumes, "If I don't go out to his SUV and give him your message soon, I'm going to be in some major trouble with multiple entities. Can you give me a break? Please!"

The hairs on my neck rise. Butterflies attack my belly. I blurt out, "He's here?"

Brax's face reddens, then he clenches his jaw.

I brush past him toward the entrance.

He stays on my heels. "Fiona, you know you can't go out there."

I don't listen, rushing through the building. I whip the door open and step out into the cold, scanning several SUVs parked on the street.

"Fiona! Go back inside!" Brax orders, tugging on my shoulder and spinning me into him.

I demand, "Which one is he in?"

"Give me the message and go back inside," he barks, the red in his face turning maroon.

A gust of wind slams into me, and I step back. "Which one?"

"Fiona, is everything okay?" Adrian's Russian accent booms from a few feet away.

The blood in my face drains. My pulse skyrockets.

"It's fine," Brax insists.

Adrian steps next to us, sternly stating, "I asked Fiona, not you."

I lift my chin, smiling. "Yes. Everything is fine, Adrian."

He studies me, his blue eyes piercing mine. "Why do I get the feeling it's not?"

"It is," I insist.

He leers at Brax.

"Don't act like I'm doing something wrong," Brax barks.

"Why are you here? This is Fiona's place of work," Adrian prompts.

I quickly interject. "It's a family matter, Adrian. Everything is fine. I promise. I'll be inside in a moment."

His gaze drifts between us. He finally steps back. "I'm inside if you need me, Fiona."

"Thanks. But everything is good, Adrian," I reassure.

He cautiously disappears.

"Damn, Blue," Brax mutters.

I scoff. "How is this Blue's fault?"

"Ever since she decided to get the hots for me, he's put me on his enemy list!"

"Don't be so dramatic."

Brax grabs the letter out of my hand.

"Hey! What are you doing?" I shriek, trying to retrieve it, but he holds it high in the air.

"Go inside, Fiona. Rules are never to be broken. I know you're learning things, but break them, and you die. So do others around you. That's what your father wanted, and that's our reality. And I don't have time for your games. Go inside. Now!" Brax orders.

I gape at him.

He softens his tone, pleading, "Please. You've known me forever. I need you to go inside."

I glance at the SUVs once more, not sure which one the man my brother promised me to is in, then back at Brax. "I need to see who he is or I can't do this."

Brax shakes his head, empathetically asserting, "You read the rules and you know what happens if you don't marry him."

My insides quiver. The people I love flash in my mind, and the thought of the twins growing up as orphans tears at my heart.

Brax puts his hand on my back, maneuvering me toward the front entrance, stating in a low tone, "No one wants anyone to die, Fiona. Please. Just go inside. Your time to meet him is soon."

Confusion, fear, and curiosity swirl within me. I blink hard and glance up.

Brax adds in a regretful tone, "I know this sucks." He puts his hand on the door.

"Wait," I blurt out.

He stills.

My voice cracks, and a tear falls down my cheek. "Am I going to hate him?"

Brax tilts his head and releases a long breath. "No. I don't think so. He has his moments, but he's not that bad."

"Not that bad?" I question.

He shrugs. "Yeah. I'm not that bad either, right?" He wiggles his eyebrows.

I choke out a laugh.

He tugs me into him and hugs me. It's not something he normally does.

For some reason, I sink into it, letting more tears fall.

He hugs me tighter and reassures, "Everything will be okay, Fiona. Just don't break any of the rules, and everything will be fine. I promise. Now, I need you to go inside. This isn't worth someone dying over. Not today."

I sniffle, step back, and nod. "Okay. I'll go inside."

"Thank you." He offers a smile, opens the door, and waits.

I glance at the SUVs for a final time, then cave and go inside, agreeing with Brax.

Today isn't the day for anyone to die.

Kirill

Chapter

TEN

"You told her I was here?" I bark at Brax the moment he slides into the SUV. Since Fiona walked outside, my pulse has been banging between my ears so hard I feel nauseous.

Brax scowls. "It wasn't intentional."

I point my finger in his face. "Not intentional? She was crying!"

"Shouldn't she?" Brax spouts, his expression turning to one of disgust as the driver veers onto the road.

My chest tightens.

He, too, feels sorry she has to marry me.

I can't focus on my shortcomings right now. Snap out of it, I order myself.

I seethe, "What did you say to her?"

He snarls, "To go inside so no one dies!"

"Why did you threaten her?"

He scoffs, bellowing, "All of us would have died had she seen you today. It wasn't a threat. It was the truth! Stop acting like I did something wrong!"

"You told her I was here!"

"I said it was an accident!"

"I should show you an accident!" I threaten.

He crosses his arms and stretches his legs. "Go ahead."

"Don't push me," I warn.

He leers at me, ranting, "This is your fault. You shouldn't have been here, and you know it."

I turn toward the window, staring at the passing buildings, attempting to calm down.

Brax lowers his tone. "You can't expect her to be happy she's marrying a stranger."

I turn toward him, hold out my hand, and order, "Give me the letter."

He reaches into his pocket and slides it out.

I snatch it from his grasp, crack the divider window, and command, "Pull over."

Ivan obeys.

"Get out," I order Brax.

Brax's eyes turn to slits. "Here?"

"Yeah. You have things to do. Go do them," I direct.

"Gee, not even a 'Thanks for getting me the letter,'" he sarcastically retorts, opening the door.

"Make Fiona cry ever again, and there won't be any warnings. And I promise you it won't be an accident," I warn.

His face hardens with hatred. He slides out and slams the door.

"Airport," I instruct Ivan and then close the divider. I sit back, staring at her handwriting on the front, with twitches erupting in my stomach. I flip the envelope over and look at the red F, smiling.

Carefully, I open the flap, pull out a piece of paper, and a nervous chuckle escapes me.

She tore the top off.

I unfold the letterhead and read.

Dear Stranger The Underworld Calls King,

Your letter only raises more questions, but in the essence of time, I will try to answer your question.

While I love the excitement around the new and upcoming, something about older things reeling with history sometimes mesmerizes me. I guess I'm a girl who loves traditions. I assumed I only got it from my mom, but as I learn more about my dad, maybe he loved it as much as she does.

I also love things that match but in a more eclectic way. Maybe you don't realize it, but everything you sent me (except those bright-white dresses) coordinates with my ring. You expertly combined new, old, and blue. Good job, by the way. Wink. Wink.

Since I don't know what you're referring to, I leave it to you to decide if the borrowed is older or newer. You did great on everything else, so I assume you will regarding this as well. Plus, I'm kind of a sucker for surprises.

Sincerely,
Fiona

P.S. If I go through with this and marry you, I retain the right to ask you my questions and get truthful answers.

P.P.S. I'm relieved you eliminated those flaws from my worries. What is so bad about you if none of those are it?

P.P.P.S. I appreciate the story about my father. I hate to admit it, but the memories of him have faded in my mind, and the more you reveal, the more I wonder if I even knew him. Did I?

P.P.P.P.S. Where are you flying to? I'll confess it's making me feel a bit more important than I am that you're taking all these long trips to select things for me. Wouldn't it be easier to video chat with people instead of putting yourself through another long journey?

You are way more important than you know, little bird.

There's no way I'd ever video chat about this, but it was nice of her to give me the option.

I reread the letter.

She's going to freak when she finds out it's me she has to marry.

I close my eyes, leaning against the headrest, letting the guilt swallow me until I can barely breathe.

She deserves to be happy.

She'll never forgive Sean or me for agreeing to this.

A claw digs deep against my gut, scraping the wounds I've carried for what feels like forever.

The door opens, and Ivan says, "Sir?"

Cold air rushes at me. I didn't realize we had stopped. I open my eyes, fold the letter, and shove it in the envelope. Then I get out, climb the staircase, and enter the plane.

Arina beams at me, curtsying and greeting, "Welcome back, Your Majesty. Can I get you a vodka? Or something else?"

"Vodka, please," I reply and brush past her. I plop down in the first seat, and a new panic hits me.

She didn't give me a definitive decision on older or newer.

I scrub my face, groaning.

"Everything okay?" Arina asks, holding a crystal tumbler in front of me.

"Fine."

"Do you need anything else?"

"No, thank you."

It isn't long before we're in the air. I spend the entire eight-hour flight deep in my thoughts. They range from my anger toward Brax for upsetting Fiona, my hope she's now okay, and anxiety over what I'll choose.

The pilot finally announces we're landing, and as soon as the seat belt light turns off, I rise, antsy to figure my dilemma out, knowing I have a tight timeline before the coronation.

The jetway is like every other one—dark and lit by the flames of wall sconces. Unlike the one in Monaco, this one only has one direction.

I get to the end of the hall, step through the door, and jog down two flights of stairs. There's another door that I open, stepping into a tiny room.

A short man in a tall, black, bearskin hat and red coat bows, greeting, "Your Majesty."

"Oliver. Nice to see you again," I reply.

He rises. "It is my honor, sir. His Majesty has been escorted to the vault." He pushes the button for an elevator.

I exhale a silent sigh of relief. Sometimes, the King of England gets tied up with more pressing matters, and I have to wait. Then again, he's had to wait for me, too, so I know the drill. "Good. I'm on a tight deadline."

The elevator opens, and we step inside. Oliver presses his hand to the screen, and we descend until we're forty feet underground. The doors open again, and we get on a golf cart. We travel several miles through winding, gloomy tunnels, then stop near a heavy, black and gold ornate door.

We get off the golf cart.

Oliver knocks on the door three times, and a whirring sound fills the air, followed by a loud pop. The door opens.

A man in a suit with deep wrinkles on his face and thin-wired glasses bows and says, "Your Majesty. I am the king's new royal advisor, Henry." He straightens, then steps back, widening his arm.

"Nice to meet you, Henry." I offer my hand.

He shakes it.

I brush past him, glancing around for the king. I turn back toward the man.

"Unfortunately, His Majesty had an important matter that just crept up. He has instructed me to give you time to decide what you would like to borrow," Henry states.

"Thank you."

He disappears behind the door, shutting it, and there's a sharp click of the lock followed by five shrill beeps.

My anxiety creeps up. I gaze around the room in awe of the crowns and tiaras glinting in the soft light.

How do I pick?

I step closer, examining each tiara and studying the nameplates underneath.

Fiona would love to see this.

I should bring her here sometime.

Stay focused. Time is running out.

With more determination, I pass over several I think she'd wrinkle her nose at, and get through half before I pause, reading the nameplate.

Grand Duchess Vladimir of Russia, 1874.

Interlocking diamond circles and large drop pearls adorn the gold headpiece. Next to it sits fifteen pendant emeralds.

My eyes dart from the pearls to the green gems.

She's Irish.

The pearls go better with her dress and ring, though.

Fuck. Another choice.

Maybe I can add only one emerald?

Jesus. I suck at this.

I knock on the thick door.

The lock opens, and Henry steps inside. "Your Majesty, may I assist you?"

I step in front of the tiara and pick it up. "I would like to borrow this one. Can I take the emeralds and pearls so my bride can choose?"

"Of course. And that's an interesting choice you selected," he adds.

"Oh?" I arch my eyebrows.

He nods. "Yes. It was created for the Grand Duchess Vladimir of Russia in 1874, and smuggled into Britain with 200 jewels from the duchess' secret safe. When the duchess died, her daughter, Grand Duchess Elena Vladimirovna, sold the tiara to Queen Mary in 1921. She's the one who had the emeralds made to swap with the pearls."

"I see."

He adds, "In 1953, Queen Elizabeth II inherited it in her coronation year and wore it often. It was said to be one of her favorite pieces. She also interchanged the look, sometimes wearing the pearls and some-times choosing the emeralds. A few times, she wore it without any drop stones."

I stare at the tiara, then declare, "I think Fiona will love this."

He grins. "I will package it up and have it delivered to your plane. I understand you're in a bit of a hurry?"

"Yes."

"Then Oliver will escort you upstairs, and your package will arrive shortly," Henry assures.

"Thank you." I put the tiara down, shake his hand, and exit the vault.

Oliver motions for me to get on the golf cart.

I obey.

He slides next to me and drives us back through the tunnels. We get to the elevator, which quickly opens for us to board, and rises before the doors open again.

I step out of it.

Oliver bows and states, "It's been an honor to see you again, Your Majesty."

"You as well. Thank you," I reply, then enter the stairwell. I climb two flights, stroll down the jetway, and board my plane.

Arina curtsies and chirps, "Your Majesty. Back so soon?"

"Yes." I glance at my watch, feeling antsy. There shouldn't be any time restraints, but I'll feel better when I arrive in Pompeii. So I add, "As soon as the package is delivered, bring it to me. And please let the pilot know I want to take off as soon as it arrives."

"Yes, sir," she replies and disappears.

I swallow a mouthful of vodka, cringing from the burn, and lift the shade. The runway is quiet, and the sun has already set. There are no other planes, but it's a hidden airfield reserved for the king's special guests, so it's nothing unusual.

I finish my drink, pull out my phone, and read my messages, replying to a few.

Arina interjects, "Sir, the package." She holds a black box with the king's seal in the corner and a gold ribbon tied around it.

My pulse increases. I take the box from her and nod. "Thank you."

"Sure." She glances at the box with curiosity.

"You're excused," I state, unwilling to share anything with her, especially before Fiona sees it.

She smiles and slips into her designated space.

The tension in my stomach grows. I carefully undo the bow, lift the lid, and pull out a glass box. The tiara rests on a white pillow, with the emeralds displayed around it. I carefully remove it, then gently run my finger over the gold, imagining Fiona in it, along with her dress.

Then, my mind torments me. All I can think about is her in the tiara, wearing the lingerie, with my fingers around her neck, and the same heat I saw in the snowstorm burning in her green eyes.

Images of her wearing the pearls, the emeralds, a combination of the two, and nothing at all appear like a movie trailer on repeat. Every image makes me harder until my cock strains against my zipper and my blood boils, rushing through my veins.

The pilot announces we're taking off.

I put the tiara back in the glass case and into the black box.

Shit. How am I going to get that ribbon to look how it did?

I groan, annoyed with my current circumstances.

We're in the air within minutes, and the plane levels off. I hit the call button.

Arina appears. "Can I help you, sir?"

"Any chance you know how to recreate the bow that was on this?" I probe, pointing at the box.

"Sure. May I?" she asks.

I pick up the box and affirm, "Please. Sit."

She obeys, and I hand her the box and ribbon. She secures it around all the edges, then says, "I need your finger."

"My finger?"

Her lips twitch. "Yep. I promise you'll get it back."

I chuckle, then hold my pointer out.

She presses it over the ribbon, and within a few moments, it looks like how it did when it arrived.

"Thank you," I sincerely offer.

She beams. "No problem. May I ask a question?"

"Sure."

Her eyes light up. "Is there a tiara in this box?" Excitement flares across her expression.

I grin. "Yes."

"How many queens have worn it?"

"Three that I'm aware of, maybe more."

"Wow." She glances at the box again.

I should let her see it.

No. Fiona hasn't seen it yet.

"I promise I'll let you hold it when it's time to return it."

She gapes at me for a moment. "You will?"

"Yes."

"Thank you, sir."

"You're welcome."

She rises. "Can I get you anything else?"

"No, thank you."

She leaves.

I need to secure this.

I rise, open the safe on the wall, and put the box inside. Since I often carry invaluable items, I added a safe years ago. Should anything happen to our flight, it can be recovered. So, even in the event of my unfortunate death, I can uphold my oath to return the tiara.

I lock the safe, sit in my seat, and stare out the window for several hours until the pilot lowers the aircraft.

My nerves reappear, mixing with something I don't feel very often. I try to decipher it and realize it's hope.

"Stop fooling yourself," I scold in a muted tone.

I try to smother the feeling, but it won't go away. My discomfort grows as my emotions conflict. Pompeii, with all of its ruins, the site of the coronation, seems to glare up at me.

I tear my eyes off the ground, glance at my phone, and my chest tightens further.

Less than two days until Fiona stands next to me or my head gets chopped off.

While I prefer not to die yet, it's not what scares me.

Ulrich's voice pops into my head. *"She can tap out and stay your queen. Or, she can choose not to tap out..."*

My mouth goes dry, my heart races, and I tighten my fists.

What scares me is that she might go through with this marriage. If she does, I'm going to have another choice to make.

Be a selfish man and keep her, allowing her to live but letting her suffocate from the misery of being mine.

Fiona

Two Days Later

Chapter ELEVEN

nother big yawn overpowers me. As soon as it ends, another one starts.

I'm so tired.

I can't remember when I had a full night's rest. It takes forever to fall asleep, only to wake up with my mind racing. My thoughts weave between dread and telling myself everything will be fine if I marry the king. It always ends with me turning on the light and rereading his letters.

The questions are always the same.

Who is he?

What are these flaws he deems so horrible?

How old is he?

Is he attractive?

Then, the lingerie dances in my mind, taunting me.

How do I get out of sleeping with someone forever?

The answers never come. Then I'll read the letters again, smiling and laughing at certain parts, and always coming to the same conclusion.

He's funny and nice.

He flew to Monaco to pick out my wedding attire, and asked me what I preferred.

He's going on another long trip to select whatever the borrowed item is, so doesn't that make him kind too?

He says we'll rule together as equals.

What does "rule" even mean?

He knew my dad.

That always tears me up. Then, the pain of growing up without a father and the thought of the twins not having both their parents resolidifies my decision.

There's no way out. I have to marry the king, whoever he is, and deal with whatever future is ahead of me. So my emotions are all over the place, night after night, resulting in me not getting adequate sleep.

I need coffee.

I set my hairbrush down, slide into my robe, and tie the belt around my waist. I exit my bedroom and stop short. My heart pounds harder. I blurt out, "What are you doing here?"

Valentina beams at me. "Don't look so happy to see us."

I glare at her, then slide my angry gaze to Zara.

She softly smiles with a sad expression. "I need to talk to you before Valentina does."

I cross my arms. "About what?"

"It's private. Please," Zara begs.

Valentina rises, pours a cup of coffee, then adds cream and sugar. She walks over and hands it to me. "Here. I'll wait in the guest bedroom."

"Just make yourself at home," I snap.

Her grin widens. "We'll be friends soon. You'll see."

I scoff. "Doubt that." I snatch the coffee mug out of her hand.

She shrugs, reiterating, "We will."

"Why don't you go home to Kirill?" I snarl.

She looks surprised at my words, and I can't deny feeling it too.

Why did I bring him up?

It's not the first time I've thought of him, remembered his fingers wrapped around my throat, the gleam in his blues, or how my body ached whenever he was near me. But he's a man I must forget, especially if I'm taking vows to tie myself to another. We have no future, even if I wasn't getting married. And I keep telling myself he's just a blip on the timeline of my life.

Maybe my husband will make me feel the same ache.

Doubt it.

Valentina studies me, and heat flares across my cheeks. I try to stop it but can't, hating myself for mentioning his name and showing her any of my cards. She purses her lips, peering at me closer.

I wait her out, not flinching.

She states, "I thought Kirill made it clear to you that he and I are friends. That's it."

I huff. "Sure didn't look like it."

"Why? Because you interrupted a conversation about a private matter you know nothing about?" she scolds.

More embarrassment hits me.

She quickly adds, "As far as I know, I'm Kirill's only friend. If I'm being open, I'll admit I can count mine on one hand. He's one of them."

"Yeah, okay," I mutter, wishing I'd shut up, but I'm not buying her story. No way she could be that close to him and not be attracted to him, so even if they're friends, I'm sure she wants him.

Anger flares across her expression. "We've never been anything but friends. You'll need to get over this notion you have about whatever it is you falsely believe is going on between us."

I grunt. "Why is that?"

She shuts her mouth, glares daggers my way, then shakes her head. "I'll be in the guest room. Take your time, Zara," she states, and strolls down the hall, enters the bedroom, then firmly shuts the door.

I redirect my irritation on Zara, closing the gap between us. "Why are you here?"

She keeps her tone soft. "Fiona, I have to talk to you about something serious. It's about the twins."

My anger morphs into worry. "What's wrong with them?"

"Nothing. But please, sit down." She points to the chair next to her.

I sigh and take a seat.

She stares at me, searching for something, but I don't know what.

I take a few sips of my coffee, then say, "I have to get to work soon. What is it?"

She takes a few deep breaths, reaches into her oversized blue bag, and pulls out an envelope. She sets it in front of me. "I need you to put this in your safe."

I glance at the yellow envelope. "What is it?"

Zara swallows hard, then blinks a few times, revealing, "Sean's and my trust."

My stomach flips. "Why do I need it?"

"We..." She blinks harder, and her eyes glisten. She looks away, pulls herself together, and releases an emotion-filled breath. She lifts her chin, squares her shoulders, and declares, "I know this is a lot, but we want you to raise the twins if something happens to us. If you don't want the responsibility, then it'll be left to our parents to decide who gets to raise them. We couldn't choose between them."

Horror fills me. My insides churn and my chest tightens. "Of course I would keep them! But why..."

Zara puts her hand on mine. "We've put you through a lot these last few weeks. We're both really sorry. Honestly. We never meant for any of this to happen. But Sean and I made choices, and those led us to this predicament. It's not fair to you. We'll deal with the consequences before us."

I gape at her, bile rising in my throat. I swallow it down.

She continues, "Our safe has letters I've written to the twins for their birthdays and special events, along with videos Sean and I made. If you want to move into our penthouse, it'll be your choice. The trust will hold the title for all properties and assets, but the penthouse will be transferred to your name. Do what you want with it. There should be plenty in the trust to raise the twins, and after they're eighteen, they'll start getting payouts on their birthdays."

"Zara..." I barely manage to get her name out, scooting closer and putting my arm around her back.

She blinks harder, takes another deep breath, then offers, "We really are sorry we put you through this ordeal. Thank you for taking the twins."

A tear escapes, falling down my cheek. "Zara, I'm not going to let you die!" I swipe my cheek.

She furrows her forehead, arguing, "It's okay, Fiona. You can't derail your entire life because of the choices we made. We shouldn't have let it get this far. Sean just thought he would figure out how to get us out of this mess."

"So you're going to let them kill you and let the twins grow up parentless?" I cry out.

Her face hardens and the color drains from her cheeks. She looks away, and her body trembles.

"Zara! Look at me!" I order.

Her chest rises and falls faster. She slowly meets my gaze.

"You're not letting them kill you. I already decided I'll marry whoever this man is," I declare.

Shock overtakes her features.

"You really thought I'd let you die?" I accuse, arching my eyebrows.

She swallows hard. "Fiona, it's not fair to you—"

"But letting your kids grow up as orphans is fair?" I hurl.

She wipes a tear off her cheek. Her voice shakes. "It's a no-win situation."

I chortle. "Right. But we're the adults, aren't we?"

She bites on her lip, closing her eyes.

"River and Willow are babies. They need their parents," I point out.

She nods, opening her misery-filled eyes. "I know. But—"

"There isn't a 'but' about it. You two got yourselves into a pile of shit, taking me with you. If there are only two options, as you say there are, then that really means there's only one. You know it and I know it," I declare.

Guilt explodes on Zara's face. She winces. "You're really going to go through with it?"

My gut dives. "Of course I am. There's no other choice. But you two owe me for the rest of your lives."

Tears of relief dampen her cheeks. She cackles, "You're sure?"

"About you two owing me for the rest of your life? Yep. No doubts," I affirm.

Another emotion-filled laugh flies out of her mouth. Then more tears fall. She sobs, "Fiona, I'm so sorry. Really. I am!"

I sigh and pull her into me, hugging her and admitting, "I know."

She weeps harder.

"Shh. It'll be fine," I insist, trying to convince myself as well.

She lifts her head, crying, "I didn't know what I was getting myself into. Neither of us did. We just wanted to know the truth and..."

"The truth? About my father?" I question.

She sniffles and straightens her back. "And mine."

"Yours?"

She nods. "Yes."

"Did you get it?"

"Yes."

"And what is it?"

She squeezes her eyes tight. "I can't tell you anything."

"Seriously?"

She pins her wet gaze on mine, quickly stating, "Not yet. But I will. I promise you, as soon as you're married, I will share everything with you."

Married.

My nerves flare again. I study her, then ask, "Can you tell me one thing?"

"If I'm allowed, yes," she answers.

I take a deep breath and probe, "Will he be nice to me?"

She hesitates, then replies, "I don't know him that well. But I believe so."

My insides quiver. I push, "Is he good-looking?"

She grimaces.

"Well that says it all."

She blurts out, "He's not...um...horrible."

"Well, that's reassuring," I mutter.

"I'm sorry. He has..."

"Has what?"

She shakes her head. "I'm sorry. I can't say any more."

A new wave of annoyance fills me.

Zara offers, "Sorry. I wish I could tell you everything right now."

I huff. "Yeah. Me too. Especially since I have to marry this man."

Guilt flashes across her expression once again. "I really am sorry," she apologizes.

I don't say anything.

The alarm on her phone blares through the air.

She reaches into her purse, pulls it out, and turns it off. She swallows hard and locks eyes with me. "Are you sure you're able to do this? If you aren't, don't go, Fiona. The minute you leave with Valentina, you're committing to it. If you change your mind, they'll kill you."

Nausea sours my stomach.

There's no choice.

I breathe through it and rise. "My decision is made."

Zara stands with fresh remorse flooding her beautiful features. "I feel horrible about this."

"You should," I agree, not willing to let her off the hook. I pick up the envelope. "I don't need this."

She shakes her head. "Please. Keep it in your safe. If anything ever happens to us, our wishes are the same."

"What's going to happen?" I fret. "I told you I'll marry him."

She holds her hand up. "I just meant for any reason. Like if an accident happens or we keel over from a heart attack."

I scoff. "Both of you at the same time?"

"You know what I mean."

"Well, nothing is happening to you," I insist.

"Please put it in your safe. I feel better as a mother having a plan in place," she confesses.

I put the envelope on the table. "Okay."

Another alarm goes off.

She wrinkles her forehead and swipes her phone. It stops and she declares, "I have to go. I feel sick over this, but I won't lie, Fiona. I selfishly don't want my kids orphaned or to die. So I know this sounds hollow, but thank you. Sean and I both thank you."

I grunt. "Make sure my brother knows he owes me."

Zara's lips twitch. "Don't worry, I will."

"Forever. If I have to commit to eternity, then tell him he's never getting off the hook with me," I add.

She bites on her smile, nodding, then states, "I'll relay the message. He'll be thrilled about it."

A laugh escapes me. I can just imagine how much my brother will hate it when Zara tells him. "I'm sure he will be."

Zara smiles and hugs me. "I have to go. I love you. So does Sean. We'll see you tomorrow."

"Tomorrow?" I question, going through my schedule in my head.

"At your coronation," Zara announces.

My stomach flips. "Oh. It's tomorrow?"

"Yes. And if I don't leave now, I might end up dead anyway." She hugs me tighter, then retreats. "Thank you."

I stay silent as I watch her leave, then pace a few minutes.

Valentina. Ugh.

I yell, "Valentina, you can come out now." I go to the window and stare out at the city. The roofs are covered with white snow but it's dirty on the streets from cars and pedestrians.

Valentina says, "So, you've made your decision?"

Anger fills me. I hate everything about Valentina. All I can think about is Kirill's hand on hers.

Stop thinking about him.

With my most confident stance, I turn to her and acknowledge, "There is no choice. I'm sure even you can agree with me on this point."

She tilts her head.

I cross my arms. "Why are you looking at me like that?"

"You're naive, aren't you?" she asks.

Insulted, I fire back, "Excuse me?"

She rolls her eyes. "You don't have to take offense to every little thing I say."

"You just called me naive," I point out.

"Yeah, I did. And you are," she insists.

"And why would that be?"

She steps closer. "You think the choice is clear. Some wouldn't see it that way. They'd save themselves over others."

I gulp. "Save? So I need to worry about the king harming me?"

She hesitates, then shakes her head. "I didn't say that."

"You just used the word 'save,'" I remind her.

"Others would choose to let Zara and Sean die. I've seen it a dozen times. That's all I meant," she claims.

"That's sad. Children shouldn't lose their parents as babies," I assert.

"No. They shouldn't," she agrees.

Silence fills the air, creating a sharp tension.

She breaks it, offering, "Maybe that's why you're meant to be queen."

My pulse increases. I still can't wrap my head around the royalty thing or what it actually means, especially in the real world. And the secret one my father created is just as big of a mystery to me.

Valentina glances at her watch. "We need to go or we'll be late."

"Where are we going?"

"To coronation," she answers.

"Where?" I push.

She winces. "Sorry. Can't tell you."

"Of course you can't," I mutter.

"Are you ready?" she asks.

My anxiety reignites. I blurt out, "What do I need to take?"

"Nothing. Everything is provided," she informs me.

"I have to go to work first," I add.

She shakes her head. "They aren't expecting you."

A deluge of exasperation drowns me. "Why is that?"

"It's been taken care of. You don't need to worry," she assures.

"It's not okay to tamper with my career," I warn.

She holds her hands up. "I haven't. Sean took care of it."

"How do you know?"

She sighs. "The Omni don't leave details overlooked. They cross their t's and dot their i's. Your father made sure The Underworld ran that way. There's always a map depending on what choice is made."

I glance out the window, fighting the urge to kick her out and not continue this nightmare.

"Time to go," she says.

I find the ability to follow her. We get to my front door, and she stops. "I forgot!" She reaches into her pocket and pulls out a small notecard. She holds it out toward me. "This is for you."

Cautiously, I ask, "What is it?"

She looks amused at my hesitance. "It's from the king."

The butterflies in my stomach take off. I gape at it.

"He said to make sure you read it," she reports.

I take it, go into the bedroom, and shut the door. I sit on my bed and stare at my name in his handwriting. I finally turn it over, release the seal, and pull out a notecard.

It matches his cream linen letterhead. The front is torn off, and only the inside of the card exists. I run my finger over the soft, uneven edges, and read.

MY DEAREST FIONA,
I FIGURED OUT THE BORROWED ITEM.
IF YOU ARE NOT 100% SURE YOU WILL GO THROUGH WITH
YOUR CORONATION, THEN DO NOT LEAVE WITH VALENTINA. I
WOULD RATHER BE BEHEADED THAN HAVE YOU SHOW UP, ONLY
TO WITNESS YOUR DEATH BY THEIR HANDS.
SINCERELY,
THE KING

My insides curl. I close my eyes, debating about staying home, knowing I can't.

I reread the note again, then rise. I put it with the stack of other letters, take them to the kitchen, and grab the envelope off the table.

"We have to go," Valentina announces.

I ignore her, return to my bedroom, and go into my closet. I press my hand to my safe. The lock whirs, then pops. The door opens.

A stack of cash, my valuable jewels, and my passport are inside. I slide the letters and trust documents on the shelf, then close the door. I lock it and then rejoin Valentina.

"Ready?" she questions, opening the door.

Nausea hits me again, but I fight through it. I lift my chin and step past her, cursing my father, Sean, and Zara.

There's no way out and only one place to enter.

The Underworld.

Kirill

The Next Morning

Chapter
TWELVE

"Y ou wanted to see us?" Sean states, entering the gym with Brax.

"Which one of you wants to fight?" I ask, grabbing my boxing gloves off the wall.

"I will," they both say in unison, with deep scowls on their faces.

It's a perfect way to greet me. I've barely slept, fighting my guilt, going over the different options before me. It all makes me feel unhinged, and the need to take it out on someone digs into the pit of my gut.

"Get out of the way, Brax," Sean orders, reaching for another pair of gloves. His hatred for me flares like fire raging in a dry forest, ready to incinerate everything in its path.

Brax whines, "You always take all the fun away."

Sean ignores him, steps under the rope, and cracks his neck. He pounds his gloves together, then warms up by jumping up and down.

My trainer, Vlad, studies him, then glances at me. "Sir, are you sure this is smart on such an important day?"

"Yep," I answer, ducking under the rope.

Vlad argues, "We don't have a referee."

I grunt. "Brax can do it."

"He's his friend," Vlad points out.

"Shut the fuck up," Brax snarls, insulted.

Vlad crosses his arms. "You aren't unbiased."

"Neither are you."

"I'm not the one calling the shots in the ring."

"You aren't qualified," Brax asserts.

Vlad barks, "A referee should have no conflict of interest."

"Does anyone in our world ever have no conflict of interest?" Brax spouts.

"Enough!" I snap.

Sean fumes, "Are we doing this or not?"

"We are," I reply, and step to the center of the ring.

Sean moves in front of me. "Good. I've been waiting to pound your face until it's bloody."

Brax enters the ring, holds his arm in the air, then brings it down, shouting, "Box!"

"Wait!" Valentina screams.

Sean turns, and I land a hard punch on his cheek. He flies across the ring and lands on his ass. Rage explodes in his eyes, and he jumps up, ready to kill me.

"It's Fiona!" Valentina shrieks.

I turn toward her. "What about her?"

Sean's body flies at me and knocks me to the ground. He grits out, "Motherfucking, Petrov!"

"Stop them!" Valentina orders.

Adrenaline courses through me. I flip Sean onto his back and reach for his throat.

He grips mine just as tight.

"This isn't the time!" Valentina cries out.

Vlad tries to pull me off Sean, but I'm too angry to release him.

Sean's just as determined to kill me. His greens burn into my stare. He increases his hold around my throat and tries to kick me.

"Brax! Do something!" Valentina orders.

He calmly replies, "Don't get your panties in a twist. They'll figure it out."

"This isn't funny! Fiona's having chest pains and can't breathe."

I release Sean's neck, turning my head, but I can't speak. The slight angle gives him the ability to tighten his hold on me and cuts off my air supply.

Brax grabs Sean's wrists and pulls, commanding, "Time to pause, bro." Sean releases me, and I gasp for air, rolling off him.

"Grow up. All of you!" Valentina scolds.

As soon as I can speak, I jump up, asking, "Did you call the medics?"

She glares at me but answers, "Yes. Of course."

"What's wrong with her?" Sean asks in panic, stepping next to me.

Valentina puts her hand on her hip and points at us. "Of all the days, you pick today to kill each other? Do you ever think of anyone but yourselves?"

Brax grunts. "It's just a friendly boxing match."

She pins her murderous glare on him. "Don't open your mouth again."

"Or what? You're going to spank me?" he taunts.

She narrows her eyes. "I'll deal with you later." She refocuses on Sean and me. "You two better cut this shit out."

I duck under the rope and jump to the ground. "What's wrong with Fiona's heart?"

Valentina shakes her head. "I don't know. The medics are there now. Zara is with her."

"She's in the queen's quarters?" I ask, stepping toward the door.

Valentina lunges in front of me. "You can't go there, and you know it."

"Like hell I can't," I declare, reaching around her for the doorknob.

She backs against the wooden door, snapping, "They'll kill you if you attempt to see her."

"So what?" I bark, turning the knob.

Valentina's eyes widen. "They'll kill Fiona too!"

I freeze, my chest rising and falling in short bursts, staring at the intricate pattern on the door above Valentina's head.

"Where's the queen's quarters?" Sean questions, stepping next to us.

She scoffs. "You aren't allowed there either."

"Bullshit. She's my sister," he claims.

"So what? You aren't special. The rules apply to you too, so deal with it," Valentina retorts.

"Such a bossy little minx today," Brax interjects, a proud note to his tone.

"Shut up," Sean and I growl at the same time.

He holds his hands in the air. "Touchy, touchy."

"Shut up," Sean repeats in a harsher tone.

"Tell me what happened," I order.

"All of you go sit down, and I will," she instructs.

I stay planted.

"Go." She points.

Sean caves first, stomping toward the weights and sitting on a bench. "Start talking, Valentina."

I stand back and cross my arms.

"I'm not speaking until you sit," she warns, pinning her challenging stare on me.

I finally break and find another bench.

She looks at Brax and Vlad.

"Sit," I bark at them.

They obey.

Valentina leans away from the door. "They wheeled in breakfast. The three of us were sitting around the table, and Zara was talking."

"About what?" I ask.

Valentina shrugs. "I don't remember. Something about the twins. Everything was normal, but then Fiona said her heart was racing. Her breathing became short and choppy, and her face turned bright red."

"Does she have a history of heart issues?" I ask Sean.

He shakes his head. "No." Worry laces his expression.

Valentina continues, "The medics gave her an EKG. Aside from the elevated heart rate and shortness of breath, they said she's fine. They think it might be a panic attack."

A feeling of helplessness washes over me, and my heart squeezes with fear.

Brax queries, "Fiona's never had panic attacks before, has she?"

"Not to my knowledge," Sean admits.

"I thought you would want to know. I'll let you know more information as I receive it," Valentina states, then slips out the door.

I race toward it and exit the gym, shutting the door behind me.

She spins to face me. "You can't follow me."

"I know. I just..."

Valentina arches her eyebrows, still upset.

I gather my thoughts and finally offer, "Please tell her I hope she's okay."

"I'll leave out the part about how her brother and you are acting like toddlers," she scoffs.

"He had it coming," I blurt out.

Her gaze darkens.

"Don't look at me like that. I saved his ass, and now I'm in the shit along with his sister. And he changed the course. All of this is because of the choices he and Zara made," I argue.

Her disapproving look intensifies.

"Stop looking at me like I'm wrong," I say.

She steps closer and reminds me, "You chose to give your token."

"To save his ass and Zara's."

"You chose." She jabs me in the chest.

My heart pounds harder. I clench my jaw.

She lowers her voice. "For God's sake, today is not the day to have blood and bruises on your face. How do you think Fiona will feel if your mask comes off and your face is unrecognizable?"

I grunt. "She might prefer it."

Valentina jerks her head back, gaping at me.

Self-loathing swirls in my gut, mixing with the disappointment I feel about relaying my inner thoughts out loud.

"Grow up, Kirill. Don't make this about you."

I grind my molars.

"We chose this life. Fiona's been thrown into it, thanks to Sean's and your choices. She's saving all your asses. And don't think for one minute you aren't to blame. So before you kill her brother, think about what it'll do to her. In fact, why don't you try to make peace with him? Hating Sean won't make this transition any easier on her."

I stay quiet, wallowing in guilt. The last thing I want to do is hurt Fiona further.

Valentina tosses another sharp look my way, spins on her heel, and disappears down the hall.

For several moments, I lean against the wall, considering all she said. I squeeze my fists at my sides, hating that something is going on with Fiona and I'm not there. I finally decide Valentina's right. The only thing I can do right now is try to make peace with Sean.

I open the door and enter the gym.

Sean scowls at me.

"Let's go," I order.

"Where?" Brax questions.

I cross the room and open another door. I step into the hall and then turn my head. "Are you coming?"

Vlad steps into the hallway next to me.

Brax and Sean exchange glances.

I shrug. "Suit yourselves." I take a few more steps.

"Wait up," Brax calls out.

I stop until they're in the hall and then lead them to my royal quarters. I open the door to the main area and pick up the phone.

"Good morning, Your Majesty. May I help you?" a woman's voice answers.

I reply, "Brunch for four, please."

"Yes, sir. Anything else?" she asks.

"No, thank you." I hang up and go to the bar. I pour two tumblers of vodka and two whiskeys. I hand Vlad the vodka, then the whiskeys to Sean and Brax. I grab mine and take too large of a mouthful. It burns all the way to my stomach, and I grimace.

"Pussy," Sean mutters, then downs a large mouthful, trying not to wince himself.

I grunt. "Who's the pussy?"

"You're all pussies," Vlad states, finishing his glass in three mouthfuls and never once making a face.

Brax chuckles. "Vlad's a true alcoholic or has no taste buds."

Vlad grins. "I'm true Russian—a real man."

Brax nods and drinks half of his, wincing slightly.

I point at the table. "Please. Sit."

Brax grabs the back of a chair, turns it, and sits. Vlad sits next to him.

Sean hesitates.

I shrug. "Fine. Stand the entire time." I grab the decanters of vodka and whiskey, set them on the table, and grab a seat.

Sean eventually gives in and takes the last chair.

I refill Vlad's tumbler, then top off the others. I take another sip and lean back, studying Sean.

"If you're going to stare at me the entire time, I'm leaving," he says.

I curl my fists.

Think of Fiona.

I resist the urge to slap him, and uncurl my fingers. I inch forward, tap the table, and challenge, "Do you want to make this harder or easier on your sister?"

Rage fills his features. He barks, "If you lay a hand on my sister, I'll slice you to pieces, then feed you your balls."

"I would never hurt, Fiona. Get your head out of the gutter."

Brax grunts. "Sounded like a threat to me."

I fling the back of my hand against his head.

"Ouch!" he cries out.

I point to him and Vlad. "You and you. Get out."

"What did I do?" Vlad asks.

"Nothing. Keep this one out of my hair. Go in the other room. Watch TV or something," I suggest.

"Come on. I'm hungry," Brax gripes.

"You can eat there. Now, don't make me tell you again," I threaten.

Vlad rises and nods toward the other room. "You heard the king. Let's go."

Brax leaps out of his chair, shaking his head. He begrudgingly follows Vlad into the other room.

When the door's shut, I turn to Sean. "You and I have some things to work out."

"Like why you're such a prick?" he mutters.

Anger courses through me. I breathe through it, remembering that this talk will either hurt or help Fiona. When I'm calm enough to speak, I declare, "You and I both got Fiona into this mess. If we all walk out of here alive, it's because she married me. That means, she'll have a lot to deal with once the outside world knows she married a Petrov."

"No shit," he snarls.

"Don't you think it's better for her if we get over whatever it is between us?" I ask.

His face hardens. He keeps his disapproving gaze on me.

The bell rings.

"Come in," I shout.

The door opens, and a server steps inside. He bows. "Your Majesty."

"Thank you," I reply.

He rises, then wheels a large cart inside. The scent of bacon, sausage, pancakes, and cinnamon fills the air.

My stomach growls. I point to the door, directing, "Set it up in the other room, please. You can leave through the southern exit."

"Yes, sir." He disappears through the door.

Once it's shut, I continue, "Is staying pissed at me worth hurting Fiona?"

Sean's jaw twitches.

"Well?" I push.

He sighs. "No."

"Good. I don't think so either. So besides the fact I'm a Petrov and marrying your sister, what else is the issue?"

"Isn't that enough?" he questions.

I shrug. "I don't know. Is it?"

He stays silent.

"Something tells me you're upset with me for more than that," I push.

"More than just that? Like that isn't enough?" he bites out.

I hold my hands in the air. "I'm just trying to get to the root cause of our issues so we can get past them."

He glowers.

I add, "For Fiona's sake. Eternity is a long time."

He grinds his molars.

I finish my vodka, then say, "Fine. Have it your way. Don't say I didn't try when your sister is suffering worse than anticipated." I rise and take a step toward the door.

"Wait!"

I slowly turn back around.

He points to my chair. "Sit."

I don't move.

"Don't make this harder for me," he warns. He finishes his whiskey and then taps his tumbler.

I return to my seat and wait for him to speak.

Hatred looms in his expression. "Your family is the lowest scum on Earth."

The pit in my stomach grows. I reply, "I'll agree that many of my family members are what you claim."

He grunts. "I'm supposed to believe you aren't?"

"I don't know. You tell me. I don't rape women, force them into brothels, nor do I mutilate females or children."

He sits back, crosses his arms, and puts his ankle on his knee. "I'm supposed to believe you when generations of Petrov men before you tortured too many women and children to count?"

Bile rises in my throat. I fight it back and say, "Your father did."

"Why did he?" Sean questions.

The numbing pain over the night Sean Sr. discovered I wasn't like my father emerges. I push past it and answer, "He saw I was different."

Sean stares at me.

"You have to choose whether or not to give me the benefit of the doubt. But I promise you, over time, you'll learn I'm telling you the truth," I state.

The tension in the room builds again. Neither of us flinch.

I add, "Your sister will be queen, and you have my word she'll always be treated as one."

"So was Anne Boleyn until King Henry VIII beheaded her," Sean notes.

"He was paranoid and psychotic," I point out.

"And you're not?"

"No. I'm not," I refute in a stern tone.

A heavy silence falls between us.

I cut through it. "Let's assume you give me the benefit of the doubt on this topic. What else upsets you about me marrying your sister?"

He pins his eyebrows together, then looks away.

The hairs on my arms rise. I swallow down years of loathing and lower my voice. "Ah. I see. It's my scar, isn't it?"

He meets my gaze. In a sympathetic tone, he says, "I don't mean to be a prick, but you're not the type of guy my sister dates."

"I know."

He taps his empty tumbler again, continuing, "Don't you think it's cruel to subject her to marrying a man she'll never find attractive?"

Never.

She will never find me attractive.

His words slice through me like the knife that slid over my face and body. It's not a new realization, but hearing him say the truth out loud hurts more than I thought it would. I work my hardest to keep my neutral expression, and wait until I know my voice will come out strong before I confess, "Yes, it's cruel. However, I didn't pick her to marry me."

"You should consider yourself lucky they chose my sister for you!" he hurls, his face turning red as he lowers his foot to the floor.

I hold my hands in the air. "Calm down. I didn't mean it like that."

He breathes harder, scowling.

I let him cool off a bit, then continue, "I meant that I wouldn't have ever chosen to put her through this. I'm aware of my flaws, and understand I'll never be the type of man she would willingly want to marry. Yet here we are, in a situation where everyone does what the Omni wants or we all die. So are you holding my scar against me for the rest of our lives?"

He ponders my question and then replies, "No. I guess that's not fair." He shifts in his seat and admits, "I'm not mad about your scar. I'm pissed at myself for involving my sister in our mess."

"You and me both," I agree.

He nods. "We fucked up, didn't we?"

"I don't know. Do you regret that you and Zara are still alive?" I ask.

He scrubs his face. "No. Of course not. But we shouldn't have tried so hard to get our seat at the table."

I pour another glass of whiskey for him. "I disagree with you on that point."

"Why?"

"Your father wanted both you and Fiona at the table. It was important to him," I insist.

Sean shrugs. "I don't even see the point. I feel more powerless than ever since we took our seats. Zara does too."

I refill my tumbler. "My guess is you won't forever."

"Why? What's going to change?"

I take a drink, set it down, and lean closer. "I am king. Tonight, your sister becomes queen. Our debt will be cleared, and things will return to normal."

"What does normal even mean?" Sean asks.

I drink more vodka and rise. I go to the desk, hold my hand over the paper to shield it from cameras and write, *You and I are going to clean house. The Underworld will be what your father meant it to be. I promise you.*

I walk over to Sean and put it on his lap, strategically blocking the cameras.

He reads it and looks at me in question.

I crumple the note, go to the fireplace, and toss it inside. The edges curl in the flames, and I don't take my eyes off it until the entire piece is incinerated.

All I hope is that I'm making some progress with Sean.

For Fiona's sake, I have to.

Fiona

Chapter
THIRTEEN

"Are you still feeling okay?" Zara frets.

"All good. You can stop worrying now," I reply. Shortly after the medics arrived, my heart stopped racing and I could breathe again.

They did an EKG and echocardiogram. Both tests were perfect. So they claimed I had a panic attack and asked if I had been under any stress.

It was the most ridiculous question anyone had ever asked me.

All day, Zara and Valentina have been exchanging nervous glances, checking my heart status, and fussing over me. It's getting old, adding to the unsettledness of my upcoming nuptials to a stranger.

The makeup artist orders, "Close, please."

I shut my eyelids, and she brushes more shadow on them.

"We just needed a bit more," she mutters, spinning my chair, then chirps, "Perfect!"

I open my eyes and stare at my reflection. My hair is sleek at the front and pulled back in a low, poofy bun. Shimmering gold, brown, and a bit of copper adorn my eyes. Soft pink highlights my cheeks, and my neutral-colored lips have gloss over them.

I praise, "You're talented, Lainey."

"Thank you. You're naturally beautiful, so I only had to enhance your features," she claims.

There's a knock on the door, and I spin in the chair.

Valentina answers it, and a woman with a long, gold, spaghetti-strapped dress, stilettos encrusted in jewels, and a matching-colored eye mask steps inside.

It's the same outfit Zara and Valentina are wearing, but their eye masks are sitting on the table. I asked them what they're for and they said I'll see.

The woman states, "I have the wardrobe."

Valentina steps back. "Please, bring it in."

A woman in the same outfit wheels in a cart. Two garment bags hang on the rack, and a shoebox sits on top.

A third woman carries a black box with a gold bow. She holds it out toward Valentina, declaring, "The king said to make sure only our future queen opens this."

Butterflies take flight in my stomach, confusing me. I don't know why I get them whenever the king sends me anything. I shouldn't when I haven't met him, and this entire situation is bizarre. Yet they always appear and mix with my apprehension.

Valentina takes the box and sets it on the table. "Thank you."

The three women line up in front of me, curtsy, and say, "It is an honor to serve you," in unison.

The same strange feeling that hit me when Vaughn referred to me as queen flares in my belly, fighting with my butterflies. Not knowing what else to do, I awkwardly reply, "Thank you."

They smile, rise, and leave the room.

As soon as the door shuts, I sigh in relief.

Zara unzips the garment bags and takes the lingerie and wedding dress out.

Anxiety builds within me, canceling out my relief.

She exclaims, "Wow! These are stunning!"

Valentina nods, adding, "I can't believe he picked these on his own."

"Why?" I snap, suddenly feeling like I need to defend the king's ability to choose my wedding attire.

She glances at me. "No need to get upset."

"Then explain yourself."

She smirks. "Already speaking like royalty, I see."

I glare at her.

"Calm down. The king doesn't have any fashion sense. I usually have to tell him what coordinates with what," she states.

That's going to end.

I point out, "He didn't need your help picking out anything for the coronation. I guess you've been wrong all these years about his fashion sense."

"No, I haven't. You'll see," she retorts.

Zara interjects, "Stop fighting, you two. We don't have time to waste. Fiona, come get dressed." She shakes the lingerie, adding, "This is a sexy little number."

The butterflies flitter restlessly, and I take a deep breath, rising off the chair. I close the gap between us, take the delicate piece, and step into it. I pull it to my waist, untie my silk belt, and tug the rest of it up.

Zara slides my robe off my arms. "Let's see." She spins me and wiggles her eyebrows. "Wow."

"He's going to go nuts over you in that," Valentina states.

I toss her a death glare, then stare at my reflection.

Will I want him to like me in this?

What does he look like?

I'm marrying a man, and I don't even know his name.

Panic hits me, and my heart races faster. I take deep breaths.

Zara puts her hand on my arm. "Fiona, are you okay?"

I lift my chin. "Yes. Help me get into my dress, please."

She studies me.

"Dress," I utter.

Valentina carries the dress to us and unfastens it. She gathers the exquisite material and arranges it on the ground in front of me.

I carefully step into it, and she slides it up my legs and over my torso, then I secure it over my arms. She carefully closes the front, secures it, and gushes, "This dress was made for you."

"Hot damn!" Zara exclaims.

I spend a long time assessing myself.

The dove is an incredible statement.

He has fashion sense; he just doesn't know it.

Zara holds out a pair of gold stilettos. "These are keepers too."

I nod, unable to disagree.

She bends and helps me into them.

Gesturing to the box, Valentina ponders, "I wonder what's in this."

I glance at the black box. The anxious feeling intensifying. I go to the table, carefully tug the gold bow, lift the lid, and freeze, gaping.

A glass box showcases an ornate tiara with interlocking diamond circles. Large drop pearls adorn the gold circlet. It sits on a white satin pillow, and fifteen pendant emeralds gleam around it.

Where did he get this?

"There's a note," Zara says, tearing me out of my thoughts.

My gaze darts to a small black envelope pressed against the box. I pick up the package, take it to the couch, and sit. I reach for the envelope, break the seal, and pull out the note.

My dearest Fiona,
Based on your response, I opted for something older for you, my queen.
The Grand Duchess Vladimir of Russia first wore the tiara in 1874. In 1918, Albert Stopford, a British art dealer and friend of the Grand Duchess, smuggled the tiara and 200 other jewels out of Russia and into Britain.
After Vladimir's death, her daughter sold it to Queen Mary in 1921. Queen Elizabeth II inherited it in her coronation year in 1953. She wore it many times, with pearls, emeralds, or neither.
I hope you love it and appreciate all the royalty before you who wore it. Undoubtedly, you will be the most memorable of all the queens.
Sincerely,
The King

Zara asks, "What does it say?"

I slide the note back into the envelope, answering, "It belonged to the Grand Duchess Vladimir of Russia. Queen Mary bought it from her daughter, then Queen Elizabeth II owned it."

"You're joking, right?" Zara asks.

I unlatch the glass lid, pick it up, and peer closer at the magnificent piece laced with history. I carefully slide my fingers over the different parts of the metal and pearls, then hold a green emerald next to a pearl.

"That's insane," Valentina comments.

For once, I agree with her, nodding at her comment.

"What are the emeralds for?" Zara prods, sitting next to me.

I pull the pillow out, set the box on the table, and put the tiara on the white satin. I reach for the middle pearl, explaining, "You can wear it with pearls or emeralds," and unfasten the jewel. I put it on the pillow, pick up the emerald, and attach it in the same spot.

Valentina notes, "They don't make jewelry the same anymore."

"You're right," I agree.

She asks, "How are you going to wear it? Pearls or emeralds?"

My gaze moves between the two options. I spend several minutes studying it with all the pearls and emeralds. Then I do a combination, rotating every other one. After a few minutes, I acknowledge, "This isn't helping." I put the pearls back on except for the middle one.

"It's pretty like that," Zara offers.

I hold it out.

"Let's go to the mirror and try it on," she suggests.

I obey, step in front of my reflection, and hold the tiara above my head.

"Let me put it on you," Zara says.

Lainey clears her throat. "May I?"

Surprised, I blurt out, "You've been so quiet, I forgot you were here!"

She smiles and closes the gap between us, repeating, "May I secure it? If you wish to change the jewels, I can do it for you."

Zara steps back. "Good idea. I'll screw up your hair. Besides, what do I know about how to secure a tiara?"

Lainey takes the headpiece, pushes it against my hair, fastens it, and says, "Valentina, grab her veil."

Valentina brings over a long, goldish-cream lace veil. She raves, "It has doves on it!"

Enthusiasm takes over as I study the intricate details, internally praising the king for his good taste.

Lainey takes it, adds it to the bottom of my hair, and grins. She spins me toward the mirror, praising, "Now you look like a queen!"

The flutters in my stomach resume. Never in a million years would I have thought I'd be standing here, in a dress made for royalty, in a tiara queens have worn, about to go through my own coronation—whatever that means.

Valentina pulls a box out of her pocket. "A final gift from the king."

My adrenaline rises. I reach for the black leather box, untie the gold ribbon, and lift the lid, gaping again.

"Holy shit," Zara breathes.

"He definitely has a knack for jewelry," Valentina commends.

A pair of teardrop pearls, similar to the ones on the tiara, encased in gold with tiny emeralds in the same shape dancing around the edges shimmer in the light.

"There's a note on the lid," Zara states, holding the top upside down.

I read it.

THE KING'S PERSONAL GIFT FOR THE IRISH QUEEN.

A smile so big erupts on my face, I feel giddy.

"Aw. That's sweet," Zara coos.

My hand shakes. I pick up an earring and loop it through my ear. I put the other one on and then stare at myself.

Lainey interjects, "Did you want to see how the tiara looks with all pearls or all emeralds?"

I shake my head. "No. I'm going to wear it with just one emerald."

Zara concurs. "It does look perfect like that, especially with the earrings."

"Yes," I affirm.

There's a knock on the door, and I turn.

Valentina moves toward it and then opens it.

The woman who brought the wardrobe declares, "It's time."

My excitement turns to panic. My pulse skyrockets and a sheen of sweat breaks out on my forehead. I reach for Zara's arm and stare at her.

"Breathe, Fiona," she orders.

I take several deep breaths, calming myself as best as possible.

"Are you okay?" she frets.

There's no backing out. Everyone will die if I do.

I pull it together and lift my chin, squaring my shoulders. "Yes."

"Ready?" Valentina questions.

Not wanting to show her any weakness, I force my legs to move. I hold the sides of my dress, brush past her, and ask the woman, "Where am I going?"

She curtsies, then replies, "Follow me, please." She guides me down a long hallway lit by the flickering flames of the candles in sconces.

With every step I take, my nerves intensify. By the time I get to the door, my insides quiver.

She pushes the heavy wood open, and vibrations from humming hit me. It's loud, unexpected, and seeps into my skin, digging into my bones until my trembling seems a natural part of the moment.

"Zara," the woman says, motioning her forward.

Zara hugs me. "I'll always owe you," she whispers in my ear, then kisses me on the cheek. She offers a remorseful smile, secures her mask over her face, and steps through the door. She disappears.

Valentina offers, "You'll do great," puts on her eye mask, and exits.

The hums turn to masculine *oms*. A stomping sound follows, then a feminine *ah*.

The hairs on my arms rise. My anxiety explodes.

The woman nods. "Your turn."

I stare at her.

"It'll be okay," she reassures.

Get it together.

I find my strength, lift my chin, and step inside.

The sounds echo around me.

A man in a tuxedo, wearing a skull mask, steps beside me. He hugs me. "Fiona, you look beautiful."

"Sean!" I blurt out, relieved it's him.

"You okay?" he questions.

This isn't the time to be weak.

"Yes," I reply as calmly as I can.

He retreats, and his eyes meet mine. The mask can't hide his guilt. "Fiona—"

"Don't," I warn, knowing if he gives me his apologies again, I won't be able to get through this.

He takes a deep breath and nods.

I lace my arm through his, and he leads me through a crowd. It takes a few minutes to realize we're in an arena with no ceiling. It's a cloudless night, and the full moon shines over the audience, competing with the beautiful glow of the candles the women hold. They're all dressed in the same gold dresses. Men are in tuxes with skull masks, holding torches and banging them on the ground.

The chanting and stomping grow louder as I approach the center of the arena. Sean leads me up the stairs toward a well-defined, tall, masked man. Zara's near him, holding roses. Another man in a robe and mask stands behind them.

My stomach flip-flops.

I don't get to see what he looks like?

I glance around the arena, and more panic hits me.

How many thousands of people are here?

Who are they?

Sean positions me before the man, leans into his ear, and says something. He turns and hugs me, then steps behind him.

The wind chooses that moment to gently blow through, and I freeze.

The intoxicating smell of leather, rosewater, saffron, jasmine, and other notes I can't identify teases my core.

He smells like Kirill.

It's not possible.

The man takes two steps toward me, closing the gap between us. I search his eyes, seeing the same heat and danger I always saw in Kirill.

It can't be him.

What if it is?

Please be him.

He reaches for my hands, and I glance down. One has my father's mark branded into it. The other has a tattoo of tiny pink hearts on top of crossed bones hanging off a black chain.

It's the same hand tattoo as Kirill's.

Happiness fills me, replacing my panic. I gasp, blurting out, "Kirill?"

His chest rises with air. He stands taller, towering over me, squeezing my hands. His Russian accent sounds thicker as he says, "You look more beautiful than I imagined."

A smile erupts on my lips. I blink hard, overwhelmed with all the hours I spent wondering who I was going to marry. I don't know much about this man, but the little I know is enough for this situation. And all the letters he wrote and the time he took to find attire I'd love, flood my memory, intensifying the attraction I've felt for him since the moment we first met.

The audience quiets.

Kirill doesn't break our gaze, rubbing his thumbs over my hands.

My butterflies go into a frenzy.

A man with a German accent roars, "We have waited for this coronation for a long time. The Underworld will once again be complete!"

A deafening applause erupts.

I cringe.

The man holds his hand up, and everything goes quiet again. He declares, "Tonight's coronation will consist of three parts: Commitment, Consummation, and Closure."

The crowd roars.

My panic returns. *Consummation? Here?*

Kirill closes the gap between us, leans down, and murmurs, "It will be as private as I could get it."

I open my mouth, but nothing comes out.

The man announces, "I am Ulrich, acting magistrate of the Omnipotence, and I am most humbled to conduct this ceremony."

The crowd cheers again.

Ulrich quiets it again and begins, "Your Majesty, do you take this woman, Fiona O'Malley, to be your eternal wife?"

The audience returns to their soft humming.

Kirill meets my eyes. He confidently states, "I do."

My insides quiver, mixing with a growing ache that expands deep in my core.

Ulrich adds, "Do you vow to adore, protect, and rule by her side for eternity?"

Eternity.

My knees wobble.

Kirill rolls his thumbs over my hands again, answering, "During our lifetime and eternity, I pledge to adore, protect, and rule by her side to further The Underworld's agenda. I promise to defend my bride's sacred role as my top priority, forsaking anyone who tries to dethrone her."

Dethrone me?

He roars toward the crowd, "From this day forward, a threat to my bride is a direct declaration of war upon The Underworld, handled only by death." He pins his blues back on mine.

Direct war?

Death?

A strange feeling comes over me. I don't flinch under his stare, realizing there's something amazingly sexy about his declaration to protect me to the end of time.

He'll kill for me.

Maybe I shouldn't feel good about that, but I do. It lights my core so hot I have to press my thighs together.

Ulrich nods.

Kirill releases a hand and holds it out toward Sean. My brother puts a ring in it, and Kirill turns back to me. He slides a wedding band next to the diamond and returns to assessing me.

Tingles run down my spine, vibrating along with the hums.

Ulrich booms, "Do you, Fiona O'Malley, take our king, Kirill Petrov, to be your eternal husband?"

"I—" I freeze.

Petrov?

I gape at Kirill.

There's no way he's a Petrov.

The look in his eyes tells me I'm wrong.

I glance at my brother.

Guilt flashes in his eyes, and he nods.

Kirill glides his thumbs over my hands again.

My family will kill me if I marry a Petrov.

"Fiona," Zara nudges.

I turn and look at her, my panic building.

"It'll be okay," she offers.

How?

Ulrich questions, "Do you take the king as yours, or do you refuse your role as queen?"

My insides quiver. I can't speak. My entire life, my family has warned me who my enemies are, and the Petrovs are one of them.

Kirill leans into my ear, stating, "I promise you I am not like the family members whose blood runs through my veins. We will figure out the logistics of everything later." He meets my eye.

For some reason, his confident stare makes me believe him.

Ulrich pushes, "Are you choosing to dismiss your vows and refuse your role as queen?"

I release an anxious breath and state, "I do not refuse my role as queen."

"Then do you take Kirill Petrov to be your eternal husband?" Ulrich repeats.

My racing heart makes me dizzy, but I state, "I do."

Kirill squeezes my hands.

Zara holds out a ring.

I take it and shakily slide it on Kirill's finger.

He grips my hands again.

Ulrich declares, "By the power vested in me by The Underworld and my seat at the table, I pronounce to you, King Kirill and his eternal queen, Fiona!"

The audience cheers so loudly my ears hurt.

Ulrich holds up his arm, and they quiet back to a low hum. He adds, "To the rest of the world, you are now Mr. and Mrs. Kirill Petrov."

Mrs. Kirill Petrov.

Oh my God.

My family will never forgive me.

"Kiss your bride," Ulrich orders.

Kirill's eyes rage with fire.

Electricity surges through my veins.

He tugs me into him and slides his hand over my throat. His scent floods me, intensifying the chaos in my core. He lifts his mask and tosses it on the floor.

Adrenaline pools in my cells. The sexiest man I've ever laid eyes on, whom I've thought about for too many hours to count, stands before me, bonded to me for eternity. His scar glows under the moon, illuminating every bad boy vibe he possesses.

He gently pushes his thumb against my pulse, then slides it up and down, staring at me.

I take short breaths as my gaze drifts to his lips.

He moves his face an inch from mine, his hot breath teasing my mouth. He studies my expression, continuing to caress my neck, to the point I'm reeling with anticipation. Then he finally closes the gap.

Our tongues collide in a long-waited battle, tangling with need and desperate for more until I'm out of breath and my knees give out.

He tightens his hold on me, his erection growing and pushing into my stomach.

I whimper, unable to take my gaze off his blues, sliding my tongue deeper into his mouth.

He retreats first, dragging his mouth to my ear, and murmuring, "Make sure you tap out, my beautiful queen."

Kirill

Chapter
FOURTEEN

The thick air burns hotter in my lungs. The chaotic vibrations in the audience grow, intensifying every ounce of anticipation zipping through me.

Fiona pins her eyebrows together and a flush dances on her cheeks. Her breath pushes past her parted lips in short bursts. She pins her question-filled greens on me.

My perfect little bird.

My wife.

Jesus. She actually went through with it and married me.

Why did she seem happy when she realized it was me?

I'm reading into things again, I tell myself, but the way her face lit up when she said my name is something I'll never forget.

Ulrich holds his arms out as wide as possible. The chanting ends, and the men frantically pound their wooden torches on the ground.

More questions flare across my bride's expression.

Ulrich booms, "The consummation will now begin!"

An "*ugh, ugh, ugh*" sound from the women fills the arena, fighting the echo of the stomps. A room with tinted glass walls rises behind Ulrich. A crossbeam runs over a bed, and thick chains with cuffs hang from it. Thirteen men in medieval battle gear and helmets kneel around the mattress, their shiny swords uncovered and pointed toward the sky.

I scowl at Ulrich.

He arrogantly smirks.

Fucking asshole. Of course he wouldn't give me the courtesy of a more private room.

Why did I assume he would?

Panic mixes with intrigue, washing across Fiona's face. She gapes at the room, then around the arena, her pink cheeks reddening as she realizes what will happen. She turns her greens on me, and the flickering flames I saw when I kissed her swirl with nerves.

Ulrich announces, "I present to The Underworld, the Knights of the Round Table!"

The chanting grows louder.

Fiona loses her balance, and I tug her against me, steadying her. Her gaze darts between the room and me.

I hold her close and lift my fist high in the air.

The arena quiets.

Ulrich asks, "You have a request, Your Majesty?"

I stand taller and point to Sean and Zara. "They must leave."

Ulrich replies, "Omni always have privileges to stay."

"Her brother will not be here to witness this."

Ulrich narrows his eyes. "It is not customary for Omni to step away from ceremonies, especially coronations."

I focus on Sean. "You must go."

He nods. "I agree."

Fiona digs her fingers into my thigh.

I look down, stating, "You will not want your brother here."

She glances at Sean, then the room.

I lean down and murmur into her ear, "You must trust me. If he stays, you will always hate that he did."

She swallows hard and nods. "Okay."

I point at the couple and order, "As king of The Underworld, I exercise my right to ostracize them. During the rest of the coronation, they will not be present. I will lift the order after closure and only after Her Majesty has accepted her royal robe."

Ulrich insists, "Zara stays."

I shake my head. "No. They are married. They both go."

"It is not customary—" Ulrich blusters, but I cut him off.

"Her father would not have wanted either of them here." I scowl at him.

Ulrich stays quiet.

I turn to the crowd, roaring, "By order of ostracization, Zara and Sean O'Malley may not participate in consummation or closure rituals. Any further discussion will result in a sacrifice by flames."

The crowd gasps.

Ulrich shuts his mouth, not happy, but drops his argument. One more word about this topic, and I'll hang him by his feet and light a fire under his face until he's nothing but a singed corpse.

I point to Zara and Sean. "You are banished to my royal quarters." I nod to security.

He steps in front of them and points toward the door. "Right this way."

They both toss Fiona another guilty look and then disappear through the crowd.

A bang sounds in the background, so loud that my wife jumps.

I secure my hold around her waist and inform her, "It's just the gong."

She releases an anxious breath.

I move her toward the room.

Ulrich roars, "You forgot to shed."

I stop, my heart pounding harder.

Fiona glances up at me.

Ulrich adds, "It's time The Underworld learns the truth about their king. And it will not be from behind the blur of the glass!"

My gut dives. I knew this moment was coming and should have known Ulrich wouldn't give me any more leeway, especially after I went over his head to ostracize Sean and Zara. I prepared for the glass to partially shield me. I assumed it would mentally allow me to cope with Fiona's disgust since the glass is mirrored inside the room.

Now, the truth of my identity will be revealed. Anyone I've fucked during ceremonies with my mask on will know it was me. My anonymity will be gone.

The gong sounds again, making me cringe.

There's no getting out of this.

Deal with it. Be a fucking man.

I take a deep breath, release Fiona, and move to the center of the stage. Bile rises in my throat, and I swallow it down. I slowly shed my tuxedo jacket, unbutton my shirt, and fight to continue to undress.

The moment I remove my shirt, the audience gasps, then a shrill hissing takes over. I toss it on the floor, tug at my belt, unfasten my pants, and shove my underwear and trousers down. The metal buckle clanks on the wood.

I grind my molars, familiar with the hissing. Ever since I was eighteen and my first and only girlfriend left me, every sexual act I've participated in has been during a ritual. My face is always covered by my mask, and my hand with my necklace tattoo shielded by a leather glove. Now, there's no protection and no more questions about my identity.

The war inside me rages. The longer I stand in front of the hissing crowd, staring at the thousands of flickering torches, the more I want to hide. But I can't.

The gong bangs three times, and my desire to hide turns into a wish for someone to shoot me. I do my best to keep my neutral expression intact and don't move.

The gong bangs four times.

I still don't move.

A final warning belts off five loud bangs, and there's no more choice. My desire to live outweighs my wish to die.

Cringing inside, I spin toward a gaping Fiona and reach for my cock, unable to avoid her eyes.

There's no hiding. She knows who she's married to now.

My breathing goes ragged. I don't break protocol, playing with myself, staring at my beautiful bride in her wedding dress, and unable to stop my erection from growing.

Her gaze darts over my body, following the ink of the tattooed saw-scaled viper with several heads. She undoubtedly saw the snake's face on my shoulder, then followed it down my torso and around my legs. Now that I'm turned to face her, she takes all of it in, pausing at the vicious heads on my thighs and shins before pinning her gaze on my thick, ten-inch cock. She swallows hard, her eyes widening with an expression I can't decipher.

The memory of being sliced over and over flashes before me, intensified by the hissing. I breathe through it, grinding my molars so hard I'm afraid they might crack.

She's disgusted, I tell myself.

The gong rings ten times, and some relief hits me. I release my cock.

Fiona tears her greens off me, taking deep breaths.

The women in the crowd moan while the men continue to hiss.

I close the gap between Fiona and me, and she looks up, but it only confuses me further.

I don't see any disgust. I've seen it on women's faces in rituals, but I always wore a mask. Instead of what I'm used to seeing, the flare in her eyes resembles the look she gave me when I held her throat in the snow.

I'm seeing things.

She slides her shaky hands up my chest, slowly tracing the knotted scars under the ink, then steps even closer. Curiosity, maybe pity, and the same flickering flame dance across her expression.

My ache for her intensifies. She traces the head over my chest until I can't take it anymore. I put my hand over hers, my heart furiously pounding against her hand.

She rises on her tiptoes, slides her hand behind my head, and grips my hair.

My cock hardens further.

She pushes my head lower, and her lips graze my ear. She seductively asserts, "I think we're supposed to be in the other room. Aren't we?" She retreats, pinning doe eyes on me.

A rush of adrenaline courses through me.

Why isn't she freaking out?

The gong bangs once, pulling me out of my trance. I carefully unfasten her dress, turn her back to me, then slide it off her arms.

It falls to the floor, pooling around her feet.

My mouth goes dry at the sight before me. The delicate lace of the lingerie showcases the curve of her ass to perfection. I drag my knuckles over her spine and push the middle one between her cheeks.

She inhales sharply. A tremble moves through her.

Unable to stop, I step in front of her, taking every part of her in, throbbing with a desire I don't remember ever feeling. I study her, memorizing the moles on her thigh, bicep, and topside of her cleavage.

The gong bangs twice. My eagerness takes over, eliminating my hesitation. I reach for her hand, help her over her dress, and lead her into the room.

The door shuts and locks behind us, the mechanics grinding like a high-end safe.

She takes a deep breath, glancing at our reflections, then at the knights.

I lean into her ear, reminding her, "Make sure you tap out."

She glances at me in confusion.

The stomping and humming resumes, vibrating around us, shaking the glass. The knights stretch out their swords, clashing the metal together.

Fiona steps closer to me.

I slide my hand across her thigh, grazing my fingertips over her slit, surprised by the heat and dampness I find.

Her chest rises and falls faster.

I murmur, "Little birds need to be chained so they don't fly away."

She opens her mouth, but nothing comes out.

The swords slam into each other again, then rise straight into the air. A tiny grunt rolls out of the knights' throats, then several more grow in intensity.

The moonlight streams directly over us, supplying the only illumination since the flickering torches disappeared when the door locked.

Seven rings of the gong sound loudly. The knights part at the end of the bed.

I move my bride to the mattress, slide my hand over her cheek, and kiss her.

To my surprise, she kisses me back as enthusiastically as the first time.

Hissing erupts with stomping, yanking me back to my role.

I step back three feet and roar, "Shackle the queen."

The women in the crowd outside shriek.

Fiona's eyes widen.

Two knights grab her wrists, stretching them in the air.

To my surprise, she doesn't fight. I assumed she would, and I'd have to beg her to calm down. Then Ulrich would have gotten involved and asked her if she wanted to stop, only to kill her if she said yes.

Thankfully, I was wrong. She keeps her eyes locked on me, her breath rolling past her parted lips.

Two other knights tug chains from the top of the bed toward Fiona. The links clink together, causing her to turn her head.

"Look at me," I order.

She obeys, swallowing hard.

Cuffs lock around her wrists. The same sound fills the air, and the length of the chain forces her onto her toes.

"Enough," I assert, and the noise stops.

A few moments pass, with tension growing between us. My body floods with an ache so deep I have to remind myself of my duties as king. I finally demand, "Display the queen's beauty for all to see."

Two knights reach for my bride, putting one hand under her armpit and another on her waist. They carefully move her toward the top of the bed and lie her on her back. Two others shackle her ankles. Metal clatters again until her legs are secured and spread open. The knights take their swords, holding them in the air above Fiona, and touching the one directly across from them.

She lifts her head, meets my gaze, and furrows her eyebrows. Her pink tongue darts out of her mouth, lightly grazing her pouty lips. Then I think my mind is playing games on me again. I swear a smile teases her face, directed at me, pushing against her flushed cheeks.

My cock throbs and pre-cum escapes the slit. She's the most gorgeous woman I've ever seen, and I don't understand why my little bird isn't giving me the same look as other women. Nothing is hiding me anymore, and my wife's taunting expression baffles me.

The gong bangs once, and the arena falls silent.

My pulse races faster. I step under the swords, kneel on the end of the mattress, and slide my hands over the inside of her legs, inching toward the damp lace between her thighs.

She shudders, whimpering, oddly enough sounding exactly how I've imagined all these months. She closes her eyes, leans her head back, and lifts her pelvis, opening her mouth.

"Sexy little bird," I praise, stopping before her pussy, circling my thumbs several times.

"Mmm," she softly moans, her chest trembling. She grips the chains and meets my gaze.

I slip my thumbs under the wet material until they touch her hole, taunting, "A queen serves her king. When she does, she gets rewarded. Is that what you want, my little bird? To have me reward you?" I thrust my thumbs inside her until her pussy hits my palm.

"Oh!" she cries out, arching her back and yanking on the chains.

I bend my thumbs, swirling my pads against her inner walls, watching her with awe, ready to remember every response she gives me.

Her whimpers turn louder. Ragged breath escapes her mouth. Green flames burn brighter in her eyes as they challenge me, not escaping my scrutiny.

The arena fills with women moaning. Men grunt and pound their torches on the ground. The room grows hotter, and the knights don't dare move, making urgent, guttural sounds.

I lower my face, keeping my thumbs inside her, and press my mouth to the lace.

"Oh!" she cries out louder.

I glance at her, swiping my tongue over the material, flicking her clit with every swipe.

"Kirill," she breathes, her body shaking harder.

I push deeper, circle faster, and curl my pointer finger over the wet material, pulling it out of the way. I suck her clit, groaning at the salty sweetness I never thought I'd get to taste.

"Oh fuck!" she rasps, grinding her pussy against my face, yanking on the chains so hard they creak.

My obsession takes over all decisions. I work her pussy with my mouth, making her come over and over, her body in a constant state of convulsions.

Her voice cracks, "I-I can't take any more."

Feeling crazed, I barely stop, arrogantly insisting, "You're the queen. Your job is to serve me."

Her red cheeks glisten with sweat. Her greens flood with exhaustion.

I return to her pussy, making her come several more times until she squirts her arousal all over my mouth. I groan, lapping it up, until I realize the gong's been clanging nonstop.

Shit.

I blink, out of breath, swiping my arm over my mouth, not taking my gaze off hers.

Her chest rises and falls in short bursts. She slowly relaxes against the bed, her fingers peel away from the chains, and she keeps her focus on me.

The gong blares four times. The knights at the end of the bed reel the chains until Fiona's ankles are in the air.

I move so my thighs are against the back of hers, dragging my knuckles over her breasts and stomach.

She quivers, opens her mouth, then shuts it.

The gong sounds two times.

A knight holds out his sword. "Your Majesty."

I create some room between Fiona and me and take it from him.

Her head jerks against the mattress.

I instruct, "Don't move, little bird."

She holds her breath with fear blooming on her expression. "Kirill—"

"Shh," I order.

She swallows hard.

I reach for the soaking lace, tug it toward me, and slice through it. Then I hold the material taut and slowly slice it straight over her belly button and through her cleavage.

Goose bumps pop out on her flawless skin.

I put the flat of the blade across her neck.

She freezes.

"I hope you remember what I told you earlier," I state, not wanting to do what I'm about to do.

It's a test. There's only one way out of it for her. If she doesn't obey and do what I told her, she's dead.

She blinks a few times.

The crowd is silent.

I move the lingerie to the sides, assessing my bride, approving of her hard, pink nipples, soft belly, and graceful, elongated neck. More pre-cum oozes from my throbbing cock. I lift the sword and return it to the knight.

The arena fills with hissing. It's the loudest it's been, and it digs into me until I sink into the zone, forgetting everything and everyone but my wife, the queen of The Underworld, and the bride I hope stays alive.

In one thrust, I enter her, groaning with short-lived relief.

She gasps, her eyelids fluttering.

Jesus. She took all of me.

I praise, "That's right, my queen. Your king's going to reward you for your good service." I slide my hand up her stomach, over her breast, and curl my fingers around her throat.

Her eyes widen.

I lean into her ear, tightening and loosening my grip, thrusting slowly, murmuring, "Remember, a queen must obey her king." I kiss under her lobe, my pulse pounding and fear mixing with my arousal.

She turns her head, meeting my stare with an equally challenging one.

It creates a new havoc within me. It digs into the depths of who I am, the overwhelming urges I've fought since the night I first met her, and the contrast between maintaining my position as king and wanting to keep her as my queen.

Even if her reaction to me is all in my head, the possibility of never again seeing the expression she's given me all night claws at my gut.

It's everything I didn't expect, and enough to make me more fearful of what's to come.

For my bride's sake and mine, she better tap out.

Fiona

Chapter
FIFTEEN

"*E*w-ah. *Ew-ah*," the knights begin to chant, tapping their swords above Kirill and me.

He instructs, "Blink repeatedly when you're ready to tap out, my little bird." His fingers press one at a time against my throat as he studies me with a new intensity. He thrusts as deep as he can, then teases me, slowly exiting until only the tip touches my entrance.

Like an addict, I lift my hips, wanting him back inside me, hating how empty it feels when he retreats. The ferocious pulsing in my core never stops. There are so many people chanting different erotic sounds, I barely realize I'm making incoherent ones of my own.

Kirill cages himself over my torso. His glistening skin slides against mine. His intoxicating scent flares around us, creating more chaos in my already overwhelmed senses. He grips my neck tighter, moving his face inches from mine.

I lean up and press my lips to his, slipping my tongue into his mouth, wanting to never stop kissing him. I've lost any sense of control I might have had. His body takes full possession of mine, and if servicing him means this is my reward, I'll be his junkie for life.

I knew he was different the moment I met him at the club. He's the opposite of the men I've always dated. I don't know what happened for him to have gotten those scars under his snake tattoos, but something about the vicious reptiles covering his body turns me on even more.

He's the epitome of tall, dark, and dangerous. I'm sure there's no one in the world like him, and everything about those two things should make me fear him. Yet I feel safe with him, even with thousands of strangers watching us do the most intimate things.

He moves his lips to my ear, pushes deep inside me, and stills. He reminds me again, "Make sure you tap out, my queen. Blink when you're ready." He locks his gaze on mine once again, stern, powerful, in charge of whatever he's about to do to me.

Fresh zings run down my spine. My pussy pulses around his cock. I'm surprised I can take all of him. The moment I saw how large he is, I thought my body wouldn't be able to handle it. But he slid into me with confidence, and I've never felt so alive.

"Show me you understand," he orders.

I blink a few times since I can't move. His large hand covers the entirety of my neck. He's already added pressure, but even though I've never had anyone fully choke me, I'm sure he's going to add more.

"Good, my little bird," he praises, giving me a chaste kiss, then pulls back enough that I can't reach him, yet his breath still merges with mine. He caresses the side of my head with one hand while he increases the pressure around my neck, studying my reaction. He resumes a slow thrust.

Tingles dance inside all my cells. My muffled moan vibrates against his hand. I can still breathe, but it won't be possible if he squeezes much more.

His chest rises and falls faster against mine. He thrusts faster and tilts his head, his eyes narrowing, then pushes his pelvis harder, squeezing his fingers tighter around my throat.

Adrenaline explodes within me, and my pussy spasms, trying to grip his gliding cock. My air supply is cut off, and my body convulses. My eyes roll, and a flash of white, then black, fills my vision.

Right as I'm about to pass out, Kirill loosens his grip so I can breathe. Choking and still reeling with an orgasm, I inhale a few short breaths before I can take a longer one.

The gong sounds, and I lose count of how many times it rings. My high recedes.

Kirill leans down, kisses my lobe, then murmurs in my ear, "Don't forget to tap out." His fingers tighten around me again, and he continues to assess me. His cock thrusts faster, pounds into me deeper, and his other hand continues to caress my cheek.

More waves of endorphins pummel me, and I can't stop moaning against his hand.

The knights' chanting turn to *oms*, the stomping outside the room gets louder, and the crowd returns to hissing.

"Sexy little bird," Kirill grits through his teeth, his face red, long hair dampening with sweat and hanging over me. He clenches his jaw and his scar twitches. He never takes his curious expression off me as he partially cuts off my air.

An orgasm hits me, and I can't stop trembling, yet it's not as powerful as the first one his cock gave me. I rasp, "More."

He furrows his eyebrows.

I manage to get out, "Please."

He kisses me quickly, muttering against my lips, "Careful what you wish, my beautiful wife," and then gives me what I want.

My oxygen disappears completely. He slams his pelvis against me, holding my throat in place, and my pussy loses all control. The most intense high of my life floods every cell I have, and I yank on the chains, violently convulsing underneath him. My eyes roll back and stay there. White light flashes twice behind my lids and then blackness takes over. The noise around me fades, and it's only Kirill's warmth wrapped around my shaking body.

"Fuck," he barks, but I barely register it.

Then his cock widens, flooding me deep with hot cum. It exponentially affects my high, taking me to a place I didn't realize existed.

Red flashes, then white, then black returns, and everything turns silent.

"Fiona!" Kirill roars, releasing his hand from my throat and stroking my cheek.

I cough, and everything is fuzzy.

"Fiona!" he frets, coming into view.

I blink a few times.

"Unshackle her," he orders.

Hissing fills the arena.

Within seconds, I'm released. They lower my legs and unclasp the cuffs from my wrists.

Kirill slides both hands on my cheeks. "Fiona!"

I reach my arms around him, sliding my hand through his hair, and take shallow breaths.

"I'm sorry," he mutters, his eyes glistening. "I'm—" He looks away, shaking his head. "Fuck."

The knights hold their swords over us again, slamming them into each other. The sharp metallic clang rings through the air.

I turn his face back to mine and pull it toward me, leaning up and flicking my tongue against his lips.

He jerks his head backward, as if in shock.

Stomping starts again, along with longer hisses.

I tug him toward me, kissing him, and he resists for a moment.

I tighten my arms around him and slide my tongue back into his mouth.

He finally relaxes, returning my affection but not taking his gaze off mine, as if unsure if I really want to kiss him. His hand slips under me, and his fingers push through my updo, gripping my head. His cock hardens inside me, and I realize he never took it out.

He slowly thrusts, and sensation flares inside me once again. More spasms ignite, but this time, it's a different type of intensity. It's not better or worse. It's just another feeling I've never experienced.

Like before, he never breaks our gaze, as if he's somehow fascinated by me, which I don't understand, but I decide I like it. Maybe it's false intimacy since we don't really know each other, but it makes me feel special, like I'm his and only his.

Since we're married, I suppose I am his now, but the way he watches me gives me the illusion he already cares about me. And maybe he does. After all, he knew who I was before we showed up for our vows, and he took the time to write the letters and pick out my outfits, so doesn't that count for something?

"You're perfect, my little bird," he mumbles between kisses, and a vulnerability I've never seen on any man's face softens his expression.

Something about it tears at my heart. So I kiss him with everything I have, holding him tighter, unable to speak or control the whimpers flying out of me, still convulsing against his hard frame.

It feels like it goes on for ages, and we're in a bubble. As if it's just the two of us, and we've been lovers forever. I can't comprehend it and don't want to. Kirill makes me feel protected, owned, and adored. But it's also like I have as much claim to him as he does to me. It's all new and confusing, but it's also freeing. And the only thing I know is that I never want this to end.

Reality hits me when he lowers his mouth to my ear, murmuring, "I need you to tap out, my queen. If you don't, you die. If you refuse to tap out and don't die from my hand, then that means I die."

Fear consumes me, but he doesn't give me time to think about it. He presses his lips back to mine and moves his hand over my throat, pushing one finger at a time over my clavicle. He retreats from the kiss, his worried expression growing.

I have to tap out.

I push past the fear and blink several times to show him I understand.

More anxiety builds on his face. He gives me one last chaste peck, then speeds up his thrusts.

My body has a mind of its own. I meet his thrusts with eagerness, falling back into the seduction of the high as soon as his grip tightens.

My pussy spasms faster. The desperation to return to the intensity level he had me at earlier floods my brain.

He squeezes so hard that he instantly cuts off my air supply.

My limbs flail on the mattress. My eyes widen, and I try to sit up but can't.

"Tap out," he orders through his teeth.

One more second, and I'll be there, I tell myself.

"Fiona," he frets.

Another high hits me. My vision distorts, my eyes roll back in my head, and I soar from adrenaline.

Tap out!

I force myself to blink, over and over, even though I can't focus on anything.

Kirill's hand flies off my neck.

I choke. My lungs try to take in oxygen, but I keep coughing.

"Move!" Kirill demands.

The knights obey.

Kirill slides to the side of the bed. He tugs me up, pulling me onto his lap. He puts his hands on my cheeks. "Breathe, Fiona. Deep breaths."

I realize I'm hyperventilating.

"Come on, my little bird." He demonstrates how to inhale and exhale deeply.

I can't seem to catch my breath. My heart races. My lungs don't want to cooperate.

"Come on, Fiona," he urges.

I take a normal breath of air.

"That's it," he praises, showing me how to take in oxygen.

Several minutes pass until I'm no longer hyperventilating.

He rubs my back. "Good. Keep breathing."

"I-I'm okay now," I insist.

He tugs me closer, continuing to look at me with concern.

I reach for his chest, putting my hand over the face of the snake. I comment, "Your heart's racing. Maybe you should breathe."

He freezes and then a grin blooms on his lips. A chuckle escapes him, and he starts laughing so hard that tears well in his eyes.

It's not that funny, but he seems to think it is. I laugh as well, until I'm crying too.

The gong bangs loudly, interrupting our amusement.

Kirill's face falls.

I question, "What's happening now?"

"Everything will be okay," he assures, and kisses me on the lips. He helps me off his lap and rises, grabbing my hand.

The gong bangs three times. The door unlocks and opens. The knights line up with their swords in the air, touching, creating a path to the exit.

Kirill slides his arm around my waist, protectively leading me past the knights and out of the mirrored room.

Ulrich and Valentina stand next to each other. They both have their masks on, but I know it's her. Another man stands with a long, golden rod. He holds the tip in a fireplace, and it glows. A wooden contraption next to it looks like a medieval torture device.

My gut flips. I grip Kirill's thigh.

He squeezes my waist. "Everything will be fine," he reassures, then leads us until we're standing in front of Ulrich and Valentina.

Ulrich accuses, "She didn't tap out."

The hairs on my arms rise.

"She did. You saw her," Kirill argues.

Ulrich shakes his head. "Not the first time. She didn't tap out, and she was as good as dead. You released her so she could come back to life."

Kirill pushes me behind him, sternly insisting, "She tapped out."

"She didn't the first time," Ulrich retorts.

Valentina interjects, "It doesn't matter. She tapped out."

"Of course it matters," Ulrich argues.

Valentina lifts her chin and squares her shoulders. She turns toward Ulrich, asserting, "She is the second-born. Sean O'Malley Sr. said his second-born has rights to the two attempts clause."

I glance at Kirill, not understanding what she means, but he doesn't take his eyes off Ulrich.

Ulrich narrows his gaze, scowling at Valentina. He rebukes, "The second-born clause is regarding certain ceremonies. Not coronation."

She scoffs. "It is for chivalry ceremonies and rituals. The second-born clause became fair game when you agreed to the Knights of the Round Table ritual."

Ulrich crosses his arms, glaring at her.

Kirill states, "Valentina's correct. It is a chivalry ritual." He nods at her with gratitude.

She smiles and steps to the side, pointing at the man near the fire. "Shall we move on to Closure?"

"Yes. We shall," Kirill answers, moving me toward the fire and wooden contraption.

My anxiety creeps up. "Kirill—"

He turns to face me, firmly places his hands on my cheeks, and leans over me.

I inhale sharply.

In a stern voice, he states, "This is the last thing you must do. It will be over shortly. I will take care of you after."

I swallow hard.

"It will be okay. It's short-term pain and won't last long. I promise I will help you now and after," he vows.

I glance at the fire and release an anxious breath.

"Trust me. And we can go home after this," he adds.

Home.

With Kirill.

He's my husband.

This is crazy.

The gong sounds, and I jump.

"There won't be another warning. We must follow through," Kirill softly states.

I nod and shakily step forward.

He leads me to the wooden contraption and instructs, "Put your head through the circle."

I wince. "Really?"

"Yes," he says in his no-nonsense voice.

I don't move.

"Short term," he reminds me.

"What will they do to me?" I gaze over at the hot fire.

Kirill answers, "You must wear your father's mark."

I grimace. "On my neck?"

He nods. "That is correct."

"Why don't I tattoo it instead?" I suggest.

He shakes his head. "It is not how your father wrote the law. Your golden color will be added via tattoo when the branded mark fully heals."

I bite on my lip.

The gong echoes throughout the arena. Stomping resumes.

"We're out of time. Fiona, please, put your head through the circle," Kirill begs.

I take a deep breath and step in front of the contraption. I put my head against the wood, my pulse skyrocketing and stomach quivering.

Kirill steps in front of me. He circles his arm around my back. He takes his other hand, holds the back of my head, and pushes my face into his chest. He murmurs, "Don't move, my little bird."

My heart pounds hard against his chest. I inhale his scent, and it calms my anxiety a tad, but not much.

Valentina steps beside me and says, "I'm going to hold your hair up more. It's gotten a bit loose."

I don't argue, not wanting to singe my hair with my skin. Plus, she just saved Kirill with her knowledge about the second-born clause, so right now, I appreciate her.

Ulrich roars, "By the power instilled in me by the Omnipotence, I brand you with The Underworld skull."

My stomach flips, and intense pain sears my neck. My muffled shriek fills the air, and tears fall from my eyes. I try to move, but Kirill holds my head so tightly that I can't.

"It's okay," he coos.

Within seconds, something cold is slathered over my skin, taking away the sting.

"There, better?" Kirill asks, releasing me.

I stare at him. "Yes."

He softly smiles. "You can step back now."

"Oh." I realize I'm still against contraception. I move away from it.

The gong rings seven times.

Ulrich booms, "By the power of the Omnipotence, I introduce Her Majesty, Queen Fiona!"

The women and men take off their masks. The audience erupts in applause.

Valentina holds a thick, ornate gold robe in front of me.

I slide my arms into it and turn.

Kirill has a matching one on. He steps forward, grabs the belt on mine, and secures it around my waist. Then he leans into my ear. "Are you ready to go home?"

My butterflies reemerge.

This is real.

His expression turns to one of panic. Then it hardens. He waits for me to answer.

I nod. "Yes, I'm ready."

Kirill

Chapter

SIXTEEN

As soon as I can, I guide Fiona out of the arena and toward the royal suite. She doesn't say anything, and neither do I. The dim, barely lit hallway seems to go on forever as I beat myself up.

Why did I forget my flaws?

When I asked her if she was ready to go home, the look on her face told me everything she was feeling.

Why did I allow myself to think it could be any different?

My heart pounds harder against my chest cavity. The air in my lungs stales. I swallow down emotions, telling myself nothing has changed. I'm the same person, and she's a woman, just like all the rest.

She's not, though. She's exceptional.

And she doesn't want to be married to me.

The door finally comes into view. A bit of relief fills me. I open it and motion for her to go inside.

"Is this where you live?" she asks.

I shake my head. "No. It's the royal quarters for the arena."

"Oh. And where exactly are we? The flight was long," she notes, not going inside.

"Pompeii. Please. Go inside. The hallway is not somewhere to have discussions," I advise.

She glances behind us, then rises on her tiptoes and whispers, "Is someone watching us?" Her lips twitch.

"Hallways are public. Many people use them. They are monitored," I inform her, then point inside.

"I see. And the royal quarters. Is that monitored too?" she prods, still not moving.

I nod. "Tonight, yes. The Omni revoked my privacy privileges until I completed my vows. After we leave, the cameras will be dismantled and the rooms returned to private."

She wiggles her eyebrows, puts her fingers on my chest, and teases, "So I shouldn't do anything I don't want others to see?"

My cock hardens, and electricity sparks between us. I glance at her pouty lips, deciding I'm addicted to them.

Sean booms, "Fiona! Are you okay?"

Her face falls. She tears her gaze off me and steps inside. "I'm not discussing anything with you, Sean," she says angrily.

Sean scowls, accusing, "What did you do to her?"

I shut the door and warn, "You will show the queen respect."

He narrows his gaze.

"I'm waiting."

He looks at Fiona, then steps before her and bows, grumbling, "Your Majesty."

Fiona arches her eyebrows, glancing at me.

I point at Zara. "You too."

She crosses the room and stands next to Sean, then curtsies. "Yes. Of course. Your Majesty."

Fiona's lips twitch.

I lean down and murmur, "You can allow them to rise or let them stay like that all night."

She puts her hand over her mouth and stifles a giggle, then asks, "What do I say to them?"

"I normally say thank you, but whatever you want. You're the queen." I wink.

Her smile widens. She stares at them and then offers a "Thank you."

They rise.

Sean repeats, "Are you okay?"

She lifts her chin and squares her shoulders. "Of course I am. No thanks to you."

Guilt floods his expression.

Zara's gaze darts between Fiona and me. Then it flickers with amusement. She taunts, "Did you have fun?"

"Eh. Don't, Zara," Sean warns.

She scoffs. "What? I had fun on my initiation night. Well, minus a few things..." Her face darkens.

I inform her, "Fiona's coronation wasn't like your initiation. Nothing like that happened."

"Nothing like what?" Fiona asks.

Relief crosses Zara's face. She shakes her head with a smile, stating, "Nothing."

Fiona's eyes turn to slits. "No. Tell me what you're referring to."

Zara swallows hard. She glances at Sean.

He stands taller, clenching his jaw.

I announce, "Zara killed several people."

"Kirill!" Zara explodes.

The blood drains from Fiona's cheeks and she gapes.

Zara blinks hard and looks away.

Fiona lowers her voice. "Zara? Is this true?"

She meets Fiona's gaze. "Yes."

Fiona's mouth drops open again.

"Thanks, Kirill," Zara grumbles.

I cross my arms, stating, "My queen has the right to know everything. She will not be kept in the dark any longer. If she asks a question, you will tell her the truth, no matter how hard it is for you. Do I make myself clear?"

Zara takes a deep breath and then nods.

"Sean?" I question.

He glares daggers at me, but says, "Yeah. I got it."

"Good." I turn toward my bride. "Is there anything else you want to know right now?"

Her greens widen. She glances between all of us, then says, "Yes."

"Go on," I urge.

She swallows hard, then directs her question to Sean. "How will I explain to Mom that I'm married to a Petrov?"

He grinds his molars.

"Well? You've known about this little fact longer than I have. Explain the solution to me," she orders.

He shakes his head. "I'm not sure."

She huffs. "You have no answer for me?"

He closes his eyes and then tilts his head back, staring at the ceiling.

I bark, "Don't look away from the queen! Show some respect!"

He jerks his gaze back to her.

"Well?" she asks.

Zara steps forward and puts her hand on Fiona's arm. "We're working on the best way to tell her. I promise."

Fiona sighs and shakes her head. She turns toward me. "How long do we have to stay here?"

"We don't. Are you ready to go?" I ask.

"Yes."

I don't hesitate. I slide my arm around her waist, telling them, "Have a good trip back."

"Thank you," Zara replies.

Sean's scowl returns.

Fiona points, snapping, "Don't look at the king like that!"

I still, pleasantly surprised by her defending me.

"Seriously?" Sean mutters.

Her voice turns sterner. "Yes, I'm serious. You will show respect toward him not just because he's king but because he's now my husband. And don't make me warn you again, Sean."

He forces himself to put on a neutral expression.

"Apologize," she demands.

Sean shifts on his feet. He takes a deep breath and locks eyes with me. "I didn't mean to be disrespectful. My apologies."

Fiona needs us to get along.

I fight my urge to gloat and quickly reply, "We're good." I refocus on my bride. "Are you ready?"

She smiles, making the blood in my veins heat again. "Yes."

Zara interjects, "Can I at least give you a hug?"

Fiona tenses, then steps forward.

"Can I say congratulations?" Zara asks, hugging her hard.

Fiona retreats. "Yes. Thank you."

Zara pins her smile on me. "And congratulations to you too. We have a wedding gift. Can you wait a moment while I retrieve it?"

"You do?" Fiona asks, shock and excitement in her voice.

Zara beams. "Of course."

"We can wait," I state, happy to see Fiona's expression.

"Just a minute," Zara says, disappearing out of the suite.

Tension builds in the air.

Sean steps in front of his sister. "You can't stay mad at me forever."

"Watch me."

"Fiona—"

"I'm not getting into this right now. You don't get my forgiveness for putting me through months of stress and everything that's to come until I'm ready," she states.

My gut flips.

She doesn't want to be married to me.

Of course she doesn't.

I silently curse myself again.

"I didn't know what would happen," he claims.

"But yet you agreed to it, as if you owned me," she seethes, her cheeks reddening.

He argues, "You don't know what happened!"

"And how many times did I ask for you to explain?" she scolds.

He bursts out, "I couldn't tell you!"

"Whatever, Sean," she snarls.

Sean glances at me, begging, "Help me out."

My chest tightens. I clear my throat, declaring, "Fiona, I will tell you what happened to have caused you to be in this position when you're ready to hear it. Is that moment now?"

She takes deep breaths, her gaze darting between us, then shakes her head. "No. I'm tired."

Sean grabs her arm. "Fiona—"

"She isn't ready. Respect her wishes," I caution.

He shuts his mouth, and misery overtakes his sharp features.

I ask, "Perhaps you'd like to hug your sister before we leave?"

His expression softens. He nods, admitting, "Yeah, I would."

"Fine," she grumbles, then steps forward.

They hug.

Zara enters the room, chirping, "Aw. That's a nice sight."

Fiona pulls back.

Zara holds a black velvet box with a silver bow. She says, "I hope you love it."

"What is it?" Fiona asks.

Zara laughs. "Open it and find out!"

Excitement builds again in Fiona's expression. She glances at me, asking, "Do you want to open it?"

"I'd like you to," I state, loving the look on her face, and step closer to her.

Zara suggests, "Why don't you hold it for her." She holds the box out in front of me.

I take it.

Fiona tugs at the bow and then lifts the lid. Her eyes widen in shock. She removes the silver and black bottle from the box and gasps, "This is a Louis XIII de Remy Martin Black Pearl Grande Champagne Cognac!"

Zara claps her hands. "I know!"

Fiona peers closer at the intricate details, gushing, "This is $150,000 a bottle!"

"Tell me about it," Sean mutters.

Zara nudges him in the chest. "Behave!"

"Ouch!"

Fiona holds it in front of me. "Look at this!"

"It's a really nice gift. Thank you," I offer.

Zara's face lights further. "I knew you'd love it!"

"I do!" Fiona admits.

"Yay!" Zara cheers.

Fiona puts it back in the box. "Thank you." She hugs Zara and then her brother.

I set the box on the table, then hug Zara and kiss her cheek. "Thank you. Very thoughtful of you."

"Enjoy," she says.

I grin. "We will." I hold my hand to Sean, offering, "Thank you."

He takes it and nods. "You're welcome. It was Zara's idea. I didn't know what to get you."

"Well, it's a great gift," I acknowledge, then ask Fiona, "Are you ready to go?"

She smiles. "Sure. But do we need to change?" She glances at her robe.

"No. We're okay." I pick up the box and reach for her hand.

She wraps her fingers around mine and waves. "See you later."

"Bye," they say, and I guide her out of the suite, down the hallways, and stop at a door. My nerves reignite. I hesitate.

"Are we going through mystery door number seven?" she teases.

"Seven?"

"We've passed seven doors. I don't know how you know where to go. This place is a maze," she declares.

I chuckle. "You'll learn it quickly."

"Will we come here often?"

"Often enough."

She stares at me. "So... Are we going through this door?"

Anxiety flares in my gut as I say, "That's up to you."

She arches her eyebrows.

I continue, "There's something I thought you might enjoy, but if you don't want to do it, we don't have to."

"Like a surprise?" She bites on her smile.

I laugh again, and it sounds strange. I scold myself and release a nervous breath, revealing, "You can choose option one or option two. If you choose the latter, we walk through door eight, get on a plane, and return to Chicago."

Her greens light up. "And option one is…?"

My stomach flops faster. "We can go through door seven and return home on the royal yacht."

Her jaw drops.

I wait, holding my breath.

"We have a yacht?"

"Yes."

"And we can go home in it?"

Amused, I affirm, "Yes. Actually, we can go on it anytime and anywhere you want."

She tilts her head. "So if I wanted to make stops at places I've always wanted to visit, could we do that?"

My anxiety disappears, and a grin explodes across my face. "Name the place, and I'll tell the captain."

She leans closer, tilting her head, teasing, "Am I going to like the perks of marrying the king?"

"I do believe so, my queen."

She reaches for the knob, taunting, "So if I turn this, we walk through this door, and the yacht is waiting for us?"

"Not quite."

"No?"

Amusement overpowers my fears. "We have to get into the elevator, go to the roof, and get on the helicopter. Then it has to take us to the Mediterranean, where the yacht is waiting."

Excitement bursts on her face. She blurts out, "You're kidding me."

"Nope."

"So I just have to choose door seven?"

"Yep."

"Great. Done!" she chirps, then turns the knob and pushes the door open. She lunges through the doorway and hits the button on the wall.

I chuckle, following.

The lift opens. We get in it, and I put my palm on the screen. The doors shut, and the elevator rises.

"This is insane," Fiona mutters.

"I'm glad you wanted to take the yacht," I admit.

She looks at me like I'm crazy. "Why wouldn't I?"

I shrug. "I try not to assume things."

She studies me. The doors open, and she softly states, "I like that about you."

"Yeah?"

She nods. "Definitely."

My heart thumps harder. I motion for her to go first.

She steps onto the roof. Dawn is approaching, but it's still dark.

I put my arm around her waist, turn the corner, and the wind from the chopper blades hits us. I shield her with my body, and shout, "I forgot to bring a pair of sunglasses for you. Keep your eyes shut so nothing flies in them."

She obeys.

I put my head down, quickly lead her to the helicopter, help her in, then slide beside her. We buckle our seat belts, and I remove her tiara. I hand her a helmet. "Put this on."

She slides it on her head and takes the box.

I put mine on, grip the tiara, and the chopper lifts off the ground.

She stares out the window in awe at the city's lights, declaring, "I've never been to Pompeii before now."

"Next trip, I'll show you around. It's full of history, and I think you'll appreciate it," I tell her.

Approval fills her expression.

It doesn't take long before we land on the yacht. I help Fiona out, the chopper takes off, and I lead her toward the staff.

They're lined up in a row. The men bow, and the women curtsy.

"Your Majesties," they offer in unison.

"Thank you," I reply.

Sergio, the head manager, steps forward. "Sir. It's wonderful to see you again. And, ma'am, it is a great honor to meet you. Myself and the rest of the staff look forward to serving you."

Fiona takes a deep breath. "Thank you."

I tug her closer, remembering how overwhelming it was when I first became king. I hold out the tiara. "Sergio, this needs to go into the safe."

"Yes, sir. I will do it right away," he replies.

"Thank you." I take the box from Fiona, adding, "And please put this on ice. I believe my bride would like a glass at some point today?" I arch my eyebrows at her.

She grins. "Yes!"

I chuckle.

"Will do. Maria," Sergio calls out.

A woman steps forward. She curtsies in front of Fiona, gushing, "Such an honor, my queen."

Fiona fidgets in discomfort, forcing a smile. "Thank you. It's nice to meet you. All of you," she adds, glancing at the entire staff, one by one.

That's my queen.

They're going to love her.

I put my hand on her back. "Shall we go to our room and change into something more appropriate?"

She glances at her robe, and a flush crawls up her cheeks. "Oh. Yes. Sorry. Forgot about our attire."

"See you soon," I say, guiding Fiona through the ship.

She takes everything in, commenting on different rooms as we enter and exit them. We get to our suite and I open the door, stating, "I'm glad you seem to approve of everything."

She stops in the doorway and scoffs. "How could I not?"

"Everyone has their own likes and dislikes," I claim.

"True, but you have good taste," she comments.

"I do?"

"Umm...yeah."

"Good to know," I say, happy with her approval.

She peers at me.

My mouth turns dry. "Something wrong?"

She studies me closer, then asks, "You honestly had doubts about whether I'd love this ship?"

My nerves reappear. "As I stated, I try not to make assumptions."

She doesn't take her gaze off me.

She's staring at my scar.

My anxiety skyrockets. I open my mouth and then shut it.

She prods, "Why'd you write me those letters?"

A lump forms in my throat. I swallow it, thinking about how to answer her question, and then blurt out, "I knew you'd never want to marry me if you weren't put in the position you were in. But I didn't want you to be more uncomfortable than I assumed you would be. And selfishly, I guess I didn't want you to hate me forever."

"But you knew it was me you were marrying?"

"Yes."

She pins her eyebrows together and blinks hard.

My pulse races so fast that a wave of dizziness hits me.

She lowers her voice. "Is that what you really thought?"

I look at her in question.

"You thought I'd hate you?"

My stomach quivers harder, and pain shoots through my chest. I reply, "I didn't want you to, but I didn't see how you couldn't."

She takes several breaths, then steps forward. She puts her hand on my cheek, running her thumb over my scar.

I close my eyes, fighting emotions I despise, and then force myself to look at her.

She continues to caress my scar, announcing, "For someone who tries not to assume things, you got that one wrong."

My insides shake harder, maybe from relief but also from something else I can't decipher. I stay quiet, not trusting my voice.

She adds, "Do you remember the night I met you?"

I find my voice, carefully asking, "At the club?"

"Yes."

I nod. "Of course I do."

"How much time passed before I ran into you in the coffee shop?" she prods.

"A little over a year."

She hesitates, then says, "Ask me how many of those days in between I thought about you."

I hold my breath, unsure where she's going with this.

"Ask me," she demands.

I find a way to fill my lungs with oxygen, and inquire, "How many days?"

She doesn't hesitate, revealing, "Every single day."

Shock fills me. My heart pounds faster.

"Not a day went by that I didn't think about you, wondering who you were and if I'd ever run into you again."

Still surprised, I stay quiet.

Her voice is laced with vulnerability when she asks, "Did you think about me?"

I don't have to think. I quickly answer, "Yes. Every single day. Multiple times a day."

A soft smile plays on her lips. "Then I guess you don't hate me, and I don't hate you." She releases my face, walks into the bedroom, and looks around.

I stay frozen, trying to process what she confessed.

She unties her belt, shrugs her robe off, and tosses it on the couch. She announces, "I'm tired. I'm going to take a nap." She saunters over to the bedroom door, then turns her head, smirking at me. She asks, "Are you coming?"

Fiona

Chapter
SEVENTEEN

Kirill slides under the silk sheets, keeping an inch between us. He stares at the ceiling, his jaw twitching.

I sink deeper into the luxurious bed and then face him. I hug the pillow, breathing in his scent and studying him.

He releases an anxious breath, then carefully turns toward me. Nerves fill his expression. He asks, "Do you need anything?"

Amused, I shake my head, biting my lip.

He glances at my mouth, then meets my gaze again, prodding, "Are you a light sleeper?"

I answer, "I don't think so. Why? Are you?"

"I often wake up in the middle of the night. Perhaps I don't require a lot of sleep," he claims.

I pout. "So I'll be left alone in bed all the time?"

Surprise flashes in his eyes. "That would bother you?"

"It depends. Are you a spooner?" I tease.

He arches his eyebrows. "Spooner?"

"Yeah."

He admits, "I don't know what that means."

I sarcastically laugh. "Sure you don't."

He shakes his head. The line on his forehead deepens. He insists, "I don't."

My smile falls. "You honestly don't know what spooning is?"

"No."

"How is that possible?"

He shrugs. "I don't know. But are you going to tell me what it is?"

"It's a form of cuddling," I offer.

His expression hardens. He blinks a few times and stays quiet.

My stomach dives. "You don't like to cuddle?"

He swallows hard.

I hold my fingers a few inches apart, teasing, "Not even a little?"

He opens his mouth and then shuts it. He looks past me, breathing deeply.

My insides quiver. I quietly state, "It's okay." I turn and face the window, trying to hide my disappointment.

He sighs, slides one arm under my head, then curls his other arm around my waist and tugs me into him. He brushes his lips against my ear, asking, "Is this how you like to cuddle?"

Tingles zing down my spine. My butterflies throw a new party in my stomach. I push my ass into his pelvis and sink into him, lacing my fingers through his. I turn my head, smirking. "So you do like to spoon."

He pins his eyebrows together. "This is spooning?"

"Ha, ha. Funny."

Silence fills the air, turning tense.

My chest tightens. I turn onto my back, asking, "You really didn't know what spooning was?"

He hesitates, then pushes a lock of my hair behind my ear and shakes his head. "No."

I cautiously ask, "So you're the type of guy who doesn't like to cuddle?"

He studies me for another moment, then reveals, "I haven't had anyone in my bed since I was eighteen."

I laugh, exclaiming, "I married the virgin king!"

"Not exactly," he states with a straight face.

I snicker for another moment, then realize he's not playing any games. I immediately got serious, staring at him.

He grinds his molars, looking more uncomfortable by the minute.

I slide my hand on his cheek. "I'm confused."

He briefly closes his eyes and then pins a shameful gaze on me. He lowers his voice, confessing, "I had a girlfriend once. Then... " He looks away, clenching his jaw.

I run my thumb over his chin, softly asking, "Then what?"

He meets my gaze, answering, "Then everything changed." The color drains from his face.

My insides quiver so hard that I feel nauseous. I wait for him to continue.

He adds, "She couldn't look at me anymore."

"Why?"

He stares at me, and more embarrassment washes over him.

I put my hand on his chest, caressing the raised scar tissue covered in ink, and putting two and two together. I answer my own question. "Because of your scars?"

He barely nods, trying to keep his expression neutral, but it's full of pain.

My heart aches. I slide closer to him, running my fingers through his hair and cautiously asking, "So you haven't had sex since then?"

His voice comes out flat. "I didn't say that."

"You said you haven't had anyone in your bed," I remind him.

He stares at the ceiling for a while.

I decide he's done talking, so I offer, "Sorry. I didn't mean to pry into your private life." I turn on my side and inch away to give him some space, thinking that's what he wants.

He immediately pulls me back into him, creating a cocoon around me with his body.

I sink into him, turn my head, and smile.

"I make it a point not to lie to people who are important to me. There aren't many on my list, but you're one of them, Fiona. So I'll be honest with you," he declares.

My heart soars. I turn to him and state, "Then I'll always be honest with you."

He smiles for a moment, but then it falls. He announces, "I've had lots of sex, but no one's been in my bed. Until tonight, only a few of my personal staff and several Omni—all of whom are sworn to secrecy— knew their king was the snake man."

I admit, "I'm not following."

A fresh, uncomfortable expression appears. He reveals, "The hissing wasn't something new."

I continue to stare at him, not understanding.

He adds, "The only time I have sex is during Underworld rituals. And I won't hide my past from you. I've taken part in many acts, but I've always had a mask on."

I process his statement, and he waits, watching me intently. Then I blurt out, "So you haven't dated anyone since you were eighteen?"

His face turns red. "Yes."

I gape at him, unable to fathom it, then ask, "Why?"

He grinds his molars, replying, "I know what I look like, Fiona."

I scoff. "I think you're sexy. Your scars give you a bad boy vibe, but that's not a turn-off."

"You don't have to say that. I'm fully aware of the disgust women feel when they see me," he claims.

I jerk my head back.

He clenches his jaw.

Anger fills me. It erupts from the way he's been treated due to whatever it is that happened to him and resulted in permanent marks all over his body. But it's also for another reason. I growl, "Don't do that to me."

Surprised, he asks, "Do what?"

"Don't talk to me like I'm pitying you. I just told you I wouldn't lie to you. And the first night I met you, I very embarrassingly blurted out that I thought the scar on your face was sexy. Or did you forget?" I accuse.

His eyes widen.

I scoff. "What about Valentina? You two seem super close."

"She's my only friend," he announces.

The claw in my gut reappears. I huff. "So she says."

In a stern tone, he scolds, "I told you at the restaurant she was my friend and nothing more."

I glare at him. "So I'm supposed to believe she's never been in your bed?"

His eyes narrow. "Of course she hasn't. And I just told you that no one has."

Internal chaos ensues from my jealousy, spinning with sadness, and thinking of how alone he must have been. Then, a new insecurity takes over. I blurt out, "So whenever we're at an Underworld event, women you've fucked are going to be trying to get your attention?"

He chuckles. "That'll be the day."

"It's not funny."

His face falls. "Every woman I've ever fucked has looked at me in disgust. Even with a mask on and tattoos covering my scarred skin, there's no escaping it."

"*Every* woman, huh?" I challenge.

"Yes. I'm being honest with you," he retorts.

I jab him in the chest. "I'm not every woman. Or am I?"

He looks at me in confusion.

My emotions ball up in my chest. In a shaky voice, I point out, "I've never looked at you with disgust. I've only ever looked at you with the exact opposite. So you're not looking close enough or not interested in my attraction for you." Hurt, I turn away from him, blinking hard, suddenly exhausted from too much stress and not enough sleep.

"Jesus, I'm a fool," he mutters, then tugs me into him and curls his body around mine.

"Yeah, Kirill, you are," I mumble into my pillow.

He sighs, and the weight of the world flares around us. He tightens his arms around me and presses his mouth to my neck, kissing me, then adding, "I don't know what I'm doing, my beautiful bride."

I take a few deep breaths, then turn onto my back. "And you think I do?"

He studies me for a moment, then slowly smiles. "I guess not." His grin grows.

I softly laugh.

He replicates my amusement until we're both fighting tears.

He gradually stops and strokes my cheek. Vulnerability floods his expression. He hesitates, then asks, "So I wasn't imagining things all night?"

"What things?"

Nervousness radiates from him. He takes his time before he reveals, "You weren't disgusted. You were okay when you realized I was who you had to marry?"

My butterflies awaken again. Anxiety floods me as I speak my truth. "No. I was elated it was you."

Happiness lights his eyes. He stares at me, then lowers his lips to mine.

We slowly kiss, lazily rolling our tongue against the other's, his body hardening and mine turning into a damp mess. Our limbs entwine, and fingers grip the other's skin until I'm whimpering underneath him.

I widen my legs and lift my hips.

He enters me, and his girth pushes against my walls, creating a new frenzy of welcomed sensations. His guttural groan dances against my ear as if in relief.

I cling to him, keeping him close, kissing him with more intensity, watching him study me with the same curiosity as before.

He thrusts to the speed of our kisses, and I reach for his ass cheek, pushing my fingers into his muscle, needing more. He responds by forcefully entering me so hard I see stars.

"Oh my God," I whisper.

He mumbles, "Is that what you want, little bird? Me deep inside you?"

"Yes," I barely get out.

He flicks his tongue in my mouth a few times, keeping his thrusts in sync, never taking his eyes off mine.

"Kirill," I mutter, closing my eyes and tipping my head back.

His hand slides over my throat, his thumb pushing against my clavicle.

I moan, my heart racing faster.

"Sexy little bird," he says against my neck while kissing it.

"Please," I beg, wanting the high I've never had before him.

He wraps his fingers around my throat, puts his face over mine, and presses each fingertip into my flesh one at time, as if I'm a piano.

I whimper louder, and a tremor runs through me.

He groans, thrusting deeper inside me.

"So good," I admit. Heat rushes through my veins, and tingles light up my core.

"The best," he praises, pressing all five fingers down at the same time.

A burst of pride floods me, tugging at my heart. No one's ever called me the best or played my body so skillfully. And I want nothing more than for it to be true and to be the best he's ever had.

"How do you tap out, my sexy wife?" he questions.

I blink fast several times.

"Good. But you've already been choked too much tonight, and you have to let your brand heal," he asserts.

Alarm bells ring in my head. I forgot I even had the plastic wrap around my neck. But I shake my head, and my voice falters. "N-no. I'm good!"

He chuckles, gives me a chaste kiss, then pulls away when I slide my tongue into his mouth. His lips twitch, and a flush creeps over his glistening skin. He leans into my ear and declares, "Don't worry, my queen. There's more than one way. And your king's going to fill your pussy so deep with cum you're going to feel my warmth for days."

"Yes," I whisper, pushing my pelvis eagerly to meet his thrust.

His determined gaze sears into mine. He thrusts harder and faster, keeping his hand in the same position, not increasing or decreasing the pressure.

Spasms overpower my core, desperately trying to hold on to his erection as it slips in and out of me. They start to slow, then viciously escalate until I'm unable to focus on anything else.

My body convulses against his hard frame and then his cock expands. I cry out, "You're a fucking god!"

His low groan vibrates against me. He thrusts through it, burying his seed deep inside me until we're both peaking with a rush of adrenaline.

He releases my neck, collapsing over me, holding himself up on his forearms. His hot, ragged breath hits my shoulder.

My chest pushes against his, trying to get air.

He rolls onto his back, tugging me into his arms.

It takes a while until my focus returns and my breath normalizes. I slowly lift my head.

He stares at me, his lips slightly curved.

My smile overpowers me. I lean up and kiss him, retreat, and tilt my head.

He caresses my back. "What's the look for, my little bird?"

I arch my eyebrows. "I'm the best?"

He grins. "Yes." Then he slides his hand in my hair and pulls me back to his lips.

We kiss for a while and then I settle into his arms. He slides his palm over my ass, and we lie here, content and sated.

I break the silence minutes later, propping myself up on my elbow. I trace the snake over his chest, saying, "You know how you said you would tell me whatever I wanted to know once we said our vows?"

He nods. "Yes."

"Is anything off-limits?"

He hesitates but then surprises me by saying, "No. Nothing is off-limits. Whatever you want to know, I'll tell you."

"What if it's not about me?"

He sits up, rests against the headboard, and gently pulls me into the same position. He asks, "What do you want to know, Fiona?"

I gather my thoughts but decide there's no easy way to ask and that direct is best. I trace the scar on his cheek and question, "How did you get your scars?"

He tenses. The remaining flush on his skin disappears, and he looks away.

"You don't have to answer—"

"I will tell you," he interjects, pinning his gaze on me.

I nod, pick up his hand, and kiss his branded skull mark.

He takes a deep breath, then flatly states, "What you've heard about the Petrovs is true. They traffic and rape women. Sometimes, children too."

A chill runs through my bones.

"I am not like them," he reiterates.

I scoot closer, sliding my thumb over his hand, insisting, "I know you aren't."

"Do you?" He peers at me closer.

"Yes."

"How?"

I shrug. "I don't know, but my heart tells me you're different."

He releases a deep breath, then continues, "On my eighteenth birthday, my father and uncles took me to one of their whorehouses. They had a new group of women in the house. My father wanted me to help break them in. I refused."

My pulse pounds hard between my ears. Disgust and shock fill me. No matter how much you're warned about something, hearing it again doesn't make it any easier.

Kirill looks away, then confesses, "To punish me for my disobedience, they strung me up by a rope. My father cut my face. My oldest uncle took the knife around my body. My father's youngest brother made hash marks under the parts where I tattooed snakeheads."

Bile flies up my esophagus. I gape at him.

His father and uncles did this to him?

He keeps his head turned toward the window. A tremor runs through his hand.

I squeeze it tighter and put my arm between his back and the headboard.

He continues, "They told me that no woman would ever want me. They said the only way I'd ever have sex again was with one of their whores."

I open my mouth, but nothing comes out.

He slowly meets my gaze with a painful but hardened expression. "That's the quick version. Do you mind if I leave it at that?"

I nod, then rise on my knees and straddle him.

He blinks hard, trying to eliminate his emotions.

I put both hands on his cheeks and kiss him.

For a moment, he doesn't return my affection, then finally does, but he retreats quickly. "Do you have other questions you want answers to right now?"

I start to shake my head but then stop.

"Go on," he orders.

I gather my thoughts and then ask, "In your letter, you said you had flaws. Is that what you think your scars are? Flaws?"

He swallows hard. "Yes. They changed the entire course of my life."

My heart hurts to learn how he got his scars and what he thinks about himself because of them. I assert, "Flaws make us who we are and influence how we deal with things."

He stares at me in silence.

I trace the mark on his cheek again, and he closes his eyes, strumming his hand across my lower back. I add, "They say strong people turn flaws into strengths."

His eyes fly open. Something passes over his expression and then a short chuckle flies out of him.

"What's funny?" I question.

He pins his blues to mine, then reveals, "They say your brother is like him, but they're all wrong."

Confused, I ask, "What do you mean? And who are you talking about?"

His lips twitch. "Your father."

The grief I feel surrounding my father creeps into my chest.

Kirill cups my chin, looking into my eyes, then declares, "You are the most like your father, not your brother."

I swallow the lump in my throat.

He arches his eyebrows. "You don't believe me?"

I shrug. "Everyone says Sean is like him."

Kirill shakes his head, insisting, "No, my queen. You have your father's heart and head more than your brother."

I stay silent, wondering if it's true.

He asks, "Do you remember in my letter the story I told you about your father and the moon?"

"Yes."

More pain fills his sharp features. His face darkens, but then he states, "Your father is the one who found me. I was still strung upside down and bleeding. He took me to safety and nursed my wounds until they clotted."

More nausea churns in my gut.

Shame fills Kirill's face. He adds, "The night he took me to see the moon was the second time he saved me. It was the night I almost killed myself. So when I say I'm only alive because of him, it's not an exaggeration."

Kirill

Chapter

EIGHTEEN

Sympathy, compassion, and worry mix in Fiona's glistening expression. I curse myself for revealing the last part and quickly state, "It was a long time ago. I'm only telling you so you understand how much I respected your father. He was a good man."

She blinks a few times and nods. She quietly says, "Thanks for sharing that with me."

I slide down onto the mattress, suggesting, "Why don't we try to get some rest?"

She follows suit, curling her body beside mine and resting her cheek on my chest.

I push a button on the wall, and the shades lower over the windows.

"Wow. Fancy," she teases.

I smile, relieved to change the subject. I stroke her back and kiss her on the forehead. "Get some sleep."

She yawns and slides her leg over mine. "Okay." She shuts her eyes.

I study her for several minutes, then realize she's passed out. Her lips part, and her peaceful demeanor calms me so much I fall asleep too.

Several hours later, I wake up, spooning her.

That's ironic.

I didn't know what that meant, but now I'm fully engaging in it while I'm asleep.

Hmm.

I move my arm, but she grabs it, pushing my hand under the pillow and digging her ass against my cock.

Surprised and amused, I grunt.

She keeps her eyes shut and whispers in a sleepy tone, "You're awake?" Then she yawns.

Against my will, I follow suit, then answer, "Barely."

She runs her thumb over my hand, asking, "What time is it?"

"Not sure."

"Is the sun up?"

"Probably. Should I lift the shades?"

She yawns again, then releases me, turning on her back. "Okay."

I reach for the button, and sunlight gradually streams into the room as the shades lift.

She blinks a few times, yawns again, then curls into me. "Should I assume there's a bathing suit for me to wear somewhere in this room?"

I chuckle. "You assume correctly. In fact, I believe there's a drawer full of them."

She arches her eyebrows. "Did you pick them out?"

"No."

She wrinkles her nose and huffs. "Don't tell me Valentina did."

I reply, "No, Zara did."

"Good." She sits up.

I rise against the headboard, asking, "Why are you so negative toward Valentina?"

Her expression hardens and she tilts her head.

"Well? Fill me in," I demand.

She doesn't speak.

"Fiona, if I'm going to be honest with you, then I expect you to be honest in return."

She sighs. "Fine. She barged into my home unannounced and uninvited. That was after our little encounter in the restaurant."

I nod, a little irritated but also in unfamiliar territory. I'm not used to any woman being jealous of my friendship with Valentina. Part of me likes it, but it would be immature not to nip this in the bud, so I reply, "Ah. I see."

Her eyes turn to slits. "What does that mean?"

I hide my amusement, sternly stating, "It means, you didn't listen to what I told you about my relationship with her. And I'm sorry she was in your house, but she was obeying orders. It's not fair to hold that against her."

Fiona scoots off the bed and motions to a door. "Is that the closet?"

I cross my arms. "Don't ignore me when we're talking about something important."

She glares, seething, "Important, meaning Valentina?"

My amusement dwindles. I sternly retort, "Important, meaning my only friend, Zara's cousin, and a future Omni."

Her forehead wrinkles. "Zara's cousin?"

I nod. "Yes."

"She never told me that."

"Correct. You couldn't know before, but now you can. However, it's not ever to be public knowledge."

Fiona leans against the desk. "But Zara knows?"

"She does," I reply.

Her eyes darken, and she looks at the floor.

"She would have told you now that you're queen."

Fiona meets my eye. "Would she have?"

"Why do you think Zara wouldn't?" I question.

She shrugs. "It feels like the people I'm closest to have been hiding some of the most important aspects of their lives."

"That'll end now," I tell her.

She glances out the window, not looking convinced.

I slide to the end of the bed. "Valentina isn't a bad person. I'm sure over time you'll learn to love her."

She narrows her greens, snarling, "Like you do?"

My chest tightens. I declare, "I've never been in love with her and never will be. But we are friends, and don't make me choose between you and her."

Fiona glares at me and snaps, "Because you'll choose her?"

I scowl. "No. You're my wife. I'll always choose you."

"You just warned me not to make you choose," she points out.

I scoff. "Exactly. So don't put me in that position. It'll only create problems between us."

"But you'd be done with her if I wanted you to be?" she pushes.

Uneasiness heats my stomach, yet I answer, "Yes. I would cut off our friendship and only interact with her if it regards The Underworld. Is that what you want?"

Fiona doesn't flinch, and tension fills the air.

I wait her out.

She finally lowers her voice and shakes her head. "No. I wouldn't want to ruin your relationship if you're only friends."

"No?" I challenge, feeling a mix of relief and caution.

"You're only friends?" Her voice holds a hint of vulnerability.

I sigh. "Fiona, how many times do I need to tell you so you believe me?"

She pushes off the desk. "No more. I'm sorry. Is this the closet?" She points at the door again.

"Yes."

Her eyes light with mischief. "Great. Assuming I can snoop around and see what's in there?"

"Of course. Plus, it's not snooping when you own it," I point out.

She freezes.

"What's wrong?" I question.

"It feels funny."

"What does?"

She shifts on her feet, glancing around the room, admitting, "That I own anything on this boat."

"Well, you own the yacht too," I add.

She opens her mouth, then shuts it. She glances around again and shakes her head, muttering, "Crazy."

I chuckle. "Maybe a bit."

She bites her lip, goes to the window, and stares out at the sea. Then she notes, "I love the blue of the Mediterranean. Don't get me wrong, the Caribbean is awesome too, but there's something about this water."

I smile. "Agreed."

She steps in front of the door and opens it. "Holy crap! This is huge!"

I grin at her shock.

She spins to face me. "This is the biggest closet I've ever seen on a yacht. Even Dante's isn't this big!"

Pride fills me. I confess, "I had it redone when the Omni ordered me to marry you."

She gapes at me.

I continue, "It was a quarter of the size. So I had the construction crew knock out the wall to the other bedroom to make more space."

Her gaze darts between the closet and me.

I tease, "You should see your face right now."

"You created a bigger closet for me?"

"Yes. Want me to show you all the bells and whistles?" I ask.

She beams. "Umm, does a girl love shoes?"

I grin, puff out my chest, and step next to her. I lean down and tease, "Do I get extra points for filling the shoe rack?"

Fiona's eyes light up. "You didn't!"

My stomach flips, and I say a prayer she likes what I ordered. My personal shopper sent an email with over a hundred choices, and I agonized for hours about which ones I thought she'd love. I grab her hand, lead her to the end of the closet, and push a button.

The door rises. Dozens of designer athletic shoes, flip-flops, fancy sandals, and stilettos appear.

Fiona's mouth hangs open. She glances between me and the racks. In a raspy voice, she gushes, "No, you didn't!"

I chuckle, loving her lit-up face, giving myself an internal high five.

She grabs a pair of hot-pink stilettos and shrieks, "These aren't even available yet! And there's an estimated six-month wait once the release happens! How did you get them?"

Trying to play it cool, I shrug. "I know people."

She practically vibrates with excitement as she asks, "You know Marco De Finnery?"

I lower my voice. "I'll tell you a secret about him if you wish."

Her eyes widen. She orders, "Don't hold out on me!"

Trying not to grin, I curl my finger at her.

She steps in front of me. "Tell me, tell me, tell me!"

I lean into her ear and whisper, "He's trying to get a seat at the table."

She stills, realizing what I'm referring to, and blurts out, "He's in The Underworld?"

"Yes."

She gapes at me.

I chuckle.

She tilts her head. "Is this a cruel joke?"

"Nope. Want to meet him?" I ask.

She playfully slaps the back of her hand against my bicep. "Don't ask stupid questions, dear hubby of mine."

"Or what?"

She reaches for my cock and cups my balls, taunting, "I'll turn these blue."

My heart races faster. Without thinking, I pin her against the wall, wrap my fingers around her throat, and lift my wrist.

Her face tilts back. She gasps, and her eyes blaze with green flames.

"Is that so?" I challenge.

Her bare tits press into my chest, rising and falling faster. She moves her hand to my cock, strokes my growing erection, and glances at my mouth. She murmurs, "Maybe."

My lips twitch. Hot blood rushes to my head so fast I see stars. I push past it and flick my tongue against her lobe, warning, "Don't start something you're not planning on finishing, my little bird." I kiss her neck and jaw and then meet her stare.

She bats her eyelashes, circles her thumb on the tip of my cock, and seductively breathes, "I'll keep that in mind." She lowers her gaze to my lips.

"Didn't you come in here to get a swimsuit?" I question, forcing myself to retreat.

A flicker of disappointment flashes on her expression but quickly converts back to excitement. She glances around and asks, "Which door are the bikinis hiding behind?"

My cock throbs. I realize I need to put some clothes on. Being naked with Fiona is going to result in us never leaving the bedroom, and she'll miss the perks of the yacht. So I push another button, and several drawers, shelves, and hanging rods appear.

She reaches for a gold mesh cover-up and removes it from the hanger. She holds it in front of her and exclaims, "This is vintage Simone LeRue!"

"Is that good?" I question.

She arches her eyebrows. "You're serious?"

"Yes. I told you I have no fashion sense."

She scoffs. "Don't say that. If you picked this stuff out, you have good taste."

I sincerely question, "I do?"

She nods. "Yes. You do."

I glance at her lush tits pushing through the mesh, and suggest, "It looks good on you. Maybe you should go topless?"

She glances down and smirks. "Or maybe I shouldn't wear anything under it."

My dick twitches. "You're the queen."

"Meaning?"

"Meaning, you can do whatever you want," I assert.

She tilts her head and stares at me.

"What's the look for?"

"Do you roam around this big yacht naked all the time?"

I smile. "No."

"Never?"

"No."

She bites on her smile.

I ask, "Is that what you want to do? Stroll all over the place while strutting your sexy ass in front of the staff?"

She puts her finger on my chest and drags it between my pecs, replying, "I bet we'd be the talk of The Underworld, huh? Tons of rumors would go flying around about us."

I blurt out, "Only if the people speaking the rumors want to get beheaded."

She looks at me, as if trying to decide if I'm serious.

I add, "I'm not joking, Fiona. You're the queen. I'm the king. If anyone speaks of you inappropriately, I'll behead them in front of the entire membership."

The color drains from her cheeks.

I open a drawer of bathing suits. "Wear one of these or nothing at all. Anything that happens on this ship is between you and me. No one else will breathe a word about it."

She takes deep breaths, studying me.

I continue, "Your call. Are we putting on suits or not?"

She hesitates, then pulls a gold bikini out of the drawer. "I guess I'll put this on...for now." She gives me another suggestive look.

I try to ignore my hard-on and open another drawer. I pull out a pair of red swim trunks.

She snatches another one and holds it in front of me. "Wear this one."

I shrug. "Okay. But is something wrong with the other one?"

She shakes her head. "No. It's totally in. But this one matches mine."

I try to stop my grin. "You want us to match?"

"Yeah. It's kind of sexy, isn't it?" A flush creeps into her cheeks.

I lean down, give her a chaste kiss, and grab the gold suit. "Whatever you say, my wife."

She keeps her eyes pinned on mine, and her smile grows.

Why does she seem okay with being married to me?

She steps back, puts a leg through the bottoms, and wiggles into them.

I toss the red trunks into the drawer, slide on the gold ones, and press another button.

A vanity slides out.

She gasps and says, "Damn. You're really after a girl's heart, aren't you?"

You have no idea.

I wink and open the mirror.

"And daddy knows sunglasses," Fiona praises.

Surprised, I question, "I thought you didn't want to call me daddy?"

She cringes. "It was a joke."

I dramatically wipe my head. "Whew. That's good. The last thing I want is for my super-hot wife to be reminded that I'm getting close to old man status."

"Super-hot?"

"Extremely hot."

She laughs. "Glad you think so."

"Oh, I do," I insist, then circle my finger. "Spin, and I'll tie your top."

She obeys and holds the cups over her boobs.

I reach around her, carefully tie the straps, then assert, "I need to put fresh cream on your brand."

She turns her head and cringes. "My mom is going to kill me. I honestly don't know how she's going to accept this. She freaked when Sean and Zara came home married and branded."

My gut sinks, and I release a deep breath. I admit, "It's going to be hard for her."

"How am I going to tell her I married you?"

"We'll figure it out."

She agonizes, "She's going to flip once she finds out you're a Petrov."

I sternly offer, "It'll be okay after the initial shock."

Fiona pins her eyebrows together, asking, "How?"

I tug her into me, kiss her forehead, and confess, "I'm not sure yet, but we'll figure it out. For now, let's enjoy the sun, okay?"

She takes a deep breath, looks up, and nods. "Okay."

Relieved she won't let our problem ruin her day, I kiss her hand and grab a pair of aviator sunglasses. I instruct, "Pick a pair. It's bright out there."

She refocuses on the glasses, her face lighting up again. She finally settles on a gold-rimmed, oversized pair and tries them on. "What do you think?"

I admit, "I think you can wear any pair, and I'll have a hard-on all day."

She giggles, then elbows me, scolding, "Focus!"

I chuckle, then grab the ointment off the vanity. I unwind the plastic wrap from her neck, then add the cream. I rewrap her neck with plastic, asking, "Ready for sunshine?"

"Yes. And thank you," she says, smiling.

My heart beats faster. "Anytime." I grab her hand and lead her through the ship. We get to the deck and lie on a double lounger by the pool, overlooking the water.

"Pinch me," she says.

I reach over and pinch her.

She yelps and then laughs.

"Your Majesties," one of the deckhands interjects, bowing.

"Hello, Matteo," I reply.

He rises and focuses on Fiona, declaring, "It's an honor to meet you, ma'am."

"Thank you. It's nice to meet you," she replies.

He asks, "May I get either of you a drink or something to eat?"

Fiona glances at me. "I'm suddenly super hungry."

I grin. "Don't worry. We have lots of meat here for you."

Her cheeks turn red, and she laughs then glances around. She asks, "Is it breakfast or lunchtime?"

Matteo grins. "Whatever you wish, Your Majesty."

"Please. Call me Fiona." She turns toward me. "People can call me by my name, right?"

I nod. "If you wish."

She grins and addresses Matteo. "Then please, call me Fiona."

"Yes, ma'am. Er...Miss Fiona," he replies, shifting on his feet.

She asks, "Can you tell me what time it is?"

"It's a little past noon."

"So lunch..." She scrunches her face.

"Or brunch," I suggest.

She grins. "Yes! Brunch is always better!"

"Is there anything special you want?" Matteo questions.

She peers at him. "What are my choices?"

He relays, "The chef will make anything you want, but we have fresh branzino that's delicious."

She chirps, "Sea bass, right?"

"Correct."

"Sounds delicious. Can I get a mimosa with it?"

Matteo gives her an approving nod. "Absolutely. I'll tell the chef. Should I have him select some sides for it? Or do you want to specify?"

"Please have him pick," she directs.

"Very good. And for you, sir?" He turns toward me.

"Same. Except I'll have vodka in my mimosa. And bring two Russian Breakfasts, please," I order.

Amusement fills Fiona's expression. "Don't you mean you want a screwdriver?"

I grunt. "No. Screwdrivers are for pussies who can't handle vodka. A Russian brunch has it in the mimosa, along with the champagne and orange juice."

She wrinkles her forehead, murmuring, "Vodka in a mimosa?"

"Yep."

She shrugs, beams at Matteo, and declares, "I'll try mine that way."

"Okay. I'll be back soon," he asserts, then disappears.

My wife leans closer, asking, "What's a Russian Breakfast?"

"Shots."

She arches her eyebrows, slides her hand over my thigh, and questions, "Are you trying to get me drunk and take advantage of me?"

The claw in my stomach scrapes my insides. The night of my eighteenth birthday, when my father made the new women they kidnapped drink to "loosen them up," flashes before me. I bark, "No. I would never do that to you. Real men don't take advantage of women."

Fiona flinches, her smile fading. "I was just kidding."

"Oh," I say, feeling foolish, and cursing myself for letting the ghosts of my past interfere in my current life.

Fiona

NINETEEN

"Mmm," I moan, taking the last bite of the branzino.

Amusement sparks on Kirill's face. "Glad you like it. The crew does a great job catching it when we're here."

"It's amazing how you can taste the difference when fish is fresh," I add, then finish my vodka-laced mimosa.

Matteo appears with another round of Russian Breakfast shots. He sets them on the table and then refills our mimosas. He asks, "Can I get anything else for you?"

"I'm good," I answer.

"Me, too," Kirill says.

Matteo nods. "Very good. I'll check on you in a little while." He disappears off the deck.

Kirill grabs my hand, pulls it to his lips, and kisses it, then declares, "I know a fabulous restaurant in Lisbon. What do you think about having dinner there?"

I beam with excitement. "That sounds awesome. I haven't been to Lisbon yet."

"Never?"

"No. I went to the Algarve once, though."

"Lisbon is a busy city. It's different, but you'll love it. There's a lot of art there. If you want, we can spend the night and sightsee tomorrow."

"I'd love to explore Lisbon," I gush.

"Okay, then that's what we'll do."

Sergio stops next to the table. "Sorry to interrupt, Your Majesties, but Brax is on the phone. He claims it's urgent and is in regard to the queen." He holds a phone out.

Kirill's expression goes stern. He takes it and answers, "Hello. This is Kirill," rubbing his thumb over my hand. Then he releases me, rises, and steps over to the rail, looking out over the Mediterranean.

My stomach flips. *Why would Brax call about me?*

Kirill snarls, "I'll kill them."

The hairs on my arms rise.

He shakes his head, listens for a few moments, then asks, "Who else is involved?"

I glance at Sergio, and I see he's wearing a scowl that's pinned on Kirill.

My husband declares, "Keep them alive and restrained until I get there. No food and only enough water to sustain them. Find out what they know."

I shiver, goose bumps raising on my skin.

Kirill warns, "I mean it, Brax. Make them talk."

Several moments pass.

Kirill's voice drops. "What do you mean they know?"

My gut churns so fast I get nauseous. I put my hand over it.

He shakes his head and states, "Thank you for informing me." He hangs up.

I rise and step beside him, place my hand on his arm, and ask, "What's wrong?"

He grinds his molars, staring at the sea.

"Please tell me. You said you wouldn't keep anything from me once we were married," I remind him.

Darkness floods his face. He turns to Sergio and orders, "Contact the flight crew. Coordinate with them the next port we can fly home from."

"Yes, sir," Sergio answers.

Kirill adds, "Have Matteo bring me Fiona's cell phone."

"Yes, sir," Sergio replies and disappears.

I repeat, "Tell me what's going on."

Kirill puts his hands on my cheeks, tilting my head up. He apologizes, "I'm sorry to have to cut our trip short. I'll make it up to you."

I demand, "Why are we going home?"

He takes a deep breath and says, "There's a plot to assassinate you."

"What?" I shriek.

He steps closer. His eyes narrow with hatred. "Don't worry. It won't happen. And I will make them pay as soon as we get home."

I gape at him, and he studies me.

I get a sinking feeling. "What else is going on?"

He strokes my cheeks with his thumbs, announcing, "Your mother and Dante know about us."

My jaw drops to the floor. I grip the railing, breathing, "What? How?"

Disapproval fills his expression. He admits, "Someone sent them photos of our wedding. The same thing happened to Sean and Zara."

"Yes, I remember. I got the photos too."

Guilt fills Kirill's sharp features. "I should have found out who sent them, but I had other pressing matters to attend to. This is my fault. I'm sorry, Fiona. I didn't want your mother to learn about us this way."

I turn toward the water and close my eyes, trying to shake off the vision of my mom upset, but I can't.

He adds, "Brax said they're flying to Chicago. I assume they've tried to contact you."

I stay silent, the blue water not in focus, still reeling inside over how badly I know my mom must be hurting.

I married a Petrov.

No one will ever understand why if I can't tell the truth.

Kirill isn't bad.

But they won't believe me when I try to convince them.

"Fiona, look at me," Kirill orders.

I slowly meet his gaze.

"I will help you make it right."

"How? You're a Petrov?" I remind him, feeling sicker by the second.

His face drops. "Yes, but we'll figure this out."

I shake my head. "You don't understand. They will never accept our marriage. Never."

Disappointment flashes in his eyes, but he quickly masks his reaction, claiming, "We'll get them to accept us."

As much as I want to believe him, I can't. The hatred the O'Malleys, O'Connors, Marinos, and especially the Ivanovs have for the Petrovs runs deep.

Crap! Adrian's going to kill me when he finds out.

"Trust me. We'll figure this out," Kirill insists.

Matteo interrupts, "Ma'am. Your phone." He offers me my cell.

"Thank you," I reply, grabbing it and turning it on.

My insides quiver. It feels like forever before the screen lights up, and text messages and missed calls pop up for several minutes. My hand shakes.

"Come. Sit down," Kirill orders, putting his hand on my back and guiding me to the double lounger.

"There are so many," I state, watching my screen display more notifications. I sit down and watch until it finally stops, then slowly raise my head.

Kirill rubs my back, advising, "Take a deep breath."

I mumble, "This is worse than an attempt to take me out."

He snaps, "Don't ever say that again!"

My eyes widen, and I cry out, "This is my family. All the people I love!"

He sighs.

I lean against the lounger, put my feet flat on the cushion, and click on my voicemail, scrolling through them but not listening to any of them.

Kirill stays silent, watching me.

"Thirty-four voicemails!" I exclaim, my dread growing.

"I'm sorry. I take full responsibility."

"It's not your fault."

"I should have investigated who sent the photos after Sean and Zara married," he insists.

I swipe on my text messages and hit the first one.

Sean: *Call me. Shit's hitting the fan.*

"Such a genius," I sarcastically mutter.

Kirill arches his eyebrows.

I tilt my head, scoffing. "My brother sent me a warning text to call him because shit is hitting the fan."

Kirill's expression is neutral. He suggests, "Maybe you should call him."

I debate, then ask, "What's the point? He's not going to offer any solutions."

A moment passes, and Kirill declares, "Everyone accepted Sean and Zara's marriage. It'll just take time."

I cry out, "You're a Petrov! It's not the same thing! They'll never accept you!"

Hurt, disappointment, and a bit of anger flash over his expression. He looks away.

I soften my tone and put my hand on his thigh. "I'm sorry. I didn't mean—"

"To tell the truth?" he interjects, pinning his pained, narrowed eyes on me.

Guilt assails me. It's not his fault he's a Petrov. What they did to him is beyond horrible. I swallow the lump in my throat.

He turns toward the sea.

I don't move, trying to figure out a solution and not hurt him further.

Sergio steps in front of the lounger. "Your Majesties." He bows.

"Yes?" Kirill replies.

Sergio informs, "I made the arrangements. We'll stop in Barcelona within a few hours."

"Thank you," Kirill says.

Sergio nods and disappears.

My phone rings, and I freeze. My heart beats a thousand miles a minute.

"Who is it?" he asks.

I swallow hard, revealing, "My mom."

My phone rings again.

"Maybe you should answer it," he suggests.

"And say what?"

The ring blares again.

"I don't know, but not hearing from you will probably hurt her further. And I didn't take my queen to be a coward."

"Coward?"

He crosses his arms and stares at me.

He's right.

In the middle of the next ring, I hit the screen. My stomach flips, and I slowly put the phone to my ear, answering, "Hey, Mom."

Her voice shakes. "Is it true?"

I blink hard, trying not to get emotional, but a tear escapes. I swipe at it and admit, "Yes. I married Kirill Petrov."

She takes a tormented breath of air.

I close my eyes, hating how much I'm hurting her.

She clears her throat, then asks, "How did this happen, Fiona?"

My chest tightens. I take a minute to think, then decide to be honest about whatever I can tell her. I confess, "We met over a year ago. It was the night I took Zara out for her bachelorette party."

She seethes, "You've been dating him for over a year?"

"No. We didn't meet again until I ran into him at the coffee shop near Sean's building. That wasn't too long ago." My pulse skyrockets.

She shrieks, "It wasn't too long ago? And you married him?"

My insides tremble, and I open my eyes. More tears fall. "Yes. I did."

Tense silence fills the line.

She lowers her voice, accusing, "How could you marry a man you barely know?"

"It...it just happened," I lie, unable to tell her the full story and hating myself for it.

Fear laces her tone. She frets, "He's a Petrov. You don't know what you've done, Fiona."

Heart palpitations rip through my chest. I struggle to breathe, responding, "He's not like the Petrovs our families hate."

"Like hell he isn't!" she declares.

"Mom—"

"You need to get away from him, Fiona. Whatever you've done can be undone. Tell me where you're at, and we'll come get you," she orders.

I squeeze my eyes shut and press my hand to my chest. I barely get out, "It can't be undone, Mom."

"It can! Whatever he's holding over you to have made you marry him—"

"He didn't make me marry him! I did it with my own free will. He's a good man. You'll see. Once you get to know him—"

"Get to know him? No! Fiona, you need to leave him," she insists.

Tears drip off my chin. I sniffle and shake my head. "Mom, I'm not leaving him. Not now, or ever."

She gasps. "Don't say that."

Silence ensues for a few moments.

She begs, "Fiona, tell me where you are. Please."

I glance at Kirill.

He studies me intently with concern shining in his eyes.

I reply, "I'll be in Chicago at some point tonight. I assume you'll be there?"

"Damn right, we'll be there," she spouts.

"I'll see you when I'm back," I inform her.

"Fiona, please. You don't know what he's capable of," she warns.

Hurt, guilt, and anger explode within me. I snap back, "Don't accuse him of things he hasn't or wouldn't do. It's not fair."

"He's a Petrov!" she exclaims.

I lift my chin, finding a new strength within me. "Yes. And he's my husband. So you will need to accept his last name, get to know him for the person he is, and not blame him for whatever his relatives have done."

She fearfully stutters, "Y-you don't know wh-what he's capable of doing. Please get away from him."

Pain shears through me. "I'm sorry, but I won't. I'll see you in Chicago, Mom. Goodbye." I hang up before she can reply.

Several moments pass, then Kirill grabs my hand, asking, "Are you okay?"

I face him, shaking my head. "This is worse than I assumed."

My phone rings. I glance at it and groan.

Kirill pins me with the same look he gave me when he spoke about me being a coward. "You might as well get it over with, or they'll never stop calling."

I answer on the second ring, "Hi, Zara." I put it on speaker and set it on the cushion.

I can hear compassion in her voice when she says, "Dante's on the phone with Sean. You spoke with Bridget?"

I curl my arms around my shins. "Yes."

"Are you okay?"

I sigh. "My mom is never going to forgive me."

"She will," Zara insists.

Kirill strokes my back.

"No. She won't. She wants me to leave him," I state.

"Oh. I'm sorry. What can we do to help?" Zara asks.

A cloud moves, and the sun shines brightly over us, warming my skin. I release my legs and curl into Kirill, resting my head on his chest and sigh. I reply, "You tell me. But on another note, there's an assassination attempt on my life."

"What?" she shrieks.

Kirill stiffens.

I glance at him, and my lips twitch. It seems amusing to me, even though it's not. I declare, "Brax didn't tell Sean?"

"No. Not that I'm aware of, and that isn't something your brother would keep from me. Who is it?" she asks.

Kirill pipes in, "I'm not releasing that information right now, especially over the phone."

"Yes. Of course. Silly of me to ask," Zara says.

He assures, "It's okay. They're detained, and I'll deal with them when we arrive back in Chicago."

"When are you back?" she questions.

"Tonight. We're docking in Barcelona and then flying home," he answers.

"Okay. Fiona, did you get any of my messages?" she asks.

My anxiety flares again. "Not yet. Why?"

She hesitates, then reveals, "Adrian knows."

"Shit," I mutter. My insides shake so hard bile moves up my esophagus. I swallow it down.

"He's going crazy. Skylar said she tried calling you and left you texts. You might want to look at those," Zara suggests.

"Ugh," I groan, and bury my face into Kirill's arm, inhaling his scent, wishing it were a few hours ago when I was clueless about the rest of the world learning about our nuptials.

"Thanks for the update. We'll see you when we're back," Kirill says and then hangs up.

I lift my head. "This is so bad."

He picks up the phone and swipes it, then lowers his voice. "You need to read these."

Dread floods me. I sit up and read the texts.

> Skylar: Fiona, I don't know what's happening, but Adrian said you ran off and married a Petrov. Is this true?

> Skylar: I didn't realize that when you said you needed to take off work for a week to deal with personal issues, it was to get married.

I cringe as I continue reading.

> Skylar: Please call me. Adrian's going nuts. I need answers so I can hopefully calm him down.

I exit the thread with Skylar and go to the next set of messages.

> Blue: Why is Dad saying you married a Petrov?

> Blue: I'm not buying this. I looked the guy up, and he has a scar on his face. Can you call and calm my dad down before he has a heart attack?

I groan and pull up the next set.

> Dante: Fiona, where are you?

> Dante: Please send me your location so I can get you. Your mother and I are worried sick.

A new message pops up.

> Sean: I'm sorry you have to deal with this.

Anger flares through me. He caused this and didn't create any solutions to help.

Me: No thanks to you.

Sean: I'm trying.

Me: By doing what?

Kirill asserts, "It's better to play nice with your brother. He's the only one who can help calm your mom's fears."

I grunt. "He's not getting off the hook that easily."

Sean: I'm heading to the airport to meet Mom and Dante. I'm trying the best I can.

Me: Try harder. Otherwise, Dante will try to kidnap me and lock me up to keep me away from Kirill.

Sean: No doubt.

In a stern voice, Kirill threatens, "If anyone tries to kidnap you, including Dante, they won't live to see the following day."

The ache in my core flares, mixing with panic. I blurt out, "You can't harm Dante."

"Then he better not touch you," Kirill warns.

I fight the throb growing between my legs, squeezing my thighs together, and argue, "You have to play nice."

"No one is taking my wife from me."

"Aren't you possessive?" I reprimand, but more chaos torments my lower body.

His gaze darkens as he silently studies me.

I put my hand on his thigh and gently add, "I want my family to get to know you. We're going to have to give them some leeway."

Kirill asserts, "It doesn't include them making decisions for you or kidnapping you."

I nod. "I agree. But we have to go a bit easy on them."

He tugs me onto his lap and pushes a lock of my hair off my face. "Fiona, you aren't just my wife. You're the queen of The Underworld. You rule the Omni beside me with as much authority and power as I have. My responsibility to protect you goes beyond you being my wife."

I stay quiet, taking in his statement, still not fully comprehending what being the queen means.

He strokes my cheek, continuing, "Your father wanted you to rule. It was important to him, and I know why."

Tingles run down my spine. I ask, "Why was it so important to him? I was only a little girl when he died."

Kirill takes a moment, peers closer at me, as if he can see deep into my soul, and finally states, "He saw your light."

Confused, I question, "My light?"

He nods. "Yes. Your radiance. It dances around you, highlighting your grace, strength, and courage."

I take a deep breath, slowly releasing it.

He adds, "Not just anyone can be sitting in our spots. Your father wanted you and not Sean here. I'm convinced of it now that I'm getting to know you."

I tilt my head. "Why do you think that?"

Kirill doesn't hesitate when he says, "Second-born, two-attempts clause."

I stare at him in question, admitting, "I don't understand."

"There are no clauses for the firstborn, only the second. That's you. Your father knew you'd sometimes have to fight with yourself to go in one direction or make a mistake and try again. That's the reality of those in power. If he wanted Sean instead of you wearing the crown, he would have created the clause for him."

"But wasn't my father the king?" I ask.

"Yes."

"So why would he think he wouldn't stay king?" I ask.

"Every royal figure eventually dies. Those who step into their shoes need to be prepared. And he constructed the tools so you'd wear the crown, not your brother. So, not only for my own selfish reasons but to honor your father, if anyone ever tries to harm you, there will be no mercy. And I won't give a fuck who they are," he warns, sending a chill down my spine, mixing with my growing ache.

Kirill

Fourteen Hours Later

Chapter
TWENTY

$\mathcal{A}$ rina appears by my seat and whispers, "Landing is in twenty minutes."

"Thank you," I reply in a hushed tone.

She nods, gives Fiona a starstruck glance, and disappears.

My wife remains peacefully sleeping against my shoulder, her hand resting on the inside of my thigh.

An unfamiliar warm joy surfaces, mixing with sharp agitation. I assumed my own blood would come after my bride, but they shouldn't have found out about our nuptials this quickly. There's only one way the word got out in under twenty-four hours—there are more traitors in The Underworld.

But who?

The claw in my gut re-emerges, scraping as it rises into my chest. I squeeze my fist until my knuckles turn white, making a new vow. When I discover who betrayed their oath, the consequences will be unlike anything The Underworld has ever seen.

My cell vibrates several times in my cup holder.

I grab it, swipe the screen, and swallow down bile.

Brax: There are two more.

Sean: Security is too tight. We have eyes on them and are ready to take them out or bring them in once it's clear. I say bring them in, but it's your call.

Brax: Agreed. Make them pay.

Rage explodes within me.

Me: Make it clear that no one is to take them out. They will pay for their sins before I grant death upon them.

Brax: Lev and Igor need a break. I don't think I can get anything else from them if I don't back off. They're not far from the corpse stage.

Me: Then back off. I need them alive when I arrive.

Brax: Understood.

I stare out the window, taking in the city lights, and my phone vibrates in my hand.

Ivan: We have a problem.

Sharp points dig deeper in my gut.

Me: What?

Ivan: Dante Marino's SUV hasn't moved from the runway since he and Fiona's mother landed and got off the plane.

My chest tightens. I glance at my wife and take a few deep breaths.

I don't need this right now.

They're her family. Of course they're going to be worried about her.

Me: Why am I just being informed about this?

Ivan: I was just granted access to the runway
and wasn't told they were here until now.

I grind my molars in frustration and irritation. Something is off with security. I've felt it since they took away my privacy. Things should have returned to normal now that Fiona and I are married.

Does the Omni still have surveillance on me?

If so, who at the table is making these calls?

I return to my phone.

Me: Find out why you weren't told they were
there.

Ivan: Already on it.

The wheels squeak, lowering for landing. I stroke Fiona's cheek, murmuring, "Wake up, my little bird."

Her eyelids flutter a few times and then she lifts her head. "Are we in Chicago?"

"Almost. Put your seat belt back on," I instruct.

She obeys, then asks, "What time is it?"

I glance at my watch. "It's a bit past two in the morning."

She yawns and stretches her arms as the wheels touch the ground.

I scan the runway, and my chest tightens. A black SUV is speeding toward mine.

"Fuck," I grumble.

"What's wrong?" Fiona asks.

I turn toward her. "Your mom and Dante are here."

Her eyes widen. "As in, at the airport?"

I point out the window at the SUV parking next to mine. "Yes. Right there."

"Oh shit," she frets.

I grab her hand, assuring her, "It'll be okay."

She furrows her forehead, giving me a helpless look.

"I'll handle it," I insist, but I can only imagine how this will play out.

The plane comes to a stop.

We take off our seat belts, and Arina appears. "Can I get you anything before you leave?"

"I think we're good, Arina," I reply.

"Yes, thank you," Fiona offers.

Arina pins another starstruck gaze on Fiona, then smiles. "It was an honor flying with you, Your Majesty."

Fiona shifts in her seat. "Um, thank you."

Arina curtsies and goes to the front of the plane. She opens the door, and cold air rushes inside.

Fiona peeks past me out the window. She groans and then declares, "This is going to be so bad."

I rise and put my Glock in the back of my pants, noting, "No time like the present." I grab her jacket and hold it toward her.

She stands and slides into it. Then she buttons it up.

I secure the top button and offer, "Might be better for your mom not to see the plastic wrap right now."

She blows out an anxious breath of air. "Good call."

I motion for her to go first. She hesitates, then lifts her chin and exits the plane.

I follow her down the staircase, quickly stepping beside her and sliding my arm around her waist.

Dante and Bridget fly across the small runway.

"Hey," Fiona greets.

"You're coming with us," Bridget asserts, glancing at me with the color draining from her face.

I push the familiar, uncomfortable feeling down and state, "I know this isn't what you wanted for your daughter—"

"Isn't what she wanted? You're a Petrov," Dante snarls, and reaches for Fiona, commanding, "Let's go."

I scowl and step between them, pushing Fiona back.

"Don't touch her," Dante threatens.

"She's my wife. You're going to need to accept it," I warn.

Bridget's voice shakes. "Fiona, please. Come with us. You can't be with him."

"Stop! Everyone, stop!" Fiona shouts, moving next to me.

I grind my molars and tighten my grip on her waist.

Bridget closes the gap between them. She reaches for her cheeks. A tear slips down her face, and she cries, "I don't know how this happened, but I need you to come with us. Please. You don't know who he is or what he's done."

My stomach flips. I stand taller, declaring, "I've done nothing worse than anything either of your husbands have done."

She snaps her head toward me, seething, "Don't you dare stand here and accuse my husbands of vile things! Or insinuate that you knew Fiona's father!"

"Mom! He knew Dad!" Fiona interjects.

Bridget narrows her eyes. She warns, "I don't know what this monster has told you, but I can assure you he can't be trusted. Now, please. Get in the car."

Fiona insists, "He did know Dad. And Kirill's not a monster!"

I squeeze her waist and suggest, "Why don't we all take a breather? It's late, and I'm sure everyone is exhausted. Let's get some sleep and meet up tomorrow. Then we can have a civil conversation."

Dante pulls his gun out, snarling, "Our civil conversation doesn't involve you. Now, get your hands off Fiona."

Ivan moves toward us and calls out, "You might want to think twice about threatening your daughter's husband." He points his gun at Dante.

"Dante! Put the gun down!" Fiona shrieks.

"Fiona, come with us," Bridget pleads.

A loud horn blares through the air, and lights from an approaching black SUV appear.

The pilot steps out of the plane, holding an M4 assault rifle, ordering, "Lower your weapon!"

Dante doesn't flinch.

The SUV races toward us, honking the horn and slamming on the brakes. Sean's voice shouts, "Put the gun down, Dante!" He opens the door and jumps out.

Dante keeps his gun aimed at me as his gaze darts toward Sean. "What are you doing here?"

Sean steps in front of Dante, sternly ordering, "Put it down."

"He's a Petrov," Dante seethes.

Sean nods. "I know. But put it down."

Dante hesitates.

"Mom. Tell him to put it down. Now," Sean demands.

Bridget glances between everyone. "Dante, put it down."

He meets her eyes.

"Please," she adds.

He slowly lowers his Glock.

Sean points at Ivan and the pilot, instructing, "Lower your weapons."

They don't move.

"Do it," I call out.

They slowly obey.

Fiona asks, "Sean, what are you doing here?"

He pins his gaze on me, answering, "We have to go."

"Go where?" Fiona questions.

"Why would you go anywhere with him?" Bridget interrogates.

Tense silence fills the air.

Sean and Fiona exchange guilty looks.

"What the fuck is going on here?" Bridget barks.

Sean pins his gaze on me, stating, "We only have a small window of time if you want to bring him in alive."

The hairs on my arms rise. I tug my bride to my side and assert, "Ivan will take you home. As soon as we're done, I'll meet you there."

"Like hell you will," Dante threatens.

"She's my wife, and she's going to our home," I snarl, fed up with this conversation and knowing how important it is to go with Sean.

Bridget prods, "What are you involved in, Sean?"

He clenches his jaw, turns toward her, and answers, "I can't discuss this, Mom. But I need to go with Kirill."

Her lips tremble. More tears well, and she flicks her gaze between him and Fiona.

"You're coming with us," Dante claims again.

I step closer, pushing Fiona back. "She needs security. Her safety is of the utmost importance. She's going home where I can ensure her safety."

Dante's scowl deepens. "The only person she needs protecting from is you."

"Enough! Fiona has threats against her life. Kirill is right. She needs security," Sean informs.

Bridget gasps. "Who is threatening her?"

"It doesn't matter. She needs Kirill's security," Sean insists.

"If Fiona is in danger, my men will keep her safe," Dante declares with worry in his voice.

I scoff. "You have major holes in your security."

Dante points and barks, "You have a lot of nerve—"

"It's true!" Sean exclaims.

Dante's eyes widen.

Bridget grabs his arm.

"Explain yourself," Dante orders.

I lock eyes with him and state, "We don't have time for this. Threats need to be eliminated. You are not a naive man. You know that windows of time disappear if not acted upon."

His gaze darkens.

I add, "When we've taken out the threat, I will sit down with you and show you the security holes."

"Fiona," Bridget says in an emotional tone. Tears stream down her cheeks.

"I'm sorry," Fiona softly offers, swiping her face.

It slices at my heart. I turn toward her. "Do you wish to go with your mom? I can have my men secure their penthouse."

More tears fall. She nods. "Please."

I address Dante. "You must agree my men are in charge. Your security can assist, but I cannot let Fiona go unless you assure your men will follow their directions."

"Petrov men?" he questions with disgust.

I shake my head. "Not all of them."

He tosses a curious and confused expression at me.

I offer, "I know this doesn't make sense. You're going to have to trust me."

He doesn't move.

"Kirill's right," Sean interjects.

Dante narrows his gaze on him.

Sean cautiously holds his hands in the air. "Fiona's safety is the only thing that matters right now."

Dante glances at Bridget.

She sniffles and nods.

I pull my phone out of my pocket and push a button. I put it to my ear, and it rings once.

"Sir," Draco, the head of my security, answers.

I reply, "I need level five moved to Dante Marino's penthouse."

"Sir?" he questions.

"My wife will be staying there with her family while I'm gone. The current security will assist the team, and I've been assured of full cooperation," I inform.

Draco stays quiet.

"Is there an issue?" I demand.

"No, sir. I'll personally handle this," he assures.

"Good." I hang up and continue, "Ivan will follow you to the penthouse, along with my other men."

Several SUVs turn the corner and race toward us.

I motion toward Dante's SUV. "It's time for us to go."

Dante hesitates, then puts his hand on Bridget's back, leading her toward their vehicle. They slide inside.

I guide Fiona to it and stop in front of the open door. I scan her eyes, unsure what I'm looking for, and try to push away a nagging feeling that I won't see her again.

Maybe she'll come to her senses when we're apart and realize she should have never married me.

I lean forward and kiss her on the forehead. "Try to get some rest." I step back, with all my insecurities flying at me.

She tosses her arms around me and rises on her tiptoes. She murmurs, "Promise me you'll be safe."

Surprise and relief lodge in my throat. I hug her tighter and reply, "Promise." I slowly release her and motion for her to get into the vehicle.

She slides in next to her mom.

I shut the door and motion to the caravan of SUVs. Two accelerate in front of Dante's vehicle. I tap the roof.

His driver falls behind my lead guys, and four more SUVs line up behind Dante's. I watch until they fade out of sight.

"Let's go," Sean states.

I don't reply as I hurry to his vehicle. I slide into the passenger's seat.

He gets in on the other side and takes off.

"Fill me in," I order.

He lowers his voice, but the disgust is still there. "Lev flipped on Gavin." He turns and accelerates onto the main road.

"Gavin who?" I question.

He grinds his molars, then relays, "O'Malley."

I shift in my seat, offering, "Sorry to hear that," knowing how difficult it is when your own blood is on the opposite side of you.

Sean grips the wheel tighter. "Never really cared for the prick. The day he arrived in Chicago from Ireland, I told Uncle Killian I didn't trust him."

"Why not?"

Sean shrugs. "Gut feeling."

"And you're sure about him?" I question.

Sean weaves around a car and merges onto the expressway. "I might not love the guy, but he's still blood. You don't think I'd double-check what a Petrov claims?"

My pulse creeps up. As much hatred as I have for most Petrovs, I'm still one. It's a fine line of loyalty and loathing.

Sean adds, "Lev claimed he secured an abandoned building on the South Side. The Petrovs already paid him $50,000 for a down payment to kill Fiona. The total contract was $500,000. He gets the remaining $450,000 once the demands are met. I hacked into his laptop. It's all in the chatterbox."

My gut flips. I already know the answer but still ask, "And what were the demands?"

The color leeches from Sean's face. He keeps his eyes on the road, gritting out, "They wanted my sister's rape and murder streamed on the darknet."

I curl my fists into tight balls, hating the blood that runs through my veins more than ever. I take a few deep breaths and demand, "Who's behind the hit?"

Sean shakes his head. "We haven't found out yet. Lev and Igor were supposed to take part. They aren't very high up. Their clearance level only involves taking and implementing orders. My guess is that Gavin isn't any higher up on the totem pole."

"Then do your job and hack into whatever you have to so we know who's behind this!" I roar.

"As soon as we kill this motherfucker, I will. I thought it was more important to track this bastard down."

He's right, but I don't say anything, turning toward the window. The thought of vile things being done to my new bride while being broadcast all over the darknet makes me ill.

And ready to kill.

Several minutes of tense silence fill the car.

Sean finally says, "I knew Dante and my mom were flipping out, but that was pretty bad back there."

"No shit."

"What's your plan to fix it?" he asks.

I turn, crossing my arms. "Not sure. You want to give me some insight?"

He doesn't take his eyes off the road, veers off the ramp, and doesn't stop at the red light, going through it.

I add, "Glad you're full of ideas."

We don't speak the rest of the way. Sean pulls into an alley and parks. He announces, "It's the house on the corner." He turns off the SUV and cuts the headlights.

My heart pounds faster. I reach for my Glock, and Sean pulls out his.

He hands me a silencer and then picks up his phone, asking the person on the end, "How many are inside?"

I put the silencer on my gun and wait.

"You sure?" he asks.

My chest tightens.

He states, "Good." He hangs up and says, "It's only Gavin. He's a skinny motherfucker, so it shouldn't be hard."

I feel a flicker of relief but there's also disappointment. I wish whoever ordered this hit were present, but that isn't reality, and I know it. So I open my door and get out, putting on a pair of black gloves.

We creep down the street, staying in the shadows. Once we're close to the corner, Sean points toward the back, and we split.

He moves toward the front, and I slip deeper into the darkness. When I get to the run-down back door, I slowly turn the knob.

It's locked, so I assess the door and point my gun at the lock, then shoot.

A crack fills the air. I push through the door, step into the dark room, and turn toward the sound of scuffling.

A soft, green glow radiates in the next room. I spot the tail end of a shadow and race toward it, lunging my body over Gavin.

An incoherent yelp flies out of him, and he falls to the floor.

Sean bursts through the front door.

I pin my body over Gavin's small frame, putting him in a choke hold.

He writhes under me, but he's no match for my strength.

"Motherfucker," I bark out as visions of my new worst nightmare flare in my mind.

All I see is a helpless Fiona, and it turns me into a crazed man. Any ounce of control I have disappears.

I squeeze his neck harder until he's barely able to fight.

"You're going to kill him!" Sean roars next to me.

I should stop so I can spend hours torturing him and assess if he does know who ordered the hit, but reason and reality are two different things.

"Kirill!" Sean warns, but his voice sounds like it's coming from a tunnel.

The green glow swirls with darkness, and the air turns thick with my rage. In Russian, I curse Gavin for everything he planned on doing to my wife.

It's only when Sean tears me off him, barking, "It's over," that I realize what's happened.

Gavin lies on the floor, his face purple, his eyes wide and lifeless.

"You weren't supposed to kill him yet," Sean reminds me.

I spit on the man who planned to do horrible things to my wife with the sickest of men watching, and order, "Call in the cleanup crew. And get hacking."

Sean crosses his arms, staring at me with a narrow gaze.

I leave, embracing the cold air, wanting nothing more than to get back to my wife and ensure she's safe.

Fiona

Chapter
TWENTY-ONE

Tension's thick during the ride to Dante and Mom's penthouse. No one speaks, and I stare anxiously out the window, wondering what I'll say when Mom and I are alone.

We pull up to the building and into the garage. The SUV stops beside the elevator.

My stomach twists as Dante gets out. He reaches in for my mom, helps her out, and I follow.

The elevator doors open, and a man I've never seen before steps in front of us.

Dante pushes in front of Mom and me, sneering, "Who are you?"

A man with an Irish accent answers, "We're filling the holes."

Dante's face darkens.

The man holds out his hand. "I'm Patrick."

Dante glances at his hand, hesitating.

Patrick pulls it back. "Suit yourself. You can't go up there right now. We're pulling recording devices."

Mom's face pales. "Recording devices?"

Dante seethes, "What is this nonsense? And how did you get into our home?"

Patrick crosses his arms. "You'll have to direct your questions at the boss. My job is to follow orders."

Dante snarls, "Let me guess, the boss is Kirill Petrov?"

"Yes, sir."

"And what are those orders?" Dante asks.

Patrick states, "To sweep your penthouse. So far, we've found four devices. We can't allow you to go up until we're assured there are no other threats."

Dante grinds his molars.

Patrick points to the SUV. "I suggest you return to the vehicle until we deem your penthouse clear."

Dante doesn't move.

Patrick turns toward me. "Ma'am, your husband wouldn't want you standing in the cold. Please get into the vehicle."

My stomach flips. Mom and Dante both shoot me disappointing looks.

Patrick points to the SUV, pleading, "Please. It's for your safety."

Horror fills Mom's expression. She blinks hard, muttering, "What have you gotten yourself into, Fiona?"

I don't answer. I open the door and slide across the seat.

She slides in next to me.

Dante shuts the door, remaining outside. He continues talking to Patrick.

Mom turns toward me. "Look at me, Fiona."

I take a deep breath, release it, then obey, stating, "I didn't do this to hurt you."

She scoffs. "Yet you knew it would and still went through with it. So, why?"

My heart races faster. I open my mouth, but nothing comes out.

Her expression turns to anger. "Don't sit there and say nothing. I want answers. How do you end up marrying a Petrov? And not just any Petrov, but one so scarred up it's clear he's into dangerous things!"

"That's not fair," I retort.

"Don't you dare talk to me about fair! How long have you known you were going to marry him?" she questions.

My stomach flips.

"Well?" she pushes.

My mouth turns dry. "A few weeks. Not too long."

"Not too long? You've been dating a Petrov behind my back and knew you were going to marry him for a few weeks yet said nothing to me!" she accuses.

"Why? So you could try to convince me not to marry him?"

"Damn right! How could you do this?" she asks again.

I shut my mouth, realizing I'm only digging a deeper hole. Nothing I have said makes any sense to her, and it shouldn't. I can't tell her the truth, so I don't know how to navigate this.

Minutes pass, and it only makes her more infuriated. She lowers her voice, warning, "You've stepped into a snake pit. You cannot stay in it."

I don't answer. Turning toward the window, I try to figure out what I can and can't say to her so I don't break any Underworld rules.

"You're getting divorced," she insists. "I don't care what you think is between the two of you. This marriage is over."

I snap my head toward her, declaring, "I'm not getting a divorce!"

"You are!"

"I'm not!"

Dante flings the door open, sits next to Mom, and slams the door.

The hairs on my arms rise. I look back out the window, feeling like I can't breathe.

In a disappointed tone, he states, "I never thought you'd do something like this, Fiona."

I don't answer, keeping my focus on the glass, hating the position I'm in.

Fucking Sean. It figures he'd leave me high and dry after causing this situation.

Mom scolds, "Don't you dare ignore Dante!"

I blurt out, "It's none of his business."

"None of my business? You've married the devil, and now his men are pulling recording devices out of our home!" Dante booms.

"And whose fault is that, huh?" I hurl back.

"Fiona!" Mom reprimands.

I cross my arms, asserting, "No. I won't take the blame for this one. You have holes in your security. That's not on me. At least Kirill is telling you about them and fixing it. Maybe you should say thank you to him."

"Thank a Petrov?" Dante seethes.

"Yes. Thank my husband," I add, pissed at this entire situation. I'm not going to allow them to disrespect Kirill.

They glare more daggers at me, so I return to staring out the window.

Time passes slowly. There's finally a knock on the glass.

Dante opens the door.

Patrick informs us, "You're free to go upstairs."

"How many did you find?" Dante asks.

"Eight."

"Eight?" Mom frets.

Dante clenches his jaw, gets out, then reaches in for Mom. She takes his hand and slides out. I follow, and we get into the elevator.

The ride upstairs is just as tense. Relief hits me when the doors open. I brush past them, happy to be out of the small box, inhale the fresh air, and continue into the main living area.

Dante tells Mom, "I need to deal with security. I'll be back later." He kisses Mom on the cheek and then turns to me. "Fiona, as angry as I am with you, I need to ensure you're okay. Did he do anything to you? Did he..." Dante swallows hard.

Appalled, I claim, "No! Stop insinuating Kirill is a vile man. Just because he's a Petrov doesn't mean that he does the things that his family members do."

Dante's eyes narrow.

Mom puts her hand on his arm. "Go take care of security."

He hesitates.

She adds, "Please go. I need to speak with Fiona alone."

He gives me a disappointed look, shakes his head again, and disappears.

I go over to the window and cross my arms, staring out at the blinking lights of the city.

Mom steps next to me, repeating the same question. "How did this happen, Fiona?"

I close my eyes, wishing this were a bad dream I could wake up from. I knew it wouldn't be pretty, but this is worse than I imagined.

She pushes, her voice turning emotional again, "Fiona, how did you end up married to a Petrov?"

I open my eyes. "Mom, there are things I can't tell you. I wish I could, but I can't."

Her expression morphs from one of confusion and concern to one of anger. "Don't you dare use the same tired rhetoric Sean and Zara used on me."

I'm assaulted by another wave of guilt. When they initially got married and couldn't tell me anything, I was hurt like Mom. Now, things make sense, even though I still have a thousand questions running through my mind about The Underworld and the intricate workings of the secret organization my father created.

Mom warns, "I mean it, Fiona."

I spin away from her, feeling hot and needing space. I walk across the room, remove my coat, and put it on the couch. I slip into the kitchen and say, "I'm having a glass of wine. Do you want one?" even though I assume it's past midnight.

She doesn't answer.

"Yes or no?" I call out as I grab two glasses.

She paces the penthouse.

My stomach flips faster. I grab a bottle of red, fill both glasses, and go back into the main area. I hold a glass out to her. " Here. Let's have a drink."

Her eyes widen, and the color drains from her face.

A shiver runs down my spine. "Why are you looking at me like that?"

Her gaze fixes on my neck. Her voice quivers when she asks, "Why do you have plastic wrap on your neck?"

My pulse skyrockets. I reach up and touch the plastic.

Mom's voice goes hollow. "Why would you do that to your neck?" She doesn't have to see it to know what's there. She knows what I did based on what Zara did to her own neck.

I swallow the lump in my throat, unsure how to respond.

She steps behind me and moves my hair, gasping. I don't have to look at her to know tears are falling from her eyes. She sobs, "What is with my children? Are you doing this to have your father haunt me? Is that what you want?"

I've never felt so bad in my life. I turn, replying, "No, Mom. Of course not."

"Then why would you, Sean, and Zara do this? I don't understand, and I want answers," she demands.

I open my mouth, but nothing comes out.

She steps closer, closing the gap between us, and seethes, "Don't tell me you did this as a tribute to your father."

I lie. "I did. Just like Sean and Zara. Why is it such a big deal?"

Shocked at my response, she points out, "You were just as disgusted as I was when you saw what they did to themselves."

I shrug, attempting to play it off as not a big deal. "Yeah, but they healed. It looks cool on them."

"It does not," she cries out as more tears stain her cheeks.

I lift my chin and square my shoulders. "You can't blame us for wanting a permanent reminder of something our father created."

"Like hell I can't," she shrieks.

I cross my arms. "It is what it is, Mom. Let it go."

She glares at me. "I don't understand this, Fiona. You, of all people—you're levelheaded. Why would you run off and marry a Petrov? And he's nothing like the type of guy you normally date! I don't understand any of this."

I hate that I can't tell her everything, but I know I can't.

Mom adds, "You have to get this marriage annulled tomorrow. I'll call Kora. She'll know what to do."

"No. I told you I'm not divorcing Kirill!" I cry out.

Disgust fills her expression. "What do you mean 'no'? You cannot be married to a Petrov. You know this."

"Mom, I'm not divorcing him. Not now or in the future," I insist.

"I don't get it, Fiona. What does he have over you?" she asks with concern.

"He doesn't have anything over me," I quickly reply.

"He has to. You would never date a man like him," she claims.

Angrily, I reply, "Don't ever speak ill of my husband again."

She glares at me.

I take a sip of wine and pace the room, trying to calm down, knowing this isn't my mom's fault. I would be confused and upset too if I were in her position, but I'm also not going to stand here while she talks badly about Kirill.

She says, "You married a man you can't even take anywhere."

"What does that mean?"

She scoffs. "He has a scar on his face. And why do you think that is, Fiona?"

I turn to face her, blurting out, "Because his own father and uncles sliced his face because he wouldn't rape a woman. That's why, Mom."

Her eyes widen and her face pales.

My heart races so fast that I feel ill.

Mom's shock glares hotter. Her lips tremble, and her face turns green. She puts her hand on her stomach.

The urge to protect Kirill overtakes me. I add, "Now you know what happened, but don't go spreading it around. It's not anyone's business but his, and now mine since I'm his wife," still angry that she dared talk about his scar.

She can barely speak. "His father and uncles did it to him?"

"Yes."

Her wineglass falls out of her hand. It shatters into shards on the floor.

"Mom!"

She steps over to the couch and sits down, staring at the floor, shaking harder.

New dread fills me. I sit next to her, asking, "What's wrong?"

She slowly looks at me, her voice quavering. "How old is he?"

I shrug. "I don't know. Forty-five, maybe."

I expect her to scold me for not knowing how old my own husband is, but she's too distraught. It's like I can see the wheels in her mind turning, so I wait.

Time drags and drags until she swallows hard. She grips her knees and then looks at me. "Your father had nightmares. They kept occurring and wouldn't stop. One night, he was drunk. He woke up from a nightmare and was still intoxicated. He was so upset. He told me about the Petrov boy whose family tried to destroy him. Did he really..." She swallows hard again, staring at me.

I quietly finish her sentence, "Did he really know Dad?"

She nods, her eyes overflowing with tears.

I try to think about whether I'm allowed to tell her, but I no longer care. I can't lie to her about everything. "Yes, Dad knew him. He was the one who saved him, Mom. So, he may have the Petrov name, but he's not like them. If he were, he wouldn't have lived his entire life since he was eighteen with scars all over his face and body."

She silently looks at me, as if she's seeing a ghost.

I finally beg, "Mom, say something, please." I put my hand on hers.

She looks at it. Then, a new shock fills her features.

The pit in my stomach grows.

She grabs my hand and examines my ring. "This can't be yours."

I yank my hand away, quickly stating, "Of course it is."

An ocean of tears streams down her face. She sobs, "How is it possible, Fiona?"

I hesitate to ask, "How is what possible?" My chest tightens.

Kirill told me she didn't know about the ring, so why is she telling me it's not mine?

She scrunches her face, as if in pain, declaring, "Your father designed a ring just like that. It was..." She looks away, and her entire body shakes.

Shame and guilt swirl so fast in me that I feel nauseous. I stay quiet, hating myself for allowing Kirill to give this to me but also not seeing how I couldn't have kept it.

She finishes, "Your father said he would make it for me when we renewed our vows." She grabs my hand again, and peers at it closer, adding, "It looks just like it, Fiona."

I open my mouth, and again, nothing comes out.

She stares at me with questions in her expression that I want to answer but can't. I finally offer, "I'm sorry this reminds you of the ring."

She insists, "It's exactly what he designed. I was in love with marquise-cut stones. I still am, but I swore I'd never wear one after your father died. And that ring is his design."

"It can't be," I lie, feeling more guilt and shame.

"I'll prove it to you." She gets up.

I rise. "Where are you going?"

"Just give me a minute," she says, entering her office.

I follow her.

She sits down behind the desk and turns on the computer. "I know that's the same ring he designed."

"Mom, you're being dramatic," I accuse, and immediately feel horrible for saying it.

Her computer boots up. She clicks the mouse a few times and then sits back. She points at the screen. "There. Look."

My hands go clammy. I cautiously step behind her, and it feels like my heart's squeezing. There's a photo of a drawing, and it looks exactly like my ring.

I ask, "Why is that on your computer?"

She admits, "This is the file of all your dad's drawings. I scanned the originals. Those are in the safe in New York."

"Why did you scan them?" I question.

She shrugs. "I don't know, but I did. They were one of the few things I kept of your father's."

"What else is on there?" I ask.

Her face darkens. She clicks a button and turns off her computer.

"Nothing."

"Mom?"

"Nothing is on there that you need to know about. Some things are meant to be private between your dad and me, and that's how it'll stay. Understand?" she asserts.

I hold my hands up. "Okay. Sorry. I didn't mean to upset you further."

She rises and puts her hand on her hip, pointing at me. "I want to know how you got that ring."

"Kirill gave it to me."

Her eyes narrow. "Yes, I understand that, but how did he get it?"

"Mom, it's just a ring."

"It's not just a ring, Fiona."

I take it off, and my finger feels empty. It's the first time I've removed it since Kirill sent it to me. I hold it out to her. "Do you want it? You can have it if you need it that much."

She stares at it and then lifts her gaze back to my face.

More pain hits me. I hate doing this to her. In all reality, it is her ring, but I continue to push. "Take it, Mom. If you need it that badly and want it, then take it."

She stares at it one more time and then shakes her head. "No, I'm not taking your ring. But that's your father's design."

Relieved she won't take it, I put it back on my finger, softening my voice and sincerely apologizing. "I'm sorry I've caused you pain."

"Caused me pain? Fiona, what did you think would happen? You married a Petrov. This isn't the same as Sean and Zara running off and getting married. That was bad enough, but this?" She shakes her head at me in disappointment.

"Mom—"

"No, Fiona. This isn't something you can just do and expect everyone to turn a blind eye at."

Kirill's Russian accent sounds from the doorway. "I think we owe you some answers, Bridget."

I spin toward him, and my heart pounds harder. I'm so relieved he's here.

He pins his gaze on Mom and declares, "I think it's best if we go sit down."

She hesitates, then brushes past him and enters the main room just as Dante walks through the door.

He booms, "How did you get in here?"

Kirill states, "You have holes in your security. I told you this."

"I thought your security was here to fill those holes," Dante accuses.

Kirill nods. "They are, and that's how I got in. And as I said, I'll ensure you understand where the holes in your security are, but not tonight. Right now, we need to discuss other matters."

Dante clenches his jaw with hatred in his dark eyes.

"We should get going," I say, feeling like I need a break from this conversation.

"No, he owes me answers," Mom seethes.

The anxiety in me grows.

Kirill motions to the couch. "Please, sit down. Everyone."

Mom sits, and Dante takes the seat beside her.

I sit on the love seat, and Kirill sits next to me. I put my hand on his thigh.

Mom's gaze shoots to my hand, then back at me.

The horrible feeling fills me again.

Kirill starts, "What I'm about to tell you needs to stay in this room, and until I have full agreement on that, I cannot disclose anything."

Mom nervously glances at Dante.

Kirill continues. "I mean it. No Moreno, O'Connor, O'Malley, or Ivanov can know what I will disclose to you. If you do share this information, your daughter's life will be at stake."

Mom gasps.

Dante warns, "Don't you dare sit in my house and threaten Fiona!"

"He's not!" I cry out.

Kirill squeezes my hand. "I will never harm your daughter. I will only protect her. But there will be times when there are threats. I won't do anything to intentionally put her in harm's way. So if you want answers, you need to promise me. Otherwise, tell me you don't want me to go further."

Tension builds again.

Dante finally grabs Mom's hand and says, "You have our word."

Kirill adds, "I don't even want you talking to Sean and Zara about this. You never know who's listening."

"This is my house. No one's listening now that the devices were removed. I will ensure it stays that way," Dante proclaims.

Kirill shakes his head. "With all due respect—"

"You have holes, Dante. You don't know who's listening," I interject.

He grinds his molars, his cheeks turning red.

Kirill continues, "As of this moment, your place is private. So it's now or never. You can agree that what I tell you will never leave this room, and I can fill you in on a few things, or Fiona and I will get up and leave. It's up to you."

Blood pounds between my ears.

Mom lifts her chin, meeting Kirill's gaze. She vows, "You have my word. Now, tell me."

Kirill

Chapter
TWENTY-TWO

The air in the room turns thicker. I rack my mind, putting information into categories of what I can reveal and what I can't. There's a razor-thin line between The Underworld's secrets and the truth about why Fiona's father meant so much to me.

It isn't an option for Bridget to understand I won't harm her daughter and that I have the utmost respect for her deceased husband. And Fiona has to maintain her relationship with her family. I won't be able to live with myself if it crumbles.

Dante sneers at me, ordering, "Start talking."

I resist the urge to tell him off. I put my hand over Fiona's, reminding myself again that this is her family. They can't hate me, even though I'm unsure if it will ever be possible for them to like me.

No matter what, I'm a Petrov. According to The Underworld's terms, Fiona has to change her last name. She'll bear a name that represents everything they despise.

I push my instincts away, and focus on Bridget, admitting, "I knew your husband very well."

Bridget's expression hardens as she grips Dante's hand.

"I'm only alive because of him. He saved me twice, not just once. So when I tell you I have nothing but respect for him and your children, I'm not lying." The claw in my stomach reappears.

Bridget maintains the same look, but fear has crept into her eyes as well.

I glance at Fiona, and she stares at me nervously.

I continue, "My father and my uncles tried to kill me. They did the damage to my body."

Bridget swallows hard, with a swirl of disgust and pity on her expression.

I hate it. I should be used to it by now, but I'm not. My stomach twists, and I force myself to go on. "They took a knife and not only scarred me on my face but my entire body. Your husband is the one who found me."

Bridget asks, "Why would Sean be the one to find you?"

"I'm sorry. There are certain things I cannot tell you."

She seethes, "Then don't sit here and act like my husband was a traitor."

I hold my hands in the air. "Whoa. Your husband was not a traitor. He was far from it, and I didn't insinuate anything of the sort."

"Didn't you?" she questions.

Fiona's relationship with her family is at stake, I remind myself.

I resist the urge to lash out, shaking my head, and firmly reiterate, "No, I didn't. If you took it that way, again, I apologize."

Bridget blinks hard, and Dante slides his arm around her, as if to protect her from me. But the truth will always hurt, no matter what I say. Sean was her husband and the father of her children; she loved him. There's always been mystery around what he was involved in that led to his death, and I wish I could clarify it for her, but I can't. My loyalty to The Underworld won't allow me to break my vows.

So I decide what I can tell her, then continue. "Your husband made sure I was okay. I was still young, only eighteen...barely a man."

"Yes, I already know this," she states.

Surprised, I swallow hard, fighting emotions that crawl up whenever I revisit the past and the horror of what my own family did to me. I ask, "He told you about me?"

Something passes in her expression and she nods. "Yes."

Dante asks, "How did Sean even find you?"

"I told you I can't disclose that information. If I do, Fiona will be in harm's way, and neither of us wants that, correct?" I challenge.

He stays silent, intensifying his scowl.

Bridget snaps, "Stop using my daughter as a reason for you not to tell me. I want to know what Sean was involved in that would put him in a position to save a Petrov!"

I sigh.

Fiona grumbles, "Mom. He's not using me as an excuse."

Bridget's eyes narrow. "What do you know about your father that you aren't telling me?"

Fiona shuts her mouth and turns her greens on me.

I squeeze her hand tighter and offer, "There are things you'll never know about, and I'm sorry it has to be that way."

"But yet my children can know?" Bridget accuses.

"I know this is hard—"

"You have no idea what's hard," she interjects, her voice shaking.

Dante tugs her closer.

My heart pounds harder. Guilt floods me. It's a cruel reality Bridget was dealt all those years ago and now has to relive.

A tense silence fills the air.

What am I trying to say to her anyway?

There's not a lot I can tell her.

She glances at our hands and questions, "Did you steal my husband's drawing?"

"His drawing?" I glance down, and Fiona's diamond ring glints back at me brightly. My stomach flips faster. I meet Bridget's eyes, adding, "Oh, I see."

Her lips quiver.

Every question she wants answers to involves The Underworld, but my conscience won't let me sit here and continue to gaslight her. I remind myself that my men checked Dante's penthouse. They claim no recording devices remain.

It was a quick sweep.

Can I still trust the team?

Who can I trust right now besides Fiona, Sean, and Zara?

Valentina.

Maybe Brax, as he's like a brother to Sean and Fiona.

Bridget accuses, "You can't even deny the ring is Sean's design."

Fiona starts, "Mom, please—"

"No, I know that ring," she claims, and a wave of pain crosses her expression.

Why did I give it to Fiona?

I should have anticipated this.

I didn't know Bridget knew anything about the ring.

Her pain radiates into me, tearing at my heart, so I try to calm her, stating, "Sean gave me a copy of the drawing. I thought it would be a nice gesture for Fiona to have something her father designed. I didn't know it was for you or that you had seen it, or I wouldn't have had it made," I lie, feeling guilty, but knowing Bridget can never know Sean made Fiona's ring for her.

Her face crumples. She turns toward the window, and more tears stream down her cheeks.

Dante's eyes darken to another level. His hatred burns right at me.

"Mom, I'm sorry you're hurt. The last thing I ever wanted to do was hurt you," Fiona cries.

Bridget glances back, sniffles, and lifts her chin, squaring her shoulders just like Fiona does. With a new strength in her voice, she accuses, "You have my husband's skull branded on your hand, and now you forced my daughter to get one on her neck."

"He didn't force me," Fiona grinds out.

"It's okay," I say to her in a gentle voice.

She shakes her head, "No, it's not. You didn't force me. I chose to get it. It's not fair for you to get blamed for things I chose to do on my own."

Every good emotion I've ever had about my wife exponentially grows in that moment. I don't know why she finds it so easy to stand up for me or act like there's no reason not to love me, even though I know it's too soon for her to feel that deep emotion.

Love.

What am I thinking?

Bridget pins her wet gaze on me. "I want to know why my children wear Sean's mark. I'm not stupid. The men have it branded on their hands and the women on their necks. What was he a part of, and what have you gotten my daughter into?"

My chest tightens. Fiona fibs, "He hasn't gotten me into anything."

I toss her a pleading look to stop talking. I'd rather do the lying here. So I quickly add, "It was a tribute to your husband and nothing more."

"Bullshit," Bridget snaps.

I remain silent, wondering how we'll ever get to a point when I can't tell the truth and she knows I'm lying.

Dante snarls, "If you're going to sit here and lie to us, there's no point talking."

I state, "I'm trying to tell you what I can. And you should know the most important thing in all of this."

Bridget scoffs. "What's that?"

"Your daughter will always be protected. I will die making sure no one ever touches her."

"No one but you?" Bridget hurls out in a mix of disgust, horror, and fear.

It's so intense it almost cripples me.

She orders, "You need to divorce my daughter. This marriage cannot become public, and you know it."

The air in my lungs turns stale. I reply, "I'm sorry, but I won't ever do such a thing."

Dante roars, "You know a Petrov cannot be married to an O'Malley!"

Frustrated, I rub my hand over my face and release an exasperated breath. "I know this is hard for you."

Bridget cries out, "Don't you say that to me. What your family has done to..." She stops and looks away.

The tension grows thicker.

I've never felt so guilty or horrible. I know the role my family played in Sean's demise and what they did to her, and it's haunted me since it happened. I've always blamed myself for not knowing about it so I could have tried to prevent it.

Fiona questions, "Done to whom or what?"

I look at her, ordering, "Leave it."

She jerks her head back and glares at me. I can't blame her. I told her there would be no more secrets, but I would rather die than tell her what I know.

Bridget's voice shakes. She barely gets out, "You know everything?"

I clench my jaw, meeting her gaze.

Horror, shame, and agony fill her expression.

Dante barks, "Enough of this. Whose side are you on, Fiona?"

Her hand trembles.

I grip it and answer for her, stating, "She's not on any side. She's the same person she was before she married me."

"She married a Petrov," Dante says with disgust.

"Yes, we've already established that fact, and we're going to all have to get over it," I claim.

Dante roars, "Get over it? You don't get over it."

My stomach flips. Before I can think, I hurl, "Then you're going to disown Fiona?"

A tense, disturbing silence fills the room.

Fiona rises, and her voice quivers. "I think I know the answer to that question. Don't worry, Dante, you won't have to deal with me now that I'm a Petrov." She turns to me. "Let's go."

I rise. "Fiona, we can't leave like this."

"I said I want to go. They've made their position clear," she firmly asserts.

I glance at Bridget, declaring, "You cannot disown your daughter."

Her gaze darts between Dante and Fiona. Her mouth hangs open, and no words come out. Tears drip off her chin.

Dante backtracks. "I didn't say we're disowning her."

A bit of relief fills me. I nod. "That's good."

Fiona hurls, "You might as well have. And since I'm not divorcing my husband, I guess there's clearly nothing left to say between us."

"Fiona—" I start.

"No. Let's go, Kirill," she demands, then grabs her coat and marches toward the front door.

Bridget calls out, "Fiona!"

She spins back to snarl at her mother, "What? I'm not going to stand here and feel bad for marrying Kirill. He's as much of a victim as everybody else, and you know it because Dad told you about it. So why don't you think about that instead of what all the other Petrovs do, because he's not one of them!"

"You're going to have his last name. There are consequences," Dante blurts out.

Fiona glares daggers at him, spouting, "You're not my father, so stay out of this."

The color drains from his face, and shock and hurt explode over his features.

"Fiona!" Bridget exclaims.

I interject, "I think we need to discuss things at a different time. This is getting too heated."

A sad, confused, fearful, and upset Bridget stares at me.

"We will discuss this at another time," I assure her. "I'm sorry we've upset you and caused you pain. Truly, I am."

She looks at me as if she's not sure what to believe.

I guide Fiona into the foyer and shut the door. I push the button to the elevator. The doors open, we step inside, and I press the button.

With tears falling, she claims, "They're never going to forgive me."

I tug her into me and hold her head to my chest, kissing the top of it, murmuring, "I'm sorry. We need to give them time to process this."

She pushes away from me, shaking her head. "No. You don't understand. They are never going to forgive me, and they have no other option except to disown me."

"Don't say that."

"It's true."

"No, it's not. We'll work through this. It will just take time," I insist.

She puts her hand over her face.

I tug her back into me, and she sobs as the elevator descends.

The doors open on the garage level. We exit and get into the SUV. We don't speak during the short drive, and we get out when the driver pulls up next to the elevator in the parking garage of my building.

It's slow as molasses like the broken one, which I'm still shocked hasn't been fixed. I vow to make good on some of my threats.

The doors finally open. I lead Fiona into the foyer and open the door to the main penthouse. My nerves reappear, and I say, "After you, my bride."

She obeys, stepping into the room and then glancing around. My heart races. I quickly state, "We can decorate it however you want."

She turns to me, and whispers, "This place is beautiful."

"You like it?" I question in surprise.

She glances around again, answering, "Yes. What wouldn't I love?"

Relief fills me. I admit, "I don't know, but I want you to feel like this is your home because it is now."

She steps forward and wraps her arms around my neck. "It's beautiful. And I'm sorry that you had to go through that." She kisses me on the lips.

I kiss her back, then retreat, assuring, "You don't have to say you're sorry. Your family is hurt, but I promise you, we will figure this out with them."

A sad look crosses her expression. "I don't know, Kirill, but I'm tired. Where's the bedroom?" She releases me and steps back.

I take her hand and walk her through the penthouse and into the bedroom.

She goes to the side of the bed, strips off her clothes, and slips under the sheets. She questions, "Are you coming to bed?"

I swear there's a hopeful look in her eyes, but I'm probably imagining it, so I silently scold myself. I reply, "I have a few things I need to do. I'll be in soon."

"Okay." She curls into the pillow.

I lean down, kiss her head, and shut the bedroom door. I call my head of security.

Draco answers, "Sir?"

"Are there any cameras or devices remaining in my house?"

"No, sir. We found four. Then we did another scan, but nothing else turned up."

"You're sure no one's watching us or listening?" I ask, feeling paranoid.

"Yes, sir." His tone is sure.

"Okay." I hang up and pace around the penthouse, trying to figure out how to get Fiona's family to come around. The last thing Sean O'Malley would've wanted was for his daughter not to speak to Bridget or even Dante.

Then, another realization hits me. A bigger problem looms.

I go into my office, turn on the computer, and open the dark web. I go into The Underworld chat room with the Royal Council. It's comprised of thirteen Omni, not all 666 that hold seats at the table. I glance at the calendar of moon phases and then type.

Me: Meeting on waning gibbous.

I send the message and sit back, worrying about how to protect Fiona, who the traitor is within The Underworld and if it's an Omni, and how to get Fiona back in good graces with her family.

Fiona

Chapter
TWENTY-THREE

The scents of leather, rosewater, saffron, and jasmine flare around me.

Kirill.

I smile, curl into him, then open and close my eyelids a few times. It's still dark in the room, but something tells me it's later in the day. I kiss the scar on the back of his shoulder, then trace it with my finger.

He stirs, glancing over at me with furrowed brows. In a gravelly tone, he asks, "Everything okay?"

"Mm-hmm." I lean closer, pressing my lips against his.

He turns over to face me, sliding his hand through my hair and gripping it tight.

I slide my tongue deeper into his mouth, the ache growing between my thighs.

He groans, and his erection presses against my leg.

I murmur, "How's my husband?"

His lips twitch. "I don't have any complaints right now."

I smirk. "No?"

"Nope." He kisses me deeper.

"What about now?" I tease, sliding on top of him and then sinking over his erection.

"Fuck, Fiona," he mumbles against my lips, adding, "You're going to make me get used to waking up like this."

I softly giggle and then dig my knees into the mattress on either side of him, taking as much of him inside me as possible. I whimper at the stretch and fullness.

He slides his hand to the curve of my breast, teasing my nipple, then moving it higher until it's brushing my throat.

Tingles explode down my spine. I warn, "Don't torture me."

One finger at a time pushes against my clavicle, as if it's a row of piano keys. He releases his hand in my hair and grabs my hip, moving me faster over him.

"Yes," I breathe, returning to his lips, feeling my body light up.

"So fucking wet, little bird," he says, then presses harder against my neck.

I moan, and a quiver runs to my core.

Retreating from our kiss, he studies me, pressing one finger at a time harder than before.

"Please," I beg, pinning him with a challenging, desperate stare.

A flush crawls up his cheeks. He grits his teeth, continuing to study me with curiosity, pressing his fingers harder and thrusting deeper.

Tingles explode in all my cells, and adrenaline pools to the point I feel like I can't handle it. "Kirill! Please," I beg, needing the rush of the high.

He continues to play my neck like a piano, banging on the keys, studying me more intensely as his cock slides faster against my walls, tormenting me further.

"Kirill," I choke out.

"Patience, my queen," he warns, slowing his thrusts.

My cells buzz with life. I close my eyes, begging, "Please. I-I need it."

"Open your eyes," he orders.

I obey.

He tilts his head, torturing me.

A wave of heat rolls over me, and sweat beads on my skin. I'm buzzing with anticipation as I attempt to move faster.

He doesn't let me, holding my hip firmly, taunting, "A queen obeys her king, little bird. You'll come slowly at first." He strokes his thumb over my pulse, gliding his cock in and out of me at a controlled speed.

"Please," I plead, on the verge of euphoria.

"Shh. Your king has you," he murmurs, kneading my pulse.

The adrenaline reaches its limit, slowly flooding my entire existence until I'm convulsing. My eyes roll, and I cry out, "I-I...oh God!" I tip my head back, but it can't move far in his grasp.

"Beautiful bride," he praises, keeping steady.

His scent grows thicker, enveloping me until there's no boundary between us. The high wanes, and he releases his grip on my hip, bringing his hand to the other side of my neck.

I moan, moving faster over his cock, chasing my orgasm. The desire intensifies, and the anticipation of all ten fingers wrapping around me tighter taunts me.

He grunts, his blues turning darker.

"Do it," I order.

His eyes narrow. He thrusts so hard, I'm sure he's inside my stomach, and his fingers curl around my neck, cutting off a portion of my air supply.

Incoherent, muffled sounds fill the air, and I realize they're mine. Zings ricochet in my core.

He squeezes so hard the remaining oxygen disappears. He forces my pussy over him by pushing me down using the heels of his hands on my collarbone just as he thrusts the hardest yet.

A rush of dopamine surges through me, making me see white, then black. My entire body soars, and it's like I'm looking down and seeing us.

He flips me onto my back, loosens his grip on my neck, and brings his lips to my ears, continuing to thrust inside me, demanding, "Come back to me, little bird."

I flutter my eyelids several times and then choke, gasping for air.

"That's it," he praises, kissing my lobe, his hot breath adding to the chaos.

I gather as much air as possible and turn my head. I flick my tongue back into his mouth, not satiated, wanting more.

He doesn't stop thrusting, and his sweat merges with mine. He takes my wrists and pins them over my head. His other hand stays on my throat.

Another wave of endorphins crashes through me. I order, "Again."

His lips twitch against mine. He scolds, "So greedy."

"Yes. I'm your greedy wife. Now, please," I beg.

He pulls his head back, pinning his blues on mine, taking shallow breaths. His pointer finger strokes my chin. He grits something in Russian, and his erection thickens.

"Kirill," I shriek just before he cuts my oxygen off. A deluge of euphoria hits me. Convulsions overpower me, and I violently thrash against him.

His guttural sounds echo around us, and I grip the gold bars of the headboard.

The white stars in my vision turn to black. The out-of-body experience resurfaces, and I don't know how long I'm out.

He sharply barks, "Come on, Fiona. Look at me."

I flutter my eyelids until he comes back into focus just in time for him to growl, "Jesus fucking Christ, Fiona," as he pumps his seed deep into me, filling me and giving me another shot of my high.

He collapses over me, releases my wrists, and we both breathe hard. Our chests push together, and our bodies lie in a pool of arousal. When I can finally breathe, I slide my hand into his hair and kiss him near his ear.

He moves his head, then rolls over, tugging me with him, and stares at me in question.

"What's wrong?" I ask.

He hesitates and shakes his head. "Nothing's wrong, little bird. Nothing."

"Then why are you looking at me like that?"

He softly smiles. "I don't know. I guess I'm happy."

I grin, chirping, "Because of me?"

He chuckles. "Of course it's because of you. Why else would I be happy?"

I bite on my lip.

He chuckles again and strokes my ass cheek. "What do you want to do today? And I promise I'll make it up to you for our hijacked honeymoon."

"Aw, that's sweet of you," I tease.

His tone is laced with remorse when he says, "I'm serious, Fiona. I feel really bad. We didn't get to stop at any of the places that you wanted."

"It's okay. Plus, it's not your fault. Besides, you said we can go on the yacht anytime, right?"

He nods. "Yes, of course."

I kiss him on the neck. "Okay, then. We'll go yachting at a different time. Speaking of time, what time do you think it is?"

He shrugs. "Probably afternoon, I would think."

"When did you come to bed?"

"I don't know. It was late."

"You probably need more sleep," I suggest.

He sits up and turns, planting his feet on the floor. "No, I'm good. And we have some things we need to take care of today."

"What?"

He pulls me onto his lap and pushes my hair behind my ear. "I think you need to go talk to your boss."

I groan. "And we were having such a nice day."

"No time like the present," he states.

I tilt my head, asking, "Why do you always say that?"

"Because it's better to get through things than to let them fester. Once it's done and over, it's over. Stalling only causes drama," he declares.

I think about what he said and then nod. "You're right."

"Then you want me to take you to work so you can talk to Skylar?" He arches his eyebrows.

I slide off him and mumble, "No time like the present. I better shower."

We shower, and he reveals a vanity full of makeup, hair tools, and perfumes. Another closet, even more amazing than the one on the yacht, displays more designer clothes. I gush, "You really do know how to spoil a girl, don't you?"

He beams, and I decide I really like it when he looks happy. He kisses me on the lips and states, "I'll spoil you all day, every day if you let me."

"Don't tease a girl," I chirp, feeling as happy as he looks. But the feeling doesn't last long.

The issues with Skylar and Adrian aren't going to be easy to work through, and I'm unsure what to expect. But Kirill is right. It's better to figure it out now rather than avoid it.

We finish getting dressed, leave the building, and slide into Kirill's SUV. His driver takes us to Skylar's office and pulls up to the curb.

Kirill asks, "Do you want me to go in with you?"

I think about it for a moment, then shake my head. "It's probably best if I go alone for the moment."

"Okay, I'm here if you need me," he states.

"Thanks." I grab the back of his head and kiss him.

He returns my affection, then groans, murmuring against my lips, "You're not motivating me to let you out of the car."

I softly laugh. "Then let's stay inside and have fun." I reach for his erection.

He grabs my hand, retreats from our kisses, and sternly declares, "Rain check."

"Ugh, you're no fun."

He winks, gets out of the SUV, and reaches in to help me out.

From behind us, I hear Adrian roar, "You have a lot of fucking nerve!" He then spits out a bunch of Russian.

My pulse goes haywire as I jump out of the SUV.

Kirill turns to face him, claiming, "I'm not here for trouble."

Adrian pins his seething, icy-blue eyes on me, then Kirill, snarling, "Petrovs are not welcome here."

"It's a city street. You don't own it," Kirill growls.

Adrian points at him and warns, "Don't you come near my wife's office ever again."

"Adrian!" I shout, stepping between them.

He scowls at me. "How could you, Fiona?"

Flooded with guilt, I offer, "Adrian, let's go inside and talk."

"Adrian," Skylar frets as she rushes outside.

"Dad," Blue cries out, hot on her mom's heels.

He doesn't look at them, just reaches over me, and jabs his finger into Kirill's chest, threatening, "If you come here again, I will kill you."

I push at his chest. "Adrian, stop."

He puts his hand on my arm. "Fiona—"

"Don't you touch my wife," Kirill shouts, grabbing me and moving me behind him.

Skylar steps between them, facing Adrian. She puts her hand on his cheek. "Adrian, go inside, please."

"He's not to be here," he seethes, hatred coming off him in waves.

"Dad, please come inside," Blue pleads.

He keeps his gaze pinned on Kirill, gritting out, "You aren't welcome here or anywhere near my family."

"Adrian, go inside," Skylar orders again.

I face Kirill. "Please, get into the SUV."

He stares at me.

"Please," I beg.

He hesitates, then points at Adrian, reiterating, "I'm not here for trouble."

"But you're here, aren't you, Petrov?" Adrian spits.

Kirill's eyes light up.

"Inside!" I shout, opening the door, afraid that Adrian and Kirill will get physical.

Kirill glances at me.

"Please," I plead.

He takes a deep breath, tosses another scowl at Adrian, then tells Skylar, "I'm sorry for the disruption. It was not my intention."

She gapes at him.

"Do not speak to my wife!" Adrian bellows.

I push Kirill toward the SUV.

He looks at me again.

"Please," I desperately repeat.

He finally caves and slides inside.

I shut the door, asserting, "Let's go inside and talk."

"So it's true? You married a Petrov?" Adrian seethes.

"Adrian," Skylar warns.

"No. She doesn't get to marry a Petrov and then come here. How could you?" he accuses, as if I've betrayed him.

Tears fill my eyes. "Adrian, please. Let's talk."

"No. How could you do this, Fiona?" he barks.

"Dad, let's go inside," Blue tries.

He spins and points to the door. "Get inside. Now, Blue."

"Dad—"

"I said to get inside. There's a Petrov around. Get inside. Now," he roars.

"Do what he says," Skylar orders.

Blue whines, "I'm not a kid."

"Get inside," Adrian shouts.

"Now," Skylar insists.

Blue shakes her head and stomps off into the building.

"How dare you bring him around my family," Adrian scolds. "And consider your employment here over."

"Adrian!" Skylar reprimands.

"No. We've talked about this, and I'm not changing my mind. I don't care how long she's worked for you or who her mother is. I will not tolerate Petrovs around my family," Adrian declares.

My insides quiver. "What are you saying?"

His gaze darkens. "What do you think I'm saying? Petrovs are not welcome here. That includes your husband, and you, if that's who you now are."

"I'm still the same person," I cry out.

"No. When you decided to marry a Petrov, you decided whose side you're on," he claims.

"Adrian, please go inside," Skylar repeats.

More anger fills his expression. "And leave you out here with a Petrov? Never." He moves Skylar behind him and then turns to her. "Go inside."

"I'm not going inside until you come with me," she says.

"I mean it, Skylar. Go inside."

She shakes her head. "No. Adrian, you're not staying out here. Let's all go inside. Fiona's right. We need to talk."

"She's not coming in the office ever again unless she divorces him and admits what a mistake this is."

Skylar's eyes widen. She looks at me helplessly.

I reach for the car to steady myself, my eyes watering and my body trembling. I try again. "Adrian, please. Let's go inside and talk."

"I'm sorry, Fiona. We've loved you like a daughter, but I will not stand for Petrovs to be anywhere near my family, especially after all they've done," he says, his jaw ticking.

Hurt fills me, but I feel horrible for him as well. I soften my tone and put my hand on his arm. "Adrian, I'm sorry for what happened to Natalia, but Kirill didn't do it. It's not his fault."

He snarls, "They kidnapped and repeatedly raped my sister in a whorehouse and then murdered her. And you want me to let that scumbag inside my wife's place of work?"

My tears fall faster. I beg, "Please. If you just get to know him—"

"I'm never going to get to know a Petrov. Never!"

"I'm sorry, but go home, Fiona. We'll talk later. Adrian, let's go inside," Skylar demands, tugging on him and giving me an *I'm sorry* look.

He looks at her, warning, "I mean it, Skylar. Petrovs will not be near my family."

She nods. "Let's go inside."

He gives me another disgusted look full of disappointment, then makes sure she's in front of him as he guides her inside. Before he disappears, he turns and gives me another heart-wrenching look. Then he slams the door.

I stand there, shaking and sobbing.

Kirill opens the SUV door, warning, "Don't ever tell me to get in the car again. I will never stand by and watch something like that again."

I look up at him, crying harder.

He tugs me into him, adding, "You will not be treated this way."

Feeling like I deserved Adrian's treatment, and still trying to process everything that just happened, I manage to choke out, "It's okay."

"Come, my queen. Let's go," he says.

Not knowing what else to do, I get into the SUV.

He slides in beside me and pulls me into his arms.

I sob until we get back to the penthouse. As soon as we step inside, my phone rings.

My stomach curls again. I answer, "Skylar, I'm so sorry."

She sighs. "Fiona, I'm sorry too."

"Am I really fired?" I ask with more tears forming.

A beat of silence follows and then she admits, "I don't know what's going to happen. We have to let the dust settle and then have a proper conversation."

I sniffle, trying to stop a fresh onslaught of tears, my face already a wet mess.

She continues, "I value and love you, but I don't know how to handle this right now."

I don't know how to respond.

She asks, "Are you still there?"

My voice shakes, when I reply, "Y-yes. I'm s-sorry."

"I wish we could talk right now, but Adrian's too upset. But after what they did to his sister, I can't go against him on this. Give me some time to see if I can get him to change his mind, okay?"

"Skylar, it's not fair," I say.

A moment of silence fills the line.

She lowers her voice, asking, "How could you marry a Petrov, Fiona? Knowing what they've done to our families and others..."

"Kirill isn't like that," I insist.

She sighs again. "Fiona, for your sake, I hope you're right, and we're all wrong."

"You are," I tell her.

"Again, I hope you're right. I'll call you when I can." She hangs up.

I stand there, unsure how I'll ever get the people I love to accept my husband for who he is and not for the blood that runs through his veins.

Kirill

Two Weeks Later

Chapter
TWENTY-FOUR

"The sweep produced nothing," Draco announces.

It should relax me, but for some reason, it doesn't. Every day, I have the security team search for recording devices, but they've found nothing since that first check. Even though everything has been clear, the gaping pit in my stomach never closes. Every morning, I wake up and make them check again.

Fiona teased me and said I was paranoid, but I'm not taking any chances.

I address Brax and Sean. "Has anything appeared in the chat rooms?"

Brax shakes his head. "No. But if the Omni finds out I'm hacking their messages, you better make sure you cover my ass."

Sean interjects, "We cover our tracks. No one will know."

I cross my arms, reassuring, "It's a direct order from me. You don't need to worry about it."

Brax grunts. "Spoken from the king who has it all."

I point at him, scolding, "Don't get smart with me."

He grinds his molars, and tension builds between us.

I ask, "Is there a reason you're continuing to worry about this?"

He scoffs. "You have to ask? You know what they'll do to me if they find out."

"No. They won't touch you. I gave you an order," I reiterate.

"To spy on Omni!" he hurls back.

"So you're a scared pussy now?"

He glares at me.

"You're fine. We know how to cover our tracks, and it is an order," Sean states, but Brax doesn't look convinced.

I ask, "You want off this project? You want me to find someone else to help protect the queen?"

His scowl deepens. "Of course not."

"Then shut up about your paranoia."

"I'm not paranoid."

"Aren't you?" I arch my eyebrows.

A moment of tense silence hangs in the air. Neither Brax nor I break our stare.

"There you are," Fiona chirps.

My heart beats harder at the sound of her voice, and I turn. My mood shifts to the happiness I can't seem to escape whenever I see my wife. I reply, "Hey, did you have fun?"

"I did." She beams, stepping closer, then leans down and gives me a chaste kiss on the lips.

"Aw, aren't you too cute?" Zara teases, wheeling the double stroller into the room.

"Ew, come on," Sean grumbles.

I ignore him and ask her, "Did you get anything good?"

Fiona reaches into her coat pockets and wiggles them. "I got something for you. Pick a hand."

Warmth blooms in my chest. It's good to see her smiling. She's been bored for the last few weeks, and depressed over losing her job. I keep telling her she should start her own fashion line, but her loyalty to Skylar runs deep. I can't blame her, and I respect her allegiance, but the tables have turned. If they're going to hold her new last name over her head and take away her career, then she needs to take matters into her own hands.

"Come on, you have to pick," she insists playfully.

I chuckle and point to her right hand. "How about that one?"

She pulls it out and wiggles her fingers. "Oops, wrong hand."

I groan. "I guess I don't get the surprise, then."

"Nope! Pick again." She puts her hand back in her pocket.

I laugh and point to the left one.

Her eyes light up. "Good job!" She pulls out a brown bag. She shakes it in front of my face, adding, "Guess what it is."

Amused, I question, "Is that my favorite oatmeal raisin cookie?"

She beams brighter. "It is." She pulls it out and asks, "Want a bite?"

"Where's my cookie?" Sean questions.

"Yeah. I want one too," Brax demands.

Fiona turns her head toward them. "I didn't get either of you a cookie. I got my husband a cookie. You two can get your own cookies."

I tear a piece of the cookie off and shove it in my mouth. "Mmm." I chew it, grinning at Brax and Sean.

Fiona reaches into her pocket and pulls out another package. "I did get you one, Draco."

"Thanks," he replies, and reaches for the bag.

"Seriously? You got everybody a cookie but me and Brax?" Sean whines.

"No, *I* got you two morons a cookie," Zara states, pulling brown bags out of her pocket. She hands a cookie to each of them.

Fiona rolls her eyes and then sits next to me. "So predictable. Have you guys figured out who wants to kill me?"

"Not really," I state, trying to contain my irritation. Hopefully, we'll get some answers tonight or at least have things in place to get the ball rolling. Then, we can discover who in The Underworld is truly a traitor. I just hope it's no one who holds a seat.

"I'm sorry. I hate how much of your time this is taking," Fiona offers, and worry fills her expression.

"And ours," Sean mutters.

I shoot him an unimpressed look, and put my arm around Fiona, declaring sternly, "Don't feel bad. And we'll find out who's targeting you."

She studies me a moment, then releases a big breath.

I rub her back and ask, "Do you have some extra time to spare today?"

Amusement lights her eyes. "Let me pull out my very busy schedule. Hmm." She pulls out her phone, stares at it, then looks at me. "I pretty much have nothing going on since I'm unemployed. Is there something you want to do?"

Zara huffs. "I can't believe Skylar and Adrian won't even talk to you."

"They have their reasons," Brax interjects.

I stay quiet. As angry as I am at Adrian, I can't blame him. What my family did to his sister was inhumane and despicable. But I wish he'd have a conversation with Fiona and not hold what my family did over her head.

Fiona's face falls. She states, "I don't want to talk about it."

Sean gives her a guilty look.

I rise and pull her up. "Well, if you're not doing anything, why don't you come with me?"

She tilts her head. "Where are you going?"

"To Morocco."

Her eyes light up. "Morocco? As in the country?"

I chuckle. "Yes. I called a Royal Council meeting to discuss the threat to your life."

Questions fill her expression. "What's the Royal Council?" she inquires.

Brax says, "It's thirteen Omni members instead of the entire 666 members who hold seats."

"Like a leadership board?" she asks.

I'm hit with a jolt of panic. She's not allowed to forget laws, rules, or her duties. So I affirm, "Yes. It was in the Royal Doctrine. Do you not remember?"

She looks confused, thinking for a moment, then scrunches her face. "I never read anything about it."

My stomach flips. "Are you sure?"

She nods. "Yes. I would have remembered it."

One of the babies cries.

"You're okay," Zara coos and picks up River. She bounces him on her hip and frets, "That should have been in your book."

Something nags at me. "If that's not in the book, what else isn't?"

The color drains from Fiona's face.

"Where is it?" Sean asks.

"In my desk drawer," she replies.

I rise and assert, "I need to see it. Let's take it with us, and I'll review it on the plane."

"Okay," she says with concern in her expression.

"Don't worry. I'll make sure we get to the bottom of this."

She bites on her lip but nods.

Sean stands. "Guess who else is going to Morocco?"

"Not me," Brax grumbles.

Sean grins, puffing out his chest, and pride fills his voice. "Zara and I recently got seats on the Royal Council."

Brax gets up. "You all have fun with your Royal Councilness. I'm going to go where all the little peons go."

"Oh, don't be like that, Brax," Zara says.

"Whatever. Just make sure I don't get sliced to pieces following your orders, Kirill. See you later," he says and stomps out of the house.

"What's up his ass?" Fiona questions.

Zara softly answers, "I think he's just ready to earn his seat."

"Not everybody can earn a seat," I remind her.

"Brax should get one. He's worthy of it," Sean declares.

I curl my fist, hating anything that resembles entitlement. I point out, "That has yet to be determined."

Sean declares, "I can vouch for him."

I grunt. "You've already done that several times. It stops meaning something after a while."

"No, it doesn't," he insists.

Draco clears his throat. "Sir, if I'm not needed, there are other matters I need to attend to."

"Oh. Yes. Please," I say, motioning toward the door.

He says to Fiona, "Thank you for the cookie."

"You're welcome. Thanks for keeping us safe," she replies with a grateful tone.

"It's an honor, Your Majesty," he says, then exits the room.

She turns toward me. "Okay. What do I pack? I assume we can stay awhile since I have so much going on here." She rolls her eyes.

I answer, "We can stay as long as you want."

She claps. "Yay. So I should pack…"

"You don't have to pack."

"What do you mean I don't have to pack?"

"There are tons of clothes in the royal quarters for you," I inform her.

She bites on her smile. "Really?"

"Yes."

Zara teases, "Oh, to be royalty."

I grin at her. "Don't worry. I had the staff fill a closet with clothes for you too."

She gapes at me.

"You did?" Sean asks.

"Yes. And you and the babies too."

Sean just gapes at me.

Fiona jumps off the couch and tosses her arms around my shoulders. She rises on her tiptoes and gushes, "That's super thoughtful of you."

I stay silent, unable to control my grin. Every time she looks at me with approval, I get giddy inside.

She tugs my head down and whispers in my ear, "I guess I need to give you more than a cookie?" She retreats and pins her greens on me.

My cock twitches. My grin grows wider.

"Ugh. Keep the PDA to when I'm not here," Sean interjects.

I ignore him, slide my hand behind her head and under her hair, and my lips brush her lobe. I murmur, "The cookie's nice, but my mouth loves your body much more, my little bird." I slide my thumb over the back of her neck and retreat.

Her cheeks flush, and she inhales sharply.

My cock hardens further.

The other baby cries.

Zara frets, "Sean, take River."

I wink at my wife and step back.

She smirks, then rushes over to the stroller, stating, "I've got Willow."

"Thanks, Fiona," Zara offers.

Fiona coos, "Aw, what's wrong, sweet girl?" She holds the baby close to her.

Willow buries her face in the curve of her neck, her cry turning into a soft whimper.

"Aw, it's okay, sweetie," Fiona says gently.

Watching her with the baby tugs on my heart.

She'd be a good mom.

I would be a horrible dad. But she would be a good mom.

It won't make up for my weaknesses.

"I'll go grab the book, and we can leave," I tell her.

"Okay." She graces me with a stunning smile.

I exit the room, find the Royal Doctrine, and return to the front room.

"Everybody ready?" I question.

"Yeah, I am," Fiona chirps, excited.

More warmth fills me. We leave the building, get into our SUVs, and meet at the private airport. We have fun on the way to Morocco, laughing often. When the flight lands, we get off the plane and step into the dark hallway.

Fiona states, "It's the same hallway as Pompeii."

"Yes. Anytime you attend an Underworld event, you will go through a hallway like this."

"Why?" she questions.

Sean interjects, "Because Dad wanted it this way."

Fiona scrunches her face. "But why?"

"Who knows why he wanted this or most of the rules," Sean answers.

We approach the door for the royal quarters. I open it and motion for everyone to go through, stating, "Karina will watch the babies."

Sean declares, "No one is watching the twins."

I spin to face him. "No children. It's the rules."

Zara insists, "There's a threat on Fiona's life. We're not leaving our babies with anyone."

My pulse pounds harder. I consider their worries, but I also know the rules.

"I won't harm your children," Karina says, then curtsies, adding, "Your Majesties."

"No offense, but no one is watching our babies," Sean reiterates.

"Thank you, Karina. Please go wait in the other room," I order.

She glances at the babies, then obeys.

The door shuts, and tense silence fills the air.

"Figure it out, Kirill. My kids aren't staying with her," Sean insists.

I sigh. "I understand your concern, but you know the rules. And you and Zara have to show up."

"The babies come with us, or we don't go," Sean states.

I scrub my face, unsure how to get around this.

Fiona chimes in, "I'll use my token."

"No, you won't," I sternly reply.

"It's mine to use, and I don't trust anyone with the babies either," she claims.

"You can't use your token for this. You need to save it for a more important event," I instruct.

"Willow and River aren't staying with anyone," Zara reiterates.

The tension increases as Sean and Zara hold the babies tightly.

Fiona snaps her fingers. "Queen's Honor."

"Yes! That's it!" Zara praises.

"Thank God," Sean blurts out in relief.

"Good?" Fiona questions, looking at me for approval.

"Brilliant," I reply, leaning down and kissing her. Then I head for the door. "Let's go so we aren't late."

We exit the royal quarters, walk down several hallways, then enter a small room.

Nine Omni sit around a table. They see us and rise. The men bow, and the women curtsy.

"You may sit," I instruct.

Everyone takes their seats.

Ulrich points at the babies, demanding, "What are they doing here?"

"Queen's Honor," Fiona answers in a strong voice, lifting her chin and pinning a challenging gaze on Ulrich.

"We weren't informed," he retorts.

I open my mouth, but before I can speak, she scoffs. "Since when do I need to inform you of my royal decisions?"

His face hardens.

Jytte, Ulrich's wife, speaks up. "Your Majesty, the normal procedure is to add royal requests to the agenda."

Fiona's eyes turn to slits. "Requests? Since when is the Queen's Honor a request for you to approve?"

Jytte's expression darkens. She doesn't flinch under Fiona's stare.

Pride fills me. The only way for the Omni to respect Fiona is for her to earn it. Her knowledge of the rules and her ability to stand up for herself is the best way to do that. I love watching her lean into her power. So I bellow, "Your queen is waiting for an answer."

Jytte's gaze lands on me, and something I've never seen or maybe just haven't noticed before swirls in her eyes.

She's jealous.

I glance at Ulrich.

He quickly states, "Apologies, Your Majesty. Thank you for your clarification."

"Jytte?" I question, not letting her off the hook.

She doesn't speak.

Ulrich nudges her.

She inhales sharply, then offers, "My apologies."

I grab Fiona's hand and squeeze it.

She replies, "Thank you. My niece and nephew will always be welcome at the table when I am here. It is an honor and privilege for them to sit in this room with all of us, and there will be no further discussion on this matter. Now, we have pending business to attend to. Kirill?" She locks eyes with me.

My cock aches, and all the things I want to do to my wife flash in my mind. I push the images away and declare, "There is an assassination plot against the queen. I'm issuing a Zenith mandate until we find and punish the traitors."

Gasps fill the room.

Ulrich blurts out, "That's an extreme invasion of our privacy."

Sean snarls, "Extreme measures must be taken when the queen's life is at stake. Don't you think?"

Tension fills the room. No one dares to argue with him.

He adds, "All members of The Underworld will be monitored until we know who is plotting to kill the queen. Reports will be given to the king three times a day and to the Royal Council weekly."

I drop another bomb. "I'm using my Sovereign Override privilege. I'm excluding Zara and Sean from the Zenith mandate."

No one at the table looks happy about this.

I continue, "I'm also declaring an Act of Accession, naming Sean and Zara as successor king and queen should anything happen to Fiona and myself."

Jytte snaps, "That is absurd. Ulrich and I are the ones who should be successors. They have barely owned their seats."

I rise, snarling, "Your entitlement is exactly why you will never sit with a crown on your head. As king, I determine the successors, and it will not be you."

Hatred radiates off her in waves.

How have I never seen this before?

I need to watch her.

I study the face of every person in the room, then warn, "Whoever is leaking information to the outside world and trying to assassinate Fiona will have hell to pay. I'm making a final declaration, so listen closely."

No one dares move, and the silence becomes deafening.

I announce, "I declare this assassination plot to be an act of war. Traitors will be made an example of in front of the entire membership. Their punishment will be conducted during a Black Veil Ritual."

Several of the members gasp in shock. The Black Veil Ritual has only taken place once. But no one is going to attempt to kill my wife and not be held to the harshest punishment.

"Any questions?" I ask, taking another glance around the room.

No one speaks.

I nod. "Thank you for your time. Safe travels home." I motion for Sean and Zara to rise, then reach for Fiona's hand. I quickly guide us out of the room and back to the royal quarters.

As soon as we get inside, I ask Sean, "Did you see what I saw?"

His eyes are pools of darkness. He scowls. "Yes. I will make sure to watch closely."

I nod in gratitude.

"See what?" Fiona asks.

I put my hand over her lips, not trusting the room to be free of recording devices. "We will discuss things later. Go put something nice on. I'm taking you out for dinner."

Fiona

Chapter
TWENTY-FIVE

"**S**omething wrong?" Kirill asks.

I slide another dress along the rod and then turn in his direction. "I don't mean to sound ungrateful, because these dresses are all beautiful, but are there any sexy cocktail dresses?"

His lips twitch. "Do you know much about Morocco?"

I shake my head.

He slides his finger on my chest above the towel while informing me, "It's customary for women to cover their legs and arms."

"Oh. I feel stupid for not knowing that," I admit.

"Not stupid, just unaware, but now you know," he assures, then a mischievous expression appears on his face, and he adds, "You'll look just as sexy in one of these dresses as you would in a cocktail dress. But I'll take you out when we get to Chicago so you can put one of those on." He winks.

I laugh. "Deal." I spin back to the rack, sliding the hangers over the rod and declaring, "These really are pretty dresses. Which one should I wear?"

"You'll look amazing in any of them. Surprise me," he replies, then exits the closet.

I sort through the large selection, then settle on a mint-green, long-sleeved maxi dress with a bohemian print of light-pink flowers scattered across the soft and breathable material. I pair it with strappy, brown sandals, gold and pink teardrop earrings, and several gold bangle bracelets.

I step out of the closet, and Kirill's eyes light up. He boasts, "See, I knew you'd look sexy."

My butterflies flutter hard. I drag my gaze over his khaki pants and white linen shirt, complimenting, "You look great too."

"Thanks. Ready to go?" he asks.

"Yes."

He takes my hand, kisses it, then leads me into the main room.

Zara whistles. "Look at you two!"

"Have fun," Sean offers, glancing up from his laptop.

"Are you going to work all night?" I question, feeling bad for Zara if she can't have fun in Morocco.

He narrows his eyes. "I'll be done soon."

Kirill nods, and I don't push further, offering, "Have a good night."

"You too," Zara replies, then wiggles her eyebrows at me.

I laugh, and Kirill leads me out of the royal quarters, through the door, and down several hallways. After a few turns, he opens a door, revealing an SUV.

The driver bows. "Your Majesties."

"Thank you," we reply.

He opens the back door.

We get inside, he shuts the door, and goes to the driver's side. He slides in and turns on the engine.

Excited to be in Morocco, I ask, "Where are we going?"

Kirill's face lights up. He answers, "There's a private spot I love in Marrakech. They have the best food."

"I love how you look like a little kid on Christmas morning right now," I blurt out.

His grin widens. "I do?"

"Yes. I can't decide if watching you in action today was hotter or right now."

He arches his eyebrows.

I tease, "Don't act like you don't know what I'm talking about."

He tilts his head, maintaining the same confused expression.

I lean closer, inhaling his delicious scent and lowering my voice, stating, "Okay, I decided. Watching you give that nasty woman a verbal slap down was the sexiest thing I've ever seen."

He slides his hand over my thigh, and tingles race to my core. He murmurs, "What was sexy was when you owned the room."

"I did?"

He studies me, asking, "Is that a serious question?"

I shrug, confessing, "I felt kind of bitchy, but I had to defend my niece and nephew."

He shakes his head. "Why is it that women who are strong are seen as bitchy?"

"Not sure, but it's a thin line," I admit.

"Well, you weren't bitchy. You were strong."

My heart skips a few beats. I softly reply, "Thanks."

We pass several miles of brightly colored buildings. Then we pull up to a deep-blue one. The side has a mural of two children's faces and an abstract background. The driver gets out and opens the back door.

Kirill steps out, then reaches in for me.

I take his hand, eager to experience a new country. I stand and look up at him. "Thanks for taking me out."

Something passes in his expression. I've seen it more lately, but I can't decipher if it's amusement, happiness, or something else. He replies, "It's my honor to take you out."

I tilt my head, smiling, trying to understand how a man so powerful can be so sweet.

"Why are you looking at me like that?" he questions.

I blurt out, "I'm glad I married you. You make me happy."

He tenses, pinning me with a penetrating look.

My heart pounds harder. The minutes seem to drag by.

He didn't want to marry me, and now I've put him in a weird spot.

"Sorry. Forget I said—"

He cuts my words off with his lips, sliding his tongue in my mouth so fast I lose my breath. His hand grasps the back of my neck, which is still tender from my branding, but it creates an ache that blooms between my legs.

I whimper, my insides quivering, clutching his shirt, and losing myself to everything I always wanted in a man but couldn't ever find.

"Don't ever apologize again for telling me you're happy," he mumbles against my lips and steals more of my breath.

My knees buckle.

He steadies me with his forearm against my back, tugging me closer. He kisses me again, then retreats an inch from my mouth, declaring, "I've never been happy before. Since I've married you, I now know what that feels like. So thank you."

I blink hard, trying to stop tearing up, and smile.

He kisses the top of my head and lowers his lips to my ear, suggesting, "We probably should let the driver get back in his vehicle."

"Oh," I say, then nervously laugh, realizing he's standing beside us. "Sorry."

"No worries, Your Majesty," he says, his lips twitching.

Kirill steers us toward the entrance.

I lean into his tall frame and ask, "What is that made of?" I point to the building, which is some type of stone with lines running across it.

He replies, "It's called rammed earth, a technique from ancient times. The Moroccans would compact soil, sand, silt, and water, creating a wall with the dimensions you see. It's very durable against weather conditions."

"Wow. It's really pretty," I say with admiration.

"I like it too," he admits, and we step inside.

A woman with dark hair and eyes looks up at our entrance. Her face lights up, and she says with a French accent, "Ah. Mr. Petrov. You're back!"

He grins and stands taller. "Good to see you, Charlotte. This is my wife, Fiona."

She focuses on me, beaming, and exclaims, "Wife! When did you get married?"

"A few weeks ago," he answers.

She steps forward and wraps her arms around me. I embrace her, and she kisses my cheek. "Congratulations. It's so nice to meet you. Your husband's been coming here alone for years. It's about time someone scooped him up!"

Kirill chuckles and tugs me back into him.

I decide I like her, and reply, "It's nice to meet you."

"Let me take you to your table. Will you need menus?" she asks.

Kirill answers, "That depends on whether Fiona is okay with letting Chef Rakan send out what he thinks is best." He looks at me in question.

"Yes. That sounds fun," I respond.

"Good. You won't regret it. Follow me," Charlotte says, opening a door.

"Wow!" I mutter, taking in the red and gold velvet ceiling, matching pillows, and padded private booths. Long red curtains hang in front of each table, pulled back with gold ropes or shut for privacy. Elaborate diamond light fixtures hang from the ceiling, and soft light shines against gold-foiled symbols. There's one vertical line and a curve pointing up and one pointing down. I motion to one and ask, "What does that depict?"

"That is the Berber. It's on Morocco's flag," Charlotte explains.

I glance around again, uttering, "This restaurant is gorgeous."

"Thank you. Enjoy your dinner, Mr. and Mrs. Petrov," she states.

I step into the most private of the rooms we've passed. It's slightly bigger than the others, and the curtains have multiple layers of velvet.

"After you," Kirill states.

I slide into the half-circle booth, and he follows.

A server appears. "Mr. Petrov. I didn't realize you were dining with us tonight."

"Hello, Salambek. This is my wife, Fiona," Kirill announces, and I note the pride in his voice and on his expression.

My butterflies flutter harder.

Salambek nods. "Mrs. Petrov. Thank you for joining us. May I suggest our Moroccotini to start?"

Excited, I inquire, "What's in it?"

"Orange-flavored vodka, mint, lime juice, and sugar syrup. I can't get your husband to try it, but I'm sure you'll love it," he asserts.

"No Moroccotini for you?" I tease Kirill.

"I'll stick with vodka, but you go ahead and try it."

"Okay, but you have to at least try a sip of mine," I state.

Kirill grins at Salambek. "One vodka and one Moroccotini."

"Excellent. And it's true you'd like Chef Rakan to decide your courses?"

"Yes, please," Kirill answers.

"Perfect. I'll be back soon," Salambek says and then disappears.

I gush, "This restaurant is so pretty."

"Agreed."

I lean closer, asking, "How did we get the best table when they didn't know you were coming?"

Kirill admits, "I own the table."

I gape at him.

"What?"

"You own the table?"

He chuckles. "Yes. I bought it long ago, and pay them enough money every year to keep them happy."

"Wow. The perks of being you."

His cheeks turn a bit red.

I lower my voice. "Wait. I meant the perks of being Mrs. Petrov." My smile explodes on my lips.

He chuckles and blurts out, "You have the best smile."

My heart takes a double beat. "Thanks."

"I mean it." He pins his intense gaze on me.

Salambek appears with drinks. He sets them down. "One vodka and one Moroccotini. Please, take a sip and let me know what you think."

I pick up the cold martini glass and drink a large mouthful. "Mmm."

Approval fills Salambek's expression. "You like it?"

"No. I love it," I reply.

"Great. The chef said fresh khobz will be ready soon."

I ask, "What's khobz?"

Kirill replies, "Moroccan bread."

"Enjoy," Salambek offers and shuts the curtains.

The room becomes darker and more seductive. The candlelight flickers, highlighting Kirill's scar across his sharp features. He slides his hand onto my thigh.

The throb in my lower body reignites. I drag my gaze to his lips. "You never brought anyone here before?"

"No," he says in a gruff tone.

Looking into his eyes, I don't think, just blurt out, "Weren't you lonely before you married me?"

His face hardens, and he hesitates.

"Sorry. I shouldn't pry." I take a sip of my Moroccotini.

"Yes. Life has been lonely," he finally answers.

My heart hurts for him. I put my drink down and refocus on him, offering, "I'm sorry you didn't have anyone loving you."

He takes a large sip of vodka.

Salambek pulls the curtain back, announcing, "Warm honey khobz, goat cheese, fig chutney, and olive tapenade." He sets a large platter on the table.

My stomach growls.

Kirill nods. "Thank you."

"Enjoy." Salambek steps back and secures the curtains.

Kirill tears a piece of bread, slathers it with goat cheese and chutney, and holds it to my mouth. "Try this."

I sink my teeth into the bread, and the creamy sweetness explodes on my tongue. I groan, chewing it slowly.

He looks pleased at my reaction.

I swallow, take a sip of my Moroccotini, and hold it in front of him. "Your turn."

He takes a sip, cringes, and swallows. "It's sweet."

"You don't like it?"

"Too sweet for me. I'll stick with plain vodka."

I tease, "You can take the boy out of Russia, but you can't take the Russian out of the boy."

He grins. "I guess not. Cheers." He holds out his glass.

I lightly clink it with mine, and we both drink.

He adds more goat cheese to the bread and tops it with the olive tapenade. "Try this."

An explosion of creamy, salty, and savory hit my tongue. I chew, swallow, and admit, "That might be better than the fig chutney."

"It probably tastes better since your drink is sweet." He takes a bite, then adds, "I think the chutney is better with my vodka."

I take a few more bites.

He drinks half his vodka and then sets it down, announcing, "I should take you to Russia soon."

The hairs on my arms rise. "Really?"

"Yes."

"Is it safe?"

"With me? Yes," he declares.

My anxiety disappears. "Okay. When do you want to go?"

He chuckles. "When we get home, let's figure it out."

A wave of enthusiasm rolls through me. I ask, "Do you go often?"

His face falls. "Not anymore. I used to when I was a child."

I put my hand over his. "Are your memories bad? Of your family?"

His eyes darken. "Not the ones of my mother."

"What was she like?"

He thinks momentarily and then a tiny curve forms on his lips. He notes, "She was beautiful. Kind. Funny too."

"That must be who you get your sense of humor from," I point out.

He leans closer. "You think I'm funny?"

"Yeah. I laugh a lot when I'm around you."

He strokes my thigh, lowering his voice. "I like it when you laugh."

"So you'd go to Russia with your family as a boy?"

His face falls again, filling with disdain. "Yes. My father was proud to be a Petrov, and loved returning home to show his family how much money and power he accumulated."

"Oh." My gut flips.

A heavy silence settles between us for a few moments.

"Did you ever think about changing your name?" I ask, breaking the quiet.

He arches his eyebrows. "From Petrov?"

"Yes."

He hesitates, then nods. "I told your father it was a curse, and I wanted a new last name, but he stopped me from changing it."

My chest tightens. "Why?"

"He told me it was a cowardly move. He said the way to eliminate the Petrov curse was to become the man no Petrov ever was, and ensure future generations knew how to behave and treat others."

I remain quiet, processing my father's words.

Kirill adds, "He was right. Running away might make some things easier, but it doesn't change them."

I blurt out, "Then our kids will be able to stand proud with the Petrov name."

"Our kids?" he says, pinning his eyebrows together.

My heart races faster. "Yes."

He grinds his molars and looks at his vodka glass, tapping it with his index finger.

Goose bumps race along my skin. I try to keep it light, but it comes out flat when I ask, "You don't want to have some babies?"

Time seems to stand still. He finally faces me, stating, "How would that work, Fiona?"

Confused, I question, "What do you mean?"

He swallows hard, takes a deep breath, then slowly releases it. In a cool tone, he asks, "How would that be fair to them?"

I jerk my head back. "I'm not following."

He closes his eyes for a moment, then sighs. When he opens them again, he looks into my eyes and sadly says, "They'd always be afraid of me."

"What are you talking about?"

More silence ensues.

Then it hits me. Anger floods every cell I have. I accuse, "Stop using your scar as an excuse to not live."

"I'm not using it as an excuse."

"Yes, you are," I insist, my voice growing louder.

"Fiona—"

"No! That's the most ridiculous statement I've ever heard, Kirill!" I glare at him.

He grinds his molars, and I shake my head at him.

"Don't look at me like that," he orders.

I scoff. "Then stop being an idiot!"

He leans closer. "Calm down. You're getting loud."

I lower my voice. "Don't tell me to calm down. I want kids. I would be a good mom."

"I know you would."

"And you would be a good father."

He clenches his jaw, shaking his head. "No. I wouldn't. They'd fear me."

"No. They'd love you," I insist.

"They wouldn't," he says, then finishes his vodka and stares at the curtain.

"So I can't ever love you either, right? Because you have a scar?" I seethe.

His breath hitches. He slowly turns and pins a sad and fearful but knowing gaze on me.

Angry, I scoot out of the booth and rise.

"Where are you going?" he demands.

"To the ladies' room. I need a moment." I huff.

"Fiona—"

"No! You have a scar. It's shitty how it happened. I get that what your family did to you haunts you, but it's not fair to let it ruin the potential of creating a family of our own." I toss my napkin on the seat, push through the curtains, and follow the sign to the bathroom.

It's not far, just down a hallway past the kitchen. I open the door, lock it, and put my hands on the sink, staring at my reflection in the mirror.

My insides crumple with something I've never felt before. It slices through me, and I realize this is what it feels like to lose a dream.

I love my career, but I always saw myself as a mother. Now I'm married to a man who refuses to have kids because he has a scar on his face?

As hard as I try to keep it from happening, a tear escapes. I swipe at it.

There's a pounding on the door.

Kirill shouts, "Fiona!"

I release an emotional breath, unlock the door, and order, "Leave me alone for a minute."

He ignores my request, pushes past the doorway, and locks the door behind him.

I step back against the wall, arguing, "Did you not hear—"

He puts his hand over my mouth, tipping my chin with the heel of his palm. His blues rage with fire. He lowers his face over mine and warns, "Don't say you want a baby unless you really want one." He removes his hand from my mouth but keeps it on my chin.

My insides quiver harder. My voice trembles just as hard when I tell him, "I don't just want one baby, Kirill. I want a big family with lots of kids driving us nuts."

His chest fills with air. He studies me, then murmurs, "Are you sure that's what you want?"

I don't flinch, answering, "Yes."

He bunches my skirt in his fist.

My butterflies go crazy. "What are you doing?"

He spins me toward the mirror, splays his hand on the back of my neck, and pushes me over the sink. He drops his pants, tugs my dress up, and pushes my panties to the side. In one thrust, he slides inside me.

"Oh!" I gasp, staring at him in the mirror and gripping the counter.

He grunts, thrusting a few times, then grits out, "I'm older than you. If you want a lot of kids, then it's time I gave you our first baby, little bird."

Kirill

Chapter
TWENTY-SIX

iona's greens widen. Her mouth forms an O, and her body trembles.

"This is what you want?" I grunt, sliding forcefully in and out of her, triple-checking she's serious about me fathering her children while conflicting fears and desires run through my mind.

Her face reddens. She grips the counter so tight her knuckles turn white. She squeaks, "Yes."

"You want my babies?" I bark, shocked I'm having this conversation, on the verge of pumping everything I have into her.

Why is this turning me on?

What am I doing?

She wants kids. I'm not going to spoil her dream.

But I'd be their father.

"Yes! Yours! Only yours!" she cries out, keeping her gaze on mine in the mirror's reflection.

Why the fuck is she saying this?

She must be drunk.

She's not.

She wants my babies.

Jesus fucking Christ!

I slow down my thrusts, knowing I'm worked up to the point that if I don't, I'm going to come faster than a teenager who just discovered how to jack himself off.

"Oh God!" she breathes, her eyelids fluttering.

I massage my hand on the back of her neck, but there's no chance of me cutting her air supply off in this position. But I also don't want to. Sometimes, I prefer to watch her come when she's not blacking out, even though she seems to crave it.

"Yes," she calls out, then licks her lips.

I lean over her, kneading her neck, murmuring in Russian, "I hope our babies look like you."

She whimpers and turns her head.

"Fuck this. Your lips are mine, little bird," I declare, then spin her, pick her up, and pin her against the wall.

"Kirill," she mumbles against my mouth, sliding her hand through my hair and gripping her arms around my shoulders.

"Hmm," I reply, sliding my tongue deep against hers, falling into the warm haze that overpowers me every time she shows me any sign of affection.

"Don't fight me, just love me," she says.

"I do love you," I mumble, returning to kissing her, then freeze.

What did I just say?

She arches her brows, full of hope, breathing hard.

I don't move, still inside her, no longer sure who I am or what I'm saying. My heart pounds so hard, I think I might be having an attack.

Is it possible?

We've only been married a few weeks.

I must be losing it.

The longer I stay still, the more fear paralyzes me.

"I love you too," she softly claims.

More shock fills me, and I press closer to her, letting the wall take our weight. I open my mouth, but nothing comes out.

She slides her hand over my cheek, caressing my scar.

I close my eyes, fighting too many years of self-loathing and shame.

She can't love me.

I'm hearing things.

"Look at me," she orders.

I obey, blinking hard.

She tilts her head, studying me, and asserts, "I'm your wife, but I don't love you because of our vows. I love you because you wrote letters to me. And you always stand up for me. Not once have you lied or hidden things from me. And no matter what you've believed your entire life, I think my husband is the sexiest man I've ever laid eyes on."

I have no words. Emotions attack me, and I bury my face in the curve of her neck, feeling like I might break down.

She tightens her arms around me and kisses my head, whispering, "Have I said too much?"

Has she?

I get control of my emotions and slowly lift my head to meet her eyes, answering, "No, my queen. I'm just a little overwhelmed by your statement."

She swallows hard, fretting, "In a good way or a bad way?" She bites on her lip.

I run my thumb over her chin, replying, "A good way."

She softly smiles.

I kiss her, and she returns my affection, pulling me back into a haze of happiness I never thought I deserved or could feel.

Another wave of emotions pounds into my heart. I slowly thrust inside her and mumble, "I do love you, Fiona. I don't know how it happened so quickly, but I do."

Her eyes glisten, and a tear escapes, slipping down her cheek. The salty wetness hits my tongue, and her body throbs against mine. She whimpers, clinging to me, adding, "I knew when I met you, I wanted you."

"I wanted you too," I admit through gritted teeth, my cock swelling bigger, but I'm not ready for this moment to end.

"Oh God," she breathes, her lips forming an O, and violent convulsions attack her. She trembles against me. Her eyes roll, and a loud moan flies out of her throat.

"That's it, my sexy little bird," I praise, studying every reaction.

She clutches me as if I'm her life raft, reiterating that she's mine.

Fiona O'Malley is my wife.

Fiona Petrov.

Mrs. Kirill Petrov.

"Kirill," she whispers in a raspy tone, shaking harder.

I continue to thrust, barely getting out, "You're mine, my queen."

"Y-yes," she agrees.

Every atom in my body buzzes. I kiss her harder, thrust faster, and all hell breaks loose.

An incoherent, muffled sound fills the air. Her nails dig into my shoulders.

I groan into her mouth, my erection swells, and I pump every drop of my seed deep inside her.

She kisses me through our orgasms, not letting me go, her tongue flicking into my mouth with desperation.

I reach a high I've never known. Sweat beads on my skin. I don't stop thrusting until I have nothing left to give.

Our labored breathing is the only sound in the room.

I retreat from her mouth and try to calm my lungs as I study her.

She does the same, and we don't move for several minutes.

Someone bangs on the door, tearing us out of our trance.

Her green eyes widen, and she giggles.

I move my hand over her mouth, not wanting to cause a scene in Morocco and disrespect their modest culture.

There's another bang.

"Shh," I tell Fiona, slowly removing my hand and setting her on her feet. Once convinced she has her balance, I pull up and fasten my pants.

She adjusts her panties and dress. Then she frets, whispering, "Do I look okay?"

I glance at her flushed cheeks, plant a kiss on one, and reply, "You're gorgeous like always. Follow my lead."

She nods.

I check myself in the mirror, determine we look presentable, and open the door. "Excuse us. My wife wasn't feeling very well."

A woman steps back and shoots me a disapproving look.

I quickly lead Fiona past her and back to our table. We take our seats in the booth, and I slide my arm around her.

She curls into me, sliding her hand on my thigh.

Salambek appears with a tray, beaming. "You're back. The chef has prepared zaalouk, otherwise known as Moroccan aubergine salad." He smiles at Fiona and sets two plates down.

My bride's face lights with excitement. She gazes at the dish and breathes in deeply, stating, "Smells amazing! And I'm starving all of a sudden."

"Me too," I admit.

Salambek points to the meat and continues, "Slow braised lamb shanks with the chef's secret tomato-based sauce over couscous."

"Yummy," Fiona chirps.

"Can I get you anything else? Another drink?" Salambek asks.

"Yes. Another round, please," I answer.

"Great," he says, then shuts the curtains just as the woman from the bathroom passes and tosses us another dirty look.

Fiona wrinkles her nose. "I think she knows what we did in the bathroom." She tries to contain her smile but can't.

I chuckle. "She's just jealous."

Fiona's face lights up further. "Do you think?"

Another wave of giddiness hits me. I grin and motion to the food. "Try the meat. The chef makes the best lamb dishes in Morocco."

"Well, you know how much I love my meat," she teases.

I chuckle.

She picks up her knife and fork, cuts a piece off, and pops it in her mouth. "Mmm."

"Told you," I boast, then take a bite, groaning.

"It's so good," Fiona adds, putting the salad on her fork and stating, "It's interesting how the salad looks like brown mush."

"It's good, though," I claim.

She eats it and nods. "It's delicious. I can never get eggplant dishes to turn out very well."

"Do you like to cook?" I ask.

She nods. "Yes. But I hate cleaning up."

"Tell you what, you cook and I'll clean up," I offer.

Her lips twitch. "Really?"

"Yes. Of course."

She suggests, "Or, we could cook and clean up together."

"Deal," I agree, feeling the warmth in my chest expand even further.

We eat silently for a few minutes, and Salambek slips in to give us more cocktails. He leaves, and we return to eating.

Fiona takes a sip of her Morrocotini and then puts her fork down. She pats her napkin on her lips, then turns toward me.

"Everything okay?" I question.

She hesitates.

My chest tightens. I put my silverware down and encourage, "Whatever it is, say it."

She opens her mouth, shuts it, then puts her hand on my inner thigh.

My cock springs back to life. I warn, "Careful where you put your hand, little bird. We might get arrested."

She teases me further by caressing her fingers higher, then leans into me. "So..."

"So?" I arch my eyebrows.

She bites on her lips, staring at me.

"You're making me nervous," I admit.

She softly laughs.

"Glad I can amuse you," I murmur.

She laughs again, then she goes serious. She finally says, "So you're okay if I get off my birth control?"

My stomach flips.

Stop being a pussy.

I put my arm around her and stroke her bicep, asking, "Are you sure you're ready for a baby?"

She slowly nods.

"My baby?"

She frowns. "Let's not go down this path again."

"I meant because I'm a Petrov."

She tenses.

"Ah. You forgot about that part," I state.

She shakes her head. "No. I didn't. I just hope my mom won't hate me forever."

I sigh and kiss her head. "I'm sorry. And she won't. One way or another, we'll figure it out."

Sadness fills Fiona's expression. She mutters, "I can't imagine my mom not being a part of our kids' lives."

"Then she will be," I insist, but I hate how I don't have the problem solved.

Fiona offers a brave smile. "I guess it'll be her choice, right?"

"Yes, but don't think anything but good thoughts. She won't be able to stay away from you or the babies."

Fiona waggles her brows. "You said *babies*."

My heart races faster. I remind her, "You said you wanted lots of babies, not just one."

She beams brighter. "I do."

What am I agreeing to?

She wants babies, so I have to give them to her.

What if they hate me?

Rehashing this isn't going to fly with Fiona.

I pick up her hand and kiss it. "If you want a houseful of babies, then that's what I'll give you."

She puts her palm on my cheek and scoots closer, then kisses me. "Good. And you know what we said back there?"

My stomach flutters. "Yeah."

She looks nervous. "I meant what I said."

I nod. "So did I."

She grins, then teases, "Good. Now I need to eat my meat. My husband made me work up an appetite, and I plan on burning more calories tonight."

I chuckle, give her a chaste kiss, and pick up her fork. I put lamb on it and hold it to her mouth. "Well, by all means, Mrs. Petrov. Please. Eat your meat."

She smirks, then runs her hand over my semi, declaring in a naughty voice, "I plan on eating lots of meat tonight, my dear hubby."

Fiona

One Month Later

Chapter
TWENTY-SEVEN

Saying I'm bored is an understatement. I haven't worked in over a month. Skylar still hasn't met with me. She claims we have to wait until after fashion week.

I can't blame her. It's the busy season, and I know how much work is involved. But I miss my career, the people in the office, and all the shows.

I keep going online and looking at different posts. All it does is make me feel worse.

Kirill keeps encouraging me to start my own line. At first, I said I could never put myself in a position to compete with Skylar. But the more time passes and I don't hear from her, the more I realize I might need to take matters into my own hands.

Before Kirill left this morning, he looked at my sketchbook. It has dozens of designs I've doodled over the last month. He'd set it down and adamantly stated, "You have talent, Fiona. And it's obvious this is your passion. Don't sell yourself short to be loyal to someone who isn't loyal to you."

I'd sighed, replying, "It would be easier if I didn't feel like a traitor."

He'd scoffed and said, "You aren't a traitor. You worked tirelessly for Skylar for years. Maybe this is happening for a reason."

I'd been unable to deny he had a point.

He'd kissed me, then said, "We have resources to make this happen. Think about it."

He'd left, and I'd turned on the TV, only to see more fabulous things I was missing during fashion week.

Then I'd gotten pissed. It'd mixed with my guilt and confusion over how to make things right with Adrian and Skylar. No answers had come, but more anger did.

Kirill is my husband. They've known me for years. It's not fair they won't even hear me out or give me the benefit of the doubt.

So, my rage turned into productivity. I've spent the day drawing designs, on a roll, with my brain seeing the next new outfit before I finish the one I'm working on.

I shade the top I'm working on and then put my pen down. I sit back, stare at the design, then flip through the notebook.

Kirill's right; I have talent. Maybe I should start my own line.

The more I review my designs, the more my confidence grows. Then I turn on my computer and compare what the reviewers are raving about compared to what's in my sketchbook.

My designs are better.

I'm not being disloyal to Skylar and Adrian.

They've shut me out.

I click on my mouse, and another review comes up. It's for Skylar's main competitor, and I roll my eyes. It's just another throwback from the '80s. I mutter, "They're so unoriginal."

The doorbell rings. The hairs on my arms rise, and a shiver runs down my spine.

I don't have plans with Zara, and Kirill didn't mention anyone else coming over.

The doorbell rings again.

Stop being silly. If they're in the foyer, they have security clearance.

I release an anxious breath and rise. I leave my office, go through the penthouse, and open the front door.

A young man with greasy, long locks and a scar on his neck, whom I've never seen before, stands there holding a yellow envelope. He raises it toward me, declaring, "This is for you."

My hands are clammy, and nerves erupt in my stomach. I don't know why my internal alarm bells are going off.

I ask, "Who is it from?"

"I'm just the messenger," he states, adding, "Here." He thrusts the envelope closer to me.

I grab it. "Thank you."

"It's urgent. You need to pay attention to it now," he declares.

"Okay," I say.

"Don't forget. It's urgent," he repeats.

"All right. I will," I assure him.

He hesitates for a moment, then turns to leave.

The elevator doors open. He steps inside, and the doors immediately slide shut.

Since when does the elevator work that quickly?

Lucky him.

I shut the door, lock it, and stroll back to my office. I step inside, look at the handwritten *Queen Fiona* on the front of the envelope, then freeze.

Since when has anyone from The Underworld not bowed and called me Your Majesty?

Dread fills me. I run my hand over the bump in the envelope, not sure what's inside. My insides quiver, and once again, I don't know why.

It's just some sort of Underworld business, I tell myself.

I open the envelope, pulling out a note and a flash drive. I unfold the paper and read it.

Queen Fiona,
This is how well your father-in-law knew your parents.
Sincerely,
A Friend

I'm racked by a full-body shiver. I stare at the flash drive and reread the note.

"Stop stalling," I mutter and then sit at my desk. I take a deep breath, staring around the beautiful space Kirill designed for me. The soft-blue sitting area, elaborate artwork, and rustic bookcases displaying my fashion books, look perfect against the stunning view of Lake Michigan. Normally, I get a sense of peace whenever I'm in this room. Right now, my gut won't stop flipping.

"I'm being silly," I mumble, then carefully insert the flash drive into my computer and wait. After a brief moment, a video materializes on the screen. It's black, and there's a play button.

My pulse skyrockets. I debate about pushing the play button or not, but I can't help myself. My curiosity wins, and I click the button.

There's a man strapped to a car. It's dark. The only light comes from the headlights of that vehicle and another one.

At first, it takes me a minute to comprehend what I'm seeing, and then horror races through me.

It can't be.

"Dad!" I cry out, leaning closer. There's no doubt it's him, especially when I hear his voice.

He's screaming, *"Let her go!"* and *"Motherfuckers!"* over and over.

The camera zooms out, then pans over to six men surrounding a woman. She's screaming, trying to break free, but isn't strong enough.

Bile rises in my throat.

Horrified, I put one hand over my mouth and the other on my stomach. My mother's face fills the screen and her voice pumps from the speakers.

Then, two men turn to face the camera, and my gut churns faster. I pause the video, looking closer.

It's my Uncle Niall and Uncle Shamus, who both died when I was a kid.

Why are they there and not helping my father?

More tears fall, and I try to figure out who the others are, but I've never seen them.

As if in slow motion, one by one, the men all rape my mother as my dad screams for them to stop.

My entire body shakes, and tears fall off my chin and dampen my jeans.

I want to stop watching but can't. Everything is blurry, but somehow, the images are way too clear.

Toward the end, a man takes off his gold chain necklace. It's a crucifix with an emerald in the center. He puts it around my mom's neck and chokes her, yelling at the top of his lungs, *"Pray!"*

Several times, my mom looks like she blacks out. The entire time, my father screams threats, but he's unable to do anything while strapped to the car.

When my mother blacks out for good, the camera switches back to my father. He's hysterical, screaming, *"Bridget!"*

The next scene is just as horrific. They kill my dad, and I watch every gruesome moment, feeling like my entire world is collapsing in front of me.

The video goes black, and I don't move. I don't know how much time passes. I can't stop shaking or crying, staring at the black screen.

My phone dings, tearing me out of my haze. As if in a trance, I glance down at it.

A text message pops up.

> Unknown: The man with the cross necklace is your father-in-law.

Bile flies up into my throat. I run to the bathroom and hug the toilet.

Kirill booms, "Fiona!" He kneels on the floor next to me and holds my hair back. He rubs my back.

More bile swirls in my stomach. I retch again, then dry heave until my body can't take anymore.

"Oh, little bird," he murmurs.

I slowly meet his eyes, still shaking.

Concern fills his expression. "You're sick. Let's get you into bed."

His father raped my mother and killed my dad.

I push him away. "Get away from me."

He gapes at me, in shock at my outburst. "Fiona—"

"No! Get away from me!" I shout, pushing at him.

He barely budges. "Fiona—"

I kick at his chest.

Confused, he jerks his head back. "Fiona, what has gotten into you?"

"Stay away from me," I cry, scooting toward the corner.

He looks horrified. "What's going on, little bird?"

"Don't," I say, and begin sobbing uncontrollably.

"I don't understand what's happening here," he confesses.

I pull my knees to my chest, accusing, "Y-your f-father. H-how... How..." Fresh sobs fly out of me. The visions and sounds of the video haunt me, and I can't push them out of my head.

Kirill moves closer. He touches my leg. "Fiona—"

I jump up, screaming as loud as possible, "Get away from me!" and run through the penthouse.

He follows me. In a calm voice, he begs, "Please tell me what's happening right now."

I hurl, "You want to know?"

"Yes." He shoots me another confused but concerned look.

"Fine," I say, brushing past him and entering my office. I hit the keyboard, and the video starts playing.

Kirill freezes, his eyes widening, and the color drains from his face.

I point to the man on the screen. My voice trembles as I ask, "That is your father?"

He glances at me helplessly, grinding his molars.

"So it's true?" I demand with tears streaming down my cheeks.

He squeezes his eyes closed tightly. "Yes, that's my father."

My insides quiver harder as I ask, "Did you know?"

He remains silent and slowly opens his eyes, pinning his guilty gaze on me.

I tremble so hard I have to sit down at my desk.

His expression turns remorseful.

I turn in my chair, unable to look at him, choking out, "You knew your father did this to my mother and father?"

His voice cracks when he admits, "Unfortunately, yes. I did."

I spin back to face him, growling, "And you didn't think this was important to tell me?"

Tension explodes between us, mixing with the screams from my mother and father.

He steps in front of me and turns the video off. He asks, "How did you get this?"

I sarcastically laugh. "How did I get this? That's what you want to know?"

He keeps his voice neutral. "Yes, Fiona. I need to know how you got this."

"It was delivered to me."

"By whom?"

"By a man."

"What man?"

"I don't know."

Kirill kneels and puts his hands on my cheeks.

I close my eyes, trying to breathe.

He softens his tone. "Fiona, I'm sorry I didn't tell you. I didn't want you to hate me."

I open my eyes and pull his hands off me. I rise, seething, "Hate you? You kept the worst thing that ever happened to my family from me."

"I didn't want you to ever know about this. Nor did I know this video existed," he declares, standing up.

"Well, unfortunately it does, and I'm never getting it out of my mind," I shriek, jabbing him in the chest, a new wave of emotion overpowering me.

"I'm so sorry," he claims. He pulls me into him.

I sob for a moment, but then I push him away, warning, "Get away from me."

Hurt and fear darken his features. He begs, "Fiona, please."

I shake my head, sternly replying, "No." I run to the bedroom, grab a bag from the closet, and begin stuffing it with clothes.

"What are you doing?" he questions, standing in the doorway.

"I'm getting away from you," I state.

He inhales sharply, then pleads, "Please. I'm not my father."

I spin and point at him. "You may not be your father, but you hid this from me. You should have told me."

"Told you what? That my father was the monster who destroyed your father and violated your mother? Did you really want to know that?" he asks.

I don't answer. The air in my lungs is thick and stale. I continue to toss random clothes into the bag, unable to shake the horror of the scenes I witnessed on the video. I zip the bag, then step in front of him, demanding, "Move."

"Fiona—"

"I said to move," I order.

He closes his eyes and then steps back. "Please, stop for a minute."

I brush past him, enter the office, and grab my phone. I return to the main room and toss it in my purse.

Kirill asks, "Where are you going?"

"It's none of your business."

"It is. I'm your husband," he reminds me.

More emotions pummel me. Love, hatred, and disappointment swallow me whole to the point I wonder if death would be a better option than having to find a way through this. I manage to get out, "You told me you'd tell me everything. I thought we didn't have secrets, but you kept the biggest one from me. So what kind of marriage do we have, Kirill?"

He stands taller, asserting, "We have a great marriage, and you know it. Don't let this destroy us. Please. I love you."

A sharp pain tears through my heart. My voice cracks. "I love you too, but I can't do this. Goodbye, Kirill." Tears drip off my chin as I exit the room.

He follows me to the elevator and grabs my arm.

"Don't touch me," I shriek.

He releases me immediately. "You can't leave like this."

The elevator doors open, and I step inside.

He follows me.

I push him, screaming, "Get out!"

"Fiona—"

"I said to get out. Get away from me, Kirill. I mean it. I can't right now. Just go. Leave me alone," I insist.

He blinks hard, his eyes glistening. In a helpless voice, he says, "Okay. I'll give you some space. I'm sorry I didn't tell you. But I love you."

"Get out," I repeat, crying harder. "Please."

He reluctantly steps out.

I hit the button. The elevator doors take forever to close. When they finally do, I lean against the wall in the corner and sob. Like always, the elevator moves slowly down to the main floor.

The doors open, revealing the redhead who lives on the floor below us. She's always giving Kirill dirty looks. With a shocked look, she asks, "Honey, are you okay?"

"I'm fine."

She stays planted in front of me. "What did he do to you?"

All the rage I'm feeling comes to a head. I step closer so my face is inches from hers, and snarl, "My husband didn't do anything to me. Mind your own business!"

Fear explodes on her face.

"Get out of my way," I say, pushing past her.

"He did something to you! I know it!" she calls after me.

I drop my bag, spin toward her, and lunge at her inside the elevator.

She backs up to the wall, gasping.

I put my hand on her throat, squeeze, and threaten, "You don't know who you're messing with, lady. Give one more nasty look to my husband or accuse him of something, and I swear to God, I will kill you."

She gasps for breath.

"Blink if you understand," I snarl.

She blinks hard.

I release her, shoot her a death glare, and add, "You're pathetic." Then I step out of the elevator and pick up my bag, rushing toward the exit.

The fresh air doesn't feel much different from the stifling air in the building. I glance around and realize I have no plan and don't know where I'm going. I pull my phone out and make a call.

Zara chirps, "Hey, girl. What's up?"

I cry, "I need you to come get me."

Her voice falls. "Fiona, what's wrong?"

"Please come get me. I need you to come right away," I plead.

"Okay. Don't worry. I have the babies, but Sean's not far from you."

"Please. I need to get out of here," I sob.

"Okay. Let me text him, but stay on the phone," she instructs.

I obey, and a moment passes.

"He's just down the street. He said his driver will be there in two minutes," she says.

"Thank you." I sniffle, trying to pull myself together.

"Fiona, are you okay?"

I try to answer her question, but nothing comes out.

"Fiona?"

"No, I'm not," I admit, and another rush of tears falls.

The building security guard comes closer, asking, "Mrs. Petrov, are you okay?"

"Yes. Please leave me alone," I snap.

He arches his eyebrows but steps back.

My chest tightens, and my heart races. I bend over, trying to get air.

Zara asks, "What happened?"

Sean's SUV pulls to the curb. "His driver's here. Thanks, Zara." I hang up, put my phone in my bag, and jump into the back seat before the driver can get out.

Conán, Sean's driver, frets, "Are you okay?"

"Yes."

He narrows his eyes, "Did he do something to you?"

"No, and don't ever speak that way about my husband again," I growl.

"Sorry," he mutters.

"Please go."

"Yes, ma'am." He pulls out in the traffic, then adds, "I have to pick Sean up."

"Fine," I say.

He travels three blocks, pulls up to a building, and Sean steps out. He rushes to the SUV, gets into the car, and slides next to me. He puts the divider window up, then asks, "What did he do to you?"

"He..." I open my mouth and shake my head.

"Fiona?" Sean asks with anger in his voice.

"He didn't do anything to me, but..." I start to sob.

Sean pulls me into his arms and holds my head close to his chest. "You have to tell me what's going on."

It takes me a while to pull back and look at him. The tears continue to fall. "Do you know how Dad died?"

Sean's face falls. "I have a basic knowledge."

I scrunch my face, barely able to ask, "Do you know about Mom?"

"Mom?" Sean questions.

"She...she... She was there!"

Sean's eyes blaze with anger and horror. "Fiona, what are you talking about?"

I cry harder. "Did you know Kirill's dad was there?"

Sean jerks his head back.

"Sean?"

He hesitates, then shakes his head. "His dad wasn't there. It was Uncle Niall and Uncle Shamus. The other men were Lorenzo Abruzzo, Anthony Rossi, Tadeg Bailey, and Daniel Abruzzo. You might have met him a few times at the Marinos'. They didn't know he was an Abruzzo infiltrating them."

I shake my head. "No. A Petrov was there."

"No, you're wrong," Sean insists.

I argue, "Kirill said it was true!"

Sean scrunches his forehead.

"Who was the one with the crucifix? The one with the emerald center?" I ask.

Sean slowly shrugs his shoulders. "I don't know about a crucifix. Why?"

I blurt out, "He was Kirill's dad."

Sean's face hardens.

I start to cry again, with visions of the video popping up in my mind and the sounds of my dad's and mom's tortured screams filling it.

Sean pulls me back into him.

I sob. "I need to see Mom. Please let me use your plane. Please."

He holds me tighter and lowers the divider, ordering, "Airport. Now."

"Yes, sir." The SUV does a sharp U-turn.

Sean puts the glass up and asks, "Fiona, what were you saying about Mom?"

Flashbacks of the video torment me. I can't speak, going into a full-blown panic attack, and the rest of the ride is a fog.

Sean somehow gets me on the plane, and more shock sets in. One minute, we're in Chicago, and the next thing I know, we're in New York.

It's dark out, and Sean squeezes my hand, announcing, "Fiona, we're here."

I blink hard, glancing out the window, and the steps of the Marino mansion come into view.

"Let's go inside," he gently says.

Suddenly, I don't know why I'm here. I blurt out, "What am I going to say to Mom?" and start to cry again.

Sean helps me out of the SUV and then leads me into the house.

He steers us to the living area and opens the door.

I step inside.

"Fiona! Sean! What are you—" The color drains from Mom's face. She rushes over to me. "Fiona, what's wrong?"

I can't speak. I fall into her arms, hugging her tightly, knowing things will never be the same again.

Kirill

Chapter
TWENTY-EIGHT

Nothing has ever made me crazier. I don't know who sent that video, but I've sat and watched it too many times with anger, hatred, and disgrace running through me at an all-time high.

Someone in The Underworld sent this to Fiona. I'm still as clueless as to who, as I was when she stormed out of here. The security footage reveals nothing. So I bark at Draco for the millionth time, "How did this happen?"

He furrows his eyebrows. "Sir, I don't know."

I slam my hand on the desk. "Stop giving me the same damn answer with nothing attached to it!"

"Sir, we're working on it. I know you're frustrated—"

"This should never have happened in my own home," I seethe.

He nods. "I agree."

"There's a Zenith Mandate out. There is supposed to be surveillance on every member of The Underworld, so why don't we know who the delivery guy was or the person behind this?" I spout.

He opens his mouth to speak, but his phone buzzes. He glances at it and groans.

"What is it?" I question.

"There's an issue in the tech room. I need to go."

I rub my hands over my face in frustration.

"Sir?" he questions.

I motion toward the door. "Fine. Go."

He exits.

I rise and pace the penthouse. I try to call Fiona again, but her phone's off, and I can't trace it. It's another security hole, and an inexcusable one. Yet I can't do a damn thing about it right now, so I do the only thing I can. I call Sean, hoping he'll finally pick up.

With disdain, he answers on the first ring, "Kirill."

I squeeze my eyes shut.

He knows.

"Where's Fiona?" I demand.

"That's not your business," he says.

I seethe, "Like hell, it isn't. She's my wife."

"Maybe you should have thought about that before you withheld information from her," Sean accuses.

Rage bubbles up within me. The same helplessness I've felt since I walked into the house yesterday and saw my bride in distress. I admit, "I thought it would hurt her."

Sean's snarls, "To know your father was Daniel?"

My stomach flips. The nightmare I tried to keep buried seems more alive than ever. I can only think of replying, "I'm not my father."

Sean scoffs. "I don't know what to say to you, Kirill, but your father has destroyed my family."

"I'm truly sorry. Your father meant everything to me," I offer, but it sounds weak.

"And are you sorry for what he did to my mother?" he snarls.

I squeeze my eyes shut, fighting my emotions. I lower my voice, responding, "It was vile and unforgivable. So, yes, I can't begin to express how sorry I am that my father did what he did."

Tension fills the line.

I finally break it, questioning again, "Where's my wife?"

"I'm sorry. Fiona needs her space, so you don't get to know until she's ready for you to know," he declares.

I roar, "Someone is trying to assassinate her! I can't protect her if I don't know where she is. Or did you forget that?"

He fires back, "I'm protecting her. You don't have to worry about it."

"Bullshit. You don't have the power I do," I remind him.

He scoffs. "I'll take care of my family."

"Fiona *is* my family," I insist.

"No, your family pretends to be one of the good guys but is really the devil. Tell me, Kirill. How the hell did your father pass himself off as an Italian if he was a Petrov?" Sean barks.

I close my eyes, trying to calm my racing heart. I admit, "His father was a Petrov. His mother was an Abruzzo. He grew up in both Italy and Russia, and learned the languages so well he could fool anyone."

The line goes silent.

"Please. Tell me where my wife is so I can make sure she's protected," I beg.

"She doesn't want to see or talk to you, Kirill. Leave her alone."

"This isn't your call, Sean. Where is she? I saw Zara, and I know she's not at your place, so where did you take her?"

"I'm hanging up now. I'll talk to you later," he says. The line goes dead.

"Goddamn it," I say, throwing my phone against the wall.

"Whoa. Calm down," Valentina orders, stepping inside the room with Brax on her heels.

"Don't tell me to calm down. My wife is missing."

"No, she's not missing," Brax interjects.

I scowl at him. "You better have something good to say after that comment."

He crosses his arms and clenches his jaw.

Valentina says, "We need you to take a breather."

Brax nods, adding, "If you want any information from us, she's right. You need to calm the fuck down."

I rush over and grab his shirt. "Don't you tell me to calm the fuck down when my wife is missing!"

"Kirill!" Valentina exclaims, trying to pull me off of him.

Brax shoves me, and I step back. "Get off me, man."

I point a finger in his face, snarling, "You better watch who you're talking to."

"I thought you wanted to know where your wife was?" he taunts.

My chest tightens and my heart pounds.

Valentina puts her hand on my bicep. "Kirill, let's go sit down. Please."

"Just tell me where my wife is," I say in desperation.

Compassion fills her expression. "She doesn't want to see you right now. I think it's best if you stay away."

"I'm not staying away from my wife," I insist.

"If you calm down, I'll tell you where she's at," Brax offers.

Valentina's head snaps toward him. "She doesn't want to see him."

"Where is she?" I demand.

"She's at Dante's place. Don't worry. Sean's there. She's fine. She needs time. I've known her forever. Give her some space," he suggests.

"Chicago or New York?" I question.

"New York. Sean took her. Don't worry, she's safe," Brax reiterates.

"She's not safe," I bark. "Someone wants her dead. Or did you two forget about that?"

Valentina pins me with a withering look. She puts her hand on her hip and points to the couch. "Kirill, sit your ass down."

I scowl.

She hisses, "I said to sit."

My insides shake harder.

"Kirill," she says in a softer tone.

I meet her eyes. "I need my wife. Home. Safe. With me."

She sighs and nods. "I know. Please sit."

Feeling defeated, I finally cave and plop down on the chair.

They sit on the sofa. Valentina looks at Brax uncomfortably, and he gives her the same expression.

Panic hits me. "What aren't you two telling me?"

Brax shakes his head. "We're coming up empty, man."

"What do you mean you're coming up empty? There's a Zenith Mandate. There is surveillance on everyone. It's not possible to have nothing!"

He groans. "Kirill, you're going to have a heart attack if you don't calm the fuck down."

"Watch your mouth," I warn.

Valentina orders, "Just sit there and be quiet, Brax." She shakes her head at him.

"Don't start with me," he growls.

"Cut the shit! You two were assigned to gather intel on whoever is threatening my wife's life," I remind them.

Brax opens his mouth, and Valentina puts her hand over it.

She offers, "Whoever's behind this, they know how to cover their tracks. But we will find out who's behind the plot. I promise."

I point at them. "You two are the only ones I can fully trust besides Sean and Zara. So I need you to do your job. Do you understand me?"

"We're—"

Valentina slaps her hand over Brax's mouth again. "We're working on it. Trust me, we will find out who's behind this."

"Find out," I demand and then rise. I grab my phone off the floor and slide it into my pocket.

"Where are you going?" Valentina asks, quick on my heels.

"To my wife."

"You can't go there," Brax states.

"Bullshit. I can go any fucking where I want, and don't forget it," I warn, pushing the button on the elevator.

"Kirill, you need to give her time on her own," he says again.

"Come on! Goddamn it!" I say, slamming my fist into the button, pissed that the elevator still isn't fixed.

Valentina adds, "Kirill, she's in bad shape. Just let her be with her family right now."

"I am her family!" I roar.

She jumps backward, her eyes wide.

"Fuck this." I go over to the staircase and jog down all the flights. I reach the bottom, push open the side door, and run to the front, where my SUV is parked.

Ivan asks, "Where to, sir?"

"Airport." I text my flight crew.

Me: Get the plane ready for New York, pronto.

Arina: Got it.

I stare out the window. The buildings go by in a blur as I wonder how I got to this point.

My wife can't hate me after loving me so unconditionally, can she?

Why didn't I tell her what I knew?

Would she hate me any less if I had?

My phone rings. I glance at the screen and answer, "Draco, what is it?"

His voice is laced with frustration. "All the video footage is out. We can't get it back up."

"Why not?" I question.

"The entire building just lost the internet," he informs me.

"So get it back up."

"It's not a typical outage."

My gut dives. "Meaning?"

He clears his throat. "Sir, we've been hacked."

My pulse skyrockets. "There's a Zenith Mandate out. This shouldn't be possible!"

He says nothing.

I curl my fist at my side. "Fix it and let me know when it's done," I order, then hang up and toss my phone on the seat next to me. I snarl, "Move faster, Ivan."

"Yes, sir." He accelerates, weaving in and out of traffic for several minutes.

"Faster," I demand.

He guns it, and within seconds, sirens blare from behind us.

"Fuck," Ivan mumbles.

"Don't stop. Go faster," I instruct.

"Sir?" he questions, looking at me through the rearview mirror.

I bark, "I said, don't stop. I need to get to the airport."

He sighs. "Yes, sir." He pushes his foot down, and the speedometer hits over 100mph.

I glance behind us.

Several cops are on our tail. When we get to the airport, Ivan parks beside the plane, and the police surround the car.

One says through the speaker, "Step out of the vehicle with your hands in the air."

The other cops get out of their cars, keeping their bodies shielded by their doors, and point their guns at our vehicle.

"Fuck," Ivan mutters.

I step out and put my hands in the air, yelling, "Stingray 88!"

No one puts their guns down.

I shout again, "Stingray 88!"

"Hold fire," an officer yells. He cautiously walks toward me and then lowers his gun. In a low tone, he says, "Your Majesty, I'm sorry. I didn't know it was you."

"Now you do. I have somewhere to be, so excuse me for forgetting the niceties," I snarl.

"Yes. Sorry, sir," he repeats, then screams, "False alarm. Time to go."

A few of the officers hesitate.

He shouts, "I said now!"

They get into their vehicles and race off the runway.

The officer adds, "Again, my sincerest apologies, Your Majesty."

"Don't let it happen again," I grumble as I push past him to the staircase.

Arina greets me and curtsies. "Your Majesty."

"Get this plane off the ground, now," I bark and brush past her. I plop down in the seat.

In less than five minutes, we're off the ground and in the air. I try to call Fiona again.

Her sweet voice on her voicemail greeting sends a pain to my chest. *"Hi, this is Fiona. Leave a message."*

A long beep sounds in my ear.

Sadness overpowers me. I try to soften my tone, stating, "It's me again. Please call me. I'm sorry. I don't know what to say, but I'm sorry. I love you, and we need to talk. Please. I promise you, I'm not my father." I squeeze my eyes shut, taking a few deep breaths.

Then I add, "I love you more than anything. Please call me." I hang up, hating how desperate I sound, how out of control I feel, and the chaos surrounding me I can't seem to get a hold of.

How the hell can I have a Zenith Mandate out, yet there's no intelligence?

My gut tells me this is bigger than just one person or maybe even two. Maybe the majority of The Underworld's in on it, and they're all out to get me. Who knows? But then again, I'm the king, and everybody always wants my spot.

A new realization hits me.

I named Sean and Zara successors.

I pick up the phone again.

Sean barks, "Kirill, I don't have time to argue with you all day."

"Shut up and listen, and that's an order, not a request," I demand.

He goes quiet.

I continue, "The Zenith Mandate isn't working. Ask Brax if you don't believe me, but there's no intel. That means this is larger than we thought, and if that's the case, they're after you and Zara too."

"You're paranoid, Kirill. There have been no threats against Zara or me," he says.

I point out, "I named you successors. Somebody wants to be king and queen."

Tension fills the air.

"Are you there?" I ask.

He lowers his voice. "Yeah, I'm here."

"Are you still in New York or back with Zara?"

"New York," he replies with a hint of fear.

My stomach spins. I advise, "You better get home to your wife and kids. Send Brax over to stay with them until you're back."

Again, he says nothing.

"Sean, did you hear me?" I ask, worried he's not taking this seriously or I lost the call in the air.

He clears his throat. "Yeah. Thanks for calling."

"Go take care of your family," I say, hanging up. I sit back in my chair.

Arina cautiously approaches. "Sir?"

I glance up at her.

Concern floods her expression. "Can I get you anything?"

I soften my tone. "No, I'm fine. I'm sorry if I was a jackass when I got on the plane."

A tiny smile curves her lips. "You weren't."

"I'm afraid I was," I admit.

She hesitates.

"What is it, Arina?"

She stares at me for a moment. "Are you sure I can't get you anything?"

"Yes, but thank you. I just need to be alone."

She nods and makes herself scarce.

The flight seems to take forever. When I finally land in New York, my anxiety's at an all-time high. The claw in my gut scraped so deep during the flight that it's now raw. Worse, there are no answers to any of my problems.

I get into my SUV and direct my driver to the Marino estate. When we arrive at the gate, Dante's men glare at me.

I announce, "Kirill Petrov. I'm here to see Fiona."

"Petrov? We don't allow Petrov's on this estate." He spits on the ground, scowling.

I squeeze my fist and demand, "Call Dante."

He doesn't move. "You're not on the list. Turn around."

"I don't need to be on the list. My wife is in there, so call Dante or Bridget!" I roar.

He stays planted, his expression darkening.

"Call them now or all hell is going to break loose on this estate," I threaten.

He narrows his eyes in disgust but picks up the phone. "Sir, Kirill Petrov is here. Says he's here to see Fiona."

Silence ensues for what feels like endless moments.

"Yes, sir," he says, then hangs up the phone and presses a button. He orders, "Drive straight. Take the first curve to the right."

My driver obeys and stops next to the ornate front porch.

I jump out of the SUV, and the front door opens.

Bridget steps outside and shuts the door. She comes down the steps, glaring at me.

Shame and guilt fill me. I take a deep breath. "Bridget—"

"She doesn't want to talk to you right now," she states.

"Please. I love her. She's my wife. I need to talk to her. I promise you, I'm not my father," I repeat for what feels like the millionth time. I blink hard, feeling like I'm going to cry, which is another thing I detest.

Men don't cry in my world.

Bridget sighs, and a flash of compassion flits over her expression. "I'm sorry, Kirill. She doesn't want to see you. I have to respect my daughter's wishes. You should go home."

Panic resurfaces. "I'm not leaving New York until Fiona's with me."

She studies me.

"Please. I love her. And if I had known what they were going to do to —" I turn my head and cover my eyes, trying to control my overwhelming guilt and shame, but I can't.

Bridget steps closer and puts her hand on my bicep. "Kirill."

I take a shaky breath and pull it together enough to face her.

She says in a non-accusing voice, "I don't understand how my daughter got to the point where she married a Petrov."

"I promise you, I'm not like them," I assert.

Bridget tilts her head, studying me. Then she asks, "How did you know my husband?"

My heart pounds harder. All the reasons I can't tell Bridget anything flash before me, but then Fiona's face overrules all of it. I glance behind us, ensuring no one is listening, and then back at her. I break my Underworld vows and admit, "He wanted the crime families to get along. He didn't want his children to suffer the way his generation did. He envisioned a world that many couldn't believe was possible. But there were people who did believe it was possible, and they dove headfirst into his utopia. I was one of them, and he didn't care that I was a Petrov. He saw my potential and took me under his wing."

Bridget's lips slightly curve. She nods. "Sounds like Sean."

I blurt out, "If I could tell you everything, I would. But if I did, it's not my life I worry about—it's your daughter's. And I've already disclosed more than I'm allowed."

She takes a deep breath and slowly releases it.

Her silence seems to last forever. I don't speak, not trusting my current state and what I might reveal.

Bridget breaks it, asking, "Did Sean have the ring Fiona wears made for me?"

My heart races faster. I confess, "Yes. He was going to give it to you when you renewed your vows. When he died, I secured it in a vault in Monaco."

Bridget's lips twitch. "Monaco?"

"Yes."

Her voice lifts. "Sean wanted to retire in Monaco."

"He did?"

"Yes." She smiles bigger, then takes more deep breaths, bobbing her head, as if remembering something.

"Do you want the ring? If I had known you knew about it, I would have ensured you received it years ago. But I thought you didn't know, so it seemed like Fiona should have it."

A moment passes, and Bridget shakes her head. "No. It's a beautiful ring, and there was a time in my life I was meant to have it. That time has passed."

"Are you sure," I ask.

She nods. "Yes. And I'm glad Fiona has it."

"You are?"

"Yes. It's not meant to sit in a vault, hidden from the world."

Emotions try to drag me under. I tear up and blurt out, "He was the best man I ever met."

Her smile weakens. She meets my eyes, replying, "And now you're married to his only daughter," but it doesn't sound harsh like in the past.

I don't hesitate, once more insisting, "I love her. And I'm not like any of the Petrovs you know."

She studies me further, then offers, "I know you aren't like them."

I freeze, cautiously asking, "You do?"

She shifts on her feet. "Yes. Sean told me about the boy whose family sliced him to pieces and left him for dead, all because of what he wouldn't do."

My breath gets stolen from my lungs.

She continues, "If my daughter was going to marry a Petrov, I'm thankful it was you."

I stay quiet, not trusting my voice.

"Is it fair to say there's something bigger out there that Sean created, and now his children are involved?" she asks.

"Yes."

She adds, "It's in their best interest if I stop asking questions?"

"Yes."

She glances at the woods, then rolls her eyes toward the sky and sighs.

I ask, "Can I please see Fiona?"

She pins her sympathetic gaze on me and shakes her head. "No. I'm sorry, but my daughter is very upset right now. I'm sure you understand why."

I clench my fist at my side. "Yes, and I'm sorry, Bridget. I'm so sorry for what my family did to you and Sean. He was one of the only people that ever actually..." I look away again, blinking hard and pushing my fingers into my eyes.

"It's not your fault, Kirill," she claims.

I freeze again, holding my breath.

"Look at me," she orders.

I squeeze the bridge of my nose, collecting tears, then slowly meet her eyes.

She adamantly repeats, "It's not your fault."

My jaw tics. I swallow the lump in my throat. I declare, "If I could kill my father for what he did to you and Sean, I would. I would do it with my bare hands and torture him longer than I've ever tortured anyone."

Her lips twitch. "If I could watch you do it, I would. But we can't live through what-ifs, can we?"

I open my mouth, but nothing comes out.

She lifts her chin and states, "Fiona needs some time."

"How much?"

A tiny laugh bursts out of her.

Confused, I look at her in question.

"Sorry. You just sounded like Sean. He was just as impatient when he was in the doghouse with me."

"I just want to talk to her," I claim.

Bridget nods. "Yes, I understand. Give her some time. She'll tell you when she's ready."

I reveal my fear. "What if she never wants to speak to me again?"

Compassion fills Bridget's face. She insists, "She will. Just back off for now."

Not knowing what else to do, I sigh and agree. "Okay. But tell Dante I need to speak with him regarding security. And I'm not leaving New York."

Bridget smiles and pats my shoulder. "I'll let both of them know."

Fiona

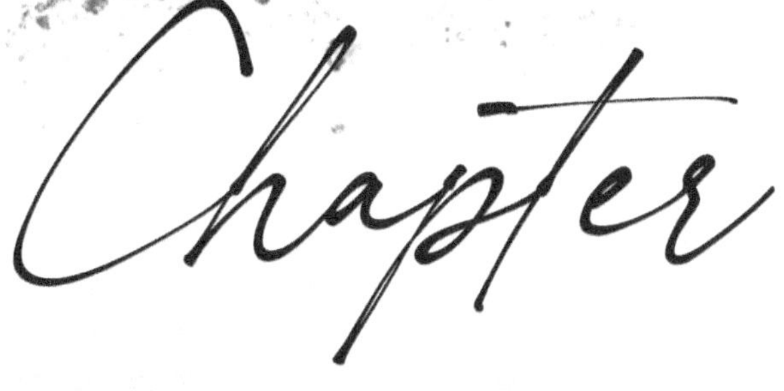

Chapter
TWENTY-NINE

Sweat drips down my face, and I grip the toilet bowl, heaving a final time. I sit back on the cold tile when I'm convinced there's no more.

Mom's voice cuts through the air. "Fiona, are you pregnant?"

My heart beats faster. I turn my head, staring at her.

She arches her eyebrows and softly asks, "Are you?"

I slowly shrug my shoulders, and my eyes fill with tears. I answer, "Maybe."

She walks to the sink, pulls a towel off the rack, douses it in water, and wrings it out. She holds her hand out. "Let's get you off the floor."

I take her hand and rise.

She steers me into my bedroom, toward the sitting area, ordering, "Sit down, sweetie."

I take a seat.

She sits next to me and presses the wet towel against my forehead. "How long have you been getting sick?"

I think back, and more tears form as I shake my head. "Every day since I've been here."

She nods. "I see. Do you think we should take a test?"

My pulse pounds between my ears. I look away, gripping my thigh.

She puts her hand on mine, sternly pointing out, "Fiona, if you're pregnant, you need to know."

I turn my head back toward her, confessing, "I wanted to be. But now... I don't know, Mom." Another round of tears falls.

She pulls me into her arms. "Shh, it's okay. Everything's going to be okay."

I freak out. "How? If I'm pregnant and I'm not even talking to my child's father..."

She pulls back. "Whose choice is that?"

I gape at her.

"Answer me," she demands.

I look away.

"Fiona, who's choosing not to speak the other?" she repeats.

I pull at my fingers, mumbling, "Me."

She continues, "You need to talk to him."

I sniffle and turn away.

She questions, "What are you mad at him about?"

My lip trembles. I blink, and more tears run down my cheek and off my jaw. I turn back. "How can you ask me that?"

She pins her gaze on me. "Tell me exactly what you're mad about so I'm not assuming anything."

I scoff. "Do I really need to spell it out?"

"Yes. So tell me."

My insides quiver as well as my voice, "I-I don't know how you can sit here and be so strong after what they did to you." Flashbacks of the video pop into my mind.

Mom's face hardens a bit. She declares, "I had a lot of therapy, Fiona. And there's no point living in the past. We can't do things over again. We can only move forward."

I choke out, "I married the son of the man who...who..." I turn away, unable to say the word.

She grips my chin, tilting my face back to hers so I can't avoid her. Sympathy is written across her features. She firmly declares, "Kirill didn't harm me. Nor has he harmed you. It's not his fault what happened, so you need to determine what exactly you're blaming him for."

"He knew and didn't tell me!"

She raises a brow at me.

"He should have told me," I insist.

Mom takes a deep breath and releases it. "I don't know, Fiona. I never wanted you or Sean to know about it, but now you do. As your mother, I also tried to protect you by keeping you in the dark. So maybe you should stop talking to me too."

I gape at her.

She points at me, asserting, "Sounds ridiculous, right?"

I ponder her question.

She asks, "Do you think knowing about it makes it better?"

I think further, opening my mouth and then shutting it. I look away, shaking my head, confessing, "I don't know."

"In my eyes, you and Sean knowing makes it worse. It doesn't erase the facts or make anyone feel any better. Now, my children have another ache in their hearts. So I don't blame Kirill for not telling you. I respect him for it. And it's not fair to blame him for what his father did."

I don't look at her, trying to get past the betrayal I feel but unsure how do it.

Mom orders, "Look at me."

I turn toward her.

She holds an envelope in front of me. My name is scrawled on the front in Kirill's handwriting.

My heart beats faster.

She lowers her voice, asking, "Don't you think it's time you read his letters?"

My heart squeezes as I stare at the envelope. She's given me one every day, but they're in my desk drawer. I can't open them.

"Take it, Fiona. You need to read this and the others. I don't know what's in them, but he comes here every day—in pain and full of apologies—with a new one. You're only making things worse, and you can't stop communicating with your husband, especially if you're having his baby," she scolds.

"He lied to me," I declare.

She jerks her head back. "How? Tell me how he lied to you."

"He—" I stop.

Mom softens her tone. "He didn't lie to you. He didn't tell you something so you wouldn't be hurt. There's a difference. Now, I suggest you take a pregnancy test and read the letters your husband has sent you."

My eyes fill with more tears.

She tilts her head, stating, "You can't heal without communication." She puts the letter on my lap and rises.

I stare at it, my body trembling.

"Fiona."

I gaze up at her.

She peers down at me. "Do you love him?"

My chest tightens to the point my heart hurts. More tears fall.

She waits for me to answer.

In a blurry haze, I nod.

She puts her hand on my shoulder, ordering, "Read the letters, Fiona." She turns and leaves my room, shutting the door.

I stare at the envelope for several moments, then open it.

> MY DEAREST FIONA,
> I NEVER KNEW TWENTY DAYS COULD FEEL SO LONG. EVERY SECOND THAT PASSES SEEMS TO STRETCH LONGER. AND I THOUGHT I KNEW PAIN, BUT I REALIZE I DIDN'T UNDERSTAND IT UNTIL NOW. NOTHING COMPARES TO THE AGONY CONSTANTLY CLAWING INSIDE OF ME, DIGGING DEEPER WHEN I THINK IT CAN'T POSSIBLY HURT ANY MORE.

Tears drip onto the letter. I reach across the table, grab tissues, dab my eyes, and continue reading.

> SINCE YOU'VE ALWAYS BEEN HONEST WITH ME, I'LL TELL YOU THE TRUTH. I'D DO ANYTHING TO PROTECT YOU. PHYSICALLY. MENTALLY. EMOTIONALLY. SO THERE'S NO WAY I COULD HAVE EVER TOLD YOU WHAT MY FATHER DID TO YOUR PARENTS. I KNEW IT WOULD DAMAGE YOUR HEART, AND I'D RATHER DIE

> THAN BE THE CAUSE OF INFLICTING PAIN UPON YOU

I close my eyes, wishing he was here to hold me, knowing it's true. Kirill always put my safety and happiness before his. I sniffle and return to the letter.

> BEFORE THAT VIDEO ARRIVED, I HAD NEVER SEEN IT. YES, I WAS AWARE OF WHAT HAPPENED, BUT ONLY VERBALLY. AND IT WAS YEARS AFTER MY FATHER'S DEATH WHEN I LEARNED THE TRUTH. SO, I DIDN'T KNOW THE VIDEO EXISTED. NAIVELY, I DECIDED TO KEEP THE TRUTH BURIED FOREVER TO SAFE-GUARD YOUR HEART, AND SELFISHLY SO YOU WOULDN'T HATE ME.
> ADMITTEDLY, I WATCHED THE SCENE TOO MANY TIMES BEFORE DISCOVERING YOU WERE IN NEW YORK. IT TORE ME TO PIECES, AND ALL I KEEP THINKING IS HOW IT HAD TO HAVE HURT YOU EVEN WORSE.

A new pain fills me. It's not for my mom or dad but for Kirill. I may not know how to overcome this, but he was close to my father. His own blood did this to my parents. The same man who scarred him both inside and out did the same to my family. So, his statement is a reminder that he's a victim too. And the realization cuts into me.

I continue reading.

> I'VE NEVER DESERVED YOU, FIONA. THE MOMENT THE OMNI ORDERED ME TO MARRY YOU, ALL I COULD THINK ABOUT WAS HOW UNFAIR IT WAS TO YOU. AS MUCH AS I TRIED TO AVOID THE DAY YOU WOULD REALIZE WHO YOU'RE MARRIED TO, IT'S COME. I STUPIDLY PUSHED IT SO FAR BACK IN MY MIND THAT I BELIEVED YOU WOULDN'T EVER HATE ME, BUT NOW YOU KNOW THE FULL TRUTH, AND THERE'S NO TURNING BACK.
> I MISS EVERYTHING ABOUT YOU. NOT SEEING YOUR SMILE OR HEARING YOUR LAUGH IS KILLING ME. DON'T GET ME STARTED

ON THE INABILITY TO HOLD YOU. IF I COULD LIE IN BED AND
SPOON YOU FOR ETERNITY, I WOULD.

I laugh through my tears, remembering how he didn't know what spooning was, and more sadness hits me. The ache to feel him wrapped around my body intensifies. I try to finish the letter.

MOST OF ALL, I MISS SEEING HOW YOU LOOK AT ME WITH
NOTHING BUT LOVE AND ADMIRATION. FROM THE FIRST
MOMENT YOU PINNED YOUR GREEN EYES ON ME, YOU LOOKED
PAST MY FLAWS AND ONLY SAW ME. IT TOOK ME A LONG TIME
TO BELIEVE YOUR ATTRACTION FOR ME, AND NOW THAT IT'S
GONE, I'M AN ADDICT, JONESING TO SEE IT ONE MORE TIME.

I put my hand over my face, taking deep breaths, hating how much this hurts. Then I blow my nose and read the rest.

WHATEVER YOU NEED ME TO DO TO TRY AND MAKE THINGS
RIGHT BETWEEN US, I WILL. I DON'T CARE WHAT IT IS, FIONA.
PLEASE. TALK TO ME. TELL ME WHAT I CAN DO.
I PROMISE YOU ONE THING. I DETEST MY FATHER. I MAY HAVE
HIS BLOOD, BUT I'M NOT HIM. NOR WILL I EVER BE.
I WANT MY WIFE BACK
PLEASE COME HOME. I'M STILL ON THE YACHT IN THE HARBOR.
I'LL WAIT FOR YOU FOR HOWEVER LONG YOU NEED.
LOVE,
KIRILL

Another round of tears leaks down my cheeks and then nausea hits me. I run to the bathroom, hug the toilet bowl, then go to the sink and clean my face. I stare at my bloodshot eyes in the mirror.

What am I doing?

It's not his fault.

He should have told me.

I return to my bedroom, open my desk drawer, and remove the stack of unopened letters. I turn over the first one, staring at his seal, then break it. I pull out the note.

One by one, I read his letters, sobbing through them as he professes his love for me, makes me laugh with little statements, and begs me to speak with him. By the time I'm done, his pain is so sharp it competes with mine.

I've never missed anyone like this or truly loved any other man.

We have to get through this.

He didn't tell me to protect me.

I stare at the stack of tearstained letters and decide there's only one answer on how to move forward.

I need to talk to him.

I need to go home.

He's on the yacht.

The harbor isn't far.

I leave my room and go to the garage. I scan the row of keys hanging on the wall and grab the set to my Land Rover. I slide into the SUV, open the garage door, and turn the engine on. I accelerate out of the garage and drive toward the gate. It opens, and I speed through it.

For several miles, I'm alone on the road. Then, a loud honk blares from behind me.

I glance in my rearview mirror. The hairs on my arms rise. Several SUVs are behind me. I slow down so they can pass, but one gets in front of me and doesn't go faster. Another slides up beside me, and I'm surrounded. The front SUV slows, and I can't do anything but stop.

I reach for my phone but realize I don't have it.

"Shit," I curse, and a cold sweat forms on my forehead.

Men in expensive suits step out of the SUVs, and my fear heightens. They circle my vehicle.

What am I going to do?

A man opens the back door of the SUV next to mine. Jytte steps out and tries to open my door, but it's locked. She orders, "Fiona, open the door."

I release an anxious breath, then open the door, reprimanding, "You scared the crap out of me!"

She narrows her eyes. "We have business matters to attend to, and you're late."

A wave of panic hits me. I know the rules. You're not allowed to be late to an Underworld summons, even if you're the queen.

"Why aren't you answering your phone?" she questions.

"It-it's been off," I reply, realizing how irresponsible I've been. The pit in my stomach grows. No matter what happens in my personal life, I have duties I'm obligated to fulfill.

Jytte insists, "Time is running out. Orders are pressing. Come with me, Fiona."

"What about my car? I can't just leave it in the middle of the road," I point out.

She rolls her eyes. "You're the queen. It'll be taken care of, so don't worry. Now, let's go."

My chest tightens.

Don't go with her.

I'm being silly.

"Okay." I follow her, slide into her SUV, and the door shuts. The vehicle takes off, and she closes the divider window.

I turn toward her, fretting, "What's going on?"

She lifts her chin, and a haughty expression appears on her face.

Chills run down my spine.

She declares, "It's come to our attention that you aren't fully aware of your duties and the rules."

The air in my lungs turns stale. I argue, "That's not true. I studied the Royal Doctrine well enough to know my duties as queen and all The Underworld laws."

She remains quiet, an arrogant look plastered on her face.

My gut flips. I insist, "I know everything inside the Royal Doctrine."

She states, "I guess we'll find out."

"What does that mean?"

Her lips twitch. "The Omni have demanded the membership to gather."

More fear fills me. "For what?"

Her smile grows. She reveals, "Tonight, you will partake in a ritual."

"Which one?" I question, putting my hand on my stomach, feeling ill.

Her smugness grows. She answers, "Tainted Crown."

"Tainted—" My mouth turns dry, and I swallow hard. The Tainted Crown can only be issued when the Omni believes a king, queen, or both aren't living up to the duties they've vowed to uphold.

They've plotted to overthrow us.

"Take me to my husband," I command.

Her lips turn up in a wicked grin.

Bile rises in my throat. I swallow it and say in a sharper tone, "I ordered you to take me to my husband."

She leans forward, grabs a crystal decanter, and pours several fingers of clear alcohol into a tumbler. She samples it, then takes a larger sip. She puts the glass in the cup holder and says, "He's already there."

I do my best to appear confident but feel nothing of the sort. If Kirill or I don't pass their test, there's only one ending for us.

Death.

Kirill

Chapter
THIRTY

"Your Majesty," Sergio interrupts, stepping into my office with a worried expression.

What now?

I shut my laptop. "What is it?"

He wrinkles his forehead and announces, "Ulrich is here with several others."

The hairs on my neck rise. I stand. "Here on the yacht?"

"Yes. He claims he needs to speak to you immediately."

I shut the door and face him, studying his face. "Why do you look alarmed?"

Sergio stands taller and murmurs, "They came on board with their guns pulled."

I freeze, taking in his statement and trying to figure out the best move. There's only one reason they would draw weapons. It's to escort me somewhere I might object going to.

That or it's an outright coup.

I pat Sergio on the shoulder. "Thank you for telling me. Please make sure the staff stays on task while I'm gone."

He scrunches his face but nods.

"Everything is fine," I reassure him.

He doesn't seem convinced.

I ask, "Where are they?"

"I had them wait in the bar," he answers.

"Good decision. Wait for me outside of the bar," I instruct and open the door. My gut flips faster, but I pick up my pace and walk into the room with my head held high, greeting, "Ulrich."

"Your Majesty," he states but doesn't bow.

The men with him rise, keeping their guns in sight.

I cross my arms. "What's your reason for bringing armed men onto my yacht and scaring my staff?"

Amusement flares in Ulrich's eyes. He picks up a stuffed olive, pops it in his mouth, chews, swallows, and takes a long drink of what I'm guessing is brandy. He taunts, "Why would members of The Underworld bring anything but pleasure to your staff?"

"Cut the shit, Ulrich. Why are you here?"

Arrogance replaces his amusement. He finishes his drink, sets the snifter down, and picks up the decanter. He pours a fresh glass, and suggests, "Shall we discuss this over drinks?"

"No," I bark.

"Fine. Suit yourself," he replies, strolling to the window. He taunts, "Such a nice yacht we supply for you."

I snarl, "I'll remind you that I'm the king. I've asked you why you're here. Stop playing games and answer my question or I'll issue a decree. And let me remind you that my men will toss you in a cell until I decide to return your freedom to you."

He chuckles until his eyes glisten.

I narrow my own eyes at him.

He wipes his cheek and states, "Look around, Kirill. You can issue all the decrees you want, but no one will adhere to them."

My chest tightens. I study each man, one by one, yet they look at me as if they can see through me. Then I ask, "Are none of you still loyal to the king?"

They don't flinch.

I scoff and threaten, "When Ulrich finishes having his fun, I will remember each one of you. The choice you've made in this room determines your fate."

They maintain their robot-like faces.

Ulrich steps closer. "It's time to go."

"Where?" I question.

"To Pompeii."

"Why?"

His lips twist before he taunts, "Didn't you hear?"

My gut flips. I wait for him to speak.

He continues, "There's a ritual tonight."

Goose bumps break out on my skin. I clench my jaw, not willing to give him the satisfaction of a response, and hold myself back from tearing him to shreds.

He leans into my ear, exclaiming, "Our ritual tonight is the Tainted Crown."

Anger and fear flare inside of me. I demand, "Where's my wife?"

"Oh, don't you worry. She's already on a plane," he informs me with an evil grin.

My gut drops further.

"Well? Shall we get going? You know how it's not nice to be late," he goads.

"Fine." I walk toward the exit.

His men fall into line behind me.

I step out of the bar and direct Sergio, "Send the royal plane to wait for me in Pompeii."

He gives me a worried glance and nods. "Yes, Your Majesty."

I make my way through the yacht, step onto the dock, and go to the SUVs waiting in the lot. One of the drivers opens a back door, avoiding my gaze. I give him the same look I gave the men, warning, "I'll remember you too."

He grinds his molars.

I slide into the back seat. Ulrich gets in next to me and shuts the door. I stare out the window, trying to determine how to keep Fiona and myself alive once we get to Pompeii.

Her copy of the Royal Doctrine wasn't an original. I've studied it for days, trying to stay busy and not go crazy waiting to hear from her. While it's subtle, the missing information is apparent. Only one who knows it inside and out can tell pertinent information has been removed.

They're going to use it against her.

The airport isn't far. We pull up next to the plane, and I get out, climbing the staircase and brushing past Ulrich's attendant. I sit and try to open the shade, but it's locked.

Rage fills me. It's what The Underworld does to new members before they've earned our trust. It's so they don't know where they're going. To do this to me, the king, is to show I have no power.

I don't right now.

"What shall we talk about?" Ulrich asks.

I lean back, close my eyes, and don't speak. I never fall asleep, spending the long flight going through scenarios for once the ritual starts. No matter how hard I think, I come to the same conclusion—Fiona and I are screwed.

We arrive in Pompeii, and I walk through the dim, barely-lit hallway. I try to open the door for the royal quarters, but it's locked.

"Tsk, tsk, tsk. That's not for you," he scolds.

I need to see Fiona.

"Nowhere in the Royal Doctrine does it state I don't have access to my royal quarters," I say, scowling at Ulrich.

He grins. "It does when the Tainted Crown gets incorporated with a Ceremony of Exposure."

My blood boils. I argue, "You cannot and will not subject the queen—"

"The Omni will do what we determine is best for The Underworld, and subject to provision 469," he roars, his eyes lighting with fire.

Provision 469 says the Omni have full authority to utilize a Ceremony of Exposure should the violation be significant enough to alter the state of The Underworld.

My mouth goes dry, and a lump forms in my throat. I swallow and look away.

"Move," Ulrich demands.

I continue walking down the hallway. We turn a corner.

He opens a door to a small room, ordering, "In."

I don't argue, stepping inside. There's one locker and a small bathroom. My crown sits on the table on top of a black pillow.

Where is Fiona?

Anxiety fills me.

"You know the drill," Ulrich says, then leans back against the wall with his arms crossed.

Begrudgingly, I strip out of my clothes, hang them in the locker, then put on the crown.

"Time to go," he declares and opens the door.

We walk through more hallways, and right as he reaches for the doorknob to the arena, I promise, "Before the sun rises, we will have one more ritual."

He arches his eyebrows.

I glare at him.

He grins. "I'll play along. Which one?"

"The Black Veil. And you'll be the groom."

He grunts. "Keep dreaming, Kirill." He pushes the door open.

My ears ring from the loud sound of lit torches being pounded on the ground. All the members in attendance are dressed for the occasion: men wear full skull masks and tuxedos, while the women don eye masks and long, white satin gowns. The stage has two guillotines next to each other. An X is painted on the floor in front of them. Dozens of roaring bonfires sizzle around them. Knights line up with gleaming swords pointed high in the air.

The crowd chants the Buddhist mantra associated with compassion and inner light, "Om Mani Padme Hum," but I already know nothing tonight will be compassionate or display an inner light.

I have to get us out of this.

Where is Fiona?

The chant morphs to hissing as I climb the steps to the stage, stand on the X, and scan the arena.

On the opposite side, I spot Fiona in nothing but a tiara. Wrath fills me like never before. I know the Ceremony of Exposure requires us both to be naked, but seeing her frightened and stripped of her clothes, paraded in front of the membership, makes it real.

I curl my fists, hating how no Omni has ever ordered a Ceremony of Exposure for a queen. It's pure disrespect, and if a miracle happens and we get through this, I vow to make all of them pay.

"Oh! Oh!" the women moan while the men continue to hiss.

Fiona's cheeks burn maroon. She climbs the steps, pins her frightened greens on me, and breaks away from the security. She flies into my arms.

I wrap my arms around her, my heart beating harder, blinking hard.

She trembles.

I shout in her ear, "We're going to get through this. I will make them pay." I kiss her head.

She quivers harder.

Silence fills the air.

Ulrich and Jytte step in front of us.

"Take your place," Jytte orders.

Fiona grasps me tighter.

"It's okay. Take your spot," I reassure.

She takes a shaky breath, releases me, and takes her place on the X.

I reach over and grab her hand, squeezing it, then stroke my thumb over her knuckles to try and calm her.

"It has come to our attention that the queen did not memorize the Royal Doctrine," Ulrich announces.

A synchronized gasp sounds from the crowd.

Jytte cries out, "Let the Tainted Crown begin!"

Torches pound on the ground in a low thud, expanding the anxiety on Fiona's expression but also inside my chest.

I hold my fist high and declare, "I demand retribution for this charade!"

Hissing erupts again.

"You cannot demand retribution for the queen's lack of responsibility," Jytte warns.

"Her Royal Doctrine was altered, and you know it!" I accuse.

Another gasp, then the arena falls silent.

Ulrich's lips twist like earlier. He holds his arms wide and bellows, "What proof does the king have of such a criminal offense?"

"The queen's Royal Doctrine is on the royal yacht. I've gone through it and noted all the places information should have been entered but isn't," I announce.

The members' shock taints the air.

Ulrich asks, "Did you bring this proof?"

My insides flip. I retort, "You know I didn't."

An evil sort of glee floods his expression. "But yet I picked you up on the Royal Yacht, and you did not ask to bring it, did you?"

I stay silent, hating myself for not finding a way out of this trap before I left the yacht.

"His answer is no, he did not bring it. So let's begin," Ulrich orders.

Jytte steps in front of Fiona, stating, "You'll have three chances to correct a wrong answer. If you cannot, the punishment for you and your husband is death."

Fiona winces, her eyes glistening, and gives me an *I'm sorry* look.

I squeeze her hand in reassurance, and try to think of how to stop them from beheading her.

Jytte asks, "What is Amendment 666?"

Fiona pins her eyebrows together and looks at me.

The air in my lungs turns stale.

She looks back at Jytte and answers, "The Royal Doctrine I was provided did not have an Amendment past 665."

The crowd gasps, then returns to pounding the torches.

"Wrong answer. Want to try again?" Ulrich asks.

"I can't answer a question when the information wasn't provided to me," Fiona argues, lifting her chin.

"Wrong! Wrong! Wrong!" the crowd chants.

Fiona shakes her head in frustration.

Jytte states, "Last chance!"

Fiona stays quiet, squeezing my hand but not flinching under Jytte's dark stare.

"Answer!" Jytte screams.

Fiona glares at her.

"Three seconds. Three. Two. One!" Jytte counts.

The crowd turns deafening. "Behead the queen! Behead the queen! Behead the queen!"

Fiona gapes at me in fear.

Before I can do anything, the knights file in between us. I'm pushed toward the guillotine, and several men hold me down. The wood shuts around my neck, and the lock clicks into place. I grip the wood, trying to lift it, but I can't.

"No!" Fiona screams, and a few tears escape her eyes.

I turn my head, and they lock the wood over her head. I roar, "Get that off of her!"

Ulrich holds his hand up, and the metal blade slides to the top.

The arena quiets.

My heart races so fast I feel nauseous.

"By the power vested in me by the Omni, representing the goodwill of The Underworld, I order—"

"Stop!" Valentina screams.

"We have proof!" Brax shouts.

I shift my gaze and catch them running toward us.

Jytte tosses a nervous glance at Ulrich.

"Stand back, or you will be next!" Ulrich declares.

"We have full proof!" Brax growls as he jumps on the stage. He runs toward Fiona and pushes the executioner aside.

Sean appears from nowhere, barking, "Get the fuck away from the king," and pushes the one next to me to the ground.

He flies across the stage on his butt.

Zara cries out, "I declare an Act of Betrayal! Jytte and Ulrich Koch, you are hereby condemned!"

"You can't do that!" Jytte argues.

Zara steps before her, seething, "I am the successor queen. I can, and I will."

The color drains from Jytte's face.

"They're lying to protect his sister," Ulrich declares, pointing at Sean.

"We're not! We have proof!" Valentina insists.

Ulrich points to the executioners. "Get in position."

"Step closer, and I'll choke the air out of you," Brax warns.

"Same," Sean snarls.

"Knights, get into position. We have an act of hostility upon us!" Jytte commands.

"No one move," Devika, an Indian woman and another Omni on the Royal Council, interjects, crossing the stage.

"We have confessions that these two plotted to overthrow Kirill and Fiona. It's all here," Valentina says, pulling out her phone and clicking on a video.

Devika presses the screen.

Screams fill the air.

Brax demands, "Tell me who paid you to kill the queen!"

Torturous, incoherent whines spill from the phone.

Valentina snarls, "Speak, or I'm taking another finger!"

The man on the video cries out, "They made me!"

"Who?" Valentina demands.

His cries ring through the arena.

"I said who," Valentina screams, and more horrific sounds echo around us.

He begs, "Please!"

Brax warns, "I told you she likes this stuff. Tell her who, or she'll dissect your balls one at a time."

"No! Don't! Please! It was Ulrich! And-and that wife of his!" the man yells.

Devika turns the video off.

"There's more on there. You're missing the best part," Brax states.

Devika shoots daggers at him with a look.

Valentina adds, "There are two other men on the video. They all claim the same thing."

Dinging sounds start to go off across the arena.

Sean adds, "That's everyone's inbox. Brax and I hacked into Ulrich and Jytte's private chats. Everything is documented."

"He's lying!" Jytte accuses, pointing at Sean.

"Free our Majesties! Free our Majesties," the crowd chants.

The knights circle the couple.

"No!" Ulrich shouts.

Sean and Brax release us from the guillotines. I rise and help Fiona up, then tug her into me.

She shakes worse than before.

I bark, "Bring the queen her royal robe! Now!"

An Omni appears with our robes. I help Fiona into hers, tie it, then put mine on. I point at the Koches, roaring, "The only ritual we'll be completing tonight is the Black Veil!"

The crowd gasps. No Omni has ever been the center of a Black Veil ritual.

Men roll out two metal poles in the shape of an upside-down L. Wire hangs from it with a noose on the end.

A bridal gown and tuxedo appear.

"Get dressed," I order Ulrich and Jytte.

Tears stream down Jytte's cheeks. "Kirill—"

"Do it," I snarl, holding Fiona tighter to me.

Ulrich claims, "This has been a big misunderstanding. We were given false information—"

"Don't make me tell you again," I warn.

Slowly, the two get dressed. Zara adds a rose to Ulrich's lapel.

Valentina positions a bouquet of long-stemmed roses in front of Jytte, instructing her, "Hold these."

Tears drip from Jytte's jaw as she begs, "Kirill, please!"

"Hold the flowers," I instruct.

She closes her eyes, squeezes the stems, and screams "Ow!" when the thorns dig into her skin.

Valentina takes a wire and pins her hands so the roses won't fall. Blood drips down her wrists.

Jytte whimpers.

Brax and Sean grab the metal nooses and place them around Koches' necks and a rope around their armpits.

Valentina adds a veil to Jytte's head.

"This is a mistake!" Ulrich yells.

"Yeah. A deadly one. Raise them into the air," I order.

Knights crank on the wheels until Ulrich and Jytte hang in the air.

"*Ayam ta idhma atma jatavedastenedhyasva,*" the crowd chants, and the torches hit the ground in unison. It's another Buddhist mantra, this one for fire ceremonies.

I glance at Fiona. "Last chance. Do you want me to show them any mercy?"

She squares her shoulders, lifts her chin, and, with shaking lips, answers, "No."

"Move them over the fire!" I shout.

The knights roll their bodies over the firepits. The flames catch the bottom of Jytte's dress first, rushing up the lace while she screeches. The roses burst into fiery buds, and the threads from the rope around her arms pop apart one at a time.

Ulrich's pants catch fire. While not as fast as Jytte, the flames travel up his body until the rope around his shoulders singes.

Jytte's rope snaps apart. Her body falls, and the metal wire cuts into her neck. Her screams turn into choking sounds.

Two more minutes pass, and Ulrich's body does the same thing, falling prey to the noose.

I point at the men standing near the stage who escorted me to Pompeii and stood by Ulrich, turning on me. I command, "Behead them!"

Another round of shocked gasps fills the arena.

I roar into the crowd, "Those who dare to be disloyal to the crown shall pay! There will be no mercy!"

The knights apprehend the men. Some of the traitors try to fight. Some hold their heads high. The knights lead them to the guillotines and force two men into the contraptions. The metal blades rise to the top.

One man shrieks, "Please!"

"Now!" I order.

The sharp, shiny metal falls, slicing their necks. Two heads fall to the floor with a thud. Blood drips over them.

The foul smell of burning corpses turns thicker.

Fiona buries her face into my chest, then moans, "I'm going to get sick." She glances up, and her face is green.

"Sean, take over," I instruct, and move her off the stage, down the aisle, and through the door. I open the first door we approach.

She flies past me, runs to the toilet, and tosses her cookies.

I grab her hair, drop her tiara on the ground, and kneel beside her. I rub her back.

She sits back on her calves, her eyes bloodshot, with tearstained cheeks.

"Are you okay?" I question, removing my crown.

She leans into me, tightens her arms around my back, and says, "Let's go home, Kirill."

Nothing in my life has ever sounded better.

Fiona

Chapter
THIRTY-ONE

Kirill steers me out of the room and down several hallways. We turn the corner, and the plane comes into sight.

"Wait," Valentina shouts.

We spin to face her.

Brax is close on her heels.

"What's wrong?" Kirill asks with alarm.

She stops in front of us, breathing hard.

"Are Sean and Zara okay?" I fret.

Brax closes in, stepping beside Valentina and affirming, "They're fine. Living it up with the hanging corpses and declaring a national chastisement for trying to overthrow you."

My heart speeds up again.

They almost beheaded us.

I blurt out, "Thank you for saving us! Both of you." I say the last part while looking at Valentina with gratitude.

Brax puffs his chest out, boasting, "Piece of cake."

"Then why did my wife almost get beheaded?" Kirill seethes, holding me tighter.

Valentina slaps the back of her hand into Brax's stomach.

I glance up, softly scolding, "He's being funny."

"There's nothing funny about it," Kirill warns.

"Kirill—"

"He's right. It's horrendous, and we need to weed out the rest of the traitors. And that's why you must give us their seats," Valentina announces.

Kirill and I stand in stunned silence.

"Please," she begs.

Kirill sighs and closes his eyes.

"Of course you can have them," I offer.

Kirill's body stiffens. "No. Unfortunately, you can't give them the open seats."

"Why not? They saved us," I cry out.

Sympathy blooms on his expression. He states, "There has to be a cleansing ritual. You know this, Valentina."

I scrunch my face. "What does that mean?"

"It was one of the missing sections in your Royal Doctrine. It's Amendment 666," he informs me.

I scoff. "The same amendment that almost got us beheaded?"

"Yes."

"And what is so special about this amendment?"

Kirill glances at Valentina and Brax, then pins his gaze on me, answering, "Seats must be refilled with the same status as those who left."

Lost, I ask, "Meaning?"

"If an individual dies unmarried, another unmarried individual takes the seat. But if a couple dies, then another couple replaces them."

I wrinkle my nose. "That's stupid."

"Agreed," Brax mutters.

"Don't belittle the rules Fiona's father created. They are to keep balance," Kirill reprimands.

"So they should get married," I suggest.

Brax shoots me a look like I'm crazy.

"No. The amendment states that the evil needs to be cleansed from the seats during a purity ritual," Kirill declares.

I admit, "I'm still lost."

"The couple can't be together due to an arranged marriage or a predetermined selection. It has to be a couple who is truly in love and has chosen to marry without outside forces. The seats must go through a rebirth period, and only love can change the energy from negative to positive," he explains.

"We're in love and getting married!" Valentina blurts out.

Brax snaps his head toward her, his eyes wide.

I gape at them.

She grabs his hand. She sternly says, "We are! Aren't we?"

Fear fills his expression.

She turns back to Kirill and me, claiming, "We check all the boxes. We'll take the seats."

Brax clenches his jaw.

Kirill chuckles and points at him. "I see. You're joking again. The look on your face is priceless. Well played."

"We're not joking," Valentina insists, tugging Brax's arm. "Tell them the truth so we don't lose the chance to take our seats."

He glances at her.

She pleads with her eyes.

He slowly slides his arm around her, tugs her closer, and stands taller. He grins, pins his gaze on Kirill, and confirms, "We're in love, and I asked her to marry me."

Kirill points to her hand. "Where's her ring?"

She interjects, "Getting sized. Brax thought my finger was a seven and it's a seven and a half."

Brax's face hardens again. He affirms, "My bad. The jeweler is fixing it."

Kirill studies them for a moment, shakes his head, then looks at me.

I bite on my smile, trying not to laugh. There's no way this is true.

Valentina reiterates, "We meet the criteria. Please! Let us take our seats!"

Kirill sighs, then gives her an apologetic look. He lowers his voice. "Amendment 666 is important. Sean created it for the sole purpose—"

"Of restoring light to the table and safety to The Underworld," I interject.

Pride fills Kirill's expression. He praises, "Yes, my queen. You're exactly right. How did you know that when the amendment wasn't in your Royal Doctrine?"

"It's part of Act 7. Balance is essential for safety, and light must always shine upon the table," I recite.

Kirill puffs his chest, gushing, "I have the smartest wife."

Brax mutters, "Don't fill her head."

Valentina elbows him.

"Ouch," he grumbles.

Kirill scowls.

I quickly add, "Which is why Valentina and Brax can take their seats as long as they get married on the next full moon."

Shock fills Kirill's expression. "You aren't buying this?"

My lips twitch. "Oh, Brax has always wanted to get married, haven't you?"

His face hardens.

"Answer the queen," Kirill instructs.

"Yeah. All day long it's all I think about," he replies.

I motion between them. "It's clear they're madly in love."

"It is?" Kirill retorts, furrowing his forehead.

"Of course," I lie.

He gives me an I-can't-believe-you're-allowing-this look.

"We are. We'll have our wedding on the next full moon," Valentina offers.

"On the..." Brax scrunches his face, then blurts out, "That's in three weeks!"

"Yes. Is there a problem?" I sternly question.

Valentina squeezes his bicep and offers, "No. No problem at all. Brax told me this morning he's dying to marry me sooner rather than later, didn't you?"

He locks eyes with her, narrows his, and slowly lowers his gaze over her body. He lewdly raises it, meets her gaze, and in a gravelly voice, replies, "I sure did, my sexy little minx."

A flush crawls up Valentina's cheeks.

I stop myself from laughing and lean into Kirill. "Sounds like our problem is solved. I'm tired and want to go home. Congratulations on your engagement and future seats at the table and on the Royal Council." I step forward and hug Valentina.

She hugs me back. "Thank you."

I retreat, firmly adding, "Thank you for saving us."

She smiles. "Anytime."

I step in front of Brax.

He glares at me.

I tease, "Give me a hug to celebrate."

His jaw tics, but he goes through the motions.

I contain my laughter and step back. "Thank you as well."

His face turns serious. He nods. "Happy to be of service."

"Can't wait for your wedding," I add, winking.

His face hardens again.

I spin toward Kirill. "Ready?"

His gaze darts between Valentina and Brax, then he looks at me quizzically, like he can't believe this is happening.

I repeat, "I'm tired. I want to go home." I tilt my head and offer a tiny smile.

With a sigh, he hugs Valentina and shakes Brax's hand. "We'll discuss this in more detail back in Chicago."

"What's to discuss?" Valentina frets.

"Nothing," I assure her, then squeeze Kirill's hand.

He glances at me.

"Correct?" I ask.

Something passes in his expression.

"Kirill?" Valentina asks in a low voice.

I wink at him.

He takes a deep breath, then points at them. "The Omni will insist on proof your love is real, and you must marry on the next full moon. If there is any doubt, you know the consequences."

My insides quiver.

Brax clenches his jaw.

Valentina affirms, "Yes. We understand. There won't be any issues. We'll prove how in love we are, won't we?" She glances at Brax.

He stays quiet.

Kirill peers closer at Brax. "And what about you? Will there be any issues? The last thing I want is Valentina dead, so tell me now before this goes any further."

Valentina glances at me with anxiety.

I interject, "Nah. He'll make sure it goes smoothly. Won't you, Brax?" My lips twitch.

His gaze slides to me.

I arch my eyebrows.

"I'm waiting for an answer," Kirill warns.

He lifts his head and smacks his palm against Valentina's ass.

She jumps with a gasp.

He grins at her. "No issues. Can't wait to be tied to this little minx for eternity."

"See. All good," I chirp, then pull on Kirill's arm. "Let's go home."

He studies them for another moment, and then his lips curve. "Then I guess congratulations are in order." He kisses the top of my head. "Let's go home."

I flick my fingers in a wave, smirking. "Bye-bye, lovebirds. Can't wait to have a double date with our soon-to-be-married besties."

Brax glares daggers at me.

Valentina purses her lips.

Kirill chuckles and steers me onto the plane.

Arina curtsies, greeting, "Your Majesties."

"Good to see you, Arina," I say.

She looks up, relief evident in her expression. "And you, my queen."

"Please. Rise," I say.

She smiles, obeys, and gives Kirill the same expression. "Sir."

"Everything is fine, Arina. Let's go home," he orders.

"Yes, sir. Do either of you need anything?" she asks.

"No, thank you," he replies.

"Okay." She nods.

Kirill escorts me to the back of the plane. He opens the bedroom door.

Exhausted, I step inside, go into the bathroom, and brush my teeth. I splash water on my face, untie my robe, and slide it off my shoulders. Then I return to the bedroom and slip under the covers.

Kirill hasn't moved. He stands against the door, appearing nervous.

My stomach flips. "Are you coming to bed?"

His chest fills with air. "Do you want me to?"

We have issues to work through.

I sit up. "Yes. Unless you don't want to?"

He comes over and sits next to me on the edge of the bed. Pain fills his expression.

I swallow the lump in my throat, offering, "I'm sorry."

"You don't have anything to apologize for," he states.

My voice quivers as I insist, "I do. I shouldn't have run away and shut you out."

He stares at me, hesitant, his breaths short.

"Say something," I whisper.

He opens his mouth and then shuts it. He releases an anxious breath and then glances at the ceiling.

I grab his hand. "Hey!"

He meets my gaze, his eyes glistening. "I'm always going to be a Petrov, Fiona." Shame floods his sharp features.

It hurts my heart. I lean forward, wrap my arms around him, and slide my hands through his hair. I pull his face to mine, blink hard, and assert, "You have nothing to be ashamed of. You aren't your father."

His face twists, and he looks toward the window.

"Kirill."

Several moments pass, and my heart beats harder. He finally turns back, stating, "I hate that you saw it. And I won't lie to you. If I could rewind time, I'd find the bastard who sent it to you and kill them before it ever got into your hands."

I rise on my knees and straddle him, putting both hands on his cheeks, breathing in the scent of leather, rosewater, saffron, jasmine, and all the other notes I still can't figure out. A warmth surrounds me, calming the chaos I haven't escaped since I last saw him.

"Fiona—"

"Kiss me," I order.

Confusion flares in his eyes.

"You don't want to kiss me anymore?"

"I'd never say that," he replies.

"Then kiss me."

"We have to work this out," he claims.

I nod. "Yes. We do. But nothing we can say will erase what either of us saw. It won't change what happened to my parents."

He stays quiet.

I add, "Is there something you have to say to me right now for us to return to where we were?"

He pins his eyebrows together.

Panic hits me. My voice shakes when I say, "You don't want things to be how they used to be?"

He slides his hand up my back and palms my neck.

I inhale sharply, my core lighting on fire.

He gruffly answers, "That's all I want."

Relief fills me. I slide closer, brushing my lips against his, ordering, "Then kiss me and take off your clothes."

His lips curve. He presses one finger at a time on the side of my neck.

I whimper, my breath hitching, but I wait.

He flicks his tongue into my mouth, and all the longing comes to an end.

I rise on my knees, gripping his hair, pressing as close to him as possible, kissing him with every ounce of love I undoubtedly have for him. My other hand reaches for his waist, untying his robe.

He slinks out of it and grabs my hip, then slides me over him.

"Yes," I whisper in a muffled tone against his lips.

He groans, thrusts inside me a few times, then flips me on my back. He lifts my thigh toward the headboard, pushing deeper inside me.

Tingles dance in all my nerves. I moan, "Kirill."

He moves his lips back to mine, urgently flicking his tongue around my mouth. His hand curves around my neck and his fingertips press down one by one.

"Kirill," I breathe through the kiss.

"Hmm," he responds, pressing and flicking with more intensity.

I blurt out, "I think I'm pregnant."

He stills, his eyes widening.

My pulse skyrockets.

Why did I choose this moment to say that?

Tense silence builds between us.

"Say something," I urge.

He opens his mouth, and nothing comes out. His heart pounds against my chest.

Fear pummels me. I ask, "Are you mad?"

He shuts his mouth, opens it again, then shakes his head hard.

"Then why aren't you saying anything?" I fret.

"I..." He takes several deep breaths, not breaking eye contact with me.

My voice cracks. "K-Kirill?"

"Is that why you got sick?" he questions.

"Maybe. I couldn't handle the smell. And I don't know for sure, but I've been throwing up every day. The nausea comes, I toss my cookies, then I'm fine," I admit.

"Since when?"

"Since I left."

He furrows his forehead.

"Why do I think you're upset?" I ask worriedly.

He rolls off me and sits up. "I'm not. Just... Just give me a minute to process this, okay?"

I sit up, declaring, "I might not be!"

He arches an eyebrow.

"What?"

"If you've been sick every day..."

I bite my lip, concerned he won't be happy if it's true.

"We need to get you to a doctor. As soon as we land," he asserts.

"I'm not dying. I can make an appointment with my gynecologist," I say.

He scoffs. "We're not waiting. If you're pregnant, you need vitamins and other things. Plus, you've been under a ridiculous amount of stress. We need to make sure everything is okay with the baby!"

I tilt my head, my mouth curving into a grin. "So you aren't upset?"

"Upset? No." He keeps his stern expression and glances at the bed.

My face falls. "If you aren't upset, then what's wrong?"

"Wrong?" He meets my eye.

"You don't look happy."

He stares at me as if I'm a ghost for a moment, then blinks a few times. "I'm sorry. I'm just..."

"Just..."

"I'm going to be a father?"

"Ummm... I don't know. Maybe. Maybe not."

He glances down, splays his palm on my stomach, and slowly pins his blues on mine. There's a mix of fear, excitement, and pride in his gaze. He firmly claims, "No. You're carrying our baby."

A relieved laugh flies out of my mouth. "Let's not get too excited until we know for sure."

He flips me onto the mattress again.

I shriek.

"Then let's make sure we don't leave any room for the doctor to tell us I didn't knock you up."

I laugh.

He chuckles, then returns to kissing and thrusting inside me.

Adrenaline ignites in a flash.

He grips my neck, pressing and kneading, inciting a pool of endorphins ready to attack my core.

"I love you, my queen," he murmurs between kisses.

"I love you, my king," I reply, digging my nails into his shoulders.

"Jesus, I missed you," he adds.

"Yes. Let's not ever be apart again," I state.

He kisses me harder, presses my thigh higher, and thrusts deeper.

Endorphins explode, rushing to my core and generating uncontrollable convulsions deep within me. My body spasms, desperately trying to hold on to him as his erection slides against my walls.

"Kirill," I cry out.

"Shh, my little bird," he coos, pressing his fingers harder against my neck.

"Do it," I order, wanting the next level I've craved since we've been apart.

"You might be pregnant," he reminds me.

"Do it," I beg.

He grunts. "No." He slides his hand under my neck.

"Kirill!"

He presses in a different spot, and the same high I get when he cuts off my air supply attacks me.

Incoherent sounds work their way out of me. My convulsions intensify, and I thrash against him. The room flashes white and then my eyes roll.

"Fuck, Fiona!" he grits out, his erection swelling, then pumping at an accelerated pace. He thrusts through it, studying me while clenching his jaw.

When the endorphins slow, and it's only our bated breath with our chests pushing against the other, his face falls. He rolls onto his back, taking me with him.

I curl into him, feeling at home, vowing to never again run from him.

Several minutes pass, then he declares, "I'm going to be a dad."

I giggle as I lean up on my elbow and put my face near his. I remind him, "Maybe."

He shakes his head. "No. No, maybe. It's happening."

Happiness fills me. "How can you be so sure?"

"You've been sick."

"Kirill, that isn't a guarantee," I warn.

Arrogance fills his expression. It's something I rarely see on him. He insists, "You're pregnant."

"What if I'm not?"

"You are."

"Humor me and pretend I'm not."

He grins, reiterating, "You are."

I roll my eyes, smiling. I relax back into his arms.

His face falls, and his voice is soft when he says my name.

"Hmm?"

He turns into me and strokes my back. I've never seen him look so vulnerable. "Don't leave me ever again."

My chest tightens. I put my hand on his cheek, rubbing my thumb over his scar near his jawbone. I reply, "I won't."

He orders, "Promise me—especially if we're having a baby. I don't want you or our baby living in a different place than me. I want to be a good husband and father."

I tear up and scoot closer to him. I adamantly state, "You're the best husband. And you'll be the best dad."

He stares at me, unsure of my statement.

"It's true," I insist, then kiss him.

He kisses me back, and I yawn against his mouth.

"Sorry!" I chirp.

He chuckles. "Turn around so we can spoon."

I beam. "Yes, sir!" I turn over, and he curls his body around mine.

No matter how horrible the past is, there's only one truth I need to hang on to now and in the future.

I love Kirill Petrov. I'm proud to be his wife and can't wait to have tons of his babies.

Kirill

A Week Later

Chapter
THIRTY-TWO

My driver pulls up to the gate outside the Marino estate. The same security guard who gave me issues before narrows his eyes at me. With disgust, he sneers, "Mr. Petrov."

Fiona leans over me. She snaps, "Have some respect, Antonio, or you'll have to find another job. Understand me?"

His eyes widen. "I'm sorry, Ms. O'Malley."

She smiles while delivering a warning tone. "It's not Ms. O'Malley anymore. I'm Mrs. Petrov. And don't you forget it."

I hold in my chuckle.

Antonio glances at me briefly and then pushes the button. The gate opens, and the driver veers around the curve and parks next to the front steps.

I tease, "Maybe you should go a bit easier on the guy."

"He's not going to treat you like that," she insists.

"It's okay," I state, my nerves spiking. The last time I was here, Fiona wouldn't come out. Dante got pissed because I kept showing him holes in his security, and I was angry it would put Fiona at risk. I wasn't as levelheaded as I should have been, and we didn't end things very well.

"Ready?" Fiona asks with excitement.

Don't be a pussy.

"Yes," I affirm and get out. I reach in for her, and my stomach flips.

Fiona wanted to announce her pregnancy to her mom and Dante in person. I wasn't going to deny her that request just to avoid discomfort.

She hops out of the car, and I guide her up the steps. Before she can grab the doorknob, the door flies open.

"There you are," Bridget chirps, hugging Fiona hard.

Fiona hugs her back. "Hey, Mom."

Bridget retreats, reprimanding, "Don't ever run out of here like that again without saying goodbye."

Fiona winces. "I'm sorry."

Bridget shakes her head but is smiling. She turns to me and embraces me in a hug.

Surprised, I tense for a moment, then hug her back.

"Kirill, how are you doing?" she asks, pulling out of the hug.

I nod. "I'm good, Bridget. It's good to see you."

"It's good to see you too. Well, come on in. Don't stand out here all day," she asserts, smiling and stepping back. She opens the door wider.

My stomach flips with nerves again. We enter the mansion, and I glance around at the ornate staircase and foyer, noting, "This is a beautiful house."

"Thank you. Dante's father, Angelo, built it. You'll get to meet him later," she adds.

My anxiety heightens. I'm sure he won't be happy I'm in his house.

Bridget suggests, "Let's go into the sitting room. Dante's there."

"Okay," Fiona chirps, grabbing my hand and beaming at me.

My heart soars. Even in uncertainty, she has an effect on me.

She squeezes my hand. She's glowing, and I've never seen her so happy. It's been an awesome week. The doctor confirmed she's pregnant, and it's been a joyful time.

We step into the sitting room, and Dante rises.

My stomach flips again.

He narrows his dark gaze on me. "Kirill. Fiona."

I don't move. "Dante."

Fiona lets go of my hand and steps forward, meeting him halfway. They embrace.

He retreats and glances at me.

Unsure how to react, and not wanting to disrespect him in his house, I remain where I am.

He steps beside Fiona and holds out his hand, greeting, "Welcome. Good to see you again."

Surprised and relieved, I shake his hand, replying, "It's good to see you too."

He declares, "I filled those holes in the security."

"That's good."

He nods. "I appreciate you pointing them out."

"Anytime," I respond, shocked over his genuine gratitude.

Bridget steps in front of the bar and pours a glass of red wine. She asks, "Kirill, what can I get you to drink?"

"Vodka, please," I state.

"Should have guessed," she teases, then asks, "Fiona?"

"I'll have a cranberry juice," she replies.

Bridget's lips twitch, and she arches her eyebrows.

Fiona practically bounces up and down. "Okay, fine! You caught me! We're having a baby! You're going to be a grandma again!"

Bridget sets down the wine, claps her hands, then rushes over to Fiona. They hug again.

"Congratulations," Dante offers, his face lighting up.

"Thank you. It's a bit scary, though," I admit.

He chuckles. "I can only imagine." He hugs Fiona and kisses her on the cheek. "Congratulations, sweetheart."

"Thanks, Grandpa," she teases with a wink.

He chuckles. "I've got enough gray hairs these days, huh?"

I glance at the silver weaving through his black locks, taunting, "You do have a few."

"Yeah, I know," he replies gruffly. Then he adds, "It's not fun getting older."

"I hear you on that," I agree.

Bridget returns to the bar and pours a tumbler of vodka. She hands it to me and then gives Fiona a glass of juice. She picks up her glass of wine and holds it out.

"To the baby."

"To the baby," we all echo.

"Salute!" Dante exclaims.

Bridget and Fiona say in unison, "*Sláinte!*"

"*Za zdorovye*," I add.

We clink glasses.

"How far along are you?" Bridget inquires.

"I'm six weeks. I was surprised, though, because I had barely been off my birth control. I thought it would take some time, but Kirill has super-strong sperm, huh, babe?"

Heat rushes to my cheeks, and I gape at her.

"Jesus, Fiona," Dante mutters.

Bridget puts a hand over her mouth, stifling a laugh.

Fiona giggles, glowing, and beaming her smile at me.

So this is happiness.

We spend a long weekend at the Marino estate, and a day longer than we originally planned. Not once does anyone make me feel unwelcome or uncomfortable. Even Dante's father and brothers engage with me in conversation, as if there's never been any reason for us to be enemies.

Every morning, Fiona and her mom go for a walk on the estate. The Marino men, including Angelo, go to their home gym and invite me to work out with them. By the time the weekend ends, I can't deny I've had a great time and like everyone.

Fiona smirks at me when we get on the plane to return to Chicago.

"What's the look for?" I ask.

She leans closer, gloating. "I think you were a huge hit."

"Me?"

She nudges me with her elbow. "Duh." She smiles and curls into my chest, quickly falling asleep.

I spend the flight asking myself how I can go from having money and power but nothing of substance, to now having an incredible wife who loves me, a baby on the way, and in-laws who don't seem to hate me anymore.

It's a gift. Don't blow it, I tell myself.

I sit back in my seat, embracing my new life.

I might not understand how I got this lucky, but I know one thing.

There's one person on Earth I'd die for with no hesitation. And the best thing is, soon there will be one more.

Fiona

Two Months Later

THIRTY-THREE

Soft music plays in the background, and the chatter of the lunchtime crowd fills the air. I step in front of the hostess and then glance past her.

She chirps, "Can I help you?"

I spot Skylar, and my stomach twists with nerves and wistfulness. I've missed my boss and friend. I shake my head, acknowledging, "My friend's already seated. I see her."

"Great." She motions for me to go through.

I stroll through the restaurant, remembering the last time I saw Skylar, getting more anxious.

She sees me and rises, waving at me.

I get to the table, lean in to hug her, then freeze. My heart pounds harder.

She winces. "We just had a weird moment, didn't we?"

"Yeah."

She holds out her arms. "Give me a hug."

"Okay," I say, relieved.

We wrap our arms around one another.

She retreats, tilting her head, and studies me.

My anxiety reappears. "Why are you looking at me like that?"

She gushes, "You've got that pregnancy glow."

I roll my eyes, groaning.

Mom and Dante can't keep their mouths shut. They told everybody before Kirill and I could tell anyone. Sean and Zara called us before we got back to Chicago. And they couldn't keep their mouths shut and told Valentina and Brax.

But it's okay. Kirill and I are so excited, being annoyed with anyone is hard. I'm glad my family's happy for us.

"Here, sit," Skylar orders, pulling out a chair.

I obey.

She takes her seat, asking, "So how've you been?"

"I'm good," I say, fighting the little bit of anger I feel toward her. I don't want to be mad at her, but the more time passed, the worse it got.

She sighs. "I'm sorry it's been so long."

"Yeah, me too," I say, a little harsher than I meant for it to come out, but I don't apologize.

She gathers her thoughts, then adds, "I didn't mean to not speak with you. I just didn't know what to do. Adrian was so upset."

"Yeah, I understand that," I acknowledge, still feeling bad that Adrian's sister went through what she did. But again, it's not Kirill's fault, so I'm conflicted on how they handled the situation.

She offers, "I've hated not having you at work with us."

Once again, my response is harsher than I want it to be. "Yeah, I've really missed it too. I wish you wouldn't have tossed me aside because of who I love."

Guilt washes over her expression. "You know I didn't want to, Fiona."

"But you did," I accuse.

She nods. "I know. And you have a right to be upset. I hope you understand the position I was in."

I release an anxious breath and admit, "I do, but my husband is not his father or any of the people Adrian knew. It's not fair to blame him."

She takes a sip of water and then nods. "I know. Adrian and I have had many conversations, and I really am sorry. I've never been in that situation. You know how he is about his sister's kidnapping and death."

I don't say anything. I don't want to talk about it. It reminds me of my mom and dad's situation. And I won't discuss that with Skylar or anyone unless it's my husband. And that's only if I need to.

She clears her throat, hope lighting her eyes. "So, I'm hoping you want to come back?"

The hairs on my arms rise. I blurt out, "I'm allowed to?"

"Yes."

"Why? What's changed?"

She hesitates, then admits, "Your mom spoke with Adrian. He's still coming to terms with this, but what she said made him reconsider some things. And you know he's stubborn, so I'm not saying he's one hundred percent there yet, but he's agreed that it's okay for you to come back to the office."

Another mix of emotions hits me. On one hand, I would love to go back and work for Skylar. I miss her. I miss Blue and everything I used to do for the company. Heck, I even miss the annoying interns.

But things have changed. I've had too much time to sit alone without her influence and think about what I want. And I have a husband encouraging me to trust my talent and take my future into my own hands.

So I square my shoulders and lift my chin. In the nicest voice possible, I reply, "I appreciate the offer. I'm glad Adrian is coming to terms with my marriage and who Kirill really is, but I can't come back to work for you."

Skylar's face falls. "I'm sorry. Fiona, really. I never meant for this to go on as long as it did...or at all."

I nod. "I believe you. And I know you were in a crappy position. So I'm sorry for that too. But I'm not okay with anyone just tolerating my husband."

She sighs. "It's just going to take some time. But I know Adrian. He'll get there. I can see the wheels turning in his head."

"I'm sure you can. But it's not going to work for me," I declare.

She furrows her forehead. "Are you sure?"

My stomach flips. I hesitate, but then Kirill's voice pops into my mind.

There's no time like the present.

I find my courage and announce, "Yes. I also had a lot of time to think while I was gone. And I don't want you to hear this from anyone else, but I have four sketchbooks full of designs. And honestly... Well, Kirill's been telling me I should start my own line." My pulse pounds between my ears.

She arches her eyebrows. "Oh?"

I nod. "Yes. And I don't want us to be enemies."

She tilts her head and softly smiles, claiming, "We're never going to be enemies, Fiona."

"No?" I question, too familiar with how this business is between competitors.

She reaches over and grabs my hand. "Absolutely not. You've been like a daughter to me. You helped my company grow more than anyone. I'll always be grateful. And if this is what you want, then I'll be in the front row, cheering you on."

Hope and happiness fill me. "You will?"

She jerks her head back. "Of course I will. Did you honestly think I wouldn't support you?"

I shrug. "I don't know what to think, Skylar. I always assumed if I did my own thing, I would be competing against you, and there would be issues."

"Well, I didn't give you a lot of choices over the last few months, did I?" she asks, falling on the sword.

I stay quiet.

She adds, "Fiona, if this is what you want, go for it. Honestly. You've worked hard, and you're talented. Just make sure I have that first-row seat at the show, okay?"

I release more anxiety and smile. "Thank you. I appreciate your kindness and support."

She leans closer. "But if you ever decide you want to come back, I'll kick out whoever is in your office."

I laugh. "Who's in it now?"

"No one, but Blue said if you didn't come back, she's stealing it."

"Aww. How's she doing? I miss her," I admit.

"She's good. She misses you too. And that's another thing Adrian and I messed up."

"What's that?" I question.

"Our actions pushed away the best mentor we ever had for Blue," she declares.

I wave my hand in front of my face. "No way, you're the best mentor for her."

She scoffs. "I don't think so. Think about you and your mom. You didn't want to listen to her when you were Blue's age, did you?"

It doesn't take me long to answer that question. "No, I did not."

Skylar laughs. "She'll figure it out, though." Her face falls. "But we do all miss you, Fiona."

"I miss you all too."

For the rest of the lunch, we talk about other things in our lives, like old times. We set another date to have lunch in a few weeks.

When I get home, Kirill's waiting.

I announce, "The elevator just moved really fast!"

He looks angry. He steps forward, kisses me, then relays, "It was all part of Ulrich's plan. They slowed it down to give time for whoever they sent into the house to get out before we got up here. But don't worry. It's taken care of now."

Relief and rage fill me. The memory of being restrained to the guillotine pops into my head.

He asks, "How did it go?"

I beam. "It was good. Skylar offered me my job back."

He freezes, arching his eyebrows. After a brief hesitation, he asks, "And what did you tell her?"

I wait a moment, gathering my thoughts. He doesn't know what I've decided to do, so I stare at him, wanting to see his reaction, and declare, "I told her thank you, but no thank you. Then I told her I'm going to be her competitor."

Kirill's eyes light up, but he's cautious. "You did?"

I grin. "I did."

"What'd she say?"

"She was the Skylar that I've always known. She told me she wants front-row seats at my first fashion show."

"Oh, that's great, Fiona," he says, hugging me. Then he leans back. There's excitement in his voice when he blurts, "Wait. So you're going to do it? You're starting your own fashion line?"

Butterflies fill my stomach. I reply, "I guess so. You still think I should, right?"

He scoffs. "Of course you should. Remember, you're the talented one in this relationship, not me."

I roll my eyes. "Whatever." I glance at his outfit, teasing, "But you did dress yourself really well today."

He puffs his chest out. "I am getting pretty good, aren't I?"

I laugh. It's a running joke between us, but he's never had any issues as far as I'm concerned.

He asks, "So, what can I help you with so you can get started?"

I bite on my lip and tilt my head.

"I need you to find a top logo designer for me."

"Okay. I can do that," he says.

I add, "I'm naming it O'Malley-Petrov Designs. I think I want something with an O and P for the logo."

Her freezes. "Petrov?"

I nod. "Yep."

"Are you sure that's a good idea?" he asks, concerned.

I smile and rise on my tiptoes. I kiss him, then answer, "Yes. Petrov is our children's namesake. We aren't going to run from it. We'll show the world who we are so our children don't carry the burden of the past."

He stares at me.

I tease, "Our kids are O'Malley's too, so we can't forget that." I wink.

He chuckles.

"Glad you're on board," I declare.

He nods, studying me further.

"What?"

He slides his hand on my cheek and tilts my face up. He leans over it and says, "This is why your father knew you were meant to be queen."

"I'm not following," I admit.

"You're one of a kind, Mrs. Petrov."

I arch my eyebrows. "And I'm still not following."

He grins. "It's okay, little bird. I understand it."

I pout. "You're not going to fill me in?"

Mischief brightens his gaze. He slides his finger across the top of my dress, suggesting, "It might take all day."

My core lights on fire. I take a deep breath and meet his eyes, taunting, "My schedule is clear."

He orders, "Then go into the bedroom and take this off. I'll do my best to make sure you understand...even if it takes us until morning."

Kirill

Eighteen Months Later

*L*ights flash, and music blares. The crowd claps as the models return behind the stage.

I bounce our baby boy, Zavier, on my lap and point, murmuring, "Look, there's Mommy."

Fiona's off to the side in the corner of the stage. Her face lights up, and she waves at Zavier.

"Gah, gah, ma," he babbles.

I pin my forearm against him, bouncing my leg, loving every second I spend with our nine-month-old.

Fiona wanted to name him after me, but I wasn't overly thrilled with the idea. One day she'd declared, "Zavier means new beginnings."

"Zavier," I'd mumbled, liking how strong it sounded.

She'd beamed. "Zavier Kirill Petrov. That's perfect!"

I'd caved, and didn't argue about my name being his middle name.

The music changes, the lights darken, and flashes of gold ignite.

More excitement fills me. I whisper, "Here are Mommy's designs."

Fiona's worked so hard for this moment. She created her line while pregnant and kept moving forward even after she had Zavier.

Several models wear her clothes, strutting down the runway.

The crowd erupts in cheers.

I rise with Zavier, cheering with others.

A horrified Fiona points at me, mouthing, *"Sit down."*

I can't. I'm too proud of her.

She puts her hand over her face, laughing and shaking her head.

Skylar glances over at me and then rises along with Adrian, Blue, and the rest of their family. I look to my other side. Bridget and Dante, Sean and Zara, and Valentina and Brax also stand, cheering. I look behind me, happy to see that not one person is sitting, making me giddier.

Fiona's models continue to swagger down the runway, and it's over not long after it started. The lights change, and the next designer's models get ready to strut.

Everyone sits, but I move through the crowd, entering the backstage area. I shout, "There's Mommy."

Fiona turns, excited. "That was good, right?"

"You knocked it out of the park," I assure her, then kiss her.

She beams at me and then leans close to Zavier's face, cooing, "Hey, sweetie. What did you think?"

He tilts his head. "Gah."

She laughs and then reaches for him, holding him to her chest. He buries his face in the curve of her neck, settling in, and my heart squeezes, filling with more love.

I put my arm around her and kiss the top of her head, praising, "I'm so proud of you."

She grins and teases, "Well, you made me do it."

"I didn't make you do anything," I claim.

"Don't you think you had a little bit of influence?"

"Nope. It was all you," I say.

She laughs.

"Excuse me, ma'am," a woman says.

We turn toward the voice.

She has a lanyard around her neck, and the name of a popular fashion magazine is on the card inside the plastic. She holds out her hand. "I'm Lynette from *Fashion Gone Crazy Weekly*."

"I love *Fashion Gone Crazy*!" Fiona exclaims, then quickly adds, "It's great to meet you!"

The woman gushes, "Yes! I'm new, but I love your line. I think we should feature it in the next issue of the magazine. I'm thinking of a four-page spread."

"Really?" Fiona asks, stunned.

The woman enthusiastically replies, "Absolutely! Those skirts were flipping incredible. My editor will fire me if I don't secure you for an exclusive."

Fiona laughs. "We wouldn't want that to happen."

"No, this is my dream job. So, can we do it? I'll make sure it's fabulous!"

"Yes, of course, I'd be honored," Fiona tells her.

"Awesome." Lynette pulls out a business card and hands it to her. "These are my contact details."

I reach into my pocket and hand her Fiona's card. "These are Fiona's."

The woman glances at me and smiles. "You're her husband. Kirill, right?"

"Oh my gosh, I'm so sorry. I didn't mean to be rude. Yes, this is Kirill," Fiona introduces.

Lynette studies us until I get uncomfortable.

"Sorry, did we do something wrong?" I ask.

She tilts her head, staying silent.

Fiona glances at me nervously.

The woman puts her hand on her hip, asking, "You know what I think would be even more awesome?"

I shake my head. "What?"

She wiggles her finger between us. "You two. We should do a piece in our exclusive on you two and your new baby."

"No, I don't think that's a good idea," I state.

"Why not? Everybody in Chicago, New York, London, and Paris will be talking about you. You'll be the 'it' couple of the fashion world. It'll be fabulous," she claims.

"Thank you. But we're private about our family," Fiona interjects, holding the baby closer.

I put my arm around her. "Yes. That's a very nice offer. But can we stick to the fashion line?"

Lynette's face falls. She sighs. "Okay. But I think—"

"It's not going to happen," I repeat sternly.

She sighs again. "Okay, but I will need to interview you, Fiona. It's fine, as long as it's about the clothes?"

"Yes. Of course," Fiona confirms.

"Am I able to mention how cute your baby is?" Lynette questions.

Fiona laughs. "Yes, that's fine. He is super cute, isn't he?" She kisses him on the head.

"He sure is," Lynette says.

"Fiona," Blue calls out.

"Okay, I'll call you later this week if that works for you?" Lynette asks.

"Sounds perfect. Thank you," Fiona replies.

Blue comes bouncing over and tosses her arms around Fiona. "Oh my God, that was freaking amazing."

"Aw, thanks," Fiona states.

"Hey there, you've missed me, haven't you?" she gushes at Zavier.

He perks up and smiles.

"Come here," she says, taking the baby from Fiona.

I grin.

Blue's been our babysitter and is obsessed with Zavier.

The rest of the family comes over and surrounds us.

At one point, Fiona takes Zavier back, hugging him to her chest.

All I can do is feel happy, wondering again how I got so lucky and truly hit the jackpot.

Fiona isn't just The Underworld's queen.

She's *my* queen. Strong. Powerful. Smart. Fearless.

Her father saw it when she was young, and while he didn't arrange our marriage, deep down, he knew she would be queen someday. Every day that goes by convinces me more that he knew all along what her role would be. And that's why he set it up so she had every advantage to earn the coveted crown.

But against all odds, Sean O'Malley Sr's only daughter fell in love with me, the broken king who hid behind his mask. Not once did she ever see my scars or the vileness of the blood that runs through my veins.

The only thing Fiona ever saw was the man her father claimed I could be; the one I strived to become even when my demons tempted me to give up on life.

Her love for me is something I'll never take for granted.

For the rest of eternity, I'll stand by my wife...my bride...my little bird.

She's Fiona O'Malley Petrov.

She's queen of The Underworld. And she's mine.

* * *

A note from Maggie Cole

Thank you so much for reading Bride by Coronation.
I couldn't wait for you to read Fiona and Kirill's painful love story weaved into a happy ending.

Up next is Bride By Ritual, the seductive tale of Brax and Valentina's fake marriage. Some Omni aren't too happy about their claimed "love" for each other, or how they're taking seats on the Royal Council. So get ready for more unveiling of dark secrets and taboo scenes of the Underworld!

Coming January 1, 2026, or possibly sooner!

Download Bride by Ritual at your favorite retailer or for exclusive collector's editions, autographed books, and discounted paperback and audio visit Maggie's bookstore at www.Maggiecolebooks.Com

No names. No personal details. No face to etch into my mind.

Just him, me, and an expensive silk tie.

What happens in Vegas is supposed to stay in Vegas.

He warns me he's full of danger.

I never see that side of him. All I experience is his Russian accent, delicious scent, and touch that lights me on fire.

One incredible night turns into two. Then we go our separate ways.

But fate doesn't keep us apart. When I run into my stranger back in Chicago, I know it's him, even if I've never seen his icy blue eyes before.

Our craving is hotter than Vegas. But he never lied.

He's a ruthless man...

* * *

Download Ruthless Stranger at your favorite retailer or for exclusive collector's editions and discounted paperback and audio visit Maggie's bookstore at www.Maggiecolebooks.Com

For exclusive collector's editions, autographed books and discounted paperback and audio visit Maggie's bookstore at www.Maggiecole-books.Com

The Underworld

Bride By Initiation (Sean Jr. and Zara)

Bride By Coronation (Fiona and Kirill)

Bride By Ritual (Brax and Valentina) - January 1, 2026 or possibly sooner.

Mafia Wars - The Ivanovs & O'Malleys

Ruthless Stranger (Maksim's Story) - Book One

Broken Fighter (Boris's Story) - Book Two

Cruel Enforcer (Sergey's Story) - Book Three

Vicious Protector (Adrian's Story) - Book Four

Savage Tracker (Obrecht's Story) - Book Five

Unchosen Ruler (Liam's Story) - Book Six

Perfect Sinner (Nolan's Story) - Book Seven

Brutal Defender (Killian's Story) - Book Eight

Deviant Hacker (Declan's Story) - Book Nine

Relentless Hunter (Finn's Story) - Book Ten

*** If you're looking for Dmitri and Anna's love story, the book that created the Ivanov and O'Malley families, then grab book six of It's complicated: Secret Mafia Billionaire - Book Six

Mafia Wars New York - The Marinos

Toxic (Dante's Story) - Book One

Immoral (Gianni's Story) - Book Two

Crazed (Massimo's Story) - Book Three

Carnal (Tristano's Story) - Book Four

Flawed (Luca's Story) - Book Five

Mafia Wars Ireland - The O'Connors

Illicit King (Brody)-Book One

Illicit Captor (Aidan)-Book Two

Illicit Heir (Devin)-Book Three

Illicit Monster (Tynan)-Book Four

Club Indulgence Duet (A Dark Billionaire Romance)

The Auction (Book One)

The Vow (Book Two)

Wilted Kingdom Duet- (A Dark Bully Romance)

Seeds of Malice-Book One

Thorns of Malice-Book Two

It's Complicated Series (Chicago Billionaires)

My Boss the Billionaire- Book One

Forgotten by the Billionaire - Book Two

My Friend the Billionaire - Book Three

Forbidden Billionaire - Book Four

The Groomsman Billionaire - Book Five

Secret Mafia Billionaire - Book Six

Behind Closed Doors (Former Military Now International Rescue)

Depths of Destruction - Book One

Marks of Rebellion - Book Two

Haze of Obedience - Book Three

Cavern of Silence - Book Four

Stains of Desire - Book Five

Risks of Temptation - Book Six

Brooks Family Saga

Kiss of Redemption- Book One

Sins of Justice - Book Two

Acts of Manipulation - Book Three

Web of Betrayal - Book Four

Masks of Devotion - Book Five

Roots of Vengeance - Book Six

ALL IN BILLIONAIRES

The Rule - Book One

The Secret - Book Two

The Crime - Book Three

The Lie - Book Four

The Trap - Book Five

The Gamble - Book Six

The Cartwright Family - Holiday Billionaire Novels

Holiday Hoax - A Fake Marriage Billionaire Romance

Holiday Hire - A Billionaire Single Dad Nanny Romance

Holiday Rider - Coming November 1, 2025

STAND ALONE NOVELLA

JUDGE ME NOT - A Billionaire Single Mom Christmas Novella

ABOUT THE AUTHOR

Amazon Bestselling Author

Maggie Cole is committed to bringing her readers alphalicious book boyfriends and fiercely strong heroines.

She's been called the literary master of steamy romance. Her books are full of raw emotion, suspense, and will always keep you wanting more. She is a masterful storyteller of contemporary romance and loves writing about broken people who rise above the ashes. Her books can often be found hanging out in the top 100, even years after publication.

Maggie lives in Florida with her son. She loves tennis, yoga, paddle-boarding, boating, other water activities, and everything naughty.

Her current series were written in the order below:

- All In (Stand Alone Billionaire Novels with Entwined Characters)
- It's Complicated (Stand Alone Billionaire Novels with Entwined Characters)
- Brooks Family Saga- A Dark Family Saga – Read In Order (Each book has different couples)
- Behind Closed Doors-A Dark Military Protector Romance – Read in Order (Each book has different couples))
- Mafia Wars (Stand Alone Novels with Interconnecting Plot and Entwined Characters)
- Mafia Wars New York (Stand Alone Novels with Interconnecting Plot and Entwined Characters)
- Mafia Wars Ireland (Stand Alone Novels with Interconnecting Plot and Entwined Characters)
- The Underworld (Next Generation Mafia Wars Secret Society with Stand Alone Novels with Interconnecting Characters)
- Club Indulgence Duet A Dark Billionaire Duet – Read in Order (Same Couple)
- Wilted Kingdom Duet-A Dark Bully Billionaire Duet
- Interconnecting Plot and Entwined Characters)
- The Cartwright Family - Holiday Billionaire

Maggie Cole's Newsletter
Sign up here!

Maggie Cole's Website
authormaggiecole.com

Get your copies of Maggie Cole
signed paperbacks!
maggiecolebookstore.com

Pickup your Maggie Cole Merch!

Click here!

**Hang Out with Maggie in Her
Romance Addicts Reader Group**
Maggie Cole's Romance Addicts

Follow for Giveaways
Facebook Maggie Cole

Instagram
@maggiecoleauthor

TikTok
https://www.tiktok.com/@maggiecole.author

Complete Works on Amazon
Follow Maggie's Amazon Author Page

Book Trailers
Follow Maggie on YouTube

Feedback or suggestions?
Email: authormaggiecole@gmail.com